THE INFINITY POOL

CLAIRE S. LEWIS

HEAD
ZEUS

An Aries Book

ALSO BY CLAIRE S. LEWIS

No Smoke Without Fire

She's Mine

First published in the UK in 2022 by Head of Zeus Ltd
This paperback edition first published in 2022 by Head of Zeus Ltd,
part of Bloomsbury Publishing Plc

9 7 5 3 1 2 4 6 8

A CIP catalogue record for this book is available from the British Library.

ISBN (PB): 9781800246195
ISBN (E): 9781789541953

Printed and bound in Great Britain by
CPI Group (UK) Ltd, Croydon CR0 4YY

Head of Zeus Ltd
5–8 Hardwick Street
London EC1R 4RG
WWW.HEADOFZEUS.COM

MIX
Paper from
responsible sources
FSC® C171272

To Friends...
especially
Sara, Sarah, Rose, Heather and Janet
and
Denise, Carol, Joely, Helena, Kerry and Jill
... for the friendship and fun

The truth is rarely pure and never simple.

Oscar Wilde

THIS SUMMER

The cicadas are silent. But there's a promise of heat in the cloudless blue. Soon the males will start up their relentless courtship calls, buckling and unbuckling their tymbals for the females. For now, the only sounds are those of her footsteps, scrunching on stone, and the smoky whisper of leaves in the olive groves stirred by the daybreak breeze.

Not a car on the roads. Not a plane in the sky. Pandemic stillness and calm...

The horizontal rays blind her vision as she crests the path leading to the infinity pool, positioned on a high ridge over-looking the valley. She looks down to avoid the glare. She's wearing only a swimsuit under her sarong and carries a towel in one hand and a notebook in the other. Her painted toenails stand out like bloodstains against the white pebbles. She shades her eyes to survey the distant circle of hills, the sun rising behind the dark mass of Monte Amiata, and closer, the undulating lunar formations of the Crete Senesi – grey Siena clays, sediments of the ancient Pliocene sea that once covered this area of Southern Tuscany known as the Val d'Orcia.

There's a timeless, infinite quality to this landscape that never fails to draw her in.

From where she stands, the pool is framed by cypress trees to the left, an old-fashioned brick well to the right and a border of fragrant 'whirling butterflies' – a wispy plant with fluttering twin white petals, fringing the deck. The water is glazed and shimmering. This is the clichéd pano shot she'd have posted on Instagram to publicise her perfect new life in Tuscany, had things turned out differently. But she doesn't possess a mobile phone anymore. He smashed her last one by hurling it against the flagstones of the new patio in a fit of rage. The screen shattered into a million tiny daggers.

In a matter of seconds, her Tuscan dream will be shattered, too. She shivers and winds the towel tighter round her chest. Wanting to prolong the peace, she closes her eyes and basks in the pools of amber light warming her eyelids and flooding her vision. There's a new sound, a gentle slapping and sucking coming from the far side of the infinity pool. Reluctantly, she opens her eyes and takes a few steps – tentative and knowing – skirting round the border onto the deck.

A dark shape breaks the surface, sending out ripples as it bumps gently against the ledge, where the water overflows into the hidden gully. As her eyes focus, the dark shape resolves itself into a man's body lying face down in the star-float position she remembers from her primary school swimming lessons. That weightless, out-of-body sensation, muffled sounds, her long hair waving in a golden halo, tickling her shoulders – it comes back to her so vividly.

This man's short dark hair is stuck close to his scalp. His halo is red, his blood darkening the water as it dissipates around his head. The sight of it makes her sway.

Her eyes fix on a long black metallic object resting on the

pristine marble at the bottom of the pool. Magnified and deformed – a hunting rifle. The hills and the olive groves and the infinite blue sky collapse inwards in concentric ripples to converge on the weapon. She sees a police officer, hurrying towards her. She takes a long, deep breath and then she screams as if to burst her lungs.

Her cries echo through the valley, jolting the sleeping cicadas into song.

In some detached part of her brain, she sees her gaping reflection in the water and knows that this is the final twist in his story.

ONE
DANIELLE

For the first time in weeks, I felt hopeful. A day in the office had been enough to lift my spirits. Being away from the flat was a treat in itself. It was only when I left the confines of my one-bedroom home that I realised how claustrophobic the atmosphere there had become. The instant I pulled the door shut, I breathed easier.

My team had set up a rota system to apply for the police permits that were rationed and required by law to travel into work. This meant that I was able to spend a day in the office every two weeks, self-isolation restrictions permitting. With the clocks going forwards the previous weekend, I preferred to make the most of the longer evenings to walk the three-mile route back from my office in the City of London to the flat I shared with my partner in Islington, rather than running the gauntlet of the dingy, germ-ridden underground. I was in no hurry to get home.

Although I knew the route back to front, there was something disorientating and confusing about wearing a mask, which made it hard for me to navigate the turns and the junctions. The mind fog it induced made me feel anxious, as I imagined someone with dementia might feel, lost in a big city. Lately, the streets around my office looked like something from a gangland film set. So many shops and restaurants had gone out of business. Their shutters were closed and splattered with lurid paint and angry graffiti. Some of it must have been there before the pandemic, but it had been concealed behind folded shutters in daylight hours, disguised by smart, well-lit and brightly coloured window displays and shopfronts. Now that anarchist, after-dark underbelly of the capital was exposed all day long.

I was struck by the reappearance of rough sleepers sheltering in the doorways of empty premises, surrounded by sleeping bags and makeshift cardboard tents. They'd mysteriously disappeared at the height of the lockdown. No one had raised any concerns or remarked on their absence. It was an open secret, rarely spoken of in the press, that for many months they'd been confined to shoebox bedrooms in cheap hotels – incarcerated like convicts. The threat from the virus having abated over the summer, once again these vulnerable people had been kicked out onto the streets to fend for themselves.

Most of the rough sleepers I passed were painfully young – the new 'lost generation'. So many of the older long-term homeless had died in the first wave of the pandemic. In the deep economic recession that followed, they'd been replaced by the young displaced and unemployed. In the harsh light of day, they looked like students suffering the effects of too much partying and alcohol and drugs – except a lot worse for wear. It was bleak. In fact, some of them probably were students – university halls of residence had been closed by government diktat – but students had been ordered not to return home for fear of spreading infection to other communities. Overnight the students had been ejected from their makeshift prisons to join the ranks of the homeless. Many had no other place to sleep but the streets.

The boy – he was just a boy, couldn't have been more than twenty – was sitting hunched over, staring at an open book.

'What are you reading?' I asked.

His eyes were dark and hooded and his skin sunken and grey. Without looking up, he began to recite in a muffled yet oddly penetrating monotone:

Hamlet... To be, or not to be: that is the question:
Whether 'tis nobler in the mind to suffer
The slings and arrows of outrageous fortune,
Or to take arms against a sea of troubles,
And by opposing end them? To die: to sleep;
No more...

He slumped back theatrically against the concrete wall.

... and, by a sleep to say we end
The heartache and the thousand natural shocks
That flesh is heir to...

He trailed off then fixed me with piercing eyes. I wasn't sure if he was taunting me. Was he an out-of-work actor or drama student? The performance arts were dead with all the West End theatres and all the drama schools closed. The streets were the new stage. I dug into my pockets and found some loose coins to drop in his cup as I walked by. In our increasingly cashless society, all those who lived off begging and tips were struggling more and more to survive. He tried to mumble his thanks, but this time his words were lost in a coughing fit that doubled him over and convulsed his body like electric shocks.

I toyed with contacting the authorities or the police. He should be in hospital or at least in warm accommodation. But I was certain that he'd resent my interference. And as for alerting a police officer, there were none on the streets these days. Occasionally a police car wailed by, its blue lights whirling. His face was covered with a government-regulation mask, distributed by the authorities, the same as worn by all the rough sleepers – a badge of dishonour. The green cloth was grimy and tattered, most likely a repository of infection. The law provided that masks should be worn at all times on the streets and the homeless could be arrested if found not wearing one. Behind the masks, no one was smiling.

When I reached the park, it was like crossing into a different country. While humanity suffered, here the natural world reaped the benefits. I quickly forgot the destitute young man. The air was clear, the birds were singing (now, you could hear them without the background drone of traffic), the daffodils were out, and the evening sun dappled the lawns and the trees. Everything was greening up. I was so relieved to see the colours of spring after the relentless grey townscape of the winter lockdown. Usually, I found the changing of the seasons unsettling – those extra hours of daylight jarred my nerves when the clocks changed – but this year I was excited. Green shoots, fresh hopes.

There was no one in sight as I walked up the tree-lined path across the park, but this didn't unnerve me. I'd got used to empty streets and open spaces. I'd always hated crowds, so the relative isolation of pandemic London suited me well. This park had been my saving grace when we were in the hard lockdown. I came here for my 'permitted daily exercise' – ten loops jogging round the park or a leisurely walk – it was the best way to clear my head and to think and to get away from Matt. Trapped together in a one-bed flat, he was an oppressive presence. This park kept me sane.

Today, the play area did look rather forlorn despite the spring sunshine. The gate was locked and boarded with a sign that read *CLOSED UNTIL FURTHER NOTICE* in forbidding black capitals.

Where have all the children gone? I wondered. Had there been a new outbreak in the neighbourhood schools and nurseries?

Even when I reached the main road, things were subdued. Although it was technically 'rush hour' (now an anachronistic phrase), there were only a few cars on the road and the occasional lonely bus, sparsely occupied, taking home the few key workers who had been allowed into the centre of town. I passed one or two pedestrians, keeping diligently to the statutory two-metre distancing and automatically averting my gaze. I'd become accustomed to my attempts at a greeting being ignored or met with suspicious eyes – as if any kind of social contact could transmit the disease. It was simpler just to look away.

I caught a fleeting glimpse of alien masked heads as a red double-decker glided past, its electric engine almost noiseless. The dehumanising anonymity of their face coverings didn't trouble me. It was the silence of the city that I couldn't get used to. No music in the cafés, no cries in the streets, no planes overhead. It was as if someone had pressed the mute switch of a movie that I was locked inside.

TWO
DANIELLE

I doubted that Matt would have bothered to leave his desk to buy food, so I stopped off at our local Italian deli to pick up something for supper. Andrea's Deli Toscana was one the few shops still open in the small parade opposite Highbury Hill. Three people were waiting outside, masked and gloved.

I came to a halt, obediently measuring my distance on the pavement and planting my feet on the yellow space marker with exaggerated precision. If there was one thing English people were good at, it was queueing, I thought wryly. I couldn't imagine the French or Italians being so phlegmatic and patient in the face of these daily restrictions on their freedom of movement.

Not everyone was so compliant, however. On the metal blind, pulled across the hairdresser's shopfront where I stood, one of the midnight anarchists had tagged the words: *Fuck yer lockdown!* There was nothing witty or poetic or street art about it. The message was stark.

When my turn came, I was the only customer allowed in the shop. I was pleased to see that at last they had pasta in stock. The shelves had been stripped bare of staples like pasta, rice and flour for weeks. I grabbed a packet of spaghetti (it felt like a small triumph) along with a jar of sundried tomatoes in virgin olive oil and a tin of black olives (ironically, non-essentials such as these weren't in short supply). Then I approached the deli counter to buy some pecorino cheese and a Tuscan salami. Matt would be happy. I paid as quickly as possible, tapping my card to minimise contact with the machine.

I was on friendly terms with Andrea. Sometimes I'd try out a few phrases of my embarrassingly bad summer-holiday Italian. 'The English are such pathetic linguists,' Matt would say, with the superiority of a bilingual Anglo–Italian, in response to my halting attempts. Andrea usually responded cheerfully, but today she avoided all eye contact with me when she bagged up the shopping. I knew why. Andrea's mother had been taken into hospital critically ill with the virus. Things weren't looking good.

The hallway was in darkness when I bent down to pick up the day's post off the frayed doormat. My flat was in one of those big old Victorian terraces with high ceilings and period features – a former grand residence converted in the 1970s into flats, most of which were now occupied by professional couples or young singles who worked in finance in the City. As I stood up clutching a handful of envelopes, I stifled a scream, startled by a small dark figure sitting on the bottom step in her nightgown watching me.

'Oh my God! You scared me,' I blurted out.

My words came out muffled. The little girl looked frightened, too. Not wanting to hurt her feelings, I took off my mask, even though it was against the rules, and continued more gently.

'Sorry, did I give you a shock? I must get that light bulb fixed. What are you doing out here? Are you OK?'

The occupants of the basement flat bucked the trend of typical residents in this street. The flat was rented by a single mother with twin babies and two little girls from more than one lowlife absentee father, who pitched up every once in a while to sofa surf for a few nights or cadge some money.

It had been bad before the lockdown. Now, their household seemed permanently in chaos. There was always some kind of row going down. Either the babies wailing or mum screaming at the little girls or some guy yelling at mum. I could hear them kicking off on the other side of the door. Mum shouting and then a crash. It was no surprise the child had crept out to escape the mayhem and sit in the shadows on the stairs.

'Do you want to come up to our flat for a bit?' I asked. 'It's nice and peaceful up there.'

The girl shook her head and shrank back on the stairs to make herself as small as possible. *Mum's probably freaked her out with talk of 'stranger danger'*, I thought. *So ironic. Her home's not exactly a safe haven.*

My flat was on the third floor. Our neighbours on the first and second floor had left in a hurry, racing to beat the lockdown and flee London at the start of the pandemic. There had been so much fear in the early days. News of tourists held hostage in their cabins on luxury cruise liners and Italian opera singers performing across the rooftops from their balconies like caged birds had stoked the panic.

So many Londoners had taken flight – the lucky ones, with family connections in the Home Counties or able to afford a second home in the countryside. The government was promising that by the autumn, things would get back to normal – or a 'new normal', as everyone kept saying. But in the meantime, London was a shadow of itself.

'Hi, darling,' called Matt as I stepped through the door. 'Danielle, is that you?'

Who else would it be? I thought to myself.

'You're twenty minutes late. Where have you been?'

'You could at least have emptied the dishwasher,' I muttered impatiently, but quietly, so quietly that Matt wouldn't hear, while eyeing a pile of mugs and plates dumped in the sink.

I didn't want to start a fight. I dropped the letters on the table next to Matt's laptop and sprayed them with sanitiser. The invisible enemy was everywhere.

'How's it going?' I asked.

Matt blew me a kiss, keeping his eyes on the TV on the wall. Then he heard the squirt of the spray.

'That's such a ridiculous waste of time and money...' He looked round. 'Hey! Watch out for my laptop.'

I plonked myself down close to Matt and stretched out on the sofa using his leg as a pillow while I looked through the post.

'What's your problem? If it helps me feel better psychologically, that's something, isn't it? Did you have a good day?'

'All the better for seeing you,' said Matt, and he bent over to kiss me on the lips – so tenderly that the memory of his previous terse words melted away.

Most of the post was junk mail – holidays, cruises mostly. Truly junk – no one in their right mind would be booking a cruise anytime soon. Then there were the inevitable bills: service charge, electricity, two brown envelopes – his and hers – chasing long overdue tax returns. Even in times of national emergency when everything was in lockdown, it seemed the bills never stopped coming. Tax collectors and credit agents were still in business.

I pushed the bills to one side. There was one letter that looked more interesting – a brown buff padded A4 envelope addressed to 'Signor Matteo Rossi' with an official-looking legal stamp on the back.

I sat up straight. 'Here, this is for you.'

With the absence of live football, Matt was entrenched on the sofa watching a replay of a World Cup football match, beer in one hand and a printed manuscript abandoned on the floor.

'What's the point of watching the match when you already know the score?' I held out the letter, but Matt kept his eyes on the game. My interruptions were beginning to get on his nerves.

'You girls just don't get it, do you?' he said without turning his head. 'It's all about the game plan and the moves and the drama, not the final score.'

I tried again. 'Shall I open this letter for you before I take my gloves off?'

'Can't you see I'm trying to relax?' he said irritably, picking up the manuscript. 'I've been hard at it all day.' He shuffled the papers together. 'Sorry, this submission is doing my head in – so long-winded and precious. I don't know why Jake accepted it... but I shouldn't take my frustration out on you.'

I decided to rip open the letter myself – several pages of closely typed Italian – and placed it on top of the pile next to Matt's laptop before peeling off my blue vinyl gloves. I was burning with curiosity but knew better than to keep nagging when Matt was in this mood.

I washed my hands above the day's dirty dishes – I'd take

care of those later – and put a kettle on to boil for the spaghetti – such a rare treat these days. Once I'd plated up and poured Matt a large glass of wine, he was persuaded to look at the letter. He blanched when he saw the legal stamp. Then, for all his scoffing at my precautions, he picked it up gingerly as if it might contain some lethal contagion and walked over to the other side of the room to read it in silence. I noticed that his hands were shaking.

'Is something wrong?' I asked. Then, attempting a joke: 'International arrest warrant? Love child?' Matt had hinted once or twice about his 'wild summers' in Italy during his reckless student days and I was, after all, an avid reader of romance and mysteries. 'Is your past catching up with you?'

Why the trepidation? As far as I was aware, Matt hadn't been to Italy for over ten years. He rarely spoke about his time there or expressed any wish to return. But I was surprised he wasn't immediately more intrigued by this official-looking letter arriving out of the blue.

I stood behind Matt with my arms around his waist, peering round his shoulder. Matt was in no mood to share.

'For God's sake, shut up and let me read it,' he said with a long-suffering smile. Then he released my hands with a friendly squeeze and walked to the other side of the room.

Eventually, I managed to persuade him to return to the table and show me the letter. He seemed to have recovered his composure, but his expression remained stony.

'I thought the police were after me,' he said without thinking. 'That legal stamp got me worried.'

The letter was in a formal and archaic style from an attorney in Siena. Matt's written Italian wasn't as good as it should have been – particularly when it came to professional and business vocabulary. It took him some time to struggle through and decipher the legalistic terminology on the closely written sheets.

'*Questo è il mio testamento... le ultime volontà di mio... Benetto Maffeo Rossi...* I can't believe this has actually happened. It's my great-uncle's will,' he said. 'He died three months ago... 15 April... at the height of the pandemic. He had no surviving children. As far as I can make out from all the legal jargon, he's left me the farmhouse.' He tapped the will ominously. That's what it says, here in black and white in his will.'

THREE
DANIELLE

Matt's pasta was virtually untouched. He'd lost his appetite when he'd opened the letter from Italy. I scraped the congealed spaghetti and tomato sauce off his plate into the bin. It was a new rule I'd made for myself. Never to put leftovers back in the fridge. All part of the depressing hygiene regime that we had to follow since the virus ruled our lives – no leftovers, no dips, no bowls of crisps, no sharing plates, no 'one pudding and two spoons, please' at the restaurant... no restaurant... no pub... At the same time, I hated waste. It hurt. That was another rule. Food was too precious to waste – especially when money was short, and you never knew what would be in the shops from one day to the next.

If anything, I think I was more excited than Matt to hear the news. After going through the legal papers, Matt had recovered from the initial shock. He was no longer agitated but seemed unusually taciturn. Normally, he was the one who was upbeat and cheerful, countering my moods of negativity. Now, our roles were reversed.

I pestered him with questions about the Italian side of his family and the summers he'd spent in Italy, which he answered mostly monosyllabically, with growing irritation and evasion. Bit by bit, with a lawyer's tenacity, I got the story out of him. Sometime back in early summer, he'd been informed (he didn't say how or why he hadn't mentioned it sooner) of his great-uncle falling ill and dying from the virus after being hospitalised for three weeks in Montepulciano, Tuscany.

'Why didn't you tell me? Night after night, we were watching those dreadful pictures on the news about the hospitals in northern Italy being overwhelmed with cases and you never said a word!'

'You were so upset about it,' he said. 'I didn't see any point in making you even more stressed.'

'I want to know everything,' I said. 'There should be no secrets between us.'

Although Matt had never spoken to me about it before, it became apparent that he knew what had befallen his Italian family in recent months. He told me that Benetto's wife, Loretta, (or Zietta Loretta, Matt's childhood name for his great-aunt), had remained on the family farm in southern Tuscany in Val d'Orcia after the death of her husband. She was cared for by their housekeeper, who visited twice a day from the local village, while the farm manager lodged in a worker's cottage and stayed on to keep the estate from falling into complete dilapidation.

'Despite her frailty, Loretta survived the infection with only mild symptoms,' he said. 'But she suffered from dementia and became more and more grief-stricken and disorientated after the death of her husband. Because she couldn't cope alone, she was moved to live with a distant cousin in an apartment adapted for older people in the suburbs of Florence.'

'That's sad,' I said.

There was worse to come.

'Benetto and Loretta had no offspring to take on the farm,' Matt went on. 'Their only son, Lorenzo, died in a tragic accident as an infant.'

'Oh my God. That's so awful,' I said.

'It was Benetto's dying wish that the farmhouse, which has belonged to the Rossis for generations, should stay in the family.'

Matt picked up the lawyer's letter again and scrutinised the last page of the will.

'So now, in the absence of an heir, Benetto has bequeathed the farmhouse to me on condition that I maintain the farm as a going concern and take up residence in Italy.' He tapped the last paragraph. 'Under the will, Loretta is granted a life interest in the farmhouse, and the farm manager – a guy called Antonio – is granted a life tenancy in the cottage.'

'This is such an amazing opportunity,' I said. 'I can't understand why you're so down about it.' Suddenly it occurred to me. 'What about your father? Surely, he's the next in line to inherit?'

Matt's jaw tightened in anger.

'Benetto fell out big time with my father years ago. Expelled from the family clan.'

I didn't want to distress Matt further, so I let the matter drop.

'What an honour to think that your great-uncle has chosen you to take on the family business and keep the family name alive in Tuscany!' I said enthusiastically. 'He must have spoken to you about this in the past, surely? This can't come as a complete surprise?'

'To be honest, I always pushed it to the back of my mind,'

said Matt. 'I knew Benetto was obsessed with carrying on the family name in the family tradition – just like every true Italian peasant. He told me his family was born from and belonged to the very earth that they farmed – *earth to earth, dust to dust*. It was stronger than a religious conviction for him – that pull of the soil. But I thought I had years to go before I'd be faced with this situation. My great-uncle was only seventy-two years old when he died. He was as strong as an ox. If it hadn't been for the virus, he'd probably have lived for at least another ten years.'

Matt grumbled on, 'The place is in the middle of nowhere. I've got no interest in agriculture. I know nothing about growing olives or vines. My only experience is from the time I spent doing casual work in the fields during my student vacations.'

'Anyone else would be jumping for joy at being gifted a home,' I said, genuinely baffled at Matt's sullen opposition to this sudden change of fortune.

Thinking back, there had been something 'off' about Matt's mood over the past summer months. This situation must have been preying on his mind since he found out about his great-uncle's demise. His persistent sulky distraction wasn't just down to cabin fever, or the relentless battering of daily updates on the pandemic, or the endless economic gloom and doom. It seemed he was going through his own personal crisis. He had some big life decisions to make – I got that. But these were decisions we should make jointly. Otherwise, our relationship meant nothing, and we shouldn't be together at all.

'I can help you take this on. Your uncle must have thought you were up to it, or he wouldn't have left you the farm in his will.'

'But it's not mine,' said Matt. 'The old woman and Antonio come with the property. I can't be rid of them or the farm until they're dead.'

'The *old woman* is your great-aunt!' I said, shocked by Matt's lack of compassion. 'Anyway, she's already gone. And the farm manager will be a godsend. This couldn't have come at a better time. You've been trying to get a novel published for years. Finally, you have an agent. With luck, you'll soon have a publisher. You could work remotely from your job in London. And to top it all, you have the gift of a new life in Italy. This is the perfect opportunity. Antonio can do all the work on the farm while you get on with writing your story. This is your chance to get it done at last.'

'Loretta's gone, but she might come back. I don't want the responsibility of looking after a geriatric.'

'Ah! that's harsh,' I exclaimed, taken aback by his choice of words.

'And as for Antonio, there's bad blood between us – history,' said Matt, ignoring my intervention. 'I don't want that man living on my doorstep.'

'What do you mean, *bad blood*?' I asked. 'Did you get into a fight with him? Why don't you like him?'

'I don't want to talk about it. Trouble over a girl – we were all just kids. He behaved badly. That's all you need to know. I never want to see the man again.' He threw the lawyer's letter onto a pile of unopened mail.

'If it makes you this miserable, you should renounce your inheritance,' I said crossly. 'There must be some way you can do that under Italian law.'

Matt paced up and down the flat, pulling at his hair. 'No, I don't have a choice. The farm will be mine. A millstone round my neck.' Finally, he slumped down on the sofa and in a flat voice, he said, 'I always knew that Italian summer would come back to haunt me.'

FOUR

DANIELLE

The more we talked about it, the more convinced I became that we should move to Tuscany.

'Together, we can do this,' became my mantra. The weather had changed again for the worse – a whole week of unseasonal wind and rain was in prospect. London was a sad and dreary place without the spring sunshine. Everyone was exhausted by the endless inescapable barrage of new and changing restrictions on daily life that were announced on radio and television broadcasts and social media by grim-faced politicians and government scientists (who looked like they'd died already) from one hour to the next. Everyone was confused and anxious and alienated. It was affecting the mental health of the nation. I just wanted it all to stop. I'd unplugged the radio and the television. But I couldn't avoid looking at the screens on my laptop and mobile.

When I checked the weather app on my phone, the forecast for Siena showed twenty-four degrees with a line of big yellow suns all across the screen. Desperate for a change of scene, I chipped away at Matt's opposition, pointing out all the positives in the project. What clinched it was the fact that the lawyer had advised that if Matt renounced his inheritance, the farmhouse would be put up for public auction. There were a number of local investors and an adjoining landowner who had already been in touch expressing an interest in the property, the lawyer had said. For some reason, Matt found it impossible to countenance the idea of the property being sold to a third party. It was as if he felt compelled to take it on, if only to stop anyone else taking possession of the place.

More papers had arrived from Italy, forwarded by the lawyer. There was a package of marketing materials prepared by a local estate agent a few years back when, on the verge of bankruptcy and facing foreclosure by their bank, the old couple had reluctantly been persuaded to put their property on the market. The sales materials had been directed to the English and American markets – to appeal to those seeking a new life or a second home in Italy. No buyers had been found and, in the end, the bank had agreed to a new loan and Matt's uncle had been able to struggle on with the business.

I read through the property brochure obsessively, poring over the plans and photographs. I loved to indulge in what Matt called my 'property porn' – my weakness for fantasising over luxury villas in exotic locations that I could never in a million years afford. This was different. There was actually a possibility of making this dream a reality. My excitement was contagious and Matt became animated as we sat, wine glasses in hand, preparing for our move and imagining our future life together in Tuscany.

'You'll love it,' he said. 'The light and the skies and the hills stretching as far as the eye can see... You can breathe. You know you're alive in that place.' Matt raised his glass.

His eyes drew me in with the magnetism that had first attracted me to him.

'Here's to new beginnings!'

He put his arm round my shoulder while we looked through the brochure:

Tuscan Renovation Property and Estate

Historic Tuscan estate with annexes and swimming pool, in the middle of vineyards and olive groves

This traditional Tuscan estate is located in an absolute dream position near the medieval village of Sangiari. In a beautifully elevated, hilly and panoramic setting, this 30-hectare estate (until recently a small working farm) has a vineyard, an olive grove and a private hunting reserve. The residential buildings of the estate (a farmhouse and workers' cottages amounting to approximately 350 square metres) currently total five bedrooms, but this number could be further increased with restoration. A storehouse/tool shelter (with working olive press), a stone swimming pool (in need of renovation) and two private wells (one functioning) complete the property. The property could easily be adapted into a small holiday accommodation business once the renovations have been carried out.

Highlights

- Stunning countryside view
- Absolute tranquillity and privacy (not overlooked)
- Natural stone farmhouse, structurally sound but in need of updating
- Traditional features: open fireplaces, stone walls,

wooden beams, rib vaults, barrel vaults, brick-built arches, stone and terracotta floors
- Outbuildings (in need of renovation)
- 12 x 8 metre stone swimming pool (in need of repairs) set in panoramic position in farmhouse garden
- Olive grove 1.4 hectare with approximately 250 olive trees
- Vineyard 1.6 hectare
- Hazelnut, almond, cypress and pine trees
- Two private wells (one functioning)
- Hilly, panoramic location
- Access by unpaved roads ('white roads')
- Electricity connected (no Wi-Fi)

Services are all available in Sangiari (4 km; ten minutes' drive on unpaved roads), where you can find supermarkets, shops, banks and post offices. From the property, it's also easy to reach some of the most beautiful cities of Italy – Florence, Siena, Montepulciano, Pienza, Montalcino and Pisa... The closest airport is Perugia (73 km; an hour's drive), but for intercontinental flights we recommend the terminals in Pisa and Rome.

I was delighted to see Matt 'embracing his destiny' at last. The poetic names of those stunning cities, centres of art and culture – Florence, Siena, Montepulciano – were enough to blow me away. Nothing could dampen my enthusiasm. Not even the pictures of the dilapidated farmhouse. The agency had given the usual glossy write-up, but even with airbrushing, the photographs told a different story. The farmhouse was in need of complete restoration. In the context of property porn, this estate was a tired old prostitute seriously in need of a makeover!

'Look at those views!' I said, pointing at the photographs and plans that the lawyer had sent through. 'We should dig out that old swimming pool and put in a new infinity pool overlooking the valley.'

The grainy photographs showed the old-fashioned stone pool – empty and cracked with a scattering of dead leaves and other debris. Nature had already begun to take hold, with suckers and shoots bursting through the gaping cracks in the green concrete. It was impressive to see the way in which the natural world could break through, allowing vegetation to overwhelm the hardest of man-made materials. The pool had just one thing going for it – the site.

'It's the perfect spot for an infinity pool. I can just picture myself there, watching the sun going down behind the mountains.'

Grudgingly, Matt turned his attention to the photographs of the pool.

'Hmm...' He topped up my glass then swiftly changed the subject. 'That mountain on the skyline, that's Mount Amiata – the highest point in southern Tuscany,' he said. 'And look, those are the Crete Senesi. Can you see the grooves in the hills, the lines of white rock? This whole area, characterised by these distinctive rock formations, is known as the Val d'Orcia. It's quite something to wake up to that view from your bedroom window, I can tell you.' Matt was unable to hide the emotion in his voice.

'Which was your room?' I asked, scrutinising the picture of the main house.

'My bedroom was there, at the back of the farmhouse.' Matt pointed at one of the photographs. 'My window looked out over the vineyards towards the mountains. But this is where I slept most of the time,' he said, tapping the image of a derelict outhouse with broken windows and a missing roof. 'In that cottage. It's almost unrecognisable.' His eyes shone. Then he recovered himself and pointed to another picture. 'There's the old olive press. Looks in need of a good overhaul. I stood over that for hours during the harvest.' He turned to the next page of the brochure, caught up once more in his memories. 'That's the workshop where my great-uncle made olive wood carvings. He tried to teach me. But I didn't have the patience.'

'It's beautiful,' I mused, undaunted by the run-down look of the place. 'I wonder why they weren't able to find a buyer.' Silently, I pondered whether the family tragedy had put people off.

Matt shrugged.

'It was 2008 – the time of the financial crisis. Not many people in the market for overseas property that year, I guess.'

Later, I was to become familiar with the meaning of the term 'stigmatised property'. At the time I was satisfied with his explanation.

It was pleasing that Matt's opposition to reconnecting with his past was weakening.

'It's vast,' I said, looking through the plans of the farmhouse and the estate. 'There's so much living space. And it's so isolated. An ideal place to shelter from the pandemic.'

I located the property on a map on my phone. It was deep in the southern Tuscany countryside.

'We could redesign the farmhouse so we can work remotely without getting in each other's way.'

During lockdown, we'd competed for elbow room at the dining table in my one-bedroom flat, annoying each other with phone calls and Zoom meetings. It was nice to have the company but impossible to find any privacy.

'You could convert that outbuilding into an office,' I said, pointing at the floor plans. 'Hide yourself away and get your book written. All the peace and quiet you could wish for.'

He grunted and turned over the brochure to hide the pictures.

Matt never followed up on my suggestion. I'd discover that an invisible cordon barred his entrance to this derelict old outbuilding, and he never crossed its threshold.

Matt worked as senior commissioning editor for Reel-Writes, a publishing and film production company in London. He'd published two fairly successful non-fiction guides to the UK publishing industry alongside his day job, but his real love was creative writing and his real goal was to write a work of fiction. I'd seen the box file of rejected manuscripts that Matt had stashed in a storage cupboard in the hallway of my London flat. He'd spent the last ten years at ReelWrites editing and promoting other people's stories. Now, he was consumed with the ambition of writing his own novel.

'You can do your writing and editing from anywhere in the world,' I went on. 'We're probably heading for another lockdown. You'll be working from home for the foreseeable future. There's no reason why you shouldn't do your work from Tuscany just as well as from this apartment in Islington.'

'I don't want to leave London,' said Matt. 'This is my home. And that place is a wreck.'

Undeterred by Matt's despondent tone, I continued, 'Look on the positive side. It would be an amazing challenge. We've both been looking for a fresh start away from the drudgery of our day jobs. I can have a studio for my painting. Antonio can stay on to look after the olives and the vines, and I'd happily take charge of project managing the renovations and the interior designs.'

'How on earth would we pay for the renovations?' Matt

said. 'You're being completely unrealistic. I'm working from home on only two-thirds of my salary. You've already taken a big pay cut. Now you've barely got enough to pay the mortgage on this one-bedroom flat.' (Matt contributed nothing to the mortgage payments but voiced no qualms about this.) 'I'm eating into my savings month by month because of this bloody pandemic. Everyone's struggling, here in London and in Italy. The pandemic ravaged their country, for God's sake,' said Matt passionately. 'The whole of Europe is still reeling and in a deep economic recession. Most people are just thinking about survival while you're getting all excited about having a second home in Tuscany. Can't you see how selfish that is?'

I was on a roll, not to be deterred by his lecture. 'Reel-Writes will keep you on when the all this ends, so you'll still be getting a salary for your editing work.'

I was a qualified lawyer working for a law firm that specialised in media and entertainment law. That's how I'd come to meet Matteo when our paths had crossed at the Frankfurt Book Fair almost a year earlier. Seduced by his suave Latin charm that bordered on arrogance and my sense of urgency to settle down (like so many other women in their late twenties fearful of never finding the perfect match), I'd fallen into a whirlwind love affair. A couple of months later, he'd moved into my flat in north London just ahead of the first lockdown.

If it hadn't been for the pandemic, we might have taken things more slowly, but owing to the restrictions on socialising, we were faced with the choice of either living together or not seeing each other at all. In those early weeks, our relationship had the intensity of a wartime romance. Like so many other couples, our relations were strained at times by the dragging months of confinement and mutual isolation. Perhaps I was deluding myself, but I believed our love had stood the test and now we were about to enter an exciting new phase. I was determined to make it work, come what may.

'I'll take voluntary redundancy,' I announced. 'The firm is desperate to get rid of some of us and even with my pay cut, I'm the most expensive lawyer in our team after the partner. We should do it!' I said defiantly. 'I've been waiting for the opportunity to take up my art again. Who knows? I might even be able to make a bit of money out of it if I can sell a few pieces. And I'll put my flat up for sale. With what we have left after I've paid off the mortgage plus my redundancy money, we'll have plenty to live on in Italy, as well as money to fund the renovation project.'

If Matt was taken aback by my willingness to put my job and my home on the line and to throw in my lot with him, he didn't show it. He was a little older than me, with more professional experience and self-assurance in many ways, but not too proud to rely on my generous financial support.

'And if we're ever short, I can do freelance work for the law firm, reviewing media law contracts. With everyone so geared up for remote working, it won't be a problem if I'm not based in London. We can sit out the next year or two in the Tuscan countryside,' I continued. 'Enjoy the fresh air and splendid isolation! It's better to be out of London at this time. There's no sign of things easing up soon.'

Matt scrolled through his emails while I enthused.

'When the pandemic is over, we could transform the farmhouse into an *agriturismo* and take advantage of all the tax breaks available in the region for regenerating farming through tourism. By the time American and English tourists start coming back to Italy, the renovations will be finished. We'll be in the perfect position to start renting it out.'

Matt looked at me sceptically.

'If we get seriously homesick, we can move back to the UK and just spend a few months in Italy each year. You'll be honouring your great-uncle's wishes to keep the farm in the family. That's important, isn't it? And if things really don't work out, we can sell the business on as a going concern and hopefully make enough money to buy ourselves a home together back here in London.'

'Since when did you become such an expert in Italian business models?' said Matt sardonically.

He was forgetting that as a lawyer, research was second nature to me.

'Oh, you know, I've been doing some research the past week or so. You can learn about anything online these days.'

Matt slammed down the lid of his laptop and went off to get a beer from the fridge. He said nothing for a while as he took a long slug of beer and stared at me.

'You've got it all worked out, haven't you? Looks like you're dead set on this madness.' He pointed his finger right in my face.

He paused and I held my breath.

'I'm warning you, if it goes badly, you've only got yourself to blame.'

FIVE

THE HITCHHIKER

BY MATTEO J. ROSSI

He notices the child first – through a dreamy fug of tiredness – a tiny figure in a white T-shirt that catches his eye against the greens and greys of the tarmac and the sunburnt verge, kicking up the dust at the edge of the road. Some distance on, a young woman stands in the shade of a tree, nonchalantly thumbing a lift while dragging on a cigarette.

Instinctively he slows – which is lucky because a microsecond later, a white flash crosses his field of vision as the child runs out. He slams on the brakes and swerves violently across the carriageway. With a sickening jolt and a screech of metal and tyres, he grinds to a halt in a suffocating cloud of dust. His head hits the dash. The music stops.

Rewind an hour...

He's in the moment yet sees himself from a distance. The sun is shining. He's wearing shades. The roof is down.

He's 'living the dream'.

He owns the rush of freedom and speed, powering along the *Route Nationale Sept* that runs between Paris and the Italian border. The Parisians know the road as the *Route des*

Vacances – or, more cynically, during the July and August race to the Mediterranean beaches, the *Route de la Mort* – road of death. Here, a few hours south of Paris, in the vicinity of Moulins, the RN7 is dead straight despite the rolling countryside. Unlike country roads in England that wind sympathetically round geographic contours, clinging to the natural boundaries of vale and hill, these cruel French roads cut through the countryside, with military precision, dissecting woods, fields and villages in a relentless stomach-lurching roller coaster strip of tarmac as far as the eye can see.

Plane trees rise like sentinels at regular intervals on each side of the road. He's tired. It's early afternoon. There are only a few cars on the road and for long stretches, it's empty. He's been driving without a break for five hours. Driving into the sun. He's tries to keep alert – knocking back a Coke and blasting out the music. At one point he strays to the left-hand side of the carriageway, only to be jolted out of his reverie when a lorry angrily flashes its headlights and hoots wildly.

'Bloody French maniac!' he shouts out before realising with a jolt that he's the one at fault, on the wrong side of the road.

The sports car is borrowed from his stepdad – the least favoured from his stable of Jaguars. This is a present for Ted's twenty-first birthday and graduation from university – not an outright gift, of course, but the use of his stepdad's car over the summer for an extended trip to Italy. Ted's not stupid. He knows his stepdad's real agenda is to get him out of the house and away from his mother for the long vacation, the longer the better – forever as far as he's concerned. They don't get on.

Pressured by her new second husband, Ted's mum has arranged for him to pass the summer working on his grandparents' farm in southern Tuscany. He'd have preferred to join his mates on a trip to Southeast Asia. But he's had more than his fair share of getting stoned at all-nighters in the clubs of Magaluf and Zante, and they'd be doing the same kind of thing, just on the other side of the globe. And anyway, three years at university have left him completely broke with an eye-watering student debt. To be honest, he's looking forward to the manual labour out in the open air after weeks of revising for finals.

* * *

But now this...

His hands grip the leather steering wheel. His torso slumps forwards, racked with coughing. His eyes are screwed tightly shut as he struggles to control his breathing. He can't bring himself to open them, terrified of what he'll see. The music has stopped. The only beat he can hear is his thumping heart.

Is this where his life pivots?

* * *

He feels a light touch on his forearm and hears a young female English voice.

'Are you OK?'

Because of his low seating position, her thighs are all he can see when he opens his eyes. They're only a few inches from his face, tanned and smooth, with downy blonde hair and a small black tattoo of a broken heart on her top inside leg. Then she bends down and smiles. Thank God, the child must be safe. Time seems to stand still. Did he imagine the child? Eventually, she lifts her sunglasses and laughs.

'Thanks for stopping,' she says.

She's very pretty with golden brown hair and blue eyes. Not much more than a girl. She must be about his age. Ted has never been lost for a chat-up line before. It could be the bang on the head. He just sits there looking at her stupidly.

A second later, she's gone. He watches her through the rear-view mirror as she saunters back along the verge. She heaves on a big rucksack and hangs the guitar over her shoulder. She calls back to the child to follow her and he trots along behind in the road. He's heard of hitchhikers using a girl as eye candy to stop a car, but her tactics were something else!

A car approaches at speed and again he can't bear to look for fear of what might happen to the tiny child, but the driver slows and winds down the window, making catcalls and whistles and obscene gestures.

What the hell are you playing at? I almost ran over the kid. He could have died. I could have died. That's what he wants to say when she picks up the little boy – not much more than a toddler, wearing shorts and a dirty T-shirt and a pair of beach sandals, with blond curls framing his face – and places him unceremoniously in his lap. But in fact, he says nothing – heart racing – stunned into silence.

While she swings her guitar onto the back shelf-seats and wedges the rucksack next to it, he notes the weight of him. He's never held a little child before – soft and solid and warm. He feels the surge of something new. You could call it tenderness.

'Where are you going?' he asks as she slides into the passenger seat beside him.

She smells musky – a heady mix of incense and fresh grass and cigarette smoke and strong French cologne and two days on the road. Her fingers sparkle with cheap rings. Rows of braided friendship bracelets colour her wrists. Her vest top reveals bruises round her neck and on her upper arms. She's made no attempt to hide them. She wears them proudly – like her tattoos.

'I don't care,' she says. 'South. Just drive.'

'I'm headed for Italy,' he says.

She takes the little boy from Ted and places him between her legs then puts the belt around them both.

'Perfect. I've heard Italian lovers are the best in the world. Let's go.'

SIX

DANIELLE

Despite the gloomy economic climate caused by the pandemic, it was surprisingly easy to find a buyer for my flat. Private green space was in high demand because of the risk of further lockdowns and the property on Highbury Hill had a decent-sized communal garden at the back shared by the four flats. The other big selling point was the flat's location – less than five minutes' walk from Highbury Fields and a fifteen-minute cycle route or short trip on public transport to Hampstead Heath.

It was the next best thing to living in the countryside, having access to these extensive open spaces almost on your doorstep. And for anyone unlucky enough to have to go into the office to work, it was an easy commute to Shoreditch or the City or Canary Wharf.

There was so much interest that in the end, the estate agent asked the five prospective buyers to send in sealed bids and the flat was sold to the highest bidder (a couple with a young baby moving from a high-rise flat in Docklands) for twenty-seven thousand pounds more than its full asking price.

'That will be going towards the new infinity pool,' I said cheerfully.

I'd expected Matt to be grateful for my selflessness in agreeing to sell my own investment so that he could enjoy his inheritance. But if anything, he became more and more bad-tempered and irritable with me as the days went by. It was almost as if the more financial independence I gave up for his benefit, the more he took it (and me) for granted. When I thought back to our carefree dates pre-lockdown – how clever and funny and considerate he'd been – I hoped that his disagreeable behaviour now was just a passing phase and not his real nature.

The slightest comment or omission could trigger an argument. If I asked him to put his dirty clothes in the basket or if I forgot to put sugar in his tea, that would be enough to start an argument. He accused me of pressurising him into making the move to Italy, but at the same time, if I ever hinted that he had the right to renounce his inheritance, he'd fly off the handle and say that he had no choice but to accept his fate.

'You've forced my hand,' he'd say. 'Why did you have to interfere?'

Our packing was fraught, as Matt was still in denial about the move and had to be nagged to do anything to help. Travel was restricted between European countries, with borders closed to all but 'essential travel', and arranging freight wasn't straightforward, so we decided to take as little as possible. We put most of our stuff into storage. Matt boxed up all his files from his three previous unfinished novels and rejected screenplays, and put them into storage. I packed up my university notes, files and legal textbooks, and went through all the 'junk' in our bedroom – my old clothes and ornaments and rows and rows of bookshelves stacked precariously with books that dated back to my childhood and had moved with me from one cramped student accommodation to another to land up here. I'd been putting off having this clear-out for almost a decade.

I made three piles: Italy, storage and recycling. At first, I found it hard to put anything into the recycling pile but suddenly, I had a change of heart. I was sick of the lot of it, especially my clothes – all those tired old outfits that had seen me through lockdown. I took everything off the storage pile and dumped it onto the pile for recycling. Then I got a roll of black bin liners and stuffed it all into the bags. If there was anything that living with the virus had taught me, it was that you had to live in the moment. All this baggage from the past was weighing me down.

For the next week, I used my one permitted exercise outing of the day to haul the black bin bags down to the recycling point. When the job was finally done, I was left with only two large suitcases containing the things that I wanted to take to Italy – one full of clothes and another full of books and painting materials. This was all I wished to salvage from my life in London, now tainted by the pandemic.

It was time to start afresh.

Leaving my employment proved to be more difficult than selling the flat. The redundancy negotiations were protracted and tense. In the meantime, I had to continue with the interminable online team meetings and Zoom calls that had become the bane of my life. At the peak of the lockdown, there had been a sense of purpose and heightened determination to get through this crisis together.

That had been the atmosphere at work as well as in the community, but as the weeks dragged by, I felt increasingly detached from my colleagues. There was something Orwellian about those virtual meetings – all human contact reduced to two-dimensional images on a screen. I missed those small cues of friendship – habits and gestures, even the familiar smell of a perfume or aftershave – that cemented normal human interactions.

In the 'new normal', I played the game, setting up my laptop in a corner of the dining room where the lighting was the best and the clutter pushed to one side, checking the titles of the books on the shelves that formed the backdrop to my profile, putting on my make-up flawlessly and wearing a flattering top over pyjama bottoms or a scruffy pair of jeans – all the usual tricks. But there was a virtual disconnect and something fake about it all that contributed to my feelings of dislocation and futility. It was all a façade, framed within the rectangle of my computer screen.

Eventually, the discussions with my law firm were concluded and I agreed to their voluntary redundancy package. The firm was contracting owing to the fall-off in business after the pandemic. My practice in media and entertainment law had been particularly hard hit as the performing arts industries had been so ravaged by the lockdown restrictions with the forced closure of cinemas, theatres and concert venues. My pay-off was generous in the circumstances and would be sufficient, I hoped, to pay for much of the renovation work on the Italian estate as well as our initial living expenses.

I agreed to keep in touch with my partner at the law firm and to make myself available for freelance work on an occasional basis once I was settled in Italy. My spirits rose the minute I signed on the dotted line of my redundancy letter. I was free! I couldn't wait to get out of London. I was sick of walking its streets, where everyone was head down and suspicious and masked. I couldn't wait to rip off my mask and look up to the sun and the sky and the splendid isolation of the Tuscan countryside.

Matt had taken on board my idea about realising his ambition to get a novel published. On the strength of his track record with his two non-fiction books, he'd successfully pulled a few strings among his contacts in the industry to land himself a publishing contract for his proposed novel. Now, all he had to do was write it!

We were set fair for Tuscany.

I just hoped that Matteo's mood would improve when he got there.

SEVEN
DANIELLE

The long hot summer seemed to go on forever until one day in September, the landline rang. It was hardly ever used anymore and the shrill rings made me jump. I stood motionless and uncomprehending, listening intently to Matt's Italian conversation. His tone was animated and he gesticulated like a native. He spoke fluently though with a strong English–American accent as a result of having grown up and been educated in the UK before doing postgraduate studies and working for several years in the USA. For the first time, it occurred to me that there was a whole other dimension to Matt's life of which I was ignorant – and from which I'd be excluded unless and until I learnt to speak Italian.

He put down the phone and turned to face me.

'Well, you got your way,' he said. Now, his voice was flat and dull. 'It's done. The farmhouse is mine.'

I wanted to dance round the room. At last, we were the owners of a 300-year-old Tuscan farmhouse on a plot of over thirty hectares. We were landowners! But his word 'mine' brought home another reality I hadn't considered until today despite my years of legal training. The farmhouse belonged to Matt and Matt alone.

I brushed the thought aside. Now was the time for celebration. I spun round to the fridge to grab a bottle of champagne that I'd been saving for this very moment – a parting gift from my colleagues at McKendricks. London law firms had extensive wine cellars, so they were still well stocked despite the new border controls.

'This calls for a celebration,' I said brightly, setting out two champagne flutes.

It was impossible to get champagne in the shops these days. Normal people were cut off from all that was fine and life-enhancing on the continent of Europe. The drink had become a rare luxury for all but the most privileged and reserved for the most special occasions.

'Not tonight,' said Matt crossly. 'I've got a pile of paperwork to get through. Save it till we get there. You might want to drown your sorrows when you see the state of the old place!'

* * *

It felt like a race against time to get travel arrangements booked and final preparations made. Infections were on the rise again in England and despite all the prime minister's denials, we knew it was only a matter of time before the country went into another lockdown. My emotions were roller-coasting as sharply as the steep curve of daily deaths displayed on the hourly news bulletins. The poker-faced medical experts who explained the graphs did nothing to calm my anxiety. My biggest fear was that international borders would be closed before we could leave London.

* * *

After a restless night, I woke at dawn full of apprehension and excitement for our escape – that's what it felt like with all the new restrictions imposed on our freedom – escape from a police state. Matt had used fifteen thousand pounds of my redundancy money to buy a second-hand Land Rover for the journey.

'We're going to need a four-wheel drive,' he said. 'The *white roads* will be impassable in winter without one. The farmhouse is very remote.'

I'd protested to no avail: 'We should ship our stuff and buy a right-hand drive once we get to Italy.'

I'd wondered briefly if Matt's insistence on buying a car suited to driving in the UK was because at some conscious or subconscious level, he had no intention of staying long in Tuscany, but put that thought aside and chose to focus on the positives. It was a spacious, sturdy car and we could use it back in the UK if we did end up splitting our time between two homes.

Everything we needed to start our new life in Italy was crammed into the back of the Land Rover. The stashed suit-cases contained all the possessions we'd decided to take with us from the London flat. I'd hauled the heavy cases down the stairs to the car while Matt paced the dining room, engrossed in an 'urgent' business call.

I'd also packed an overnight bag containing a file of all the new supporting documents required for the border crossings, in addition to our passports (freedom of movement was a thing of the past), as well as a 'survival pack' of masks, vinyl gloves, sanitisers, snacks and bottled water. It had taken me a whole day to fill out the many forms required to exit the UK and to enter France and then Italy. Of course, I'd done the forms for the pair of us, since Matt relied on me to deal with all the tedious administrative stuff. It was as much as he could do to sign on the dotted line where I pointed.

As well as submitting forms to show that our travel was essential and for a legitimate purpose (travel to a main residence of which Matt was the legal owner), we had to provide certificates and permits proving that we were financially solvent, virus-free and fit to travel, and with no previous criminal record. This last requirement had particularly outraged Matt and had been complicated for him to comply with, since his dual nationality obliged him to supply certificates from both the British and the Italian police authorities.

'How are we supposed to prove a negative?' he'd stormed. 'It's such an invasion of privacy.'

'Why worry? You've never done anything wrong,' I soothed.

The British permits were no problem – other than a few points for speeding on Matt's driving licence, neither of us had been in trouble with the law. Dealing with the Italian police was another matter. There was some hold-up – concerning certain 'minor misdemeanours' on his record for possession of drugs – or so Matt told me. He railed against their 'inefficiency'. In the end, the lawyer who had dealt with Matt's inheritance jumped through many hoops to procure the necessary Italian certificate of *good character and non-criminality*. I suspected that a bribe had been paid to make this happen.

The borders had reopened in a limited way, but international travel was still disrupted. Although there was very little traffic on the motorways, at every customs post there were long delays. I understood how it must feel to be a refugee travelling through a war-torn country. Armed border police in bulletproof vests, masks, gloves and visors patrolled the queues of vehicles with sniffer dogs. I breathed a sigh of relief when we rolled off the Channel Tunnel train onto French soil. I wanted to jump out and kiss the tarmac. But our ordeal wasn't over.

Our progress through France was slowed by police patrols and road checks at every payment station on the motorway. The UK number plate attracted their attention. The French police were if anything more intrusive and intimidating than the British because they asked more questions. Repeatedly, we were asked to show our documents and on one occasion, the officers ordered us to empty out the entire contents of the Land Rover for a search. What were they looking for? Was it smuggling – now rife again because of the imposition of exorbitant tariffs for trade between the UK and other European states? Or drugs? Were the police officers so hard up owing to the pandemic that they were angling for a bribe in return for allowing us to go unimpeded on our way?

I remembered my trip the previous summer touring round Europe with a group of my girlfriends – you could cross from one country into another without so much as showing your passport. Unlike Matt, I was no longer a European citizen. Those freedoms I'd known and taken for granted since birth to roam freely across Europe had disappeared overnight. My right to live, work and study in any European country had been stripped away by the privileged old men who governed our country. To my mind, that was reason enough to leave it. Great Britain had become Little England and it wasn't funny.

Again and again, we repeated our story in halting French. Matt showed the border police his Italian passport and explained that he'd inherited a property in Tuscany. He spoke passable French thanks to his fluency in Italian, but mine consisted of no more than schoolgirl phrases. His journey was 'essential travel' within the meaning of the regulations, as his stated purpose was to take possession of his new home.

He showed copies of the lawyer's letter and the legal documentation relating to the transfer of the Tuscan property into his ownership, in addition to his 'permit to travel' as a dual national with Italian citizenship. Then the police officers would nod in my direction and ask for my papers, too. Because I wasn't named on the property transfer and wasn't married to Matt or in a formalised cohabiting relationship with him, my status and permission to travel in this new order of restrictions was precarious and ambiguous. The clock had been turned back.

'You should have bought me a ring,' I said despondently. 'It would have made things so much easier if nothing else.'

I had to rely on my powers of persuasion to convince the police that we were in a genuine relationship and that my journey, too, fell within the definition of 'essential travel'.

As we pulled away in the queue, Matt turned to me.

'I didn't want to buy you some stupid trinket from the internet. You deserve the best. When we're all settled, I'm going to take you somewhere special. We'll go to Venice for the weekend and not far from Venice there's a beautiful little town called Vicenza, which is famed throughout Italy for its jewellery and gold – that's where we'll choose your ring!'

He took my hand and kissed my fingers gently, sending a surge of warmth through my body with this unexpected declaration. Sadly, this moment of tenderness was short-lived. Some way further on, there was another halt. When a particularly officious policeman asked Matt to produce the documents for the Land Rover, I was annoyed to discover that Matt had bought it in his name and hadn't even bothered to put my name on the insurance.

'That would have been an extra three hundred and fifty pounds,' he said by way of explanation.

He gave me one of his winning smiles, shrugged and squeezed my hand. For fear of starting an argument in front of the police, I didn't dare to point out that both the car and the insurance had been bought with my redundancy money. Instead, I let him kiss me on the lips. This time his touch left me cold.

A doubt came over me like a passing shadow and for a fleeting instant, I regretted both leaving my job and my decision to sell my London flat. I had thought we could leave our troubles behind us. Was I wrong? *Moving house doesn't fix what's broken,* I mused. *Unhappy couples pack up their troubles into suitcases and then unpack them all again at the other end.* Should I believe promises of engagement rings and weekends away in Venice? Right now, I was in limbo. With no guarantee of safe passage and no place to call home, I was entirely dependent on Matt.

We'd heard reports of hours of delay at the Mont Blanc Tunnel. Northern Italy had suffered so acutely in the first wave of the pandemic that movement into the region was restricted to a few hundred cars a day. Having almost eliminated the virus over the summer, the authorities were determined to control their borders to prevent a recurrence. So, to avoid the long queues at the tunnel, we decided to take the longer coastal route, driving to Aix-en-Provence and then east along the Côte D'Azur to the French–Italian border at Menton–Ventimiglia.

My spirits rose as we sped along the motorway, known as *La Provençale.* Matt was in high spirits, too – rolling down the windows and belting out the songs playing on the radio as he pushed the car to its limits. I glanced at his profile, backlit by the setting sun. *He fits all the clichés,* I thought. *Dark eyes, high forehead, strong jawline, sensual lips.* No wonder I'd fallen for him that first weekend away in Frankfurt when we played truant from the book fair, alternating between the bars and his hotel room.

There was little traffic, and I was able to take in the scenic route bordered by rugged terrain, umbrella pines and the craggy foothills of the Alpes-Maritimes. Even the names on the road signs conjured up glamour and romance from a pre-pandemic era: Saint-Raphaël, Cannes, Nice, Monaco. I wanted to detour down to the beaches, but we knew it was too risky to stop with a full load of suitcases in the back. With the collapse of the tourist industry and so many unemployed, the rates of crime on the Côte d'Azur had skyrocketed and our (or rather Matt's) UK-registered Land Rover would be a sitting target.

When we reached the *Haute Corniche* I cast all my insecurities aside. The approach to the Italian border was dramatic and exhilarating on the spectacular coastal route of tunnels and bridges cutting through the foothills of the Alps. Each time we emerged from the gloom of a tunnel, the intense sunlight and glittering expanse of the Mediterranean stretching to the horizon hit me with a renewed and thrilling sense of infinite possibility.

EIGHT
THE HITCHHIKER
BY MATTEO J. ROSSI

After a couple of hours, they stop for fuel. The hitchhiker leaves Ted minding the boy, while she goes into the service station.

'Give me a minute,' she says.

She comes back with a Pepsi, aniseed chewing gum and Gauloises cigarettes for herself and, for the little boy, a bar of chocolate and a sugary drink. While she lights a cigarette, Ted spreads out the map of Europe that his stepfather gave him.

'We're about an hour's drive away from the entrance to the Mont Blanc Tunnel,' he says.

The hitchhiker's having none of it.

'Are you crazy?' she says. 'We're not driving through a ten-mile tunnel in this.' She gestures extravagantly, drawing a circle above her head with the smoke from her cigarette. 'It'll be dark and claustrophobic and full of car fumes.'

She puffs a cloud of smoke over the child's head. He clocks the irony but doesn't say a word.

'We're going over the top. The views will be fabulous.'

Her smile is irresistible in both senses. It's all he can do to resist leaning in to touch her sensuous lips with his own.

'I've always dreamt of crossing the Alps in an open-top sports car.'

Luckily, he's always been pretty good at map-reading and instantly he knows she's right. He remembers taking the route once before as a young child with his parents when they went to visit his Italian grandfather's farm in Tuscany. He'd been so excited at the prospect of seeing the St Bernard rescue dogs at the top of the mountain, but his father had been in one of his sullen rages and had refused to allow them a stop despite his mother's pleading.

It seems normal – the hitchhiker laying down the law like this. He's already under her spell. The stunning mountain road will be the perfect start to their Italian adventure. He spreads out the map on the bonnet of the car.

'The Great St Bernard Pass – Colle del Gran San Bernardo...' He sing-songs the words like a proper Italian, throwing his hands in the air.

The little boy, balanced on her hip, catches the mood, grabbing her hair and joining in the laughter.

'The route takes us round Lake Geneva. The climb starts from Martigny in Switzerland. It'll take us at least an hour to get to the top.'

Ted looks it up on his phone. At an altitude of almost 2,500 metres, the mountain pass is the third highest road in the Alps, marking the convergence of the snowy peaks of France, Switzerland and Italy, linking the Valais canton of Switzerland with the Aosta Valley and the Piedmont region in Italy. With the optimism of youth, Ted is unrealistic about their timings.

'We'll be at the Great St Bernard Pass before sunset,' he

says. 'We can stop for an hour or two – get some supper maybe and see the monastery and the dogs – then cross over the border and drive down the mountain to Aosta on the Italian side. It's a scruffy little town, but there should be some places to stay the night.'

The views are spectacular, the road winding up green slopes towards the immense craggy grey peaks and glittering snowcaps scissoring the sky. They pass sheer drops, bare rocks, open galleries and dark tunnels opening out onto vast wild-flower meadows. It's like entering a landscape from *Lord of the Rings*.

Ted forces the car, taking the hairpin bends at speed. Exhilarated by the ride, the hitchhiker grips the child, throws back her head and laughs – inciting Ted to further risks. Suddenly, as the sports car emerges from a short tunnel at reckless speed, a cyclist – like a giant swooping bat in black Lycra – is there right in front of them. Ted slams on the brakes and the car squeals across the road, by some miracle towards the mountain and not the drop, slamming into a small stone shrine at side of the road – a memorial to a road accident victim. The shrine brings the car to a stop and prevents it from skidding towards the precipice at the next bend. His second emergency stop of the day. And again, she has something to do with it. Is she working a spell – or a curse?

'What the fuck's going on?' the hitchhiker screams at Ted, hysterical laughter turning to outrage.

Ted is too shocked to speak. While she calms the child, Ted gets out shakily. The cyclist is nowhere to be seen. He looks over the 300-metre rock face drop in horror. A few seconds later, he sees the cyclist rounding a bend and watches him fleetingly until he disappears into the next tunnel. Horror turns to anger. Why didn't the crazy bastard stop?

Ted retches into the void then steps back to inspect the damage on the car. The impact with the stone shrine has slashed the front tyre and made a big dent on the wing. The car should be drivable if he can change the wheel. That's a big *if*. Ted has never changed a wheel before. He empties out the boot. Luckily, there's a spare wheel and a jack. Eventually, he finds the wheel nut, jammed at the back of the glove compartment.

'I need a cigarette,' she says while he fumbles about on the ground trying to work out how to fix the jack.

Ted imagines that her need is less to calm her nerves (she's a high-adrenaline junkie) and more to satisfy her cravings and stave off boredom. She wanders up the road. This time at least she's holding the little boy's hand. There are no other cars in sight. Few drivers would be foolish enough to start on the mountain crossing this late in the day. He wonders if she's planning to hitch another ride. Will she abandon him here alone on the mountainside?

In the end, it's more than two hours before a car pulls up. Ted has long given up struggling with the wheel change. He watches her talking to someone through an open van window. She leans in flirtatiously, resting her elbows on the sill, and he thinks this is it – her next lift has arrived. Any second, she'll walk back to the car, grab her rucksack and guitar, and she'll be gone from his life forever. The pain in his gut is visceral.

But, to his surprise, the driver parks up, gets out and starts strolling towards the car. Turns out he's a mechanic and has taken pity on the girl. Within minutes, he's elbowed Ted out of the way, jacked up the car, mounted the spare wheel and stowed the broken wheel back in the boot.

'Aren't you glad you picked me up?' she beams triumphantly.

The light is fading fast and the temperature has dropped by the time the monastery comes into view after the last turn in the road to the summit. The Great St Bernard Pass is named after the founder of the monastery and the iconic mountain rescue dogs that were bred by the monks. Grey stone cloisters built of rock hewn from the mountain straddle the highest point of the ancient road. This was once a place of refuge and rescue for travellers lost in the snow. But it looks eerie and forbidding in the rocky wasteland in the gathering dark. As the car draws level, they have a view of the lake, the colour of slate, mysterious and impenetrable.

The boy shivers in his T-shirt and shorts. She doesn't notice or doesn't care. The cold doesn't seem to bother her. She's leaning back in the seat staring up at the stars.

'I've never seen them so bright,' she says.

'We should go somewhere warm and get something to eat,' says Ted.

There's only one bar at the top of the mountain and when they try the door, the barman barks, '*C'est fermé.*'

He's wiping down the surfaces and stacking the stools upside down on the tables with stoic indifference. He waves them off in the direction of a shabby-looking Alpine chalet a little further down the road.

'You can try there,' he says in perfect English.

The Auberge Saint-Bernard has seen better days, but the food is good. They order the one dish on the menu – a traditional rustic supper of rösti potatoes topped with salty bacon, fried egg and melted raclette cheese – washed down with a pitcher of sticky red wine. The little boy is restless and whiney. Ted tries to entertain him by making faces across the table.

The little boy isn't impressed. He spits out his food and throws a glass onto the floor.

'He must be exhausted,' says Ted.

She ignores the child while Ted makes a half-hearted attempt to pick up the pieces. By the end of the meal, the toddler has smashed three glasses and a bowl, the contents of which he tipped out over the head of the hotel cat waiting under his chair for scraps. The long-suffering waitress hovers with a dustpan and brush, looking pained and desperate for them to leave so she can clear up all the debris. Ted can't keep his eyes open. The hitchhiker smokes and sips her coffee as if she hadn't a care in the world. She's in no hurry to break up the party.

'I'm dead,' says Ted. 'Been up since four in the morning. I'm going to ask for a room for the night.'

'I'm skint,' she says. 'I thought we'd be spending the night on the road.'

And that's all she needs to say. Ted understands that he'll be paying for supper and the room.

'I can make it worth your while,' she says.

And he's not sure if she's teasing.

* * *

'I'll sleep on the floor,' says Ted, surveying the room, the cheapest in the hotel, on the top floor under the eaves.

The style is austere and monastic – wooden walls and a tiled floor, with only a narrow double bed on one wall, and a table and chair on the other.

'Don't be daft. We can share the bed. Harry can sleep in the middle,' she says. 'That way, he won't fall out.'

Ted stands awkwardly at the end of the bed while she

settles the sleeping child on the hard mattress. After two hours of hyperactivity, crying and tantrums, the little boy has finally worn himself out. It's the first time Ted has heard her refer to him by name. She checks herself and Ted guesses that she hadn't intended to let his name slip out.

'Is he yours?' says Ted.

'You think I kidnapped him?' She looks at him defiantly. 'Do I look like a baby snatcher?'

'You're so young,' says Ted. 'Are you his sister or his mother?' He realises how patronising he must sound.

'He's mine,' she says. 'We're running away.'

That doesn't really answer his question but then, it's none of his business.

He wants to ask her what they're running from. What situation could be so desperate as to lead a penniless teenage girl to hitch-hike across Europe with a toddler in tow?

'I don't even know your name,' he says.

'Shush,' she replies. 'You'll wake him.'

She comes to the end of the bed where he's standing, kisses him like she's done this before, then puts her finger over his lips and starts to undo his jeans.

'Wait,' he says. 'You know nothing about me. I don't expect you to make love to me. I could be a serial killer for all you know.'

'At least I'd die happy.' She laughs.

When it's all over, she collapses back on the bed next to the boy and motions for Ted to join her. The baby lies between them on the narrow mattress. He feels an overwhelming sense of tenderness for this beautiful mysterious girl and her baby (if he is hers?) who have crashed into his life.

He wants to know everything about her.

'Please let me sleep,' she says, irritated by his questions.

'At least tell me your name,' he says.

She kisses him sleepily then pushes him away.

'What happened on the mountain?' she says, changing the subject as if she just remembered that she'd been meaning to ask him. 'You flipped out.'

'It wasn't my fault,' he says. 'If I hadn't swerved, that crazy cyclist would have crashed right into us.'

She turns to him. 'There was no cyclist, Ted,' she says, looking long and deep into his eyes. 'You're just a bad driver.'

She silences his protest with another warm, slow kiss. Then she rolls over to face the wall.

'You can call me Nikki,' she says. 'That's double "k", "i". And now I'm going to sleep.'

NINE
DANIELLE

My friends (those few I was still in touch with through the lockdowns) were judgemental and bemused about our plan to emigrate to Italy when Europe was still in the throes of a pandemic.

'Don't you think it's selfish moving to another country when they're in such difficulties?' said my 'best friend' Jenna. 'You'll be adding to the burden on Italian public services just when they're stretched to breaking point.'

My 'next best friend', Amy, questioned whether or not I was being impulsive, moving abroad with a man I'd only been living with for a few months.

'You need to be really sure he's the one,' she said. 'You haven't been together for long.'

'Ignore them,' Matt said in rare moments when he was feeling more positive about the move. 'They're just jealous that you're starting a new life while they're stuck in *the Big Smoke*.'

I suspected there were other reasons why my girlfriends were less than positive about my move. Yes, they were sorry to see me go and perhaps a little jealous about me spreading my wings in Europe while they were stuck at home, but I also sensed a strange mix of jealousy and disapproval of my new relationship with Matt.

By 'pre-pandemic' norms, he was certainly a catch on the social scene. When he arrived in London from New York, he'd caused quite a stir with his classic good looks, his colourful Italian shirts and snappy suits, and his educated, smooth Anglo–American accent. I'd see him with his friends at the pub or a work event, always the life and soul of the party – a warm and attentive host bringing everyone into the conversation, treating everyone with respect and entertaining everyone with his witty comments and quirky anecdotes. He appeared unconscious of his exceptional charm and the fact that each woman in the room was aware of his presence and wanting to please him. At least that was my view of him.

He had his detractors. He'd gained a reputation for arrogance on account of his sharp wit and famed intelligence (Oxford University, then Harvard Business School – frankly, overqualified for the world of publishing, he often made out). And for being a womaniser, because every time he was seen out socialising, he was with a different woman (attractive, self-possessed) or surrounded by a gang of pretty, giggly young things competing for his attention. Yet, he could be disarmingly funny and gallant in an old-fashioned brusque 'Darcy-esque' kind of way. Many of my friends admitted that they found him devastatingly attractive.

So, when we began dating, I knew I'd ruffled some feathers among my friends, who also had him within their sights. I got wind of backchat suggesting he was 'out of my league' and I was 'punching above my weight' and 'bound to get hurt'.

At the time, Matt was an important client of my law firm and my female boss seemed conflicted in her approach to him. On the one side, she flirted with Matt outrageously and resented the attention he gave to me. On the flip side, she took me aside one day to warn that one of the new trainees had come to her with serious allegations about sexual harassment and inappropriate behaviour occasioned by him. Fearing she'd said too much, she then back-pedalled, said the girl was mentally unstable, suffering from depression, and that soon after she'd been signed off on sick leave for 'unrelated reasons'.

'The poor girl is an unreliable witness,' she said. 'Yet, I felt duty-bound to tip you off.'

Crossing the border from France into Italy, I put all that water-cooler gossip and hypocritical concern behind me. I experienced not only the thrill of anticipation, but also the uplifting conviction of being on a mission. I had a renewed sense of purpose. It was as if by moving to this country, which had suffered so poignantly and been so ravaged by the virus, I could participate in its national effort to regenerate and rebuild. The Italian government was reaching out to overseas investors and to its own citizens who lived abroad to return to the motherland and work for the prosperity of the nation. I was excited to be a part of this.

Not far beyond the border, we entered the spaghetti junction of suspended motorways and bridges that circled the town of Genoa. Despite my positivity, for a few instants I was gripped with panic. My chest was tight. It was like a scene from a bad dream. Would I be forever lost and stuck on this infernal roundabout? But once we'd navigated the knot of roundabouts and tunnels at the juncture of the Maritime and Ligurian Alps, the motorway opened up and I began to breathe more freely.

With little traffic on the road, we sped through the open plains north-east of the now deserted seaside resort of La Spezia and on past the dazzling white slopes of Carrara, famous for its marble quarries. Massive glistening blocks of marble lined the route, piled high in open storage facilities.

I marvelled to think these quarries were the source for the stone used to build the Pantheon temple in Rome and for Michelangelo's timeless, iconic sculptures. They'd been used for so many architectural and artistic masterpieces throughout Italy and the world. These vast blocks cut from the earth would endure infinitely beyond the current turmoil affecting the fine arts, the performing arts and all pleasure-giving, life-enhancing sectors of society. Funnily enough, their solidity seemed to symbolise the substance and dura-bility and infinite malleability of all things of beauty and architecture. A mere pandemic couldn't rob humanity of those.

It wasn't long before the motorway cut in from the coast towards Lucca, Florence, San Gimignano and Siena. I'd never visited Italy, but the names on the road signs held such reso-nance for me. I knew Tuscany through the technicolour haze and hues of the books and films I'd loved as a teenager: *A Room with a View*, *The English Patient*, *Under the Tuscan Sun* – these were my favourites.

The timeless landscape through which we drove was unscathed by the pandemic – or at least so it seemed from our fleeting and distant views over the rolling hills. The olive groves were green and silvered – heralding the late autumn olive harvest. They'd been there for generations – surviving savage world wars and fascist repression and unrecorded mutations of deadly viruses through the centuries. Fortified hilltop villages topped with feudal towers and castles dominated the skyline. This ancient land had weathered many storms.

The landscape changed again as we drove south of Siena towards Pienza. Here, the focus was less on viticulture and more on the cultivation of grains. I'd done my research and had read in the tourist guides that from spring through to late summer, the hillsides of the Val d'Orcia were an ever-changing tableau, moving through light greens to dark green to shining swathes of golden wheat as far as the eye could see. But now, the wheat fields had been harvested and ploughed into clods of baking brown earth. The effect was strangely moving – both lunar and biblical – the fields of bare clay glowing in the autumn sunshine. As we drove between San Quirico d'Orcia and Pienza, this elemental moonscape of earth and dust invoked in me not only feelings of exhilaration, but also a sense of my own mortality. *For dust thou art, and unto dust shalt thou return...*

Eventually, we came to the medieval hilltop city of Pienza – the jewel of southern Tuscany that in recent years had become so popular with tourists. It was the closest substantial town to the isolated farmhouse Matt had inherited. I wanted to stop to look around this place that I'd read so much about ('a perfect miniature of Renaissance architecture recognised by UNESCO as a World Heritage Site') and to pick up some provisions. Matt was keen to press on.

'Marcella will have some food and essentials to get us started,' he said.

Reluctantly, he pulled off and found a parking space near the supermarket. It was closed and shuttered. A police officer was walking up and down the car park. He stopped a few feet away from our loaded car and stood watching. Matteo was visibly on edge. He fumbled with the glove compartment and dropped the car key down the side of the seat, cursing profusely as he struggled to retrieve it. We put on our masks and gloves, got out of the car and nodded nervously to the policeman before strolling into the city walls.

There was no one about – not a tourist in sight – even though it was a Saturday afternoon. It seemed things were even stricter here than in London. The cathedral was locked, as were the three palazzos that framed the main square. Matt had told me about the famous ice-cream shop ('the best pistachio ice cream south of Siena'), but that was closed and shuttered, too. There was a notice on the door. I picked out the words '*pandemia*' and '*chiuso*'. Other than that, I couldn't decipher it and Matt was too impatient to translate.

'I need to learn Italian,' I said.

Although I'd never admit the same to Matt, I worried that with my pathetically limited knowledge of the language, I'd lose my independence.

Matt led me through the narrow streets to the ramparts that circled the town, giving a 360-degree view of the Tuscan countryside. The thick stone wall was solid and cold beneath my fingers as I leant into the wind and lifted my chin. It felt good to be far from the contagion of the metropolis, to take long, deep breaths and to stand with the breeze whipping through my hair. On impulse, I took a selfie of us standing there, side by side, big smiles and crazy hair.

'This is as good as it gets, isn't it?' I laughed.

I gazed out over the sea of rolling hills formed of ploughed wheat fields and olive groves crested with farm buildings, white roads snaking along the contours to the distant mountains on the horizon.

'Freedom at last,' I shouted into the wind.

After months of being confined, our lives had opened up again, like the landscape.

Although the historic little town was still in hibernation, it too seemed on the brink of coming back to life, like a theatre set before curtain-up.

Matt took out a map from his jacket pocket.

'Haven't seen one of those for a while,' I joked.

All navigation took place on screens these days. The map was stained and creased and had been folded incorrectly. I guessed it must be a relic from Matt's summer vacations in Tuscany all those years ago. He spread it out on the stone surface and held it down with his elbows. The corners flapped in the breeze. He studied the map for a minute or two, checking his bearings against the hamlets and solitary farm-houses visible from the viewpoint. The Rossi estate was circled in red biro.

Then he looked up.

'Now, if I'm not mistaken, it's that one.' He pointed to a hillock in the distance. 'See that track,' he said, 'winding up between the trees to the bridge over the river? Now, on the top of that hill... See there – the line of cypress trees? That's the driveway. And you can just make out the rooftops of the farm buildings hidden behind.'

Without warning, he swung me up onto the rampart so that I could see better. My legs hung over the ledge and I clung to him, my eyes brimming over with love and excitement.

'I think we made the right choice,' he said.

As Matt bent to kiss me, a gust of wind blew the map and he made a grab for it, sending me lurching forwards, perilously close to tipping over the edge. I scrambled off the wall, my legs like jelly, while he watched the map fluttering down onto the rocks below, cursing softly.

'You bloody idiot,' I screamed, close to tears. 'You almost killed me.'

Matt was already walking away.

'Come on. Let's go,' he said with no word of apology, his voice sullen and flat. 'I can remember the route without the map. Marcella will be waiting to hand over the keys.'

TEN
THE HITCHHIKER
BY MATTEO J. ROSSI

Ted lies awake listening to the noises of the night. He's been awake for hours – overcome with euphoria and too enervated for sleep. He can't believe what just happened. He has the taste of her in his mouth – a mix of Gauloises and aniseed that leaves him longing for more. Next to him, Harry snuffles in his sleep.

He touches the downy cheek of the boy. Ted doesn't know much about kids, but he guesses Harry must be about two years old – just a baby really. He can hear the girl breathing softly, too. Mostly, he can hear the howling gale rattling the shutters and battering the wooden structure of the hotel with all its force. Then there are creaks and tapping on the other side of the door and scuffling in the rafters above his head. *'The house is breathing,'* his mother would say. *You could say that, or you could say it's haunted,* he tells himself, not quite disbelieving it.

It's a narrow bed and the girl lies sprawled across it, taking up most of the space. He finds it hard to take his eyes off her. Then there's the child. Ted is on the very edge, keeping as still as possible. He's desperate to hold the girl in his arms, but he can't bear the thought of any more tantrums in the middle of the night. Harry looks like a sleeping angel now. Over supper, he was like a little devil.

Ted needs to relieve himself after all the beer and the wine, but the communal bathroom is at the very end of a dimly lit corridor. He prefers to hold on. He knows he's being pathetic. But this place gives him the creeps. His emotions are aroused to a pinnacle of intensity – good and bad. He listens to the wind, closes his eyes and waits for the night to pass...

He's perched on the ledge of a cliff above a rocky bay. A giant black bat swoops towards him and circles away, screeching and flapping its wings with the sound of a hurricane. Each swoop forces Ted closer and closer to the edge of the cliff until he falls backwards and hurtles into the rocky sea below...

Ted wakes with a bump on the tiled floor next to the bed. His shoulder hurts and his shirt sticks to his legs. A flush of embarrassment. Did he wet himself? Surely not.

He gets up off the floor and quietly changes his top before creeping down the corridor to the bathroom. The stars are still out, though there's light in the sky and the wind has calmed. The storm is over.

When he climbs back in bed, he discovers that the mattress is soaking. Harry is asleep, but his pyjama bottoms are drenched. The girl must have forgotten to put a nappy on him. Ted tries to shake her awake.

'Harry needs changing,' he whispers.

But she's dead to the world.

He can't leave the child in this state. He rummages in her rucksack and finds a nappy. There are no wipes. He makes his way back down the gloomy corridor to the bathroom and then improvises with wet paper towels. He's never done this before. The child's bottom is red and sore. She's been neglecting him. He cleans him up as best he can and finds some nappy cream in the bottom of her bag. He puts on a thick layer and then the clean nappy. He's pleased with a job well done, bonded to them both by this simple act of intimacy.

Neither Harry nor the girl have opened their eyes through his whole performance. He covers the wet patch on the bed with a spare quilt that he finds in the cupboard and gently puts the child back into her arms. He watches them sleeping. *Nikki... Nikki...* He tries out her name in his head. She looks scarcely more than a child herself, lying there so innocently. She told him over supper that she's nineteen years old, only a couple of years younger than him. Watching over them in the darkness, he feels suddenly much older. He feels like a man.

Slipping back into bed beside her, he says softly in her ear, 'Right now, everything I care about in this world is here in this bed,' hoping his words will penetrate her dreams.

'That's the most romantic thing anyone has ever said to me,' she whispers back.

She'd been pretending to sleep the whole time.

* * *

The room is empty when she wakes up the next morning. For a moment she doesn't know where she is. Strips of sunlight fall on the bed sheets, shining through the slats in the shutters. She jumps out of bed and even though there's nowhere in the spartan room that he could be hiding, she calls out Harry's name.

'Oh my God! He's taken him.'

She throws open the shutters and scans the parking area

and the road beyond. The mountain sun is streaming down. Thank God! Ted's blue sports car is still there, gleaming in the sunshine. She takes the stairs two at a time. By the time she clatters down the four floors and reaches the breakfast room, she's flushed and out of breath. It's only when the waitress gives her a strange look that she looks down to see she's wearing nothing but Ted's oversized T-shirt and a pair of briefs. She's barefoot. She hasn't brushed her hair or washed the make-up off her face from last night. She looks a fright.

Harry's beaker is on the table. The hitchhiker stares at it with panic in her eyes. Seeing her anguish, the waitress smiles uncertainly and nods towards the open door.

'*Il est avec son papa*,' she says. He's with his dad.

ELEVEN
DANIELLE

Marcella was waiting by the road, leaning against a rusty iron gate, in the shade of a cypress tree. She was in her late sixties, her face kind and open and lined by the southern Tuscan sun. She had the look of someone who had worked close to the land for years. Still upset and shaken after my scare on the ramparts, the homely appearance of Marcella lifted my mood. Matt braked sharply, jumped out of the car and ran over, forgetting the social distancing rules. Marcella called out, '*Teo, Teo... ciao... dare il benvenuto... ciao,*' – welcome, welcome – and instinctively reached out for an embrace.

I smiled to hear Matt's Italian name – *Teo* – and reflected that here in Tuscany, he had a different identity to the Matt I'd known. Then I laughed as Matt swept Marcella off her feet while she squealed like a child. But the second he put the old woman down, she backed away, turning her head and gesturing wildly for him to keep his distance.

I knew arriving Brits were treated as high-risk. But her reaction was more than fear of the virus. She looked emotionally conflicted, as if she regretted her instinctive impulse to

71

hug him. Now, tears were streaming down her cheeks. She resisted the urge to wipe them away, government health warnings to avoid face-touching having been ingrained from months of self-control.

Matt pointed at me. 'This is Danielle.'

'*La tua fidanzata?*' – ah your fiancée? – said Marcella in Italian, her eyes darting from my masked face to my wedding finger... and finding it without a ring.

'She's my girlfriend,' Matt replied. '*La mia ragazza.*'

I looked away, hurt he thought it necessary to correct her.

Marcella beckoned for us to turn into the driveway. The cypress trees that lined the stony track stood like watchmen guarding the entrance to the farmhouse at the top of the hill with an air of solemnity that seemed somehow out of place and ominous. Marcella locked the gates behind us and got back into her own car – a dented and scratched dark-green Fiat Panda that had seen better days and that bounced along, navigating the ruts and humps of the rough track with more ease than our four-wheel drive.

'I think that might be the same car she was driving fifteen years ago.' He laughed.

'I thought cypress trees were a symbol of mourning and death,' I mused. 'I've only ever seen them in cemeteries before.'

'They're everywhere in Tuscany,' said Matt. 'Part of the scenery. Some say they were introduced by the Etruscans, but others believe they were brought here by the Romans. For the ancients, they signified the underworld as well as mortality. I think the locals think of them as a symbol of life and death. You know they can live to a thousand years.'

I glanced at him approvingly. It was great to see him engaging with his Italian roots.

'There's been a lot of death in this place, that's for sure,' he concluded, a grim expression clouding his features.

And suddenly, a shadow passed over me.

* * *

Marcella walked up to the old oak door and turned the key in the lock. I noticed that even in this remote spot, she was wearing thin disposable rubber gloves. No doubt the farm-house had been disinfected and scrubbed and left empty for weeks, but fear of the silent enemy was endemic. She stood aside and waved us in.

The flagged stone floor was cooling through my flats after the heat and dust outdoors. It took a while for my eyes to adjust from the brightness of the autumn sun to the gloom of the hallway. Despite her mask, Marcella's distress was plain. She couldn't bring herself to look at Matt. Perhaps seeing him again after all these years reminded her of happier times, throwing recent sufferings and losses into sharp relief.

Soon, she recovered herself and while Marcella babbled away excitably with Matt in a torrent of Italian, I cast my eyes around, taking in every detail of the place I'd now be calling home. The estate agent's description had focused on the 'period features' and 'rustic charm' of the property. At first glance, the reality was rather more challenging. Small windows, dim lighting, sagging walls, cracked surfaces, stained ceilings – it looked as if nothing had been updated since the 1950s.

I was already making a checklist in my head, planning how I'd remodel the kitchen, rewire the electrics, refurbish the wood-burning stove, upgrade the bathrooms, install solar panels, refresh the faded yellowing paintwork and wire-brush the blackened beams. And that was before we even went upstairs. I couldn't wait to get started.

Despite his English–American accent, once he got going, Matt's fluency in conversational Italian was impressive. In the coming days and weeks, I was to discover that he was a different person when he was speaking Italian – more animated and expressive, more youthful and engaged. Even the Italian variant of his name signified a more vibrant personality. The first time I'd been charmed to hear Marcella refer to my 'Matt' as 'Teo'. Later, it made me think that the Matt I'd lived with in the London lockdowns was a lesser and muted version of his younger self. I looked forward to reconnecting with the real Teo now that we were here.

For my own part, on this first encounter with Marcella, I felt excluded and slightly at a loss. With my smattering of Italian, I struggled to follow the gist of the conversation or contribute to the lively exchange. I felt separated as if by one of those acrylic screens that were now everywhere, able to see but unable to participate or reach out in any meaningful way. I remembered some months ago 'visiting' an elderly aunt in a care home from behind a screen but not being allowed to touch or hold her hand. My aunt's confusion and upset had been only too visible. See-through barriers intended to bring us together serving only to signify her isolation.

While I sat taking in my new surroundings, Marcella gave Matt an emotional and tearful account of what had happened at the farmhouse during the first wave of the pandemic. Matt did his best to include me in the conversation, with quick asides and summary translations of Marcella's unstoppable, animated stream of Italian. Deep in the southern Tuscan countryside, the locals had held out against the virus for longer than most Italians, she said. Infections were concentrated in the cities. Of the nearby towns, Siena and Florence had been the first and hardest hit – understandably because they were important centres of commerce as well as being overrun with tourists (until they all fled or were ordered home just before the lockdown).

Montalcino, Montepulciano and Pienza had been protected for longer. But when the restrictions were lifted after the first wave subsided, wealthy Italians from the major cities such as Milan and Rome with second homes in the Tuscan countryside had started to travel out of town, bringing with them the disease. Even the most remote farming communities hadn't been spared. (Marcella pulled anguished faces and waved her hands in gestures of despair.) It was when the seasonal workers arrived to pick the olives in the late summer, travelling by train from regions all over Italy and from Eastern European countries further afield, that disaster struck at the farmhouse, she said, just when they thought they'd been shielded from the storm.

With no one from the local community to help bring in the harvest, Matt's elderly relatives let down their guard in the mistaken belief that the danger had passed. A Romanian student brought the infection onto the farm and it spread like wildfire among many of the seasonal workers. (Marcella raised her hands high to simulate the raging *incendio*.) And then Benetto became infected. Great-Uncle Benetto was a lifelong smoker and each winter, with no central heating and the wind blowing through the hills, he suffered from bronchitis in the cold, damp months. Aged seventy-two, he still had muscles of steel, but the combination of the virus on top of his bronchitis was too much for him. (Marcella crossed herself.)

When he was taken away to hospital in an ambulance in the middle of the night, Marcella knew she'd never see him again. Loretta, who was a few years older than him and prematurely senile, had been beside herself with grief, crying like a child. (Marcella's own tears began to flow again as she recalled the scene.) Loretta didn't understand what was going on – why her husband was wrapped up like a spaceman and why she wasn't allowed to hold his hand or kiss him goodbye.

He succumbed three months later, having battled to the end with the stubbornness characteristic of a Tuscan peasant determined to hold on to his land and his fortune and his life. At least, in his English translation of Marcella's words, that's the spin Matteo put on it.

Marcella tried to care for Loretta at the farmhouse, but she had her own family to look after and it soon became clear that the old lady couldn't live alone. (Marcella's voice became shrill as she recalled the old lady's distress.) Loretta's dementia worsened and she wasn't safe without supervision. She wandered at night.

Early one morning, she was found at dawn by the baker in a nearby village. She was calling out desperately, not for her husband but for her lost son, Lorenzo – killed when he fell down a well, aged only two years old. (Marcella crossed herself rapidly three more times and I shuddered inwardly to hear Matt's translation of her words revealing the horrific way the little boy had died.) When Marcella received the policeman's phone call asking her to collect the distraught Loretta and take her back to her bed, she decided that enough was enough. She contacted Loretta's cousin, who lived in a spacious apartment in the suburbs of Florence and was willing for Loretta to come and live with her until other arrangements could be made.

'I just hope to God the cousin doesn't kick her out.' Matt grimaced behind his hand. 'We don't want her back here.'

Dismayed by his lack of empathy and compassion, I pretended not to hear Matt's aside and instead nodded sympathetically at Marcella while I absorbed the shocking revelations.

Having recounted the whole tragic tale, Marcella somehow pulled herself together and gave us a tour of the farmhouse.

'I apologise it's in such a state,' she lamented in Italian.

During the lockdown, the property had lain empty both because of the restrictions on movement and because the lawyer acting as executor of the trust didn't want to grant access until Matteo returned to Italy to claim his inheritance. Violent storms the previous week had blown down an apple tree, she said, broken some terracotta pots and dislodged tiles from the roof.

When she took us upstairs, we found that the main bedroom was in disarray. Marcella stood in the doorway, exclaiming loudly. Rainwater had leaked through the damaged roof, leaving both the floor and the ceiling buckling and in danger of collapse. She promised to get her husband, a retired builder, to come in and look at it the next day. I watched Matt's expression becoming blacker and blacker as we inspected one dilapidated room after another, but I refused to be disheartened.

At last, Marcella led us to a bedroom at the back of the property that seemed to be habitable straight away – a big, beamed room with an oak bedstead in the middle, an old-fashioned washbasin in one corner, a desk, a high-backed chair and a huge antique *armadio* – wardrobe – of the kind, as a child, I'd have imagined could lead to Narnia.

Marcella gave Matt a smile that was both awkward and

conspiratorial. Then she left us to freshen up and settle into the room, indicating that she'd meet us again downstairs.

As the door closed, I took off my mask.

'Well, this will do fine,' I said with exaggerated cheerfulness, patting the bed and looking inside the *armadio*, whose shelves were piled high with cardboard boxes and spare bedding.

Matt threw himself backwards onto the bed, causing the old mattress to sag down to the floor and the frame to creak alarmingly.

'I guess the springs have gone!' He laughed.

He caught my arm and pulled me onto the bed.

'At last, I've got you all to myself.' He began to undo the straps of my sundress.

'So, this was your bedroom that summer,' I said playfully (in truth I was beginning to feel like the young wife in *Rebecca*). 'Time to meet your ghosts?'

He looked at me intently as if taking in every feature of my face. Then he shook his head.

'Come here,' he said. 'I prefer the land of the living.'

TWELVE
DANIELLE

When we re-joined Marcella a short time later, she took us down to the cellar to explain the controls and switches for the house. It was cavernous, with dripping brick arches and dark recesses. It smelt of damp cement and fermenting wine and something pungent, rotten – a dead rat, perhaps. I noticed that there were old-fashioned rodent traps behind the brick pillars. The boiler looked a hundred years old and, even to my untrained eye, the bare wires hanging from the ceiling flashed 'fire risk'.

'We're going to have our work cut out here,' I said despondently, wondering how far my redundancy money could stretch.

As ever, Matt left all the practical stuff to me. Unperturbed by the state of the cellar, while Marcella demonstrated the archaic workings and quirks of the farmhouse utilities with lots of hand gestures and facial expressions, he ventured further into the gloom to rummage around the dusty old estate barrels and bottles of vintage wines stored on the racks.

He returned brandishing two bottles of red wine triumphantly.

'I'd forgotten old Uncle Benetto had such a good collection,' he said, suddenly upbeat and determined to cheer me up. 'If we get locked down again, at least we'll have plenty to drink!' Without ceremony, he handed the bottles to Marcella and pulled me into his arms for a kiss. 'We'll be OK,' he said.

And in that instant, all I could feel in the cold, dank stairwell was his warmth and his ripped, solid chest.

We're not such a bad team, after all, I reflected. Matt certainly knew how to raise my spirits when I was down.

The sun was low in the sky by the time we came up from the cellar. I hoped that Marcella would show us the grounds, but she seemed impatient to leave before nightfall and Matt did nothing to persuade her to stay. I was particularly keen to see the swimming pool. When I said the words, *'Dov'è la piscina?'* learnt from my Italian phrase book, she blinked her eyes nervously.

'Domani, domani.'

She glanced at Matt. Then she bustled out to her car and came back with a basket, which she set down on the oak refectory table. It contained a 'welcome pack' of pistachio nuts and olives, breadsticks, salami, pecorino cheese and plum tomatoes, fresh basil, olive oil and balsamic vinegar. There was also a loaf of that rough Italian bread that feels stale when you bring it home from the bakery but tastes out of this world when toasted and piled with Tuscan bruschetta. I longed to hug her.

'We'll have a feast tonight,' I said, smiling from ear to ear.

Marcella blew me a kiss to show that she understood and with that, she made her escape.

When we were alone, I stood behind Matt and put my arms around his hips.

'We made the right decision, didn't we?'

With the lengthening shadows, the atmosphere in the kitchen had changed. Matt was rummaging in a drawer for a corkscrew to open the dusty bottle of estate wine he'd brought up from the cellar.

'There must be a bloody corkscrew here somewhere! I need something to drink. Then I'll give you my answer,' he grumbled.

I looked round his shoulder. The drawer was rammed with an assortment of vintage kitchen utensils and cutlery.

'We could make a fortune selling this lot on eBay,' I said.

You could tell the farmhouse had had elderly occupants. Eventually, Matt pulled out a rusty corkscrew. It was a crude straight-pull design – a simple twisted metal helix embedded in a hand-carved olive wood handle. The feel of it in his hand seemed to reignite some memory and he looked down at his palm for a second or two. I could see the initials 'T' and 'N', with a heart shape in the middle, crudely carved and inked into the wooden handle.

He put it down by the wine bottle then struggled to close the drawer, which had come off its runners. As he rammed in the drawer impatiently, the whole thing fell apart. He cursed loudly.

'This place is a wreck,' he said. 'It was madness taking it on.'

I wanted to snap at him for being such a killjoy, but I managed to bite my tongue.

'Well, I'm going to take a look around outside,' I said, 'before it gets completely dark. Are you coming?'

I left Matt grappling with the drawer, knowing that if I

stayed in the kitchen, we'd get into a futile round of fighting and recriminations.

In the fading light, I could still make out the overgrown borders and lawns in front of the farmhouse – and beyond, the ploughed wheat fields and olive groves forming the part of the estate that I'd seen on the way here. The sweet scent of flowers I couldn't identify wafted on the breeze and I made a mental note to ask Marcella to give me the names of the plants.

A stone path led from the back of the farmhouse up a slight incline to the top of the hill. I was curious to explore this side of the estate, as it was hidden by the topography of the land. Some distance from the main farmhouse, I passed three dilapidated outbuildings. The estate agent details had at least been honest in saying they required complete renovation. Looming in the deepening shade, there was something uncanny about their emptiness and abandonment. Stupidly, I had that clichéd feeling of being watched from the gaping eyes of glassless windows and I hurried on up the path through a glade of ancient oak trees.

As I walked through the wood, my nerves jangled and every creaking branch or rustle in the undergrowth made me turn my head. I quickened my steps. Matt's flash of bad temper had released a cloud of bad vibes that seemed to lurk in the glade.

When I came out of the trees, I found myself on an exposed high ridge, which I realised must be part of the Crete Senesi – those distinctive dry clay hills with white dome shapes or *biancane*, and steep-sided valleys or *calanchi*, which Matt had told me about. Surveying the sparse and dramatic rippling landscape, I could see why the tourist guides described it as 'lunar' – as much for the odd shapes formed from the clay as for its grey and off-white luminosity. A full moon rose in the sky, lighting up the rugged terrain. The whole effect was otherworldly and a far cry from the picturesque Tuscany I'd seen on so many postcards over the years.

The path now skirted the ridge and I carried on a little further until it broadened out to a terrace. Again, I had the feeling of being watched and kept glancing back over my shoulder towards the trees. Suddenly, I came to an abrupt stop when my shin cracked against a sharp stone ledge. In my distraction, I'd narrowly avoided tripping over the low stone wall of the abandoned swimming pool. I'd spotted the cavernous pit in front of me only because the foot or so of rainwater at the bottom of the pool glimmered a ghostly grey in the moonlight – but not soon enough to avoid cutting my leg.

I put my foot up on the ledge and gripped my shin, moaning. Looking down into the water, I saw it was almost opaque and layered with green spores. I felt weak from the shock of the injury. For an instant I swayed, my eyes narrowed, and in my semi-faint I imagined the figure of a young girl floating Ophelia-like beneath the surface. The surge of adrenaline caused by this fearful vision revived me instantly and as my eyes focused, the image of the girl resolved itself into the pattern of spores on the surface of the water.

Stop being such an idiot!

I soothed myself by gazing at the impossibly bright stars and the vast moon rising above the mass of Mount Amiata on the horizon. I'd never seen so much sky – so black and so dense.

'This will be such a wonderful adventure,' I said out loud, willing it to be true.

I couldn't wait to see the view in the daylight. I couldn't

wait to bring up my easel and install myself on this spot for the day. I couldn't wait to indulge in sunset dips on beautiful summer evenings. The location was perfect. But this derelict old sewer had to go. I'd start to research designs for a new infinity pool the very next day.

When I returned to the farmhouse, my injury forgotten and my good humour and optimism restored by contemplation of the stars, Matt was grappling with a second bottle of wine.

'The other one was corked,' he said. 'I poured it down the sink. What happened to you?' he asked, seeing the deep gash on my shin and blood running down to my ankle.

I looked down at my hands. They were covered in blood, too. The pain flooded back.

Matt gave another yank with the corkscrew. Suddenly, the handle snapped and his wrist caught and scraped on the exposed end of the helix while the bottle rolled and smashed on the terracotta floor.

'Look what you've made me do!' he yelled unfairly.

Now, we were both tainted with blood.

My euphoria dissolved. I watched as Matt's blood dripped from his wrist into the dark red pool of wine on the floor while he picked up the pieces of broken glass. My head swam from the heat and exhaustion of the journey, and the excitement of seeing our new home, and the shock of what had happened to me at the swimming pool and the throbbing pain in my shin and the sight of another person's blood, which always made me feel sick.

The swirling reds of blood and wine were the last thing I saw as I crumpled to the floor.

THIRTEEN
THE HITCHHIKER
BY MATTEO J. ROSSI

On the far side of the parking area, Ted comes into view, walking to his car hand in hand with Harry.

The little boy toddles along beside him like a young puppy, trusting and confident.

The waitress holds out the beaker. Nikki pushes past her and runs out, shouting Harry's name. Ted turns and smiles and keeps walking, as if pretending not to notice her panic.

'We're just going to get ice creams,' he calls, 'and see the dogs... over at the hospice.'

Nikki is mad at him. 'You should have woken me,' she yells.

'You were sleeping so peacefully,' he says. 'You look so pretty sleeping. Just didn't want to wake you. We didn't want to wake you, did we, Harry?'

Ted smiles at him and Harry laughs for no particular reason – just because he's happy. Nikki doesn't want to dampen the little boy's spirits – she knows how quickly he can spiral into a tantrum. Ted smiles his winning smile and kisses her on the cheek – like he's a part of the family, like they've known each other for years. Now he's made her look a fool, ranting in the car park with everyone turning their heads.

'Don't ever fucking mess with me like that again,' she says, but this time quietly, like a caress.

There is hope of a future in her words.

They take Harry to see the St Bernards. These days the dogs are mainly a tourist attraction and Harry is excited to have the chance to pet them. Neither Harry nor Ted has the patience to listen to the talk, so when Harry gets sick of stroking the dogs and starts to wail because he's not allowed to ride one like a horse, Nikki lets Ted take him across the road to the café for ice cream.

Nikki is as wide-eyed as a schoolgirl, listening to the visitor guide, a fat old monk in a brown hassock. She learns that before the road crossing was built in 1906, the dogs were trained by the monks to search for avalanche victims and travellers who had lost their way while going over the pass. The monk tells them what a treacherous journey this was and how many souls had perished on the mountain in the snow or down some ravine. She delights in the story of Barry, the St Bernard dog, who lived between 1800 and 1814 and saved more than forty human lives. The monk explains that the dogs would search in pairs for travellers lost or buried in the snow. They wore small wooden kegs on their collars that held brandy or wine. If a traveller was found on a rescue mission, one dog would stay close to keep the person warm and sustained with liquor while the other ran back to the monastery to fetch help.

When the talk is over, Nikki joins Ted and Harry at the café. Ted has been chatting cars to the Italian waiter, who was taken with his borrowed vintage Jag. The French waiter speaks perfect English with a slight Mancunian accent.

'I worked there for two years,' he says. 'Best place in the world, Manchester.'

The talk turns to the dogs and the mountains. The waiter cracks open three beers 'on the house' and an apple juice for Harry then sits down at their table.

'I had no idea so many people had died making the crossing,' says Nikki. 'No wonder this place has such bad vibes.'

Ted laughs at her.

'You don't believe in ghosts, do you?'

'All those lost souls... buried in the snow. Such a painful, lonely and lingering death. I don't know about ghosts, but I do believe places hold our feelings. It's the hippy in me. Human feelings don't reside just in our minds and bodies but settle into the places where we live and die, leaving reverberations behind. There's a sadness in these mountains. I felt it last night when the sun went down.'

Normally, Ted would rubbish such thoughts, but coming from her...

It was easy to dismiss notions of the supernatural sitting here drinking beers in the crisp Alpine sunshine, but last night something desolate and forlorn hung like a pall over the mountaintops. And he has to admit he'd felt inexplicably uneasy in the hotel room. Even their lovemaking had been tinged with desperation, as if their passion was the only way to stay in the here and now and keep the spirits at bay.

'There are plenty of ghosts up here,' says the waiter, making a ghoulish grimace. 'You should hear the stories. The old villagers are very superstitious. They say that on nights of the full moon, you can see their shadows moving along the road and in the mountains, completing the journey they never made.'

'Oh my God! It was a full moon last night,' says Nikki,

clapping her hand to her mouth. 'We should have kept watch for them.'

'Even your famous writer, Charles Dickens, wrote about the frozen dead in these mountains,' says the waiter, enjoying the girl's rapt attention.

'Tell us, tell us,' says Nikki with the excitement of a child.

The waiter goes into the back and comes out with a well-thumbed copy of *Little Dorrit*.

'An American tourist left this for me last year,' he says. Then he points to an austere grey building some way up the road. 'See that old outhouse? That used to be a mortuary for people found frozen on the mountain.' He turns to a page where a passage has been highlighted. 'Read this. See how he describes the ice statues.'

Nikki pushes the book over to Ted, who reads aloud, his voice resonant and clear, while Nikki listens with her eyes half-closed, twirling her hair:

... The mother, storm-belated many winters ago, still standing in the corner with her baby at her breast; the man who had frozen with his arm raised to his mouth in fear or hunger, still pressing it with his dry lips after years and years. An awful company, mysteriously come together! A wild destiny for that mother to have foreseen!

She opens her eyes wide and leans forwards. 'That gives me the shivers,' she says, only half-joking. 'To think of those corpses, standing there, frozen solid.'

The waiter gestures to the auberge where they'd spent the night.

'They say it's haunted,' he says. 'Guests report hearing a newborn baby crying in the middle of the night, footsteps pacing the corridors, sightings of a breastfeeding mother in the corner of the room, strange smells and cold draughts.'

Nikki shivers for real this time and lifts Harry onto her knee.

'Or they've been reading Dickens and drunk too many beers!' says Ted, jealous of the attention the waiter is getting from Nikki.

'And then there are the road accidents,' continues the waiter. 'These mountain roads are so treacherous in the winter months. There's a hairpin bend on the Swiss side about two kilometres before the summit, where there have been three fatal accidents in the past ten years. The locals call it "*le virage du fantôme*".'

'What does that mean?' says Nikki, hanging on his every word.

'*The ghost's bend*, literally,' says the waiter. 'It sounds much better in French. There have been sightings of a phantom cyclist, speeding round the bends.'

Nikki looks at Ted, who stares at his beer.

'C'mon,' he says kicking back his chair, 'we should get on.'

* * *

Ted says he wants a walk to clear his head after the beer before they set off down the mountain to Aosta. Nikki knows it's the ghost stories he wants to clear from his thoughts, but she doesn't let on.

'Let's have some fun!' she says, picking up Harry and whirling him round.

They scramble up a long stretch of snow and ice that remains on the mountains all the summer long. Harry's plump little legs disappear into the snow. The three of them tumble over and make snow angels and touch hands like a row of paper cut-outs and shut their eyes against the blinding sun. The phantoms are forgotten. Ted is on top of the world.

She squeezes his hand.

'I wish we could stay here forever,' she says. 'So close to the sun and the sky.'

But the snow begins to melt against their skin. And Harry is writhing in the snow, shouting, 'Wet, wet,' and trying to rip off his trousers.

'Let's go,' says Ted, jumping to his feet. He grabs Harry and slings him effortlessly over his shoulder. 'C'mon, I'll race you to the car.'

FOURTEEN
DANIELLE

I was woken by autumn sunshine streaming through the curtainless windows. The catch on the wooden shutters was broken and they'd swung open in the night. Despite the sunshine, I shivered when I threw off the duvet. There was no central heating in the house and the electric heater in the corner of the bedroom wasn't working. I rolled out of bed, aching and stiff – not the way I wanted to feel on my first morning in Tuscany.

After I passed out in the kitchen, Matt had spent the evening of our arrival pampering me. First, he patched me up with iodine and bandages that he found in an old first-aid box in the cupboard above the kitchen sink.

'Takes me back to the cuts and scrapes of my childhood,' he said. 'That old box has been there as long as I can remember ...and Marcella, wiping away my blood, sweat and tears.'

He seated me at the table and prepared supper with the basket of goodies Marcella had brought and plied me with estate wine (having eventually managed to uncork a bottle that was finely matured and ready for drinking). He regaled me with stories of his summer holidays at the farmhouse as a boy. At last, he scooped me into his arms and insisted on carrying me all the way up the creaking stairs to our new bedroom. I was touched by these moments of tenderness, revealing a gentler, more caring side to Matt's nature that contrasted with his bouts of abrasive bad temper and gave me hope for our future together.

After we'd made love – there had been something hasty and desperate about our lovemaking on that lumpy old mattress – it had taken me a long time to get to sleep.

While we were down in the cellar, Marcella had pointed out a carved walnut high chair belonging to the little boy who died. It was an unusual item and Matt had admired the fine workmanship and clever design.

'It must be worth a lot of money,' said Matt. 'Let's bring it up to the dining room. It'll get damaged down here in the damp. You never know, we might want to use it soon.'

He'd squeezed my hand and a warm glow had suffused my whole body.

Seeing the high chair had prompted me to prod Matt for more information about the tragedy before we went to sleep. Of course, I already knew the old couple had lost a child and that's why Matt was the heir. But learning the manner of his death disturbed me in a vivid and visceral way. My guts were in knots. I couldn't get the image out of my head of the boy screaming and flailing about in the water at the bottom of the well. Had I known the full story before Matt accepted the inheritance, would I have encouraged him to take on the farm? That night our new home seemed tainted by the tragedy. When we turned off the lights, I clung on to Matt.

'He died long before I was born,' said Matt. 'No one spoke of the accident when I was a little boy. It was a taboo subject for my great-uncle and aunt. I only knew it was bad and it made them very sad.'

'You should have told me the details,' I insisted quietly as we lay there in the dark.

'I didn't see the point,' he said angrily. 'I knew it would upset you and I've never really had any choice about taking on the family farm. It was always my destiny.' His voice almost broke. 'God knows, I don't want to be here. But I bear the burden of the Rossi name – it's my duty to take on the estate.'

I shrank under the blankets, dismayed by his abrupt change of mood. It chilled me to think that Matt was embarking on this challenge under duress and that unwittingly, I'd helped to force him into it. And it chilled me to think of what had happened in this place.

Sensing that I was genuinely distressed, Matt reasoned with me calmly.

'This happened more than forty years ago, Danielle. Death is all around us now. There can't be a family in this part of Italy who hasn't lost a loved one in the past few months.'

This wasn't exactly cheering and didn't serve to calm my nerves for sleep. Moonlight quivered over the big old-fashioned furniture with a sinister, disconcerting effect that put me on edge. I kept glancing over at the antique *armadio,* whose bulk possessed one corner of the room like the entrance to Narnia. The key was missing from the lock and it seemed each time I closed my eyes that the wardrobe door swung open, its hinges creaking eerily.

'Stop being pathetic,' Matt said when I jerked and gasped.

Tired of my fretting, he got out of bed to wedge it closed with one of his T-shirts.

'The floor is uneven and there are draughts everywhere. This is an ancient house. What do you expect?'

That night, my dreams were filled with anguished scenes. I was locked in the wardrobe, hammering on the door, in a desperate attempt to break out and save the drowning child.

The banging of the shutters in the wind must have found its way into my nightmare.

* * *

After breakfast, Matt installed himself in what used to be his great-uncle's study – the most comfortable, if antiquated room in the farmhouse. It was where Benetto had spent most of his time when he wasn't out in the fields, dealing with the farm bookkeeping and paperwork now filed away in rows of brown leather binders on a large oak bookcase.

Matt spent the morning raging at the local telecom companies, trying to get the landline at the property reconnected and a broadband connection set up. The mobile network was so poor at the farmhouse that the signal on his iPhone kept breaking up. The more frustrated he got, the louder he got, and for much of the morning I overheard him shouting into his mobile in Italian, trying to get hold of someone who could make it happen. Knowing that Italian bureaucracy was notoriously complicated and arcane, I empathised. There would be so many officials to convince and forms to complete for something as simple as installing a phone line. It was maddening.

Now, all was quiet. I pushed open the door and stood holding a tray with his cup of freshly brewed coffee and a sweet pastry. Matt's papers were spread out on the faded and stained leather top of a grand old walnut desk. He was sitting in front of an open laptop with his headphones on. I knew he liked to listen to loud music when he was writing. I stepped into the room and stood looking over his shoulder at the words on his screen. It was the first time I'd seen his work. He'd been so secretive about it.

For a minute or two he was unaware of my presence. He leant back, took a sip of cold coffee and stared at his document. He put his hands on the keys, sighed and typed a few words, stared at the screen, took another sip of cold coffee and typed a few more words.

'I brought you a nice hot cup of fresh coffee,' I said.

'Just put it down on the desk,' said Matt.

A 'please' or a 'thank you' would be nice, I thought to myself, but it wasn't worth picking a fight. Now that Matt seemed at last to be getting into the headspace for writing, I didn't want to be the one to break his concentration. He remained engrossed for a minute or two while I read what he'd written:

DRAFT ONE
THE HITCHHIKER
by Matteo J. Rossi

He notices the child first – through a dreamy fug of tiredness – a tiny figure in a white T-shirt that catches his eye against the greens and greys of the tarmac and the sunburnt verge, kicking up the dust at the edge of the road. Some distance on, a young woman stands in the shade of a tree, nonchalantly thumbing a lift while dragging on a cigarette. Instinctively he slows – which is lucky because a micro-second later, a white flash crosses his field of vision as the child runs out.

He slams on the brakes and swerves violently across the carriageway. With a sickening jolt and a screech of metal and tyres, he grinds to a halt in a suffocating cloud of dust. His head hits the dash. The music stops.

Below the paragraph, the screen was blank.

'How's it going?' I asked.

He looked up crossly, as if he expected me to have gone already. I wondered if this was how he'd treated his secretaries at work. When office working was a thing, ReelWrites had been one of those elitist companies where successful editors still had secretaries – or PAs as they were now called, with a nod to feminism, which meant that the job description included booking flights and tables in fancy restaurants, and going out to buy the sandwiches for lunch in addition to all the secretarial and administrative work.

'Is that all you've written?' I blurted out, thinking of the many hours Matt had spent fixated in front of his laptop in the London flat, avoiding other chores.

He closed the lid with a snap.

'Well, it's a good start!' I laughed awkwardly.

Matt kicked back his chair and walked over to look out of the window.

'No, I'm serious. It makes me want to read on...'

For a moment he seemed lost in contemplation of the olive groves whose silvery leaves shimmered in the breeze.

'It would be a lot easier if I didn't have you breathing down my neck the whole time.' He turned to glare at me.

'Sorry I asked!' I shrugged. 'Sorry for taking an interest.'

Matt's eyes softened. 'I'm not ready to share it with you yet,' he said in a more conciliatory tone. 'You'll just have to wait and see. It's the story of a love affair. That's all you need to know.'

There was no point trying to push him further.

'I just came in to ask what you want for lunch,' I said. 'I can do more bruschetta with what Marcella left for us yesterday. We'll have to make a trip down to the supermarket this afternoon.'

'Yes, that would be great,' he said, content this morning to limit our interactions to the practicalities of life. Matt took a bite of the pastry. 'You're going to make me fat!'

He stood up and folded me into his arms. His body was firm and lean.

'What does the 'J' stand for by the way?' I asked.

He groaned. 'Jacopo. So now you know. I never use it.'

He gave my shoulder a squeeze.

'I'm sorry I was grumpy. I've just received another message from my editor banging on about the publication schedule. Now that I'm on the other side of the table, I understand it's not such a piece of cake being a writer. I think he's doing it to wind me up.'

After lunch, I decided to go for a walk round the property while Matt retired again to the study. It was a blustery day with the wind lashing the derelict farm buildings and banging the loose shutters. The tops of the hills to the south of the property were shrouded in fog. This wasn't the sun-kissed *Under the Tuscan Sun* version of Tuscany I'd longed for in my imagination. The reality that autumn day was harsh and inhospitable. Mount Amiata was hidden behind a band of storm clouds moving almost imperceptibly towards me. The olive trees had morphed into a sea of twisting grey waves as their olive-laden branches flailed in the wind. I judged I had about thirty minutes before the downpour.

I wanted to see the swimming pool again, if only to put to rest the bad feelings I'd experienced on that spot the night before. I'd been overwrought and overtired after the long journey. In the cold light of day, I knew all of my fears of the night before had been irrational and absurd.

Whipped by gusts of wind, the fetid water was sloshing up against the cracked sides of the pool. I looked down into the murk, wondering how my brain could have resolved the scum and spores and fallen leaves on the surface of the water into the haunting vision I'd imagined.

I thought about the larger picture – the economic and health emergency in which we all found ourselves struggling to survive. I wondered if we'd made a big mistake in moving to Italy. Was it selfish, as some of my (so-called) friends had hinted, to have come here at a time when the country had been so cruelly afflicted by the pandemic? I pushed the thought away. What the country needed now was rebuilding and investment to kick-start the economy again. And in a small way, I intended to do my bit to reinvigorate the local economy with our redevelopment project here at the farmhouse – starting with the swimming pool. Matt might label me 'superficial, entitled and materialistic', but if there was anything that would transform the place, it was a new infinity pool.

I planned to spend the evening researching designs and local builders. My lack of Italian might be a problem, but hopefully Matt would relent and help me out. Then once the heat of the summer was with us again, we'd have somewhere to unwind and enjoy the stunning views while we took our time over the rest of the estate.

The storm reached our ridge sooner than I expected. Raindrops stung my face. The rain was horizontal now as the sodden clouds seemed to funnel and swirl through the valley before surging up and over the exposed ridge. Wearing only a light jacket, I knew I'd get soaked. I made my way to the glade of trees from where I'd conjured someone watching me last night. Today, it held no menace.

Finding a sheltered position under the canopy of an old oak tree, I got out my phone and took some arty shots of the driving rain and a panorama of the stormy landscape. I was impatient to set up my studio and start on my first sketches of Tuscany. When the weather was more settled, I looked forward to bringing out my easel and spending the days painting '*en plein air*'. Until then, I'd have to make do with painting from photographs.

I concentrated on composing an image with the swimming pool in the foreground and a traditional stone well at the end of a row of cypresses in the background. And then it hit me. I gasped. This must be the well where little Lorenzo died. Such a shocking and tragic death. So close to where I want to install the new infinity pool. Immediately I checked this thought, profoundly ashamed of my selfish and superficial response.

I wasn't generally one to believe in supernatural phenomena, but I remembered the old wives' tales about ghosts being attracted to water. Last night there had been something uncanny in the air. I was so distracted and tense that when, out of nowhere, a human shadow appeared in my viewfinder, I screamed out and dropped my phone. The man was dressed for the weather in waterproof oiled jacket and trousers with what looked like a hunting rifle slung over one shoulder. His face was covered with a black mask. His eyes were dark and severe underneath the hood of his jacket. He was carrying a black folded umbrella, which he brandished in my direction. Without taking his eyes off me, he stooped to pick up my phone.

Where had he sprung from and how long had he been watching me? Should I run?

FIFTEEN
THE HITCHHIKER

BY MATTEO J. ROSSI

It feels good. The sun high in the sky, the air crisp and dry, and the roof down.

Nikki is wearing Ray-Bans and bright red lipstick, like a starlet in a 'road-chick' movie. Harry is relaxed and happy, pleased with his new St Bernard baseball cap and doggie soft toy – one of thousands piled up in the souvenir shop. The drive down the mountain on the Italian side is more open, with big wide bends and glorious views of verdant valleys. With the foolish confidence of youth (convinced of his own invincibility) and undeterred by the accident of the day before, Ted puts his foot down. Nikki is a thrill junkie – he's worked that out already – and he wants to impress her. At the same time, he wants her to think he cares...

'Do you know why I gave you a lift?' he asks.

'Because I'm hot.' She laughs.

'Because I was worried about your safety – yours and the little one. I didn't want some psychopath to come by and pick you up.'

'Takes one to know one,' she says.

He turns to stare at her and the car veers dangerously.

'Seriously, you should be more careful, you know – especially with looks like yours. You're too trusting.'

Halfway down the mountain, they stop at a viewpoint and stand, shoulders touching, contemplating the valleys and peaks, and he kisses her properly – lovingly – for the first time while Harry squirms in her arms. Then they spread out a towel on the grass and eat their picnic lunch of fruit and baguettes. The scars and bruises on Nikki's upper arms and thighs stand out in the sunshine.

'Are you running away from something?' he asks. 'Or someone?'

She smiles enigmatically. 'You first! What are you running away from?'

'Nothing,' he says. 'Driven away, in my case. Banished to Italy for the summer. My stepdad was so keen to get me out of the country that he lent me his car.' He takes a bite of his sandwich. Pauses. 'I suppose I am running away in a sense, from my situation at home. My dad died a few years ago and my mother got remarried last year – to one of his cousins. It's a bit like *Hamlet* at ours, if you know what I mean.'

She raises an eyebrow.

'My stepdad and I don't get on. He can't stand it when I'm around because he knows I upstage him in my mum's affections. And I remind him of my dad. They despised each other.'

'Are you going to kill him?' she asks, inscrutable. 'Like Hamlet?'

Ted stares at the dent in the front of the sports car. 'Now there's a thought,' he says, unsmiling. 'Unless someone kills me first.'

'Your stepdad won't be too thrilled when he finds out you've smashed up his Jag,' she says.

'He's not going to find out,' says Ted. 'He'd kill me for sure. I'll get it fixed up before I go back to England.' Ted takes another bite of baguette. 'Your turn.'

'Dads,' she says bitterly. 'Life would be so much simpler without them. Mine was a waste of space.'

She takes out a flick knife and cuts up an apple for Harry. Ted watches her closely.

'I'm running from his dad,' she says, pointing the blade of the knife casually at the boy.

'Careful,' says Ted.

She ignores him.

'Harry's dad is a lot older than me – old enough to be my dad almost. He's been abusing me since I was a child. I've been living with him since I was sixteen.' She runs her fingers over the bruises on her thighs. 'It never stops.'

There's a long silence.

Ted wants to ask more questions, but from her body language, it's clear she's got nothing more to say on the subject. He doesn't want to think of his home in England, either. She's all that matters to him right now. Nikki and Ted on this Alpine mountain – that's all he wants in his headspace.

Nikki gets her guitar and plays. She plays for her own pleasure, with no self-consciousness or posturing. He's surprised to find that she's truly talented. The music is Harry's lullaby. He snuggles up to his mother like a puppy and falls asleep. Ted stretches out, hands behind his head, eyes staring into the piercing blue while her guitar playing penetrates his soul.

It's a long time before they speak again once they get on the road.

Eventually, Nikki says, 'Let's have some music.'

She rifles through the glove compartment and pulls out some old CDs: The Smiths, The Killers... She puts on The Killers.

'If nothing else, you've got good taste,' she says.

Along with the CDs, Ted's passports are in the glove compartment – one British, one Italian.

'Cool!' she says. 'Like you can be two different people – two identities.'

They hadn't shown their passports at the frontier, waved through by the border guards on both sides. Nikki flicks through Ted's passports and giggles at the mugshots taken some years ago – Ted, a scowling young teen, with acne and a bad haircut.

'That's your surname: *Innocenti*?' she says quizzically. 'That's ironic – with your devilish looks!'

'As you can guess, I was crucified at school for that name.' He grimaces. 'My mother's maiden name. She got my name changed after my father walked out. She couldn't bear for us to keep anything of his.'

'Half Italian. That explains why you're so good-looking – and good at the lingo. Wish I had two passports.'

She doesn't show him hers or Harry's.

'My grandfather has a farm in Sangiari – a village in Tuscany near the city Pienza. That's where I'm going. I'll be there all summer until harvest time, working in the vineyards and the olive groves. I've just graduated from university, but I'm not in any rush to get a proper job. I'm taking a year out. It was my stepfather's idea to get me out of the house.

'But I'm looking forward to it. Sun, fun, good food and wine – the most beautiful girls in the world – you excepted!'

He squeezes her knee teasingly. 'Italians know how to enjoy themselves. My mother's hoping I'll get a Florentine girlfriend and come back speaking like a real native – she always regrets the fact that she spoke to me in English instead of Italian when I was a child...' He trails off. 'Enough of me – what about you?'

She ignores his question. Maybe he's offended her with talk of Italian girls. Maybe she's sick of his questions.

'I'd have thought a boy like you would already have a girl,' she says, matter-of-fact.

He laughs.

'Where are you going?' he tries again.

'We're going south,' she says vaguely. 'Then I don't know. Maybe we'll take a ferry. I've always wanted to go to the Greek islands. Can you drop us at the railway station in Florence?'

Her tone has changed. The intimacy is gone. She's already planning the next leg of her journey.

'So, I'll never see you again?' says Ted sadly, hurt by the pragmatism of her request.

He feels used. For the past twenty-four hours, she's been pretending to have feelings for him. Now, it seems her tenderness was fake.

'Easy come, easy go,' she replies. 'I don't go in for long goodbyes – or false promises.'

'I thought you were broke,' says Ted. 'How are you going to pay for the train?'

'I'll find a way,' she replies coldly. 'I know how to take care of myself. Quite honestly, it's none of your business.'

Abruptly, Ted pulls off the road into a lay-by. He cuts the ignition and grabs her wrist, twisting his fingers into the tasselled rows of woven friendship bracelets. He feels the roughness of scars against his fingertips. He squeezes until he sees her wince.

Harry starts to cry.

'What if I won't let you go?' he says.

SIXTEEN
DANIELLE

'*Signora, signora.*' His tone was both insistent and impatient.

With outstretched arm, he handed me my phone and the folded umbrella, keeping the statutory two-metre social distance and raising his free hand in a gesture of comic despair to the falling rain. I couldn't work out where he'd sprung from, this sallow, masked man. It was as if he'd been stalking me silently through the trees.

For an instant, my impulse was to run back to the farmhouse until it occurred to me that it was unlikely that a man offering to lend me an umbrella wished me any harm. I stared at the large hunting rifle hanging off his shoulder. A man out hunting wouldn't usually take an umbrella. He must have seen me from a distance and come out specially to meet me.

'Antonio,' he said, introducing himself with a formal nod of the head.

Of course, Antonio – the man named in Benetto's will, who had been gifted a life interest to remain living in one of the farm cottages. Matt had fallen out with him for some reason. What was the phrase he'd used? *Bad blood?* That was it. 'Don't talk to that man. I don't want anything to do with him.' In all the excitement of the move to Italy, I'd put 'that man' completely out of my head.

Unfortunately, I couldn't ignore his presence any longer. I fumbled with the catch of the antiquated umbrella.

'Danielle,' I said stiffly, holding out my free hand instinctively and then withdrawing it quickly when I remembered the new social code. *Hands, face, space.* Reaching out to a stranger was strictly off limits. No touching, whether physically or emotionally – that's what it came to – not with our hands, or our smiles or our breathing.

Like it or not, we were stuck with Antonio as a neighbour and would need his help on the farm. It was absurd to make an enemy of the man, no matter what offence he may have given to Matt in the past. I've never approved of holding grudges. If I formed a good rapport with Antonio from the outset, I thought, this would build a bridge for their reconciliation.

We sheltered from the rain, waiting and watching as the skies darkened and the drops turned to icy hail. A sudden gust almost ripped the umbrella from my hand. A second blast of wind turned the umbrella inside out and sent it whirling above my head before it crashed into the trees.

After the rain came the storm – a storm like no other that seemed to catch even the gamekeeper unawares. A flash of lightning speared the valley beyond the ridge and a clap of thunder exploded above our heads, sending vibrations through the very tree trunks.

'*Vieni qui, vieni qui...* Come, come,' he ordered me urgently.

Though I was still wary, it seemed impossible to refuse. I was now in pain and trembling from the cold.

Antonio grabbed me by the arm and dragged me hurriedly

down a short track bordered by the line of cypress trees to a stone cottage at the bottom of the hill. He pushed me inside, followed me in and bolted the door against the wind.

I looked down at my muddy trainers, my drenched clothes dripping onto the flagstone floor. My hair was stuck to my head and drops of water ran down my face. I couldn't stop shaking – as much from the cold as from the creeping realisation that I'd put myself in a vulnerable position with a man Matt had warned me about, probably out of concern for my own safety. A man who could be a criminal or worse.

When I looked up, Antonio was watching me. He ripped off his mask and laughed at my dishevelled state, baring wolfish white teeth and at least two days' worth of black stubble. His features were striking, with chiselled sensuous lips and a strong jawline. He was a different man behind the mask. He peeled off my jacket and hung it to dry over the back of a chair. I could feel his breath on my bare arms – all pretence at social distancing abandoned.

I stood there stupidly, my teeth chattering while he crouched down to pull off my trainers. Dizzy and weak, I put my hands on his shoulders to steady myself as he lifted my feet. Perhaps because of the months we'd been forced to keep almost everyone, even our nearest and dearest, at arm's length, there was something disturbingly intimate about this touching, like lying on a couch for a medical exam.

Taking in my surroundings, suddenly I felt very far from home. In fact, it was as if I'd walked into a peculiar fairy tale. There wasn't a single softening hint of femininity in the room. No rugs and pictures, or coloured mugs and cushions, or soft lighting and sweet smells. It was all male – unadorned, elemental and earthy. A wood-burning stove crackled and hissed in one corner of the room, casting flickering shadows over the beamed walls. Three wild boar head trophies displayed above the stove seemed to grimace in the firelight. They say there's a resemblance between animals and their owners. Antonio had no pets, but I clocked a likeness between his grinning face and his hunting trophies above the fireplace.

I became aware that I was surrounded by Antonio's accoutrements and implements of death. His leather boots and walking shoes were lined up against one wall, and above them a selection of hunting rifles hung by their leather shoulder straps from a row of hooks. A handful of knives, with different styles of blade – some thin and sharp, some serrated, some thick and blunt, some elegant and curved – lay on a bloodstained wooden table along with a steel mallet and a pair of bloodstained leather gloves. It must be here that his gruesome hunting kills would be split, crushed, skinned, hung, drawn and quartered, roasted, boiled and devoured. A meat casserole was simmering on the iron stove. The smell of death was heavy in the air.

Antonio disappeared into another room and came back with a towel and a change of clothes for me. It seemed that his English was even worse than my Italian, but it was easy enough to understand each other. He motioned for me to go into the bathroom to change. My hands trembled as I took the things, powerless to refuse. The bathroom was too intimate a space and too confined. I didn't want to remove my clothes in this man's house. But this man, with his rifle and his knives, had stripped me of agency. I couldn't say no.

The bathroom was as unloved as the rest of the house, with scum rings round the plugholes, cracks in the basin, damp flaking paintwork and a single light bulb filling the small space with harsh, garish light. I peeled off my clothes and put on Antonio's faded, oversized Harley Davidson T-shirt that smelt of his kitchen and cheap cologne, together with a pair of women's soft grey jogging bottoms that smelt of cedar mothballs.

When I went back into the kitchen, Antonio gave me an approving smile (this time less wolfish and with a strange, swiftly suppressed glimmer of surprise and recognition), muttered the words '*Molto bene, molto bene,*' and handed me a chipped mug of black tea. Knowing the British tea-drinking habits, he offered me milk, but when he opened the door to his fridge and I caught a glimpse of the bloodied meat cuts filling its shelves, I shook my head.

When I finished sipping my tea, I got up to go. The storm had passed over as quickly as it had hit. Antonio seemed reluctant for me to leave. Slowly, he put on a hunting jacket, picked up his rifle and accompanied me up the track as far as the swimming pool. The skies had cleared and the freshly washed hillside was now bathed in autumn sunlight. The whole landscape had changed.

I tried to suggest that Antonio should come with me to the farmhouse to see Matt, but he shrugged off my invitation – whether through lack of understanding or the pretence of it (because he knew he wouldn't be welcome), I couldn't tell. He took his leave and set off in the opposite direction through the woods.

When he'd gone, I paused to take more photographs. I wanted to paint a series of landscapes showing the same scene before, during and after the storm, so I went back to the well, where I'd been accosted by Antonio. The spot was a stunning vantage point for the surrounding views. At its base, I noticed something I'd previously missed – an iron plaque on a small stone plinth. Although I couldn't understand what it said, I guessed that it must be a memorial to Loretta's little boy who had fallen to his death.

My heart sank. If not for the tragedy, I wouldn't be standing here. In the natural order of things, that little boy should have grown up and become a man. He'd have taken over the management of the farm and had a wife and a son and so on through the generations. It was only because Lorenzo had lost his life that Matt and I had emigrated to Italy. *This place is cursed.* I cast away the words the instant they formed in my head. Instead, I resolved we should prove ourselves worthy of Matt's inheritance by making something good of our lives here, in honour of the little boy's short existence.

The well captured my attention and I took several photographs showing different perspectives. Was there something ghoulish in my fascination? I noted that the opening was protected by a rusty grate bolted to the stone. I couldn't stop obsessively rattling the grate to check how secure it was. The grate and its bolts were well worn. I wasn't sure if the bars or fixings would withstand the weight or determination of a headstrong child. In future we'd have our own children here, and I imagined them playing out in the fresh air and running wild on the estate. Fixing the grating would be added to the 'top priority' list I was compiling in a fat leather ledger dedicated to the renovation of the house.

I came in through the back door of the farmhouse, hoping to slip upstairs and get changed before seeing Matt (who would inevitably quiz me about my long absence), but he was waiting for me in the hallway. He must have been keeping watch for my arrival. I could tell he was in a bad mood from the way he was scowling at his phone. He looked up from the screen as I pushed open the door.

'Where the hell have you been?' he said sourly, looking me up and down. 'I was worried about you. And what the fuck are you wearing?' He stared at the Harley Davidson T-shirt and grey baggy jogging bottoms.

Suddenly, I remembered that Matt had offered to cook me dinner and told me to 'wear something cute'.

'I got caught in the storm,' I said defensively. 'I've been taking photographs from the ridge – for my landscape painting project.' Before Matt could block my way, I ran up the stairs and locked myself in the bathroom. 'Just give me twenty minutes,' I shouted through the door.

I stripped off my borrowed clothes and got under the shower. This was another thing that needed changing. The showerhead was impossible to regulate, so the water ran either freezing cold or scorching hot. Today, it was almost unbearably hot, which was just what I needed.

When I stepped out, steamy and pink, I opened the window a crack and stood for a long time wrapped in my towel listening to the sound of gunshots coming from the far side of the estate.

Antonio?

I shivered.

It was only then that I realised that in my distraction I'd forgotten my own wet clothes on Antonio's bathroom floor. *Damn it*. I couldn't be bothered to field Matt's questions. Before leaving the bathroom, I stuffed the clothes Antonio had lent me into the space behind the loose bath panel. Then I went into our bedroom and put on my favourite red dress.

Matt was waiting for me in the dining room. I was touched to see how much effort he'd made. The table was set with his great-aunt's best china and silverware, the lights were dimmed and he'd lit the candelabra, which sent shadows and light into all the corners of the room as the flames flickered in the draught.

'Mmm... That smells delicious,' I said.

Since arriving in Italy, I'd discovered that Matt was an excellent cook – far better than me – certainly when it came to the local cuisine.

'You look gorgeous,' he said.

He pulled out my chair, spooned a generous helping of wild truffle risotto onto my plate and handed me a glass of chilled white wine.

Matt's anger was gone. This was how it always was with Matt. He'd fly into sudden rages that just as quickly dissipated and he'd become again the perfect gentleman.

'*Cin cin.*' He clinked my glass and kissed me gently on the lips. 'So, tell me, how did you spend your afternoon?'

Just at that moment, a gust of wind battered the farmhouse, and all the candles went out.

SEVENTEEN

THE HITCHHIKER

BY MATTEO J. ROSSI

The ethereal peaks of the Alps are behind them now. They're down in the plains, where the air is thicker and dreams solidify into dust. Ted eases off the accelerator to prolong their five-hour journey along the Italian *autostrada* from Aosta to Milan to Bologna to Florence. He doesn't want it to end. But he knows it's over. She's already gone.

'My wallet is in the glove compartment,' he says as they pull up at a motorway toll station. 'Can you deal with it?'

They've settled into their roles already. Taking the ticket and paying the toll is her job, because the sports car is right-hand drive and all the tolls are designed for Continental road users. She leans over to feed a ten-euro note into the machine. It hasn't escaped his notice that she hasn't once offered to contribute to the cost of petrol or the toll charges. Is she really that broke? If so, how will she and Harry survive? Or is she just tight?

Ted doesn't complain about the detour off the *autostrada* and the long drive through the congested suburbs of Florence to reach the *Firenze Stazione di Santa Maria Novella* – one of the busiest mainline stations in Italy used by about 60 million people a year and the departure point for the Florence-to-Rome high speed railway. Each red light, each queue is a reprieve – another few minutes to be spent in her company. He hasn't lost hope that before they get to the station, she'll change her mind.

When it comes to it, there are no long goodbyes. It's a circus at the station. The taxis behind him hoot their horns, and a policeman blows his whistle and makes frantic, angry hand signals. Italians aren't good at queueing.

She performs a rewind of the movements she made when he first gave her a lift. She dumps Harry in his lap like a package, hoists on her backpack and hangs her guitar over her shoulder. She comes to the driver's side. Ted lifts Harry up into her arms. She settles him on her hip, gives Ted a quick smile, her face half hidden behind her hair.

And then she's gone. This time for real.

* * *

After dropping Nikki and Harry at the Florence railway terminal, Ted is on autopilot for the next two hours. He drives fast. Tunnel vision. Mouth dry. Eyes fixed on the road ahead. It's only when he sees that the fuel gauge is deep into the red that he re-engages with himself. He pulls off at the next service station, looks at a map – is surprised to see how far he's come and can't recall anything about how he got here. The entire journey is a blank.

Ted fills up the car. His final destination must be within 30 kilometres, but he doesn't want to break down in the darkness on the twisty white roads leading to his grandfather's farmhouse and he knows that this is the only service station in the vicinity of the place he'll call home for the rest of the summer. A great wave of weariness crashes over him. He had less than four hours' sleep last night. He goes into the garage to pay for the petrol and get an espresso from the coffee machine to keep him going.

At the till, he opens his wallet. There were two fifty-euro notes in his wallet when he left the Auberge Saint-Bernard this morning – emergency money his mother had given him for the journey across Europe. Now, all he can find is the few coins they got in change from the tolls. The coins drop out and roll across the tarmac. He looks through the folds of his wallet once more, not wanting to believe that she's stolen from him – one hundred euros is missing. He's skint.

He fingers the wallet one last time. The notes are gone – that's for sure – but she's left him something in exchange: a braided friendship bracelet tucked into the fold where his money should be.

EIGHTEEN
DANIELLE

We began to settle into our daily routines. Matt worked for hours at a time shut up in his study or took long walks around the estate glued to his mobile phone. It irritated me to see him constantly tapping away at messages or staring at the screen. Even when we went for walks together, he spent more time looking at his phone than talking to me or communing with nature. What was the point of living in such beautiful surroundings if you never lifted your eyes to take in the view?

'We're three in this household,' I said, picking up on the new vocabulary of the lockdown. 'You, me and your mobile phone. Can't you just live in the moment? You're married to that bloody phone!'

I fell into the habit of walking down most mornings to our nearest village, Sangiari d'Orcia, to buy provisions for the day. I loved the forty-minute hike along unpaved white roads through the undulating countryside. I made a point of taking only my SLR camera and leaving my phone behind. I wanted absolute freedom. The phone was a tether to Matt, to chores at the farmhouse, to the emotional demands of my family and friends pinging me messages from the UK (these remote inter-actions no substitute for face-to-face gatherings and drinks at the pub). It was a good feeling to 'cancel' it all, if only for part of the day, by leaving my phone in a drawer.

Outside, the early morning air was crisp and invigorating and cleansing. I filled my lungs with it – so grateful to be far from the dust and grime of the city. Although there were still many local restrictions in place owing to continuing infections, it didn't feel like a lockdown when we had access to such stunning countryside the instant we stepped out of the door.

On my first solitary morning outing to the village, almost every shop and building was shuttered. But that wasn't only because of the pandemic. I hadn't realised it was a *giorno santo* or saint's day, which meant that the schools and most of the shops and businesses in the area were closed. In a normal year, however, the streets would have been full of people. It would have been a time of celebration and there would have been colourful rival, *contrada* flags hung out from windows and traditional pageants and tournaments in the streets – but this wasn't a 'normal year'. The streets were empty.

In happy isolation, I wandered with my camera for company, pausing at medieval churches and street corners and fountains and squares to capture the essence of this unbeliev-ably photogenic little gem of medieval architecture.

Although the flags were missing this year, the narrow streets were brightened with an abundance of flowers in terra-cotta pots positioned on the terraces of closed restaurants and stone balconies and porches of shops and homes. The festivity of the flowers on this sunny autumnal day contrasted strangely with the absence of people. I wondered where they all were, and pictured curious eyes looking out at me through beaded screens and slits in the shutters as I circled the village.

There were some shaded corners that were more sombre. Italians are in the habit of posting obituary notices on the walls of their buildings. I'd noticed one or two of these customary death notices displayed in streets next to a church or secluded square on previous visits to Italy. But now I came to a sepulchral alleyway where the entire wall of a building was plastered with obituaries. The posters bore the faces of the deceased – old-fashioned black-and-white photographs, mostly of men in their prime of life, sometimes in military uniform or in formal suits and narrow ties, stiff and unsmiling, whose dark, earnest eyes stared out at me. Below the photograph, the name of the deceased was given, along with the date of birth and death followed by a long eulogy.

I tried to decipher some of these notices. It was beyond me to translate many words from the eulogies to these men, but I was moved to read their names – *Alessandro, Federico, Jacopo, Gabriel, Emanuele* (the sounds rolled off my tongue, a bittersweet romantic chant). And to note the number of deaths clustered in the springtime (the time when Italy had been hardest hit). And to calculate the ages at which these victims of the virus had died, ranging from 41 to 101 years old. Some obituaries had already started to peel away from the wall; others had been obliterated by water damage from a leaking drainpipe; others were defaced with graffiti – every one of them was beginning to fade having been exposed to the elements all the summer long.

The fragility of these death notices seemed to represent the transience of life itself. There were so many of them. Even in this remote Tuscan village, the virus had struck a very heavy toll. And it wasn't over yet. I hoped that the people pictured before me had more permanent memorials elsewhere – a marble headstone or an iron plaque that would endure beyond the next storm. I hoped that their memorials in the hearts of loving friends and family would last longer than the posters on this wall.

Before turning away, I scanned the walls of the alleyway for the name I was hoping to find: *Benetto Maffeo Rossi*. It was nowhere. I was shocked to think that there was no one competent or caring enough in Benetto's family to have performed the simple service of writing a eulogy and publicising his passing to the community. Then it occurred to me that as his surviving heir, this should fall to Matt. I resolved that, even now so late in the day, I should get Matt to put things right. So far, Matt had avoided all contact with officialdom down in the town. But as the new owner of the estate, he had certain duties and responsibilities. In my view, honouring his benefactor was one of them.

In the end, I didn't have to nag Matt about putting up an obituary notice for his great-uncle. Just as I was about to go on my way, a picture of a young couple on their wedding day caught my eye. It was partly obscured by other notices, but there was something familiar about the image. I leant in and read the name – *Benetto Maffeo Rossi* – and recognised the same image I'd seen at the farmhouse, framed on a side table in the old dining room. Benetto was posing in a three-piece wedding suit, standing stiffly next to his young bride, Loretta.

The poster was coming away from the wall and I was tempted to pull it off and take it home for Matt to see. But that seemed wrong. Instead, I got out my camera to take a photograph. I turned on my flash as the light was so dull and that's when I saw it – purple graffiti scrawled across the notice in ugly, angry letters: *pedofilo*. I could make a pretty good guess at what that word might mean, but I couldn't understand what could have possessed someone to deface an obituary with such a horrible insult.

Unless, of course, it was true... and that was even more uncomfortable.

* * *

It was time to head back to the farmhouse. I'd been out for more than two hours and Matt would be fretting over where I'd got to. Not being able to contact me by phone would drive him nuts. I tried to retrace my footsteps to the arched gateway of Sangiari and found that I'd completely lost my bearings in the twisty lanes. Rounding a corner, at last I saw some people. I wasn't the only person out on the streets.

By chance, it seemed I'd stumbled across the only shop that was open in the village that morning: the bakery. Sweet smells of fresh bread and pastries filled the air. Four or five people were queueing patiently outside. All were wearing masks.

I joined the queue, conscious of suspicious sideways glances as I passed by the shoppers. A fat old lady dressed all in black with an incongruous bright pink mask turned and hissed at me. I couldn't make out her words so, at first, I had no idea what I'd done to cause offence. When she pointed at my face and then tugged at her mask, the penny dropped. I'd been so engaged with my surroundings that I'd forgotten to put on a mask. Mask-wearing wasn't such an ingrained habit for the English as for the Italians. Shortages of personal protective equipment at the start of the pandemic had led our government disingenuously to discourage people from wearing masks by saying they provided little protection outside medical settings and should be reserved for key workers. Later, of course, the narrative had changed.

I scrabbled through my small backpack, avoiding eye contact, muttering, '*Scusi, scusi,*' acutely aware of my embarrassing English accent.

Eventually I found a grubby, used paper mask in one of the pockets and hastily covered my mouth and nose.

Taking my place, I became aware that my clumsy spoken Italian had marked me out as a foreigner. There was an uncomfortable shifting and stirring in the queue and I got the sense that I wasn't welcome. News about a recent mutation of the virus that had taken hold in the south-east of England was circulating in the Italian media. I'd seen images of overrun NHS hospitals on the old-fashioned television that Matt was in the habit of slumping in front of in the evenings.

There was something else, too. A couple about my own age turned to stare at me, then looked at each other meaningfully and then straight ahead. I sensed an unspoken understanding – as if I'd been recognised as the subject of an earlier conversation. I supposed that the news must have spread through the village that old Benetto's farmhouse had been taken over by 'the English' – *gli inglesi*. Was it something about the old place that aroused hostility, or was it the fact that we were outsiders? I wanted to tell them that Matt was an Italian, that the farmhouse was his rightful heritage. But, of course, I didn't have the language to communicate this. I stood there awkwardly, avoiding eye contact, conscious there would be something particularly offensive about foreigners taking possession of ancient Tuscan landholdings at this time.

Local resentments hung in the air like contaminated breath.

At last, it was my turn. I pointed to a loaf of *pane Toscano*.

Matt had taught me the words for this Tuscan bread – a coarse, dense loaf cooked in a wood-fired oven (great for mopping up a Tuscan soup or stew, he said) and nothing like those soft and springy British loaves, the mere memory of which made me feel homesick. The baker – masked, gloved and wearing something like a shower cap over her head – passed the loaf out through the hatch on an ancient wooden pizza peel whose long pole enabled her to keep the statutory social distance from her customers.

Only a few loaves and one pie remained on the shelf. Guiltily, I pointed to the pie, sensing a quiver of annoyance from the woman behind me next in line, which not even her mask could conceal. She was holding hands with a boy aged about seven who was playing up, kicking at stones and swinging on her arm.

Matt had a weakness for *crostata* – a traditional treat in this region of Tuscany. The latticed pie was filled with sticky plum jam, and the pastry was sweet and doughy with added eggs and citrus zest. I knew Matt would be riled by my long absence. If, on my return, I could treat him to a slice of *crostata* and a steaming cup of Italian black coffee, he'd be pacified, and the rest of my day would be more pleasant.

I waited while the baker carefully wrapped the *crostata* in white paper. Meanwhile, the boy started to protest loudly. I looked away, pretending to be unaware of the fact that I and the vanishing pie were the cause of his distress.

My eyes fell on a poster taped inside the glass pane of a small hotel *pensione* next door to the bakery. It was amateur – handwritten in English – and the message was stark and simple: *no Americans, no English, no tourists*. It was reminiscent of those disgusting racist notices that were displayed in the windows of lodging houses in England in the 1950s: *no*

Irish, no Blacks, no dogs. This echo of xenophobia was deeply disturbing and upsetting. I grabbed the *crostata* and turned on my heel. As I walked away, I heard the boy start to wail. Suddenly, he yelled after me, his high-pitched, frantic voice ringing out in the quiet square:

'*Go away, English.*'

NINETEEN
THE HITCHHIKER
BY MATTEO J. ROSSI

He knows he should have explained his predicament to the dour, pudgy garage attendant and given his grandfather's address – maybe left his passport as security. But on impulse, he slams his espresso down on the counter, turns on his heel, runs to the car and screeches out of the petrol station. The garage attendant lumbers onto the forecourt and in his rear-view mirror, Ted catches a glimpse of him taking out his phone, no doubt to call the local police. Ted accelerates and it's not fear but exhilaration that sends a tingling shot down his spine and makes his heart pump faster and his breath come in short gasps.

He tears round the bends on the dirt roads, tyres skidding on the loose chalk, kicking up a cloud of white dust in his wake and laughing like a maniac. Stealing is so easy. She's shown him the way. That man was an easy target. *You snooze, you lose...* The service station must have security cameras and maybe there would be trouble down the line, but for now he's the master of the universe – and the whole world can go to hell.

He arrives at his grandparents' farm just as the sun is setting behind the hills. He's still in high spirits, an adrenaline high, bending to kiss his grandmother on both cheeks and spin her off her feet so that she squeals like a young child. She's fragile and light as a feather. Back on *terra firma*, she holds him at arm's length and smiles up at him, eyes crinkling in her wrinkled-apple face: '*Teo, Teo, mio grande ragazzo!*' – my big boy.

Ted's grandma is the only one to use the Italian diminutive of his name. Reawakening memories of her own lost child, she's always had a soft spot for her blue-eyed English grandson, now towering above her. Ted's grandfather is more interested in the sports car. He marvels at its sleek lines and laments the ugly dent in its side.

'*Che peccato, che peccato!*' – what a shame – he exclaims.

Soon, the car is safely parked out of sight in one of the barns and Ted lugs his trunk up to the guest bedroom at the rear of the farmhouse, where his grandmother has made up the bed for him. Once installed, Ted hands over the gifts of English tea and shortbread and ginger biscuits that his mother packed for the family and settles in to soak up the magical stillness of evening out on the patio.

The sunset is stunning – he hasn't seen so much sky since the last time he was here. His grandmother's rich Tuscan cooking tastes as good as he remembers and his grandfather's wine cellar, even better. He leans back to survey the rolling wheat fields and vineyards and savours the earthy tones of last year's blood-red vintage from his grandfather's estate swirling over his palate.

But for the feeling that his 21-year-old heart is breaking, he could be happy here all summer long. His mind swirls with poetry and clichés. His entire body aches deliciously for the hitchhiker, his lover of one night.

Parting is such sweet sorrow.

Over the next few days, Ted gets stuck into work on the estate. His grandfather is a hard taskmaster. He puts Ted to work in the fields, alongside the estate manager's son, Luca, green pruning and thinning the vines, cutting the grass, spraying the crop, and repairing the posts and trellises. The idea of spending days out in a vineyard sounds idyllic but in reality, it's long hours of back-breaking manual labour under the Mediterranean sun.

It's not long before Ted is tanned and muscular, with scratches and scrapes on his shins, callouses on his hands and creases round his eyes. He looks more like an Italian peasant than an Oxford graduate. When Ted isn't in the vines, he works on jobs around the estate, repairing a fence, demolishing an old outhouse, digging out the foundations for a new terrace surrounding the ancient swimming pool.

He's not the most practical of adolescents, having spent the better part of his teenage years sitting at desks in front of screens. But Luca, a few years his senior and undeniably more experienced when it comes to *sex, drugs and rock 'n' roll*, takes him under his wing. Soon, Ted and Luca are thick as thieves, labouring together from sunrise to sunset and drinking the nights away down in the town.

Ted soon finds out that Luca has a well-deserved reputation as a local playboy and troublemaker. Wherever he is, there's drama. Whenever there's a fight, you can be sure he started it. Whenever a girl is upset, you can be sure he had a hand in it. Yet, he's popular with the packs of girls who hang around the bars on a Friday and Saturday night. There's something they find sexy about his wolfish looks, '*devil may care*' attitude and predatory generosity. He's always good for a drink (at least if you're young and pretty) and he's always on the prowl for a one-night stand.

Luca is happy to share. He introduces Ted to a selection of the more accommodating girls. But Ted has lost his taste for casual sex. The only girl Ted lusts after when he collapses into bed and closes his eyes after a long day working in the vines under the Tuscan sun...

... is Nikki.

Nikki... with her long brown legs and her soft pink mouth.

The one who got away...

The rest of them can go to hell.

TWENTY
DANIELLE

'Honestly, Matt, I didn't feel welcome,' I said over steaming black coffee and *crostata*. 'I was shunned. Like an alien. People actually moved away from me in the queue for bread.' I was close to tears.

'Don't let it get you down,' said Matt. 'It takes time for foreigners to be accepted in these remote hill towns.'

'It felt personal,' I said.

I showed Matt the photograph of Benetto's obituary notice and pointed out the graffiti insult scrawled across it: *paedophile*.

'What's all this about?' I asked. 'Did your uncle have enemies? Was he a bad man?'

He dodged the questions.

'The villagers always resented him for his wealth. The big local landowner. They're mostly halfwits and inbreds with nothing better to do than gossip over old jealousies and imagined wrongs,' he said flippantly.

Even in jest, I was shocked to hear him speak that way.

'Look, I'm sorry you were upset,' he said. 'You should keep away from the place.'

In fact, that's exactly what Matt did.

* * *

Before the pandemic struck, Matt had been an outgoing and gregarious man, his social ease and ready conversation among the things I found most attractive about him when we first started dating. He'd drifted into social isolation during the London lock-downs. I'd hoped that the move to Italy would bring back the man I'd fallen in love with, but instead since our arrival in Tuscany he'd become a recluse. He said it was because he wanted to stay focused on his writing and keep in the headspace of his story, but I suspected that he rarely ventured beyond the perimeter of the estate because he wanted to avoid meeting people from his past.

At the farmhouse, Matt avoided all contact with Antonio. He even kept out of Marcella's way – our main link to village life. Since their conversation the first night, he'd exchange only the barest civilities with 'that old scandalmonger', as he now called her.

Unlike me, rather than rebelling against the restrictions of the lockdown, Matt was using them as an excuse to withdraw from all forms of social contact and putting pressure on me to do the same.

'If there's one thing the pandemic has taught me,' he said, 'it's that most of the social activities I engaged in before were a worthless waste of time and I don't miss them in any way.'

Matt spent long hours locked in his office. In theory, he had all the time in the world to write his novel, especially as he'd offloaded most of the chores relating to the day-to-day running of the house and the estate to me. But I could see that he was preoccupied and struggling to write. He seemed paralysed by his change of fortune.

The fact is, he had writer's block. It was as simple as that. Unfairly, he seemed to blame me for his inability to string a sentence together on the screen. He said he couldn't concentrate because I was forever 'interrupting his train of thought' or 'getting inside his head'. Though his door was shut virtually all the time, he accused me of 'watching over him' or 'spying on him'. He insisted he could 'hear me breathing on the other side of the door', even when I was nowhere near his office.

Whenever I asked how he was getting on, he snapped at me for 'checking up on him'. But when I tried to give him space, he accused me of 'neglecting him'. I couldn't win. Matt's paranoia and unpredictable mood swings began to get me down. When he was low, I could do nothing right. Then everything was my fault.

In normal times, we'd have been fine, I told myself. We couldn't be the only couple having a few difficulties in lockdown. Truth is, for all my bravado, I was lonely. Lonely – and perhaps, although I scarcely dared admit it to myself, a little broody. Without the distraction of my job and my social life, the physical and emotional isolation of living deep in the countryside with only one companion, in a foreign country, when we were still in the grip of a global pandemic was... well, quite simply, depressing. Probably that made me clingy and needy. I hadn't been the best company myself. It was hardly surprising tensions were running high.

Once his book is written, everything will be OK, I thought.

October was drawing to a close. We'd been in Italy for over six weeks and so far, there had been little time for romance and relaxation. That night I persuaded Matt to come to bed early. We'd both been working too hard, Matt on his manuscript and me on the renovations.

'We should take time to stop and breathe and enjoy the beauty of this place,' I said.

The evenings had lost their balminess and the nights were closing in.

'It'll be winter before we know it.'

The sunset glowed crimson, but dark clouds beyond the mountains heralded a storm. Matt said he needed some exercise and went out for a long run along the white roads surrounding the estate while I retired to our bedroom. When I heard his steps on the driveway, I called down from the open window.

'Come up here – the view is stunning.'

During the afternoon, I'd picked armfuls of lavender and brought them up to the bedroom in an old clay vase. The smell of lavender filled the room. Tuscan lavender bore no resemblance to the cloying lavender scents of talcum powder and papery-skinned old ladies that I recalled from my grandmother's vanity table. No. This wild lavender was oddly seductive, conjuring honey and bees, purple sunsets and rainwashed dawns. I'd also picked the last of the pink roses on the front terrace to save them from the coming storm. The roses were almost blown and the petals I brushed against fell to the floor as I breathed in the heady fragrance.

I took off my clothes, lay on the bed, placed a rose between my breasts and waited.

* * *

Matt was on a high after his run. We made love urgently that night as if we were rediscovering our bodies and our love for each other. Instead of the saggy old passion-killer we'd been sleeping on, we now had a quality mattress bought online from one of the factory outlets that had reopened as life returned to normal. The new mattress had been delivered that afternoon and I'd made up the bed with crisp white sheets of Egyptian cotton, also ordered online.

I didn't want this night to end. Afterwards, I wandered out onto our bedroom terrace. The brickwork was weathered by time but still structurally solid and the view of the night sky overhead was spectacular. The sun had long since sunk behind the olive groves, leaving only a peachy glow above the line of hills. The hills were alive with the sound of cicadas, whose endless thrumming and drilling reminded me that we were not alone – the place was teeming with life.

While I watched the stars emerging from the violet haze to shine with greater intensity, the sound of the cicadas took on an extraterrestrial quality. It felt like supernatural forces were at work in the elemental landscape as darkness deepened. Suddenly, I felt very small and insignificant in the vastness of the universe and overcome with a not unpleasant spine-tingling surge of melancholia.

I'd never paid much attention to the night sky in London. Like most Londoners scuttling to and from work, I spent more time looking down at the pavements than up at the stars. During lockdown, we'd taken to going out for walks late at night and for the first time in years, I'd been moved to tears by the luminosity of the moon and the vast universe that encircled me. But even in lockdown, the planets and constellations had to compete with artificial lighting from street lamps and all-night shopping. Here in the Val d'Orcia, there was no ambient light pollution to dim their brightness. The configuration of constellations stood out clearly against the dense dark blanket of night. The moon hung like a huge orange fireball and I could almost see it moving as I watched.

I called Matt out onto the terrace. I wanted us to share the intensity of this experience.

'Show me the stars,' I said.

I threw myself down onto the old mattress that we'd dragged onto the terrace earlier to make way for the new one (Covid regulations meant we'd have to dispose of the old one ourselves). Matt had let slip that one of his former girlfriends had taught him the names and configurations of some of the constellations: she was into gemstones and stars – all that kind of thing – bit of a hippy.

Matt was so uptight and strait-laced these days that I couldn't imagine him hanging out with a hippy girlfriend. He wasn't into counterculture or flower power or psychedelic drugs or the philosophy 'make love, not war', or any of the other hippy stereotypes. He was a man of action, not contemplation. He'd only half-teasingly call me a 'lazy slut' if I left my bra draped over the towel rail at night, or my clothes in a bundle on the floor. He generally rose punctually at 6 a.m. and liked to see me washed, dressed and made-up by 8 a.m. Even in the London lockdowns, there had been no breakfasting in pyjamas or sitting around in loungewear in our household.

This night was a rare exception, with Matt unusually relaxed and revealing a deeper and more reflective side to his personality. He came out holding a duvet, lay back on the mattress and rolled us into a cocoon.

'This is a great place for stargazing. Did you know that Galileo invented the telescope here? That's the Big Dipper,' he said, tracing a line of stars with his finger. 'And that's the

Milky Way.' He pointed out the arc of bright stars pulsating above. 'There's Orion – the hunter.'

I stared hard (joining the dots in my mind) to make out the shape of the hunter drawing his bow.

'And look – planets. See... there's Jupiter and that's Saturn.'

'How do you know which ones are stars and which ones are planets?' I asked, thinking that Matt could be telling me anything and I wouldn't have a clue if it was true or false.

'Planets look a lot like big bright stars,' said Matt. 'It's partly knowing where each one is positioned in the sky, but one clue is that planets don't sparkle like stars – they give off a constant shine.'

'That's weird,' I said. 'What makes the stars sparkle?'

'Million-dollar question,' said Matt, to avoid having to admit he didn't know the answer (something he never did).

'I had no idea you were so into this kind of thing,' I said, resting my head just below his ribcage, where I could hear his heart beating.

'There are lots of things you don't know about me,' he said as he pulled me gently on top of him.

While we made love once more, our bodies gleaming in the starlight, I thought about how little I knew this man.

TWENTY-ONE
THE HITCHHIKER
BY MATTEO J. ROSSI

It's Luca who picks up the girl and brings her back to the farm. He's at the village bar drinking beer and watching a football match with his mates when not long before midnight, he notices a car pulling up in the square and a young girl gets out with her little boy propped on one hip and a guitar slung over her shoulder. As she struggles with the door, he approaches in rolling cowboy gait, takes her rucksack (ever gallant when a pretty blonde stranger is in need) and helps her to a seat at the nearest table. Once she's installed, he buys her a beer and goes back to the game. He likes to play it chilled. From the side-lines, his drinking buddies watch the beautiful young foreigner with hungry eyes.

In a Tuscan village like Sangiari, the bar is the hub of local life. It opens at the crack of dawn, serving up cappuccinos and pastries to commuters and local businessmen on their way to work. All day long, it sells newspapers, cigarettes, bus tickets, scratch cards, chocolate, gum… In the afternoon, it's *gelato* – ice cream – for the children and creamy *dolce* – sweets – for their gossiping mothers, then espressos and beer served to soft-bellied middle-aged men with nothing better to do than sit and smoke and put the world to rights. In the late afternoon, old men stop by for their *apertivi* – appetisers – and the tables are occupied by out-of-town diners drawn to the excellent wood-fired pizza and home-made pasta.

Most of the drinkers leave after a few glasses to go back to their wives and their dinner tables. The usual suspects keep drinking all evening and slump into corners, where they merge with the fixtures and fittings. Once the tables are cleared, a younger crowd takes over the space. Some are there to get drunk and/or laid, but mostly they're there to get out of the house, hang out with their friends and watch live football matches on the screen on the wall.

In the course of one day, the full spectrum of local life, good and bad, passes through the bar. The owners are the eyes and the ears of the Tuscan village. The bar really *is* the place where everybody knows your name, for better or worse. If you've got something to hide, God help you!

Luca has one eye on the match and one eye on the girl at the table by the door. Exceptionally, Ted isn't by his side tonight. It's his grandfather's birthday and a special meal has been laid on at the farmhouse, with uncles and aunts invited from the far corners of Tuscany. The old man didn't invite Luca to join the celebrations. Luca made out he was offended, but having seen the girl, he's secretly pleased to have the night to himself. At half-time, he watches her go up to the barman. He sidles across and listens in on the conversation. The girl's Italian is bad. She switches to her own language, English.

'Do you have rooms here?' she asks. 'Is there a hotel in the village?'

Unusually, the barman's English is even worse than the girl's Italian. He shrugs and shouts out to another member of staff to come over. At this point the little boy, red-faced and wriggling in her arms, lets out a howl and, kicking his legs, sends a glass of wine shattering to the floor. Luca dives in to pick up the pieces and offer his services as interpreter. He tells her that the bar has no accommodation and that the nearest hotel is in Montepulciano, ten kilometres away.

'Stay here till the end of the match,' he says, nodding up at the screen where the players are getting into position for the second half of the game. 'I have a car. I can drive you.'

Luca speaks English fluently, though with a strong Italian accent and a cultivated 'cool' American twang from the Hollywood movies and pop music all the young Europeans grow up with. He buys her another beer and one for himself and a juice for her kid, which she takes without a word of thanks – and no qualms about accepting favours.

'What's a pretty girl like you doing in Sangiari?' he asks, in no hurry to get back to the football this time.

She pushes back her golden hair and Luca's eyes fall on her slender wrist circled in friendship braids.

'I'm looking for a job for the summer,' she says, unfazed. She's used to being the centre of male attention. 'I've come to work at the farm belonging to the Innocenti family. Do you know it? It's not far from here.'

Luca almost chokes on his beer. She pulls out a ragged map from her rucksack. Another thing she stole from Ted along the way. The Innocenti estate is circled in red biro. Luca gives her a big smile. It could be his lucky night.

'I'll give you a lift,' he says. 'I'm going in that direction.'

TWENTY-TWO
DANIELLE

The weeks turned to months. The nights closed in, and a wet and windy November gave way to a cold and bright December. Each season had its colours and its charms. We both settled into our new routines, and life began to feel more balanced and domesticated – almost normal. Matt helped with the renovations in the main farmhouse, taking time off his writing to organise the contractors and chat with me about the plans. We were a good team – me driving the project forwards and making the design and construction decisions, and him dealing with third parties to get them implemented.

Work was well under way on rewiring, heating and plumbing. I wanted to make our new home as environmentally friendly as possible, installing solar panels and a small wind turbine, together with compatible heating and air conditioning systems. I was delighted that Matt supported my commitment to transforming the farmhouse into a beautiful sustainable home. But all this came at a cost and the major works were rapidly eating through my redundancy pay-off and the modest proceeds from the sale of my flat. Meanwhile, there was one project over which Matt did nothing but procrastinate – the infinity pool. In fact, he preferred not to talk of it at all.

I was impatient for the work to get started on the infinity pool so that we'd be able to use it in the hot summer months. But I hadn't reckoned on how difficult it would be battling with the local bureaucracy. It had been so much easier, I discovered, negotiating and structuring complex legal contracts at my London law firm than it was circumnavigating the twists and turns of Italian officialdom and its spider's web of petty rules relating to planning consents. There were so many layers of regulation to be complied with, so many officials to be satisfied and so many boxes to be ticked before any progress could be made.

The fact that I couldn't string a sentence together in Italian didn't help, so I had to rely on Matt's help. Tired of my badgering, Matt finally got in contact with a swimming pool company. He refused to use the local pool engineers recommended by Marcella's nephew. Instead, he telephoned a national chain specialising in swimming pool construction and design that catered to the second-home expat community. Increasingly, it seemed as if Matt wanted to keep us and our lives here as separate as possible from village affairs.

The day before the appointment with the company's representatives, we clashed over the swimming pool. Matt was worried about the expense, as we were both on a reduced income and the renovations up at the farmhouse were spiralling out of control. The foundations of the old pool were sound, he declared. It would save money just to put in a new pool liner and tiled surround rather than having to dig new foundations and then dig out and resurface the existing site.

I understood his logic but had set my heart on the idea of

an enlarged infinity pool whose design would maximise the impact of the stunning views over the valley from the ridge, the seamless blend between the edge of the pool and the sky beyond giving the illusion that the water continued indefinitely into the distance. If he was pragmatic, I was the fantasist.

I'd done the sketches and drawings... I imagined myself – as if on the cover of a holiday brochure – stretched out on a sunlounger sipping chilled cocktails, soaking up the views of the Crete Senesi that stretched from the ridge to the horizon in our beautiful corner of the Val d'Orcia. And at night, I visualised myself floating in the water... stargazing. Here, where the stars hung bright, undimmed by dust or ambient light, heavy and low, throbbing in the black sky as if they might fall down at any instant among the shadowy wheat fields and silver olive groves.

I knew that I'd be sinking the better part of my redundancy payment into the redevelopment of the farmhouse. A big chunk would be spent on boring but essential renovations that wouldn't enhance the aesthetics of the place.

'Since I'm paying for it all,' I insisted, 'I don't want to compromise on this. I'm determined to realise my dreams at least when it comes to the pool, which I want to be stunning – the jewel in the crown of our estate.'

'Listen to yourself,' said Matt quietly. 'What a princess!'

In the long, dark winter evenings I obsessed over its design and features, poring over photographs of the most iconic infinity pools around the world. Matt called it my 'infinity pool porn', claiming that it had displaced my previous obsession with 'property porn'. *The world's best infinity pools are all about blurring the lines between the man-made and the natural,*' I read. I researched with lawyerly diligence:

An infinity pool is a reflecting pool where the water flows over one or more edges, producing a visual effect of water with no boundary. Such pools are often designed so that the edge appears to merge with a larger body of water such as the ocean, or with the sky.

I researched photographs of award-winning pools in celebrity homes and stylish hotels. This would be a feature that we could highlight if we ever decided to develop the property as a holiday villa. One international chain of boutique hotels claimed in its marketing materials:

Hanging out in an infinity pool allows swimmers to immerse themselves in stunning landscapes and seascapes at the same time. Add in great cocktails, amazing food and fun in the sun, and these are the types of swimming pools that can make your entire vacation.

From elephant-spotting in the Serengeti National Park and floating over the Bangkok skyline, to revelling in epic Santorini sunsets, there's so much to do, beyond simply swimming and soaking, at our favourite hotels with infinity pools across the globe.

With most countries around the globe having closed their borders and international leisure being pretty much at a standstill, this holiday advertising read like something from a lost world – a long-forgotten fantasy obliterated by the pandemic. Still, I picked out the features and finishes that appealed to me most. If I couldn't travel to the Serengeti to immerse myself in the liminal space between water and sky, then I'd build this illusion right here on our doorstep.

Finally, Matt's patience ran out. I sat at the old oak dining table, eating toast and reviewing my paperwork. He looked over my shoulder.

'It's immoral, you know, when the pandemic's still raging,' he lectured, 'to be investing so much time, money and emotional energy into such a frivolous enterprise.'

I resented his patronising tone.

'We're contributing to the Italian economy,' I said. 'It's important for everyone who has the means to do so to engage in economic activities again.'

I'd heard the economists and politicians using such phrases on the BBC World Service radio station. I didn't really believe in my own borrowed rhetoric. Secretly, I was plagued with a nagging guilt about the project.

After breakfast that day, I followed Matt out to the old pool with our coffees to take a final look before the arrival of the pool engineers.

'I spent most of that summer floating around in this pool,' Matt said to me in an aside as I drew level.

He was looking down into the putrid water. His eyes were dreamy and distant.

'So that's why you're so sentimental about keeping it the same,' I said.

Then, as I handed him his coffee, his eyes clouded over as if an unpleasant memory had come to mind.

Shortly, we heard a car engine and saw a trail of dust rising from behind the slope.

'Let's get this over and done with,' said Matt.

He strode down the track to the main entrance of the estate to open the gate. We'd become so isolated and cut off from the outside world during the lockdown that we kept the gate padlocked for much of the time. Because Matt had refused to use a local company, the men doing the pool installation work had had a two-hour drive from the other side of Florence and the first thing they wanted to do on arrival was use our toilet.

This annoyed Matt. I'd noticed that he'd become increasingly paranoid about the virus in recent weeks. All the talk of 'mutations' and 'variants' that he picked up on the Italian news channels must have fuelled his anxiety. He disliked having workmen coming onto the estate, let alone having them inside the farmhouse or using our facilities.

He followed the engineers out of the house, assiduously rubbing the door handles with antiviral wipes. Once outside, he insisted on 'man-marking' them up to the pool, and then stood keeping watch while they surveyed the site and poked about with rulers and rods.

I tagged along. Although I couldn't take an active part in the discussions because of the language barrier, I didn't want to be sidelined. Perhaps this was my vanity project, but at least it meant I was emotionally invested in it.

It wasn't long before Matt asked the men if they wanted a drink and when they asked for water, he nodded in my direction. Not wanting to appear discourteous to the workmen, I dashed back, grabbed my project file from the kitchen table, and two chilled bottles of mineral water from the fridge, donned my mask and gloves, and made my way back to join the group huddled deep in conversation at the edge of the old pool.

I marched up to them and held out my file of drawings to the man who looked like the boss.

'Tell them this is what we want,' I said to Matt.

Not wanting to divert his attention from the male head of the household to me, the man hesitated for a second or two, waiting for a cue from Matt. I'd noticed the 'macho' approach to anything to do with building work or construction that subsisted in this part of Italy and it seemed far worse than anything I'd encountered when doing up my flat in the UK.

Matt put his arm around my shoulders and continued smoothly in Italian while I stood by stupidly, shut out from the conversation. The men wore their masks dangling below their noses and stared at my tense, masked face with thinly veiled amusement and disdain. I knew I was right. My proposed design was the best for the pool. It was the way Matt brushed aside my intervention so publicly in front of these two men that upset me. He made me feel worthless. I was the artist, after all. I was the one with an appreciation of landscapes and angles and perspectives. I was the one who had spent hours visualising and sketching out the site.

Refusing to be sidelined, I took out my drawings. My plan was to do away with an ugly, raised stone terrace that blocked the view from the water and to double the surface width of the pool to extend as far as the ridge. The existing terrace was made up of big, uneven concrete paving stones and broken cement.

'The cement is at least six inches deep and will be a nightmare to dig out,' Matt had said. 'Believe me, I know what I'm talking about. I built it with Antonio the summer I was here. It was back-breaking work. Those flagstones weigh a ton.'

It was clearly an amateur job, done on the cheap.

'Well, you didn't make a very good job of it,' I said cuttingly.

As far as I was concerned, it was an eyesore.

My concept was for a sustainable deck paved in local stone and landscaped with wildflower borders and rockeries to be built alongside the new infinity pool.

'This is what we want,' I insisted, brandishing my drawings and gesturing for the men to follow me. 'Your first job will be to dig out this hideous terrace and remove all the rubble from the site.'

The two pool engineers ambled after me nonchalantly, keeping the statutory distance. My abrupt behaviour was out of character, but their attitude infuriated me. The older man looked towards Matt as if expecting him to translate my words. Suddenly, Matt flipped, as if he felt humiliated by my defiance. His anger flared and in a macho gesture, he marched over, grabbed my drawings and ripped them unceremoniously in half.

'It's my house, Danielle. I get to decide.'

TWENTY-THREE
THE HITCHHIKER
BY MATTEO J. ROSSI

Ted is dozing luxuriantly in bed, when his rest is broken by the sound of screaming – shrill, breathless, hoarse. Not the lustful screams of a young woman, or the angry squealing of an infant, but the pitiful screams of an old woman. He opens his eyes. The sun streams through open shutters, filling his room with speckled light as the rays catch on flecks of dust in the hot air. It must be almost lunchtime.

Ted leaps out of bed and rips back a gauze curtain that partly covers the window opening. His grandmother runs towards the pool waving her arms. The water is disturbed by rings and bubbles. Ted recalls hearing a soft splash immediately preceding the screaming as he surfaced from his dreams. He springs into action, vaulting down the stairs in his boxer shorts and sprinting to the edge of the pool, where a small orange shape is visible beneath the water. Without pausing an instant to reflect, he dives in and retrieves the tiny body of a young child writhing at the bottom of the pool.

When he breaks the surface with the child lifted above his head, the first thing he sees is a pair of legs – legs that are familiar: tanned, smooth and shapely, rising up and up, it seems. All the way to the sky. Then slender wrists, banded with colourful braids that only partly conceal the faint criss-cross of scars, and hands that he's held, that have touched the most intimate parts of his body, reaching down for the child. Then a face, etched in his memory for its luminous beauty, now twisted in anguish and fear.

Nikki.

She's oblivious to him. All of her attention focused on her baby boy, breathless and blue against her chest. She crouches down and places him across her knees head down, frantically tapping his back until at last he takes a breath and starts to cough and splutter – and then to vomit water and bile onto the stones. A few steps behind her he sees Luca, who must have come from the same direction, following in her shadow, running up to see what all the fuss is about. Luca, like Ted, wearing only his boxers.

Ted is in shock. Despite the heat of the midday sun, his body judders and he turns away to retch into the flower bed. The excesses of rich food from the family gathering of the night before (the centrepiece had been a roasted wild boar shot by Luca on a recent hunting trip with his grandfather). And alcohol (he must have drunk at least two bottles of estate wine, followed by liqueurs and the malt whisky he brought from home). Together with the adrenaline rush of the rescue. All had combined to provoke an attack of projectile vomiting.

It's only when he looks up again at Nikki cradling Harry, now sobbing loudly in her arms, that he notices she's wearing nothing but Luca's favourite Harley Davidson T-shirt. The T-shirt drowns her slim frame but barely covers her modesty. His eyes meet those of Luca, who looks away quickly, and in that instant he knows.

She spent last night in Luca's bed.

* * *

At the end of the day, Nikki and Ted are reunited in the ramshackle worker's cottage adjoining the almost equally dilapidated one where Luca sleeps. Harry is curled up in an ancient carved wooden crib fast asleep. Ted and Nikki sit side by side on a coarse, hard couch, not touching, watching Harry's little chest rise and fall. Nikki startles at every snuffle or wheeze. For a long time, they sit without speaking. Tears are running down Nikki's face. Ted's face is blank.

'That's the second time you saved his life,' she says. Then five minutes later: 'I'm a bad mother.'

'Yes,' he says automatically.

She sleeps around, drinks too much, takes drugs, is reckless, irresponsible, endangers the welfare and life of her child. Ted worked that out already. But Ted doesn't care whether or not Nikki is a good or bad mother. All he can think about is that when Harry wandered off from the cottage and fell into the pool, Nikki must have been asleep in bed with Luca. The image sears his brain – the two of them, all night long, drunk and stoned, making love in the cottage next door, oblivious in the heat of their passion to the tick-infested mattress and the dingy surroundings then finally succumbing to sleep at dawn. It's not like she's his girlfriend or anything, but *fuck*...

For a second, he wants to strike her.

As if Nikki can read his thoughts, she takes Ted's hand and squeezes it hard.

'He slept on the floor,' she says. 'It was late when we got back from the bar. We didn't want to wake everyone up at the house.'

Ted hears only one word: *we*. The *we* that she insists upon.

It hurts.

He should be a hero...

He feels like a fool.

TWENTY-FOUR
DANIELLE

The next morning was cold and blustery with glinting sunshine. A fierce gust slammed the shutters against the outer walls as Matt, bare-chested with a towel wrapped around his hips, leant out of the window to hook them back. Even with my eyes half closed, the sight of his athletic body gave me pleasure.

'*La Tramontana*,' he muttered ominously. 'It's going to be bitter today.'

He'd warned me about this chill, dry wind meaning 'from beyond the mountains'. It was a frequent occurrence in Tuscany in wintertime, blowing down from the northern Alpine peaks of Italy and originating as far away as Albania. Its icy blasts sent the temperatures plummeting.

When I came down from my shower, Matt was nowhere to be seen. Marcella was on her knees in the kitchen with a scrubbing brush and a big metal bucket. I made her a strong black coffee the way she liked it and got myself a cup of Earl Grey tea – English-style with milk – along with a slice of toast and marmalade. Old habits die hard. Fortunately, I'd had the foresight to pack enough stocks of English preserves and tea to last us until the easing of travel restrictions. Then we could make a trip to Siena to replenish our supplies at 'The English Grocery' that catered to the British and American expat community in the region.

I could tell Marcella didn't really want to carry on house-keeping for us up at the farmhouse. Out of pity for the old lady, she'd stayed on to care for Great-Aunt Rossi until she moved in with her cousin near Florence. Now, she was getting old and tired herself. Cleaning was hard work in the big, ancient property. In wintertime, it was a struggle for her coming out over the rough white roads to our remote location. No doubt she'd have preferred to quit her job altogether, but there was very little work in the village with no tourists and many businesses having closed. She was left with no choice. She needed the money.

I resolved that while Marcella was still coming to work for us three times a week, I'd make every effort to be on friendly terms with her. The language barrier didn't make it easy for us to get to know each other. But there was more to Marcella's stiffness and reserve than mere communication difficulties. While not openly hostile, I got the sense she didn't like me or felt sorry for me or disapproved of my pres-ence in the place that had for so many years been 'her' domestic domain. In turn, this made me awkward and uncomfortable around her. She gave me imposter syndrome. Nevertheless, I decided to persist. If we were to make a home for ourselves in this part of the world, I wanted (unlike Matt) to be integrated with the locals as well as under-standing their perceptions of the family whose ancestral home had become mine. Marcella had worked on the farm for decades. If anyone could let me into the slanders and secrets of the Rossi household that she guarded so jealously, it was she.

After clearing away my simple breakfast, I looked up a recipe for *crostata* on the Tuscan cookery app I had on my phone and began to gather the ingredients. Since it was always in short supply in town, I was planning to ask Marcella to show me how to make the perfect Tuscan jam pie – one that would meet Matt's exacting standards. While we were baking, I was hoping to get the chance to ask Marcella about Matt's great-uncle, the brother of his paternal grandfather. I was still curious to know if there was anything behind the offensive graffiti scrawled across Benetto's memorial notice that I'd seen on my first visit to the village shortly after we arrived. On my last visit, I'd noticed that the poster had been further defiled with splodges of red paint.

I found flour, sugar, butter and eggs in the cupboards, and lemons in the fruit basket that Marcella had replenished with fresh produce from the weekly village market. I was missing only the plum jam. I remembered seeing some shelves of dusty jars down in the cellar when Marcella had shown us round the property on the first evening. I helped Marcella up off her knees then in my broken Italian, asked her to find me the key to the cellar door.

The cellar was creepier than I remembered. I hadn't been down there for weeks. There was only one flickering light bulb to illuminate the cavernous space. The jam pots were on a stack of shelves in the far corner, deep in the gloom. I made my way over, pushing past old tools and empty suitcases and boxes piled high on all sides with the detritus of years gone by. I found the jar I was looking for – *marmellata di prugne* – and turned round. A figure stood at the opening at the top of the stairs.

'Matt, is that you?' I called out. Against the light, I could see only a dark shape. 'I'm down here.'

At once, I heard a commotion and a rat scuttled past my legs. I screamed out, dropping the jar, which smashed, spewing its purple gloop onto the concrete floor. There was another crash behind me. Disturbed by my shouting, the sudden movement of the rat had dislodged an old guitar, which fell, clattering down. To my horror, as it landed, two more rats scuttled out of the sound hole from their nest in the body of the guitar.

I fled.

* * *

As I reached the top of the cellar stairs, I heard the click of the front door closing, followed by the sound of the Land Rover being driven away. I gripped the bannister, my heart thumping. *He can't have heard me calling him,* I told myself.

Once I'd pulled myself together, Marcella came down to the cellar with me to see what all the fuss was about. With no nonsense, she cleaned up the broken glass and scattered rat poison pellets in the corner where the guitar had fallen to the floor. I wanted to get rid of the broken instrument – the wood was warped and cracked and three of the strings had snapped. She motioned for me to leave it there. I understood why – the rats would scatter if their habitat was disturbed. But I shuddered at the cruelty – the baby rats would die in their nest. *Marcella must think I'm pathetic,* I thought.

Soon we were back in the kitchen armed with a new pot of jam (which I'd washed assiduously under the hot tap before opening) and up to our elbows in flour. I initiated an impromptu Italian lesson, urging Marcella to tell me the names of all the ingredients and utensils, and the words for measuring and pouring, mixing and rolling. Dropping her usual reserve, she proved to be a good-natured and patient teacher, in contrast to Matt, who refused to help me because my 'dreadful accent' grated on his nerves.

When the pie was in the oven, I rinsed off my hands and got my phone. These days it was unusual for Matt to venture out and this was a rare opportunity for me to quiz Marcella away from his controlling presence. I scrolled through my recent pictures and clicked on the close-up image of Benetto's memorial notice. I pointed to the word *pedofilo* and mimed a confused expression while raising my hands in a questioning gesture.

Immediately Marcella's face dropped. She tutted loudly then turned her back to me and began to wash up all the used spoons and bowls energetically in the sink. That was the end of our convivial cooking session. *Was this obstinate loyalty or something more sinister such as silence born of fear?* The conversation was closed. I was left wondering what kind of family I'd got myself mixed up with.

While Marcella cleared away wordlessly, I tried the door to Matt's study. Unusually, he'd left it unlocked. I intended to ask Marcella to come in and clean. Guiltily I entered, knowing that Matt would be annoyed but thinking I should make sure his papers were put safely to one side before Marcella got going with her dusters and mops.

Since our arrival, Matteo had become very secretive about his manuscript. I'd seen nothing of his novel, save for the opening paragraphs, which I'd read over his shoulder some weeks previously. Matt refused to show me what he was working on or to discuss his progress. During his past attempts at writing, he'd liked to try out plot ideas on me, or to boast about his word count tally at the end of the day. In truth, I used to get irritated, as he'd get so obsessed with the process of writing that his story was the only thing he could talk about. But this time he was being very private about it all. Sometimes I fancied he was locked in his study watching porn – or having an online affair. Perhaps the novel was just a cover for endless exchanges of illicit images and texts.

In fact, there were no papers or sheets of Matt's manuscript lying around. The shredder was almost full. He must have disposed of the hard copies of his latest drafts. My curiosity piqued, I switched on his computer screen. I told myself I absolutely needed to see right now if the infinity pool construction company had responded with costings for my plans. I used the computer occasionally for household admin, so I knew Matt's usual password – 'Bundy', his pet dog when he was a child – but this time it didn't work. Not to be deterred, I tried 'Bundy' with various combinations of Ted's birthday, which I knew was the 9th of December.

'Bundy0912.'

Wrong password.

'Bundy912.'

Wrong password.

I switched the month and the date around.

'Bundy1209.'

I struck lucky. The computer started up and Matt's most recent novel draft topped his document list.

I clicked on the document, but it was code-protected. After several failed attempts, I gave up trying to crack the code and turned instead to Matt's email which was what I was really interested in. We'd resolved our differences over the infinity pool. Matt had relented, apologised and forwarded new copies of my drawings to the pool company, but I could find no reply from them in his inbox.

Feeling frustrated and annoyed, I lingered over Matt's latest messages – a friendly message from his agent asking how he was getting on with the novel and a less friendly message from his publisher rescheduling the publication date as he'd missed yet another deadline. *If he's made so little progress with his writing, what's he been spending all his time on, shut away in this study?*

I turned to Matt's search history and scrolled down his '*recently visited*' and '*recently closed*' list of sites. There weren't any dating or porn sites but it didn't make for the most comfortable reading:

Ten Most Deranged Serial Killers of All Time – Infopoint
The Beast of Siena – Italian Serial Killers – Wikipedia
No motive found as Italy's worst serial killer gets life – World...
The Nine Most Famous Italian Serial Killers – Ranker
Infamous Couples Who Killed Together – Insider
Santa Rosa hitchhiker murders – Wikipedia
A serial killer who kills hitchhikers picks up a serial killer – Reddit.com
The Moors Murderers
Ted Bundy: Falling for a Psychopath...

Now, I understood why Matt had been so preoccupied the last few days. *Research.* He'd been filling his head with all these sick and upsetting reports about monstrous people and traumatic events.

Ted... Ted Bundy... I mused. *Ted... the main protagonist of his novel... Why?*

I was genuinely confused.

'I thought he was writing a love story?' I said out loud.

I shut down the computer.

Come to think of it, 'Bundy' is a weird choice of name for a pet dog... He must've lied about that...What else is he lying about?

TWENTY-FIVE
THE HITCHHIKER
BY MATTEO J. ROSSI

Ted's grandmother is in the vegetable garden picking runner beans for lunch. She has a view over the pool as the land slopes away slightly towards the ridge. She looks up from the beanstalks. Something catches her eye – a movement close to the old well. A blur of orange. The sun is in her eyes. Her eyesight is weak. Could it be a fox? She fears for her chickens.

She'll send out Luca later with his gun.

As if by magic, her sighting of the fox transforms into the shape of a tiny child. Now, she sees the toddler wandering over the grass towards the pool. His hair gleams in the sunlight. Is he a dream or a ghost – this golden-haired apparition? She's transfixed by the vision of her beloved son – lost in infancy in a tragic accident – drowned in the well all those years ago. It feels like yesterday. She's very still, expecting this apparition to glide across the water towards her.

He comes to her in dreams and nightmares. He's visited in her waking hours, once or twice in recent years. The cherubic figure approaches the pool, runs up and down the stone patio, haloed by the sun, leans out over the edge to reach something on the surface. She opens her mouth. A sound comes out, visceral and high-pitched, more like a puppy's howl than a scream, as he topples in and slowly sinks to the bottom of the pool, swallowed up by the water.

* * *

When the drama is past and Harry is changed and dry, playing on the grass, Nikki leads him to where the old lady is still sitting on the low stone wall onto which she collapsed. She's crying quietly to herself, with Luca at her side. The hitchhiker comes over and strokes her shoulder gently.

'I'm so sorry,' she says quietly.

Watching from a distance, Ted thinks Nikki resembles an angel, her features lit with sunlight and tender concern as she leans over his grandmother.

Harry laughs at the old woman's wrinkled face and she pinches his cheek with shaking fingers. She feels foolish and faint and confused – but also angry at this foreign intrusion onto her private property and into her private grief.

That afternoon there's a family conference over almond biscuits and wine to decide what to do about the hitchhiker and her little boy. They speak in Italian, so the girl can't understand. Ted asks his grandparents if Nikki and her child can stay for a few days. His grandparents are suspicious and disapproving.

'What's a teenage girl doing running around Europe half-naked with a child in tow?' they say.

'Is it even her baby? We know nothing about her. She could be telling lies. She could be in trouble with the police.

She could be running from the law. *Madonna mia!* For all we know, she could have abducted the child.' Ted's grandfather becomes more animated, raising his voice and gesticulating wildly.

Ted knows his grandfather could be right, but he can't let her go.

Ted tells them Nikki's life story as she told him – the boy's father beats her... she's running away from him to join a girl-friend working in a hotel in the Greek islands. She's been offered a summer job there and wants to start a new life where she and the baby will be safe. She won't be any trouble – she only needs a place to stay for a few nights until her friend can transfer some money over for the journey and then she'll be on her way. He doesn't tell them that this girl means more to him than anything in the world, that she stole his heart away that ghostly night between Alpine peak and sky, that he can't live without her, that he'd die for her... that he'd kill for her... He doesn't have the words to say those things in Italian. And anyway, his grandparents would dismiss him as a hysterical young fool, bewitched by a teenage siren.

At the kitchen table, Nikki plays quietly with Harry, moulding pizza dough into animal shapes. His grandmother glances at them nervously. Ted can't take his eyes off Nikki's hands. Oh! to be that lump of dough she shapes between her fingers...

Ted's grandparents look more and more uncomfortable. His grandmother wrings her hands. She attends Catholic Mass every Sunday. She doesn't want a scandal or lectures from the village priest. His grandfather paces the room. He doesn't want more mouths to feed or trouble from the boy's father or anyone else. The concept of domestic abuse is beyond his comprehension. He's not running a charity, he shouts. Or a bloody women's refuge. The girl should go home to England, back where she belongs... and behave herself...

Ted, or Teo, as she calls him affectionately, is the apple of his grandmother's eye. Perhaps he's a substitute for her dead baby son lost so many years ago.

'Just a few days,' pleads Ted.

The young man squeezes the old lady's gnarled hands, his expressive dark eyes brimming with love and concern. Ted's grandmother is almost persuaded. And little Harry, playing quietly in the kitchen with his teenage mother, has already touched her heart in more ways than one. She can't turn the girl away because her *dolce bambino* – sweet baby – has reawakened a torrent of maternal love and sorrow.

Eventually, a compromise is agreed. The girl is not to sleep at the farmhouse. Absolutely forbidden. Catholic propriety must be preserved. She and the baby can stay in one of the old workers' cottages until she gets her money transfer, then she must go. Ted will clear it out and make things ready for them. While she's staying at the farm, she must earn her keep. She'll help Ted's grandmother with the cooking and cleaning and work in the vegetable garden.

Nikki agrees to everything.

Later that afternoon, Ted's grandmother beckons for him to follow her upstairs. She unlocks a heavy oak door in the corner of her bedroom, which opens onto a side room. Ted has never seen inside. As a child he believed it was haunted. Whenever the cousins played hide-and-seek in the house, his grandmother's bedroom was always out of bounds.

The décor in the side room is pastel and faded. Next to the wall is an ornate, antique carved and turned walnut crib made up with pale blue brushed cotton sheets and a crocheted woollen blanket. Ted knows nothing about antiques, but he can see the crib is old from the tiny wormholes in the wood and from the vintage carvings of roses and cherubs.

'This crib belonged to me,' she says quietly in Italian. 'And then to Martina – your mamma – and at last, to my beautiful son, Alessandro.' The old lady's eyes fill with tears. 'The girl can use it for her baby.'

TWENTY-SIX
DANIELLE

'The day of the rats' (as I always thought of it later), I was shutting the door to Matt's study, when I heard the Land Rover coming up the track. I hurried out to meet Matt on the driveway where, looking pleased as punch, he was unloading a state-of-the-art mountain bike from the boot of the car.

'Well, you've been nagging me to take more exercise.' He laughed. 'I'm getting fat with all your delicious cooking.' He tapped his perfectly flat stomach. 'What do you think?'

'So that's what you were doing this morning,' I said. I checked the bike over admiringly. 'Looks good. Must have been expensive.'

He ignored my comment, leapt on the bicycle and pedalled off joyously up and down the track. I watched him go. Soon, he skidded to a stop by my side.

'Here, give it a go. We should get one for you, too.'

The bike was too big for me, but gamely I tried it out.

'Yeah,' I said, 'maybe. I prefer walking. Cycling up the hills round here would kill me. But I think the bike is a great idea for you.'

In the weeks that followed, Matt took to cycling along the white roads and trails that surrounded the farmhouse. I imagined this would be a sociable activity and that his word count would actually benefit from him getting regular exercise and fresh air away from his desk each day. In the mornings, he remained shut up in his study. In the afternoons, he set off on his mountain bike. Sometimes I went with him, riding a rickety old bike that Marcella had dug out from one of the outhouses and asked Antonio to repair and oil for me. I found it hard to keep up on that old boneshaker. In the end, we hadn't got round to buying a mountain bike for me.

Matt cycled for miles, pedalling furiously, never pausing to speak to people or linger in the villages. He carried his own supplies, refusing to stop at the local bars for a drink or to refill his water bottle at the fountains. With his luminous orange helmet (which I'd purchased for him for visibility since all his other gear was black) and the mask he wore whenever out, he was shielded from all greetings or contact with the locals. I grew impatient with him.

'You're being absurd,' I protested. 'We've got to learn to live with the virus. What's the point of living here if you don't have any interactions with the local community?'

'I don't believe in taking any chances,' he said.

The next weeks passed in mundane harmony at the farmhouse. We each had our own absorbing work and occupations. Matt: his novel-writing as well as editing work for his publishing company. Me: freelance legal work reviewing media contracts along with my photography and artwork. Matt was feeling confident about his writing. In the evenings, he notched up his word count for the day on a noticeboard pinned above the fridge before helping himself to a cold beer.

The ongoing renovations meant that most days we had workmen on the estate. If it wasn't the electricians, it was the plumbers or the plasterers or the roofers or the decorator. I escaped the builders for a couple of hours most afternoons to work on my paintings, setting up my easel wherever the light and scenery took my fancy before joining Matt for an evening drink. Between them, Marcella and Antonio kept things more or less functioning on the estate, much as they had done for the last few years, with little interference from us, while Matt and I kept the builders more or less on track. Sometimes we sat together and watched a movie at the end of the day, cuddling up together for warmth on the threadbare sofa in front of the fire.

Then one day in late February the peace was broken. I was in the kitchen when I heard raised voices outside the window. Through the glass, I watched Matt and Antonio. It was clear from their angry intonations and expressive hand gestures that things were getting heated. As they were using Italian, I couldn't work out what they were arguing about. It was the first time I'd witnessed a proper confrontation between them. Antonio mostly kept his distance from the farmhouse, our only contact with him being if Marcella asked him to help her with a repair or some chore about the house or garden, in which case Matt generally made himself scarce. Soon, Antonio turned away and I watched him stride off in the direction of the woods.

'What was all that about?' I called out as Matt marched up the stairs.

He didn't answer.

Minutes later, he came down in his cycling gear and stormed out without a word.

'Don't you want lunch?' I called after him lamely, carrying

a bowl of salad and a plate of salami and sliced cheeses to the table.

Again, he seemed not to hear me...like a man possessed.

* * *

The sun was going down and I was starting to get anxious. I phoned Matt, but the phone rang then went to voicemail. A couple of hours passed. It was pitch-dark. I went out to the porch and stared fruitlessly in the direction of the track for a glimmer of his bicycle light, wondering if I should take the Land Rover to go in search of him. I was now insured to drive the car but didn't often use it and was unfamiliar with the back roads.

From the hallway, I called Matt's mobile once more and this time I heard muffled rings coming from behind the door of his study.

'Damn it! He's forgotten to take his phone,' I said out loud, recalling his manic departure.

There was no point me trying to find him if he didn't have his phone. I had no idea which route he'd have taken.

'He's a grown man,' I told myself. 'He can look after himself.'

The truth is, I didn't like being on my own in the farmhouse at night. It put my nerves on edge, in such a remote spot, surrounded by the woods. Marcella had written Antonio's mobile number for household emergencies on a scrap of notepaper that was pinned to the noticeboard. *Did Matt's sudden departure have something to do with their argument?* I hesitated to call Antonio after witnessing the men's row on the driveway earlier that afternoon. Whatever they were arguing about, had triggered Matt's silent rage. At the same time, I knew that if Matt was in trouble, I'd need Antonio's help.

'If Matt's not back in an hour,' I resolved, 'I'll call him.'

I was on the point of dialling Antonio's mobile, when just before midnight, I heard bicycle wheels on the gravel in the yard and the security lights came on. I threw open the door. Blood was running down Matt's face from a gash above his eye and one side of his face was gouged with long grazes.

'What on earth happened to you? You look as if you've been in a catfight.'

'I got knocked off my bike,' he said. 'Some maniac driver clipped my back wheel on a bend. I lost control, hit a rock and face-planted in the road. The bastard didn't even stop. I could be dead for all he cared. I had to wheel my bike all the way back. The front wheel is fucked. Luckily, I remembered a shortcut through the woods.'

I glanced at the bike. The front wheel was buckled and punctured, and the chain was hanging loose. The orange helmet that I'd bought Matt online was hanging off the handlebar by its straps – crushed.

'Oh my God! That's dreadful,' I said, helping Matt into the kitchen. 'Thank God you were wearing the helmet. Did you see what make of car it was? I hope you got the driver's number plate. We must report him to the police.'

Matt didn't want to talk about the accident and didn't want me fussing over him. He refused absolutely to contact the police.

'They're all crooked bastards over here,' he said.

I tried to help him, swabbing his wounds with brown iodine antiseptic that I found in a wooden medicine chest in the old laundry room. I got ice for his forehead and his knee.

The cut above his eye was deep and looked as if it needed stitches. The gaping flap made me queasy.

'I should drive you to the hospital,' I said. 'You're being so brave, but you need attention.'

I pleaded with him, feeling helpless. The local hospital was in Montepulciano, about nine miles' drive along the white roads. Again, Matt refused point-blank.

'They've got more important things to deal with than putting a couple of stitches into a wound right now. I don't want to be waiting around all through the night and I don't want to risk catching the virus. The emergency department will be a hotspot of infection.'

He brushed me aside and hobbled up to the bathroom to strip out of his cycling gear and take a shower.

Matt was still bleeding profusely when he came down again after a long shower, a bloodstained white towel pressed to his temple. He wore pyjama bottoms and a black fitted T-shirt, which showed off his pecs. His face was ashen grey.

'You need to get that seen to,' I insisted, feeling on the point of passing out myself. I've never been good with blood.

'I'm not going to the hospital.' Matt gritted his teeth. 'Get Antonio over here. He'll know what to do.'

* * *

Antonio arrived a few minutes later carrying a weathered green canvas bag marked with a big white cross. I guessed it was a rudimentary field first-aid kit used for hunting trips and the like. He nodded to me briefly and went directly to the study, where Matt was waiting for him. He closed the door.

I stood in the hallway and listened. Antonio and Matt began talking in hushed voices in Italian. This was the first time I'd heard them having a civilised conversation. There had been a thinly veiled hostility in all of their previous dealings. I supposed Matt's immediate crisis had forced the change.

I opened the door. Antonio was standing over Matt with a needle poised in his hand and the first-aid kit open on the desk.

'Get out!' shouted Matt. 'I don't want you fainting on me. If you want to do something useful, get us a bottle of brandy from the cellar.'

Antonio glanced at me sympathetically.

'Should be in a wooden box in the far corner on the right – the old man stockpiled the stuff,' Matt continued more calmly.

Reluctantly, I ventured down into the cellar, fearful of being ambushed by another rat or some other horror that lurked there. A fetid smell hung in the air. The poison pellets had done their work. On my hunt for the brandy, I spied a dead rat next to the broken guitar.

Where have all the other bodies gone? I wondered, giving the rotting corpse a wide berth.

Warily, I forged a path, moving broken furniture and accumulated junk to reach the far corner, where I found a precarious stack of wooden boxes. The first one I opened, long and rectangular, turned out to be not a case of brandy, but a collection of hunting rifles, which must have belonged to Matt's great-uncle. The cellar was a repository for death and its instruments. Eventually, I found what I was looking for and retreated to the cellar entrance. I couldn't get out fast enough.

I hovered outside the study door with an ancient bottle of brandy retrieved from the cellar, balanced on a silver tray alongside two antique crystal tumblers I'd found in a side-board in the dining room. Inside I heard Matt groaning, followed by more hushed conversation in Italian. I turned the handle with my elbow. Antonio took the tray from my hands before I had the chance to set it down.

'You took your time. I could have done with this earlier,' Matt grumbled.

Antonio had done a surprisingly good job with the sutures. The cut above Matt's eyebrow was closed with a clean line of five or six stitches, individually looped and tied with black thread. On reflection, I supposed Antonio's job as gamekeeper gave him skills in the business of trapping and killing and plucking and skinning small creatures that developed a good eye and deft fingers. Those attributes transferred well to intricate tasks such as sewing and stitching up wounds. I admired Matt's fortitude in bearing the pain without the help of local anaesthetic. It was no surprise to see him gulping down the brandy.

* * *

Matt slept in the next morning, sleeping off the effects of his accident and the brandy. I took up a strong black coffee just before noon.

'I'm going down to town to stock up with provisions, so I'll be taking the car,' I said. 'Would you like me to drop your bike off to be fixed?'

Matt shot upright. 'No, it's all sorted,' he said brusquely. 'Antonio took it away last night. He's going to repair it for me.' He took a sip of coffee. 'But thanks for the offer.'

After my trip to the supermarket for supplies, I stopped at the *rosticceria* for marinated zucchini, salty black olives, sundried tomatoes and a roast chicken. I wanted to spoil Matt that evening after his ordeal. In the event, he seemed to rebound stoically from the dramas of the day before. He'd apologised for being 'such a beast last night' and was now upbeat and cheerful. He met me at the door and helped me in with the packages from the car.

I roasted potatoes with rosemary from the herb garden and made a *bruschetta* with deep red plum tomatoes that tasted nothing like the tasteless pulpy variety bought in the UK. Ripened on the vine in the Mediterranean sun, they were succulent and sweet, and for the first time I could appreciate why they were classified as a fruit. I worked cheerfully, content to be assimilating the culture, learning to cook like an Italian. I added crushed garlic, torn basil leaves and fresh oregano, a splash of olive oil and balsamic vinegar, and spooned the mixture on to toasted *ciabatta*, savouring the characteristic smells and textures of Tuscan cuisine. I was beginning to feel at home at last.

Matt poured me a glass of vintage estate wine.

'That looks good. By the way, I've invited Tonio to join us for supper tonight,' he said. 'As a thank you for what he did last night, you know.'

I raised an eyebrow. So now it was Tonio. Matt and Antonio had reached an accommodation, it seemed. Our estate manager was such a practical man – unlike the pair of us – who were both, I guess you'd say, literary, arty types. It was certainly in our interest to be on good terms with him. But I preferred to keep relations at arm's length. His watchful presence made me feel uncomfortable.

'Oh, I was hoping it would be just the two of us,' I said.

I was exhausted from the late night and had been looking forward to a cosy supper with Matt followed by Netflix.

'He's going to help me with the pool,' said Matt, knowing this would silence my objections.

Antonio arrived on the dot of 8 p.m., wearing pressed

denim jeans, a button-down collar shirt and a black leather jacket. He was clean shaven with his hair slicked back. I hardly recognised him. He handed Matt a box of Italian beers and me a bottle of limoncello.

At first, the conversation was awkward. Matt was overly hearty, perhaps to compensate for his former antipathy. Antonio seemed almost diffident – in contrast to the confident, overbearing stranger who had sheltered me in his cottage on the day of the storm. Mostly, he spoke to Matt in Italian and glanced at me furtively from time to time. To break the ice, Matt filled our wine glasses to the brim. He drained his own glass and topped up all three relentlessly.

'So, you'll be pleased to know,' he slurred, turning towards me, 'that Tonio's agreed to help me with the infinity pool. We worked it out last night, man to man.'

Antonio shifted uneasily in his chair.

'You win, my darling, as always!' Matt raised his glass extravagantly and leant over to kiss me on the lips. 'We'll double the size to create a new infinity pool overlooking the ridge as you've set out in your plans. But to keep costs down, Antonio and I will do the groundworks.'

I knew that would involve breaking up and digging out the old patio and the concrete structure and foundations of the existing swimming pool.

'Are you sure? It'll be such a big job.' It sounded dodgy to me. 'Wouldn't it be better to get in the professionals?'

Matt laughed. 'Trust me, we'll do a much better job than most of the so-called professionals round here!'

I bridled at Matt's tone, though he continued more soothingly.

'We can't just throw money away,' he said. 'Be reasonable, Danielle. Antonio and I can install the new terrace, too – we helped my great-uncle lay the old patio. Tonio's done odd jobs for building contractors during the winters here for many years. He's a skilled workman.' He toasted Antonio, who nodded briefly at me. 'It'll be good for me to do some manual labour alongside my writing. And the money we save by doing the demolition and groundworks ourselves can be put towards the cost of your fancy new pool.'

We all loosened up and became very drunk as the bottles went down. Disinhibited by alcohol, the men reminisced raucously about their wild pool parties 'that summer'. Antonio's spoken English was unlocked by the wine and soon I discovered that he was far more fluent than he'd previously let on. For my benefit, the conversation was mostly in English while they joked about crazy times dancing on tables in village bars, casual sex on the back seats of cars and nights under the stars inhaling cocaine. Or rather, Matt did most of the talking and Antonio nodded and laughed along. At times, Matt reverted to Italian for some private joke or memory too obscene to share with me.

Amid the hilarity, I wasn't so far gone that I failed to notice Antonio watching me from time to time with that peculiar mix of stillness, alacrity and intensity that you see in the eyes of a predator. At one point Antonio actually gestured at my face, then turned to Matt, to make some comment in Italian, which I was sure related to me. For a second, Matt's face froze and I thought he was going to hit him. *Did he say something offensive about me?* I wondered. Then Matt laughed and took my hand and stroked my cheek and the conversation moved on in English.

* * *

Matt slept deeply after our drunken supper. But I had a broken night. For a long time, I lay pressed up against his back with my arm around his chest, feeling the bulk of his torso moving as he breathed in and out. I always felt closest to Matt when he was asleep. The evening played out in my mind. I wondered why Matt would have engineered this sudden reconciliation with Antonio if he'd behaved so badly in the past. Surely Matt could find some other labourer to help him with the groundworks for the swimming pool? Did the man have a hold over him for some reason? I wasn't ready to welcome Antonio into our home like a long-lost friend.

Eventually, I dozed off into uneasy dreams.

Sometime later I woke with a start, unsure what had disturbed me. Matt hadn't moved. He was snoring lightly, sleeping off the wine and limoncello. *The sleep of the innocent.* Alcohol had the opposite effect on me – leaving me restless and on edge. I noticed we'd forgotten to close the shutters, so maybe their knocking against the stone casement had woken me.

I went out to the terrace to close them. The garden, so entrancing on long summer evenings, now looked sinister. The trees were shrouded in mist, creating ghostly chambers between the tree trunks under the canopy of branches. The darkness of night magnified every sound. An owl hooted in the distance and closer in, I heard a branch snap and a rustle in the undergrowth. The security lights came on, beaming across the grass and into the trees in a shimmering arc. I started, fearful of what had set them off.

Matt had teased me for wanting to install security lights and a house alarm.

'We're in the middle of nowhere here. Who do you think is going to bother to come all the way out here to break in?

We've got nothing to steal. And no one would hear the burglar alarm if they did.'

I knew he was right, but despite the pandemic regulations, I'd insisted on getting the work done as a priority.

'It might act as a deterrent. Anyway, it makes me feel safer to have some outdoor lighting.'

My throat was dry and I could feel a headache coming on. Matt was right. Beyond the estate, there was no other property within sight or shouting distance. Shivering out there on the terrace in my skimpy nightdress, I knew that if a car were to pull up in the middle of the night, we'd have to defend ourselves alone. Or not quite alone – there was Antonio on the other side of the estate, but that didn't exactly quell my nerves.

Sure, we'd had an entertaining evening, but I still couldn't make up my mind. I found it strange that his English had seemed almost monosyllabic on our previous encounters and yet it turned out his conversational English was in fact pretty good – at least when he was drunk. There was something shifty and defensive about him that I couldn't quite put my finger on. Was the man trustworthy or 'the enemy within'?

Maybe I should learn to shoot? I thought, my mind going back to the wooden box of rifles I'd stumbled across in the cellar.

I was desperate for a glass of water but too spooked to go down to the kitchen in the dead of night, though rationally I knew I was being pathetic. My thirst morphed into feelings of vulnerability and loneliness, and not for the first time I wondered if we'd done the right thing coming here. Especially now, when it was so difficult to make new Italian friends and with international borders closed, making it impossible to have visits from family and old friends back home. In normal times, my girlfriends would have jumped at the chance of coming

out for a few days' holiday under the Tuscan sun. But sponta-
neous socialising was a thing of the past. Now, I was left with
a creeping sense of isolation.

Beyond the trees, the visible half of the old pool shone in
the moonlight, casting a spectral aura. I heard the faintest
slosh of water ripples – as if someone had dived or jumped
into the pool. My stomach tightened. Was it my imagination?
Surely, it wasn't Antonio taking a midnight swim in the fetid
water. Perhaps nostalgia for those lost summer nights of his
youth had put the notion into his head.

I craned my neck over the wall to see if I could spot him,
but the water was now glassy still. Scanning the trees, I
thought I saw a dark shape moving in the undergrowth and
seconds later, the security lights flashed on for a second time.
Again, that stomach-clenching fear.

I was about to run into the bedroom and jump into bed
with Matt, when I saw our intruder: a wild boar, rooting
around on the patch of burnt-up grass below our bedroom that
we called the lawn.

I chuckled to myself. 'So that's what's been digging up my
herb garden and eating my vegetables.' I had thought it was
rabbits.

I'd never seen a wild boar before. The creature reminded
me of the childhood book character the Gruffalo. It was the
shape of a domestic pig, with a long, blunt snout, small eyes
and large ears. But it was dark, with a coarse, bristly coat that
gave it a bearlike appearance. The boar looked up at me like a
co-conspirator, held my gaze and then carried on munching
something it had dug up.

I'd gleaned from my expat online news subscription, *Your
Tuscany*, that these beasts were taking over the countryside in
the lockdowns, decimating the local farmers' crops. Over

supper, Antonio had complained about them too, damaging the roots of trees in the olive groves. Their only natural predators were wolves, but these were declining in numbers.

I decided not to tell Matt about the wild boar. I feared that if I did, he'd tell Antonio and then Antonio would hide in the trees, lying in wait with his rifle, the following night.

Antonio is a wolf, I thought, recalling the way he'd looked at me over dinner.

And that's when the idea came to me... It was counterintuitive but not dumb. *Confront your fears. Befriend your enemies.* I'd make a friend of the man and at the same time learn a new skill that would make me feel safer living on a remote country estate in the heart of Tuscany. Now that Matt was on speaking terms with him, there was no reason why he should remain a stranger to me. That abandoned box of hunting rifles down in the cellar could be put to good use.

'I'm going to ask Antonio to teach me how to shoot.'

TWENTY-SEVEN

THE HITCHHIKER

BY MATTEO J. ROSSI

'Why did you come back?' asks Ted.

They leave Harry sleeping in the crib and go to sit in the dark on some deckchairs near the pool. Ted pours Nikki a glass of wine from a bottle stolen from his grandfather's cellar.

'I came back for *you*, of course,' she says.

Ted gives her a wary look.

'And because, well, I ran out of money.'

'Now I believe you,' he says.

'We had an adventure, – three days in Rome, then Sorrento then Naples.'

'When you say *we*...?'

'I mean me and Harry, of course.' She laughs. Then more seriously, she says, 'Look, I don't want to lie to you. I did meet someone in Rome.' (*No kidding*, thinks Ted bitterly.) 'He showed me the city. Then he took me to the beach in Sorrento, then he drove me to Naples.'

'I thought you were headed for the port of Brindisi to catch a ferry to Greece. That was quite a detour. I'm jealous.'

'Ted, I don't owe you anything,' she says. 'I'm a free spirit, remember? Anyway, you've got nothing to be jealous about. He's a lying shit.' Nikki drains her glass and pours herself another. 'He told me Naples was where his family came from. He told me I could stay the night at his mother's house, but when we got there, the "house" was a one-room squat in the suburbs of Naples where he lived alone. He forced me to have sex with him.'

Ted thinks back to the night they spent together on the Saint Bernard mountain pass and how she'd come on to him.

'Like I "forced" you?' he asks cynically.

'He raped me,' she says angrily. 'We were trapped. I was scared of what he might do to Harry if I tried to resist. He was adorable in Rome and Sorrento, but when we got to Naples, he turned into a monster.

'He went out to work early the next morning – told me he worked at a pizzeria – and left us locked in the room. I smashed open the bathroom window and carried Harry down the fire escape. We almost broke our necks. I'd been hoping he'd give me some money to pay for the ferry, but he was a tight bastard. And there was none to steal at his place.'

Ted thinks ruefully of the hundred euros that she stole from his wallet.

'And don't you dare judge me!' she says. Her eyes flash in the moonlight. 'He treated me worse than a whore. He deserved to pay.'

'He deserved to die,' he says forcefully, 'for abusing you that way.'

'By that time, I was skint,' Nikki continues. 'Not a cent to buy milk or food for Harry. We walked out to the ring road to hitch a lift and waited and waited for someone to stop who was heading in the direction of Brindisi. I thought that once we reached the port, I'd find a way to get money to pay for the ferry crossing.

'Anyway, I must have been looking rough yesterday morning, because the cars didn't even slow. Eventually, an old couple pulled up on the other side of the road to see if we were OK. They didn't stop for me – they were worried about Harry. Turned out they were driving to Milan. I guessed they'd have water and food in the car and Harry was starving. So, I changed direction. I took the lift and they drove us all the way to your town.'

'How did you know where to find me?' he asks.

'I'm psychic.' She laughs.

'I don't remember telling you where I was going.'

'You told me your grandfather had a farm near Sangiari and I saw your passport – *Innocenti*. How could I forget that? I figured there couldn't be that many farming families called *Innocenti* in Sangiari.'

She leans over to take a long drag of Ted's roll-up.

'I missed you,' she adds like an afterthought, watching the smoke curling up to the stars.

Then she takes off all of her clothes and dives naked into the pool.

* * *

Nikki is banned from staying at the house. But that doesn't stop Ted from sleeping over at the cottage. The arrangement suits her. When she's not doing chores for the grandparents, she spends her time in bed or lounging in the hammock strung up by Luca in the yard behind the cottages. Ted is her caveman, bringing food and drink to his mate.

When he cries, Nikki gives her son biscuits. Sometimes

he's left in the crib, in his dirty nappy, wailing inconsolably, while Nikki and Ted have steamy sex.

Ted feels bad for Harry but not bad enough to change his nappy. Nikki loves her little boy, but not as much as she loves herself. Ted knows nothing about babies, but even he can see that Harry is difficult and different... *Is the kid mad or possessed?* One minute all laughter and smiles, and the next screaming blue murder, with a determination that seems unnatural in one so young.

This morning Ted – unshaven and wearing only his boxer shorts – sits at the table with Harry balanced awkwardly on his knee. Nikki is nowhere to be seen. She's sprawled out in the hammock, her head hidden under the blanket Ted threw over her last night after they made love. He went indoors to sleep. She stayed out under the stars in a stupor of alcohol and cocaine.

Harry wears only a nappy and a vest. The little boy screams for his mamma, who is dead to the world. Ted tries to shush the child but doesn't know what to do. He swears to himself under his breath in between trying to calm the little boy.

'Your mamma is a useless fucked-up bitch,' he sing-songs tenderly, half to Harry and half to himself.

With one hand he balances Harry on his knee and with the other he spoons pureed baby food from a jar into Harry's mouth. He misses and the orange sludge goes over Harry's nose and cheeks. Harry is red in the face and splutters with indignation. He's too old for baby food. But something out of a jar is about all Nikki can come up with.

As Harry squirms, Ted feels a sludgy wet patch on his suntanned leg – the child's dirty nappy is leaking. Even Ted knows Harry is too old for nappies and should be potty-trained by now. Poor thing must be raw, left in a dirty nappy since last night. The child flails around and knocks the jar of baby food out of Ted's hand. The glass smashes into shards, scattering across the tiles.

Ted loses it then. He yells at Nikki to get her ass out of the hammock and come deal with her child. He fills the metal tub on the floor with water from a plastic hose. Crouching down beside the tub, he's doing his best, but this is above his pay grade. Meanwhile, Nikki rolls out of the hammock and stumbles into the kitchen, shielding her eyes from the bright morning sun. Even hung-over and dishevelled, she exudes sex appeal.

'Coffee would be nice,' she says.

Ted can't take his eyes off her. She moves like a lithe cat. Any second, she might pounce. Suddenly she screams, then she shouts and swears – pulls a spike of glass from the arch of her foot and the blood drips everywhere.

'Why the fuck didn't you sweep up the glass?' she snaps at Ted.

TWENTY-EIGHT
DANIELLE

One Friday evening in late March, Matt announced that he and Antonio would be driving the trailer the next day to collect a mini digger and jackhammer they were hiring from one of Antonio's mates who owned a construction company.

'You'll be pleased to know, we're going to make a start on the excavations for the infinity pool next week,' he said cheerfully.

He told me that the pick-up location for the hire equipment was close to Bagni San Stefano – a series of natural hot springs running through a wooded valley deep in southern Tuscany – which we'd visited in the autumn soon after arriving in Italy.

'The weather forecast is great for tomorrow,' he said. 'Let's make a day out of it. You can go ahead to the springs in the Land Rover. I'll get Antonio to drop me off once I've checked out the equipment and paid for the hire, then he can drive the trailer back to the farm on his own.'

'Can't he deal with it all on his own?' I objected. 'We haven't had a day out together for ages.'

'Oh, you know, there'll be the usual haggling over prices. The man wants to be paid in cash, of course, and I'll have to help load the equipment onto the trailer. I need to be there... Sorry... I should be clear well before lunch.'

I was excited at the prospect of a day at the springs. On our last visit, I'd been captivated by the unusual natural phenomena of the hot spring formations, with calcified rocks and cascades paradoxically having the appearance of glacier mountains and snow-filled gullies against the cerulean blue pools of pure hot water. Hidden in deep woodland of pine and chestnut trees, these hot springs had been known and used for curative purposes since Etruscan and Roman times, and in normal times were popular year-round with the locals for bathing and picnics.

Owing to the social distancing rules, the natural springs had been officially out of bounds with the car park closed and big police notices nailed to the trees warning of criminal offences and fines for trespass and law-breaking when Matt had taken me to visit them soon after we arrived in Tuscany. Of course, that hadn't stopped Matt. For him, the prohibition simply added a frisson of excitement to our adventure. He'd parked our car on the far side of the woodland. Then he'd insisted on wrapping the silk scarf I'd been using for my face covering that day around my eyes and leading me blindfolded down his 'secret path'.

'I want to surprise you,' he'd said gaily.

When he'd removed the blindfold, my eyes had opened onto the most spectacular of the bathing pools, the *squalo bianco* or white shark. It was an immense formation of white rock face gleaming like the marble quarries of Carrera and overhanging a turquoise pool shrouded in steam and mist that added to the uncanny and mythical atmosphere of the scene.

'It's quite something, isn't it?' he'd said while I gasped in wonder.

Then he'd folded me into his arms.

We'd had the place to ourselves. We swam naked and floated on the surface of the pool looking up at the sky. We played and made love in the water like lovestruck water nymphs. When we were exhausted, we stretched out on the warm rocks, our bodies touching. Matt told me he loved me. I was living the dream.

The day had been perfect, romantic, magical, save for a few moments of tension.

'Did you come here with that girl?' I'd asked lightly, thinking of the teenage girlfriend he'd mentioned once or twice.

Abruptly, Matt's mood had changed. He'd looked at me with a cold blue light in his eyes I hadn't seen before. He'd dived down to the bottom of the pool coming up with a handful of black sludge.

'One of our old haunts,' he whispered, wiping the sludge all over my face. 'It's good for your skin,' he said in honeyed tones. 'You'd pay a fortune for this in the spa.'

There had been nothing friendly in his touch.

I didn't speak of her again.

* * *

I'd grown used to doing things on my own – walks, cycle rides and trips to the shops were mostly solitary affairs these days. I packed up my bikini and a towel, some cold drinks and a book to read, as well as my sketch pad and a tin of graphite pencils. This would be a good opportunity to do some preparatory sketches for paintings of woodland scenes that I planned to start working on once my studio was set up. It was nice to be in the driving seat of the car for a change and I enjoyed the feeling of freedom as I sped along the empty roads with the band *Coldplay* at full volume, following the satnav directions to Bagni San Stefano.

Matt had pinpointed the exact parking location for the 'secret path' he'd led me down on the previous visit. We'd agreed that he'd pick up a takeaway from the nearby pizzeria and join me at *squalo bianco* when he'd finished his business with Antonio.

I found the spot with no difficulty. Some barbed wire had been strung across the entrance to the little path and there was a new police notice telling people to keep out. But the place was deserted and I doubted that the police patrols would come to anywhere so remote, so I decided to chance it and climbed carefully through the rows of barbed wire. I followed the winding path down through the trees, my sandals getting caught up in the vegetation that had grown across the path. Save for the birdsong and the sound of bubbling water from the springs, it was eerily quiet. I imagined the babble of Italian voices and children's laughter and shrieking that would have filled the air in normal times.

The *squalo bianco* lived up to its name, as dramatic and imposing as I remembered. In the spring sunshine filtering through the leaves, the jagged protrusions of the rock face shone like white shark's teeth, gaping over the pale blue waters of the pool. I changed into my bikini and clambered carefully over the rocks into the water. The heat felt almost scalding against my cold skin but gradually, my body adjusted and I sank down into the water, feeling as if I were slowly melting away.

I cleared my mind and floated weightlessly, looking up at

the canopy of new leaves stirring in the breeze – and beyond that, the pale blue sky as hard and bright as a porcelain plate. I settled on a stone ledge ideally positioned to enjoy an invigorating natural massage while the spring surged over a fall of rocks, jetting hot water onto my shoulders. It was bliss.

After bathing, I spread out my towel on the grass and took up my sketch pad. I did a few rough sketches of the bathing pool. Then I settled down with my novel, a tense psychological thriller recommended by Matt, involving the abduction of a young woman by the Sicilian Mafia. It was just about warm enough to lie out in the sun. *Matt should be here soon,* I thought. I looked forward to bathing with him again and our picnic on the rocks.

I'd read a chapter or two (not the ideal storyline for solitary reading in the woods), when I began to hear gunshots in the distance and dogs barking. It must be people out hunting – perhaps for wild boar. Or a police patrol, checking for bathers breaking the lockdown rules... The men's voices unsettled me. They moved closer. I was exposed and fearful of getting into trouble for trespassing, since the hot springs natural park was closed for the pandemic. I knew the Italian police were more hard-line about rule-breaking than the British police, who generally adopted a light-touch approach to policing the new regime.

I glanced at my phone. It was almost midday. There was still no word from Matt, who should have been with me by now. I sent him a message.

Where are you? Thought you were joining me for a dip.

Seconds later, I heard the faintest ping – like that of a

mobile phone receiving a text. *At last! That must be Matt,* I thought. I checked my phone again. No messages.

There was more barking and shouting. Louder than before.

Sensing movement in the trees behind me, I called out, 'Matt, Matt, I'm over here,' but there was no answer.

I shivered and hastily put on my clothes. My imagination took over. I couldn't resist the urge to look over my shoulder. Was someone stalking me – a lone hunter? A rogue police officer? Was I his quarry? The sun had gone in and the sky was now a flat, impenetrable tombstone grey. The wooded valley that had seemed so peaceful took on an air of malice.

Typical of Matt to get me into an awkward situation like this and then leave me in the lurch, I thought crossly.

When we were dating in London, he was always late for everything. Then he'd seemed to me so busy and so important and so full of charming excuses that I always forgave him. Now, there was no excuse. I wouldn't have broken the lockdown rules if I'd known I'd be here on my own.

I peered into the trees in every direction. I couldn't shake that uncomfortable feeling of being watched. When you stop to listen, woods are noisy places – the snap of a twig, the creaking of tree trunks, a rustle in the undergrowth, birds squawking and flapping their wings. Suddenly, there were noises everywhere. I'd had enough. I was ready to go.

I grabbed together my things. Too bad, he'd missed his opportunity.

'Damn him.'

I ran all the way back to the car, jarring my ankle on the way on a tree root.

Just as I unlocked the car door, a text came through from Matt:

I'm at the pizzeria having a beer. Come and join me.

* * *

From a glance at my satnav, I realised when I pulled up outside the pizzeria that the place was only five minutes' walking distance from the 'white shark' hot spring where we'd agreed to meet. The pizzeria was located at the top of the main path that led down into the hot springs. He could so easily have joined me. Antonio and Matt were seated at a table on the terrace. Matt didn't apologise for failing to show. He broke off an animated debate with the waiter.

'Hey, Dani, over here. I ordered you a margarita and a Diet Coke.'

I could see he was in high spirits. I limped over to the table. Matt switched back into Italian to continue what I gathered was a debate over the relative merits of Italian versus English beer while Antonio stood up and pulled out a chair for me. Restaurants were still only allowed to sell food and drinks for takeaways, but Matt was good at persuading people to bend the rules. We had the outdoor space to ourselves.

There was no point making a scene at the table, so I sat down quietly. While the men exchanged banter in Italian, I read the cover of the book Matt had left on my seat: *The Beast of Siena*. I'd seen it lying open on the floor by his bedside only the night before. From the blurb on the back cover, I saw it was a true crime story written by an American investigative journalist documenting a series of murders that had taken place in the Tuscan hills over a period of two decades in the Eighties and Nineties.

I opened the book and read on. The preface spoke of horrific attacks targeting young lovers at local beauty spots 'making out' in their cars on romantic dates after the bars had closed. It had never been proven whether one serial killer was responsible for all the murders or if they were the work of many. Suspects had been arrested and released over the years – some had even served prison terms – but the police had never solved the crimes, which had sparked many conspiracy theories, not least involving the Mafia. With the passage of time and the failings of the Italian justice system, the cases had gone cold. The killer or killers were referred to collectively as *The Beast of Siena*.

Having finished his conversation, Matt turned to me and took my hand.

'I'm so sorry, darling. I had to go to the bank to get cash for the equipment hire. Half the banks were closed – business not back to normal yet. I wasn't expecting that... queues everywhere.'

I put the book down on the table next to Matt.

'Let's go for a walk this afternoon instead.'

'This is cheerful,' I said, tapping the book, unwilling to forgive him yet.

'Ah, yes,' said Matt. 'Research.'

'I thought you were writing a love story,' I said coldly.

'Killers fall in love too, you know.' He held my gaze. 'I'm sorry I didn't make it to the springs.' He kissed me softly on the lips. Then, with a boyish grin, he put his hand in his pocket. 'Ah! But I did get you this...' He handed me a small jewellery box engraved with the brand name *Pietra Dolce Vita*. '*Sweet life stones*,' Matt translated.

'Oh, Matt, they're beautiful.'

The box contained a pair of delicate silver earrings set with pretty blue gemstones.

'A perfect match,' said Matt, staring lovingly into my eyes.

TWENTY-NINE
THE HITCHHIKER
BY MATTEO J. ROSSI

On hot summer nights, the swimming pool becomes the hub for drinking and socialising after the grandparents have gone to bed and the day's work is done and Harry's asleep in his crib. Despite Ted's nagging doubts and his ever-present jealousy concerning Nikki, the three of them get on like a house on fire.

When he's not in one of his foul moods, Luca is the life and soul of any gathering, with his boundless energy, acid wit and arrogant Italian charm. He can party all night long then work all day from sunrise to sunset. He's the perfect hustler – knows everyone's business and though he's always broke, somehow has access to endless supplies of alcohol and recreational drugs – no questions asked. Oh! and he's a great cook – as long as you're a carnivore.

They're tight and conspiratorial. *'The three mutineers.'* Nikki coins the phrase. Usually, it's just the three of them hanging out together. Luca fires up the barbecue and grills wild boar steaks and other cuts from his latest kills in the woods. They drink cheap booze from the village Supermercato24 and pop pills (of doubtful provenance) and fool around by the pool. Luca's an irrepressible testosterone-fired flirt, stretching Ted's tolerance to the limits.

Nikki's game. She's a consummate attention-seeker and likes to play the boys off against each other. She thinks it's a laugh watching Ted torturing himself. Sometimes Luca brings back a girl to even up the numbers. Nikki's OK with that – as long as the girls aren't too pretty or too smart. Sometimes she fools around with the girls, too. Her tastes are pansexual when the girl is to her liking. If she's not cool, Luca's girl is subjected to ritual humiliation, victim of the mutineers' malicious humour and cruel games. Then she never comes back for more.

July is a big month for festivals, with the biggest of all being the Palio di Siena held each year in the heat of summer – a wild festival of pageantry and sport. As the climax to the day, ten horses and their jockeys – bareback and decked out in the colours of rival city wards whose flags hang from the buildings and flutter in the crowd – gallop around the medieval shell-shaped Piazza del Campo, 'renowned worldwide for its timeless beauty and architectural integrity'. For once, the guidebook isn't exaggerating. The tickets are like gold dust. Luca got his hands on three of them – something about the mate of a mate in one of the *contradas* who owes him something.

'You'll see,' Ted tells Nikki. 'Siena is out of this world. And the Palio is one of those mind-blowing experiences that must be on your bucket list.'

'I'm not planning on dying anytime soon,' shoots back Nikki, who resents being told what she must and mustn't do.

Ted's grandmother offers to babysit Harry at the farm-house so Nikki can have the day off and go to the Palio in

Siena with the men. The threesome mingle, crushed against excited flag-waving revellers. Luca's old metal hip flask is passed around. He eyes up a pixie-faced young woman in the crowd. He gets her talking and soon he's up close and personal and has made a new friend. She's Irish, strawberry blonde and petite. When bodies surge as the horses gallop round, he lifts the pixie girl, festival-style, onto his shoulders out of the crush. Her bare thighs squeeze against the sides of his neck. By the time he puts her down, she's accepted an invitation to go back with them to the *fattoria dell'amore,* as Luca has renamed it: *the farmstead of love*.

Nikki ignores Ted all day – star-struck with the dashing young jockey who rides the winning horse in this most macho of contests. When the race is over, somehow she manages to push her way through the crowd, pat the horse's neck and steal a kiss from its rider. She's euphoric.

Luca, who's been drinking since breakfast and can't wait to get the pixie girl's legs round his neck once again, is like a man possessed on the drive home from Siena. Ted is off his head too, but that doesn't stop him from bracing with his feet and gripping the door handle as Luca throws his battered old Fiat Panda round the bends. In the back, the girls shriek with laughter like teenagers on a roller coaster. Somehow, they make it home in one piece.

Festivities continue under the stars out by the pool. Nikki and the pixie girl – Sinead – are no match for Ted and Luca when it comes to drinking games. It's not long before the girls have each forfeited every item of clothing and are splashing around naked in the swimming pool. The men stay by the pool drinking whisky and watching them. The pixie girl was no match for Nikki when it came to inhaling cocaine. The pixie girl is off her head.

The next morning, Ted wakes in his bedroom in the farmhouse. His head is bludgeoned and he aches all over. His last memory of the night before is watching Nikki (naked) and Sinead (wearing only Luca's boxer shorts) walking hand in hand into her cottage. Nikki turns around and winks at him. Then nothing. The rest of the night is a blank.

Luca's boxer shorts are on the floor next to the bed. And his aviator sunglasses. When Ted stumbles out of bed, he almost steps on Luca's shades.

He finds a used condom on the bathroom floor.

WTF happened?

He scrubs himself under the shower until his skin is raw.

When he puts on his clothes, he discovers that the treasured Breil wristwatch that his grandfather passed on to him as a gift for his twenty-first birthday is missing from his bedside table.

* * *

Later that day, Ted proposes to Nikki. He doesn't mean to do it. It just happens. Maybe because he's tortured with thoughts about what he might have done – and what Nikki might have done – and where is Luca? He needs to speak to Luca, but Nikki tells Ted that Luca and his grandfather drove off in the truck at the crack of dawn. She knows too much for his liking. Yet, she gives nothing away.

Ted and Nikki have the day off to recover from the Palio. They're lying in an old double hammock strung up between two ancient trees in the furthest olive grove. The little boy naps on a beach towel in the shade. He stirs and starts to cry. Ted picks him up and lays him across Nikki's chest then gently, he slides in beside them, taking care not to tip up the hammock.

The sky is very blue above the lustrous canopy of olive leaves. Everyone he loves, all he wants in this world – this girl and this child – are strung together in the hammock. He'd be happy to stop the clock right now, innocent and ignorant of whatever happened last night – to stay forever, gently swaying, listening to her breathing and gazing into the cloudless blue sky. Nikki's young enough that the catalogue of self-abuse – drinking and drugs and sleep deprivation – hasn't yet spoilt her iridescent loveliness. Her hair smells of cigarette smoke and weed from the night before, but her breath smells of something sweet – mint and the wild strawberries that he picked for her breakfast.

Harry snuffles against Nikki's shirt, still hopeful that she'll feed him, even though she stopped that months ago. The boy will keep that hopefulness until he's a grown man and finds another woman's breast to satisfy his needs. Though it feels wrong, Ted is aroused by the sight of the little boy, whom he thinks of as his surrogate son, nuzzling his lover's chest. He can't help it. He slips his hand up between Nikki's legs and strokes her thighs gently, then more firmly. She turns her hips towards his and their legs intertwine.

'Marry me,' he says quietly. Then louder, as her eyes stay closed. 'Marry me.'

Her eyes open slowly, but she's not smiling.

'I want to take care of you and your son. I'll be a good dad to him and a good husband.'

She turns her head away, looking out over the valley towards the horizon.

'Harry already has a dad,' she says. 'And I already have a husband. And if he found us here together, he'd kill you and beat me to a pulp – and I can't bear to think what would happen to Harry.'

'I promise I'll keep you safe,' says Ted. 'We could disappear together... Drive off into the sunset and never come back.'

'This isn't *Thelma & Louise*,' says Nikki impatiently. 'We can't just drive into oblivion. You've got a life to go back to in England at the end of the summer – your family... your friends... a proper new job. I can never go back. I've burnt my boats there – I'm done with England.'

'I would give it all up for you,' says Ted.

'I'd be toxic for you. Our love won't outlast the summer. Then I'll be out of your life forever.'

Ted wants to make love, but Harry has other ideas. When Ted puts him back on the blanket, his face puckers and he starts to howl. Nikki is furious.

'Why did you have to move him? Just when he was finally calm and quiet. I'm exhausted. You all want a piece of me. I wish everyone would just fuck off and leave me alone.'

Her words are like a punch in the stomach. Why has she suddenly turned? He's never experienced this gut-twisting pain of rejection before. His conquests have always been easy and light. Now, he must deal with the child. His feelings of tenderness give way to frustration and despair.

I'm too young for this, he thinks as Harry lets rip, ignored by his mother. Ted picks up Harry and swings him around wildly above his head until Harry is all giggles.

* * *

'What happened to the girl?' he says, putting Harry down.

'She had a name, Ted, for God's sake – Sinead. Can't you even remember her name?'

Ted looks at her sullenly.

'I think she stole my watch,' he says.

Nikki ignores the accusation.

'I don't know, Ted. I don't know what happened to her. You tell me.'

Her eyes bore into his head.

'When I woke up, she was gone.'

THIRTY
DANIELLE

Matt donned rubber gloves and came down with a black bin bag. We found three dead rats. Trying not to gag, I looked away while he picked them up and dropped them into the sack. He'd interrupted his writing to help me clear them from the cellar.

'It's not fair to ask Marcella to do this,' I said. 'She's been complaining of arthritis in her knees and struggles with the stairs.' The guitar lay on the concrete floor covered with droppings and bits of chewed-up cardboard from the nest the rats had made in its hollow body. 'We might as well get rid of this, too,' I said, kicking the instrument lightly with my foot. 'No one will want it now.'

Matt lifted the guitar gingerly and carried it up the stairs.

'We can use it for firewood,' he said. 'I'll put it on the woodpile and break it up later.'

'While we're at it,' I suggested, 'we could take up your great-uncle's old hunting rifles.'

Antonio had offered to clean up and recondition them for us when I'd expressed an interest in learning how to shoot.

Together, we lugged the heavy box up the stairs. It contained six firearms.

'This is quite an arsenal old Benetto kept stashed away down here,' I joked. 'Are you sure he only used the guns for shooting wild boar?'

'What are you saying?' Matt wasn't laughing.

'You know, was he part of the Mafia?' I kept my voice light.

'I wouldn't mock things you don't understand,' said Matt seriously.

* * *

The following Sunday, we woke at dawn to the peal of church bells carried on the air. Marcella had told us that a national event was taking place to honour the lives of victims of the virus, each chime commemorating someone who had died in the district. While the good people of Sangiari were making their way to church for the service of remembrance, Antonio set up a field target practice in the woods and, to the sound of tolling bells, gave us our first shooting lesson.

It turned out I was a bit of a natural, while Matt seemed to have two left hands. Antonio had cleaned and polished the rifles until the barrels gleamed. He'd picked out the lightest for my use and after showing us the principles of safe handling, he handed the weapon ceremoniously over to me.

He was in his element and showed himself to be a patient and conscientious teacher. He drew diagrams to demonstrate the principles of trajectories, land contours and range, and the effect of gravity in pulling the bullet off the target. He taught me how to breathe when lining up the shot and to exhale before squeezing the trigger. He was tactile in his methods, standing close to position my arms and my legs and adjust my fingers, hand over hand – and leaning in to check my breathing and share my sight line, his cheek almost touching mine. I discovered there was something disturbingly sensual about learning how to shoot and to kill.

By mid-morning, Matt had lost interest and went back to the farmhouse to continue with his writing. He was up against a tight deadline and this time his editor had refused to push it back, saying further delays would derail the publication schedule. Meanwhile, I was mesmerised and hitting the target five times out of ten.

We packed up at noon. Buoyed up by my enthusiasm, Antonio offered to give me a lesson the following week and said that if my progress continued over the summer, he'd let me join a 'hunting party' at the start of the next hunting season.

'Oh no.' I recoiled in horror. 'I'd never shoot an animal for real. I'm just doing it for the sport.'

'Ah, fair play! That's what you English say'–he laughed–'*è vero?*'

We walked out of the woods in the direction of the farmhouse. Neither of us spoke.

Then, out of the blue, Antonio said, 'I want to tell you – Matteo didn't go to the bank. He went for a walk in the woods. I hear him... at the pizzeria. He lies to you.'

I was taken aback, unsure how to respond to Antonio without being disloyal to Matt. *Why would Matt have lied to me? And why would Antonio have thought it important enough to tell me about his deception?*

'OK... I understand,' I said. 'I'll see you next week. *Ciao.*'

* * *

When I arrived back at the farmhouse, Matt was loading a wicker hamper and a rug into the back of the car.

'Well done, darling, you were superb. I was proud of you,' he called back over his shoulder. 'I think Antonio's taken a shine to you.'

'This is a treat. I thought you had to work this afternoon,' I said, choosing to ignore Matt's previous comment and happy with the unexpected turn of events.

'I've spent long enough staring at the screen,' he said. 'It's Sunday. It's a beautiful day. We should be enjoying the great outdoors.'

I thought that he was looking more and more Italian every day, so sharp in his aviator sunglasses and his freshly pressed outfit, a white linen Italian shirt and tailored jeans.

'I need some inspiration. I can justify it as research. Come here,' he said. 'Seeing Antonio with his hands all over you is driving me mad with jealousy.' He took me in his arms and spun me round. 'Why don't you change into a pretty dress,' he murmured softly after we embraced. As I walked into the farmhouse, he called after me: 'But wear your trainers. We're going for a walk.'

* * *

Matt whistled softly as I got into the car five minutes later wearing my favourite red sundress.

'Wow! Aren't I the lucky one! You look gorgeous – and smell gorgeous, too,' he said, nuzzling into my neck.

He drove fast on the dirt tracks, accelerating round the bends and wheel-spinning the Land Rover on the steep inclines.

'We're not in a rally.' I laughed, clinging on to the door handle.

'I've planned the walk,' he said. 'A circuit of about six miles. Takes us through the vineyards and past a ruined abbey, then over an old crumbling bridge and along the riverbank, where we can stop for lunch. It's a pretty walk. I've done it before, years ago.'

We followed trails marked out with red-and-white signposts. Matt pointed out the features of the landscape and we stopped at various landmarks for Matt to take photographs.

'Look at those fields over there,' he said. 'In a couple of months, the poppies will come out – a sea of red. It's spectacular. You'll see.'

When we reached the river, Matt laid out the picnic rug and we tucked into the hamper of wine, bread, cheeses and seasonal fruits he'd packed. After our early start for shooting practice, and the mental and physical effort I'd put into learning a new skill, suddenly I was very sleepy. The wine went straight to my head and soon I was horizontal, dozing in the spring sunshine while Matt teased me with wild strawberries that he'd picked that morning until my lips and his fingers were crimson with juice.

Matt had stolen a handful of loquats (or *nespola* as they call them in Tuscany) as we walked by a fruiting tree.

'You have to try these,' he said.

Carefully, he peeled the oval fruit, its shiny apricot-coloured skin pocked with brown flecks, and popped it into my mouth.

'Delicious, aren't they? Bitter and sweet at the same time – like my love for you!' he joked.

It was a perfect afternoon – until it wasn't.

Matt said he was going to explore the path along the riverbed while I took a nap and stayed with our stuff.

'What did you put in that wine?' I murmured, curling up on the blanket.

I'm not sure how long I slept, but sometime later I became conscious of movements close to me. I sensed Matt's shadow blocking the sun until I shivered in the cool spring air while the pools of amber light that had suffused my closed eyelids darkened.

I half opened my eyes but lay very still watching him through a languorous haze as he moved around taking photographs of me with the SLR camera which I used for studio photography. I couldn't rouse myself to move. For one shot, he bent low and gently pulled up the skirt of my flowery sundress so that it bunched around my thighs. His behaviour struck me as strangely tender, though undeniably weird. I closed my eyes and must have drifted off again.

When I stirred once more, Matt was standing over me with his feet straddling my torso, extending the blade of a knife that glinted in the low rays of afternoon sun. He was staring straight down at my face. I sat bolt upright – this time, aghast.

'What the fuck are you doing?' I gasped.

Matt laughed and lowered the knife.

'I'm just packing up,' he said. 'The sun's going down. It's almost time to go.'

The knife was short and serrated – a hunter's knife like one I'd seen in Antonio's cottage, designed for skinning and slicing, for disembowelling dead carcasses – the knife Matt had used for peeling the *nespolas*. Now, he held it in his left hand, which hung down by his side, the blade resting against the denim of his jeans.

'Don't move for a second,' he said.

He had that flinty blue look in his eyes that I'd seen once before at the hot springs.

'I want to photograph you, in that pose, with that expression. I need a scene like this in my novel. I'm trying to visualise it in my head.'

'You are joking, aren't you?' I said, backing away and jumping to my feet.

He lagged behind as we completed the circular trail back to the car while I walked briskly ahead, desperate to get on the road before nightfall.

'You're being hysterical,' he muttered as he got in and started the engine.

I couldn't look at him.

'Haven't you heard of "*method acting*"?' he said, reversing the car on the track to turn in the direction of home.

Matt loved to impress me with his extensive general knowledge. While I sat staring ahead at the road, not trusting myself to speak, he explained to me in a calm, quiet voice that 'method acting' was a technique, pioneered by the theatre practitioner Konstantin Stanislavski, in which an actor aspired to complete identification with a character.

'So, for example, imagine an actor has been given the role of a murderer,' he said. 'Of course, in their own life they've never killed anybody, but they draw from their own experiences of feeling anger or aggression or anything else they feel is relevant. They then use their own personal experiences and memories to imagine how their character is feeling and relate these emotions to their portrayal of that role.'

His condescending tone irked me.

'Lots of great actors do it when they're preparing or filming a role. They inhabit the mind of their character, both on set and in their day-to-day life off set. Then they use this preparation to feed into their performances on camera.'

'But you're not an actor, you're a writer,' I said, unconvinced.

'We're not so different,' said Matt. 'Both writers and actors embody the lives of other people. I want be a *method writer* – inhabit the mind of my character so I can write a true and authentic characterisation that will feel real to the readers.' He gestured towards his copy of *The Beast of Siena*, which I'd tossed onto the back seat of the car. 'Many novelists read books about real-life murderers to try to understand and portray what's going on inside their protagonists' heads. True crime books like that one.'

'You're obsessed with that book,' I said angrily.

'I want to go one step further,' continued Matt, 'to recreate the mindset of a killer inside my own head. I want to know how it feels. You know, heart pumping, guts clenching – the visceral reality of it all.'

He spoke with passion, but I wasn't persuaded.

'That's sick,' I said. 'And you didn't just feel it, you acted on it. You took pictures of me without my consent. You lifted my skirt, for God's sake, while I was half asleep. That was predatory and degrading.'

'You think that way because you don't understand the creative process,' said Matt smoothly. 'You can't imagine what was going on inside my head.'

'It's not all about *you*,' I snapped indignantly. 'Imagine how your behaviour makes *me* feel!'

'Well, exactly! That's the point of it,' said Matt crisply, as if he'd won the argument. 'As a *method writer*, I have to get inside the heads of *all* my characters. I need to see the fear in your eyes – to feel my power over you and to imagine what's going through *your* head. To do that, I have to get *you* to embody the part of the victim.'

'Now you're really freaking me out,' I said. I helped myself to one of his cigarettes from the glove compartment – the first time I'd lit a cigarette since before the pandemic – and took a long drag. 'I'm not a bloody character in your story. I refuse to play the part of "victim" in real life or in fiction.' I jabbed the cigarette at him. 'I swear, if you ever use me in one of your twisted mind games again, I'll be on the next plane home to England.'

Matt winked and patted my leg.

'Don't be silly, darling! There's nothing sinister about it. I'm just using you as a prop for my creative genius.'

'You are joking, aren't you?' I shook my head and stared at him in disbelief while he gave me one of his most winning smiles. 'You've been warned,' I said, blowing smoke into his face.

'Be an angel and light one for me,' he said.

'If you're so keen to get me involved in the creative process,' I said, handing Matt my cigarette and lighting another for myself, 'why are you so secretive about your writing? I'd happily read your draft novel and give you my comments.'

'It's too soon,' he said uncertainly. 'Too much early scrutiny can kill the spark.'

For the first time in the conversation, his words sounded authentic and I warmed to his vulnerability. Then he recovered himself.

'But, sure, why not? One of these days, I'll print you a copy.'

* * *

Later that evening while Matt was writing in the study, I noticed that he'd left his book *The Beast of Siena* on the table in the hallway next to my camera. I wanted to delete the images that he'd taken of me while asleep, but I knew that this would annoy him. He'd want me to print them off for him when my darkroom was set up for his peculiar 'method writing' project.

I got them up on the display screen and scrolled back. I compared Matt's compositions to the reproductions in the book. They were uncannily alike. He'd framed me in such a way as to recreate the original photographs perfectly. Now, I understood what he meant by embodying the experience of the victim. Looking at the images made me feel physically sick.

I scrolled back further. There was worse to come. Pictures of me in the woods. Antonio was right – Matt had lied to me. Matt hadn't been to the bank. He'd lured me to the woods and rather than joining me there, he'd left me alone, going for a solitary walk, with the sole purpose of taking clandestine photos of me at the bathing pool. While I'd been waiting anxiously for him, he'd been hidden behind the trees, behaving worse than the most aggressive paparazzi or most pathetic of voyeurs. He'd been only metres away from me when I sent him the text – close enough that I'd heard the ping on his text. There I was – preserved in black-and-white – isolated, lonely and fearful.

I could see that he'd zoned in on the tension in my eyes. He'd captured me, clutching my towel to my chest, looking over my shoulder, glancing at my phone. What had been going through his head as he recorded my distress? The thrill of the hunt?

Antonio had been concerned enough to tip me off about

Matt's strange conduct that day. He'd known Matt as a very young man. Were there things he knew about Matt's character or his past that made him fear for my welfare or safety? Antonio was a hunter and a tracker himself. Had he been tracking Matt about the estate these last months, watching him behaving in this way before?

The thing that confused me is that Matt had made no attempt to prevent me from finding these pictures. Technically, this was my camera. A Christmas present from him. I was the one who took most of our holiday shots (back in the day when holidays were a thing!) and I also used the camera for my artwork. It was obvious I'd see his pictures of me. Did he really think his behaviour was OK?

No. He wasn't that stupid. This was all part of Matt's thought experiment. He wanted to know how these photos would make me feel. If Matt intended to confuse and unsettle me, he'd certainly succeeded. I'd lost all sense of what was for the purpose of research and what was for real. Perhaps that was the whole point of his writing, I reflected – to blur the boundaries between fiction and truth.

That night, my nerves on edge, I lay looking up at the ceiling, consumed with paranoia, thinking of the historic murders in the Siena countryside and of all the serial killers that Matt had been researching for his novel. Of course, I knew that books don't sell if they're about a mundane couple falling in love one summer, having a perfectly pleasant time in a nice place and then going their separate ways. Matt needed to add elements of mystery and drama to heighten the suspense. But it wasn't just his story. There was something about this old place that exuded bad vibes. It was as if the estate buildings themselves harboured dark secrets that were being released into the air with the dust from the renovations.

Even Marcella who had worked at the house for decades had made some cryptic comments about *scavando nel passato* – digging up the past – and then refused to elaborate. At first, I thought her reserve was simply down to the language barrier, but lately I'd got the impression that she was hiding something from me too.

THIRTY-ONE
THE HITCHHIKER
BY MATTEO J. ROSSI

Ted and Nikki are in the back of Luca's old Fiat Panda, parked up alongside a tiny church dedicated to the *Madonna di Vignoni* at the top of a hill, protected by cypress trees. The church is one of a string of beauty spots along the route of the aptly named *Via Dell'Amore* overlooking a breathtaking panorama of the Crete Senesi. It ranks top among the most photographed spots in Tuscany, with the hills rolling off to the left and an ancient ruined abbey in the distance. It's one of the spots favoured by young Italian lovers and because of that, a magnet for local perverts and voyeurs.

It's almost sunset – a glorious pink-and-grey banner stretched out over the hills. Ted and Nikki aren't looking at the view. She's wearing only a miniskirt and a strappy little top. She thought it pointless to wear a bra and Ted has already removed her thong with his teeth. Now, she's straddled on top of him, one knee on either side.

The back of Luca's car isn't the most conducive space for an evening of passion. It's dirty and cramped. Empty cigarette cartons and beer cans and the foils from used condoms and an old blanket covered in dogs' hair litter the seat. But the lovers are determined to put on a good show. They've been here every Friday night for the last five weeks. They're hopeful tonight will be the night when the fish will bite.

Luca's hidden in an alcove at the back of the chapel, patient as a monk. Every Friday he's been there, chain-smoking Marlborough Reds, armed with a film camera and a crowbar in case things turn ugly. Once or twice, a car pulled up and someone looked in through the windows, curious or shocked. But no one stayed for long enough to fall into their trap. Luca's got a good feeling about tonight – the sunset, the balmy night air, the sap rising in nature and in men. It'll bring out the *guardoni* – voyeurs – in hunt of a cheap thrill.

Nikki's bored and Ted has cramp in his left foot. The sun's going down and the moon's rising in the sky and they're about to call it a day, when Luca sees a car in the distance moving slowly towards them, long and low, headlights off. It stops at the bend, down by the river, out of sight. Luca stamps out his cigarette and pulls up his hood. Then he texts one word to Ted:

Incoming.

THIRTY-TWO
DANIELLE

Matt avoided travelling to Montepulciano and discouraged me from making what he described as 'frivolous trips' except for specific errands such as food shopping. He'd been stopped once or twice at 'pop-up' police roadblocks used for monitoring people's movements in and out of the biggest local town.

'This country has become a police state,' he fumed. 'We'd better keep our heads down.'

Being fluent in Italian, he'd quote all the latest rules and statistics in support of the restrictions he imposed upon both himself and on me, and I had no idea whether or not he was making it up as he went along. It seemed to me he broke the rules whenever he wanted to, but always had a ready justification when I challenged his double standards. In any event, on Monday morning, I was pleasantly surprised when he told me about the new freedoms.

'The shops are reopening today,' Matt said, 'and the bars are allowed to serve drinks indoors or outdoors.'

Marcella always brought us the local Sunday newspaper

after her family had finished with it when she came to clean on a Monday morning. Matt picked up the paper and translated for me.

'*Virus levels in the sanitary district* 12 – that's our district – *have fallen dramatically, permitting the regional council – consiglio regionale – to ease certain restrictions on retail and hospitality.*' Matt tossed the paper to one side. 'So basically, all the *non-essential* shops will be open for business and you can have a drink in a bar.

'Feel free to take the Land Rover. I don't need it today. It'll do you good to have a change of scene,' he said. 'Go and get some retail therapy. You seem very stressed at the moment.'

I was happy with the prospect of a day's shopping by myself. I'd been wanting to order fabric for curtains and blinds for some weeks, so though I bridled at his patronising tone, I didn't react.

'Don't you just hate that feeling,' I'd complained when undressing late the night before, 'that someone could be watching us out in the dark when our lights are on.'

Matt had been sitting up in bed reading *The Beast of Siena*.

'God, you're obsessed. I think your next book should be *The Psychopath's Guide to Tuscany*,' I'd said flippantly.

'I think the Italian tourist board might have something to say about that.' Matt had laughed. 'They're trying to encourage the tourists to come back!'

Then he'd leapt up and grabbed me from behind, dragging me squealing with laughter backwards onto the bed.

'And you're paranoid. Let's turn out the lights, then no one can see inside – problem solved,' he'd murmured into my ear.

And we'd made love.

But there was one small problem when it came to shopping – I had no access to my money. When we arrived in Italy, Matt had transferred all of our savings and the proceeds from the sale of my flat into an Italian bank account. It was supposed to be a joint account – as we'd agreed. But thanks to Brexit, including my name on the account had become a bureaucratic nightmare, since I was neither a citizen of the European Union, nor an Italian national. Matt was supposed to be chasing up the bank for me to get around this impasse, but somehow it was never at the top of his list of priorities. For now, the account was in Matt's name only.

'When are they going to get my bank card sorted out?' I railed. 'I'm sick of relying on handouts.'

After breakfast, Matt handed me a wodge of fifty-euro notes. I pocketed the cash with irritation, knowing it was rightfully mine.

'Here, this should be enough to pay for those curtains you've been going on about.' He eyed my ripped jeans and faded T-shirt. 'Treat yourself to some new clothes while you're at it.' He softened the words with a smile. 'You've let yourself go.'

I bristled at his jibe but didn't bother to retort, knowing it was true. I hadn't made much of an effort with my clothes or personal grooming lately. I needed a haircut... And a manicure – my hands were suffering from all the manual tasks involved in renovating an ancient building. We never went out and never saw anyone, so there didn't seem much point getting dressed up, meaning I'd lived for most of the winter in jeans and a sweatshirt.

On the other hand, I could take pride in my fitness. Since arriving in Italy, I'd lost several kilos and my body was toned and firm from all the walking and cycling, as well as the yoga and HIIT classes I followed religiously online. Now that it was getting warmer and social restrictions were easing, the idea of buying some pretty skirts and dresses to show off my new figure lifted my mood.

'We're going to make a start on the terrace today. It's going to be a noisy job breaking up all that old concrete. Don't feel you have to hurry back.'

I couldn't help wondering if Matt had some ulterior motive for getting me out of the way. Clearly, he didn't want me interfering in the swimming pool excavations. He'd made that very plain. But I had my own agenda, too. While Matt was in his study, I quickly packed my easel and paints into the back of the Land Rover. On my way back from town, I was planning to stop to paint the wildflowers and thistles that were out in abundance in an area of uncultivated land we were rewilding on the far borders of the estate. I knew that there was a little-used stony access lane where I could slip in unseen. The land on the far side of the estate fell away behind a hillock planted with olive trees. I wouldn't be in the sight lines of the men working on the terrace and could get on with my painting in peace.

Beyond the gates, I tasted freedom – chalky white road cutting through the olive groves, luminous green of young wheat, splashes of red poppies already in bloom in our part of Tuscany. I rolled down the windows, turned up the music, set the satnav and accelerated away in the direction of Montepulciano. The less time I spent on the road, the more time I'd have in the poppy fields. I glanced up at myself in the rearview mirror. I looked different. I was smiling.

Montepulciano was a fashionable hill town with elegant shops and impressive historic monuments. It had been used as the location for several movies and shows over the years, most recently a popular vampire series. At this time of year, its steep, winding streets would normally have been crowded with tourists, their tour buses parked up on the narrow roads outside the city walls. But now I heard only Italian voices as young couples and family groups mingled around the cafés and shops. It was more civilised and – even with the masks – paradoxically more normal not having throngs of foreigners. I felt privileged and excited to be a part of the reopening of the town.

I knew exactly where I was going. The *Casa dei Tessuti* or House of Fabrics was situated in a shady courtyard behind the cathedral. Marcella had recommended it to me and I'd checked out the website, on which the establishment declared itself 'the finest fabric shop in the whole of Tuscany'. Marcella had told me to ask for Sofia. I gathered that she was a distant relative of the Rossi family, daughter of a cousin or something along those lines – I'd lost track in Marcella's convoluted explanation. But then, here everyone seemed to be in some way related to everyone else.

Sofia knew everything there was to know about fabric and design, according to Marcella, and she'd give me a good price, too, because of the family connection. Marcella had smiled in complicity and rubbed together her fingers. She could also tell me the best places to buy clothes.

I hadn't mentioned to Matt that I was meeting Sofia. We'd spent so much time in each other's company recently that it was nice to feel that I was striking out independently to make a new acquaintance.

From the Casa dei Tessuti website, I'd already picked out a striking poppy chintz print on a linen Tuscan weave. It would be perfect to add instant colour to our neutral and currently dilapidated décor. I'd called ahead and spoken to

Sofia, asking her to put aside a swatch. It was a good-quality fabric but not the most expensive. Matt had little interest in home furnishings and there was no point antagonising him by spending more than necessary.

Sofia looked about my age. She was wearing a green silk shirt and black leather trousers. I became conscious of my faded jeans and oversized T-shirt next to her polished Italian chic. As soon as I greeted her in my broken Italian, she welcomed me in perfect English.

'Danielle. It is Danielle, isn't it? It's so lovely to meet you. Marcella has told me all about you.'

Her face was covered by a washed silk mask that blended with her shirt and set off her dark eyes. I'd noticed that you could form an impression of the way people looked behind their masks from the timbre of their voices and the expression in their eyes. Sofia was undoubtedly attractive and all smiles beneath hers.

For a second or two, she looked into my eyes intently – as if she recognised me – almost like a long-lost friend. She muttered something in Italian, then she looked away and became all businesslike.

She was helpful and efficient, with only a touch of conde-scension. She showed me the swatch and a range of other options. Because of the lockdown, the shop was unable to offer its usual measuring and fitting services, but she'd arrange for one of the fitters (brother of one of the girls she worked with) to come out in his own time.

She tilted her head slightly and her eyes crinkled mean-ingfully as she smiled again behind her mask. I got the message. These unofficial ways of getting around the lock-down restrictions were commonplace in Italy. People needed to eat, after all – and get on with their lives.

Once I'd paid for the fabric, Sofia ripped a sheet off her order pad and scribbled down the names of her favourite shops, along with a rough map of how to find them.

'And you must stop here,' she said. 'Caffè Angelo. The waiters are rude, but they have the best pastries in town and a beautiful view from the balcony.' She flicked her wrist at the queue of customers lining up restlessly behind me. 'I wish I could come with you, at least for a coffee... We're so busy today. The grand reopening!'

I went on a quick tour of the shops and found an embroidered white cotton summer dress that I fell in love with and a pair of white linen trousers. I tried on a 'new season' deep plunge Versace bikini. I glanced very quickly at the price tag. For once I didn't cringe at my reflection in the dressing room mirror, now that I was slim and tanned. Already I was fantasising about swimming in our new infinity pool. Spurred on by the enthusiasm of the overly attentive shop manageress, who clapped her hands in wonder each time she pulled back the dressing room curtain, I bought the bikini, along with the dress and the trousers, a flowery cotton miniskirt and a pale blue silk shirt. I must have been her biggest sale since the start of the pandemic.

Feeling rather giddy (and more than a little guilty – it was such a long time since I'd been out on a shopping spree), I headed for Caffè Angelo, stopping en route to buy a copy of *Your Tuscany* from a newspaper seller in the main square. I managed to get a seat on the balcony and browsed the magazine while a surly waiter took his time with my latte. I turned the pages, idly scanning through the endless advertisements for restaurants and bars in the food and culture section, the statistics and updates on the 'health emergency', and news items dealing with the closure of a regional bus service. Most of it was prosaic and dull, though a short news article made me chuckle as I sipped my coffee.

Lockdown felony – man gets himself arrested and sent to jail to escape his 'insufferable' wife... Mario Conti, garage attendant aged 43, said he stole a car and deliberately crashed it because he wanted to be sent to prison to get away from his nagging wife. It was *'la moglie o la macchina'* (the missus or the car) he told the magistrates, indicating how desperate he'd become. The car was a write-off...

I folded the magazine into my bag. It was the sort of quirky news story that would appeal to Matt.

I switched my phone to 'aircraft mode' as I left the café. I was looking forward to an afternoon of painting without interruptions or distractions and didn't want to be disturbed by Matt or anyone else. While Matt considered his writing a 'vocation', I knew he thought of my painting as a 'hobby' – and a self-indulgent one at that, which got in the way of my responsibilities project managing the renovation work. He'd let his true feelings slip only the other day.

'It doesn't bring in a penny,' he'd said when a large delivery of art materials appeared on our doorstep. 'In fact, it's a very expensive hobby – all that money you spend on canvases and paint. It would be different if you had any talent...' He checked himself. 'I mean, you know, commercial success. I think you're very good, don't get me wrong, but you haven't actually sold any paintings.'

When Matt spoke like this, sometimes in the moment, it made me hate him.

What possessed me to throw in my lot with this egotistical, entitled, patriarchal bastard? I seethed internally. Then he'd say something funny and loving and disarming, and the moment would pass. Yet, deep down, his criticism corroded something in my love for him.

The hypocrisy of Matt's words still rankled. He hadn't earned a penny from his writing so far. His costs mounted month by month. I knew this because I was the one who had to make the payments: the paper and the ink and the broadband charges for his obsessive research – it all added up. So why his 'vocation' for creative writing should be deemed 'a business venture' while my painting was dismissed as a 'vanity project' was beyond me.

I parked at the end of the stony access track and when I turned off the engine, I could hear the digger rumbling over by the terrace on the other side of the hill. *Good!* I guessed Matt would be working there with Antonio until late afternoon, so that gave me about three more hours of freedom.

I got started immediately, setting up my paints and creating the composition for my painting by sketching out the scene in front of me. In the distance there was a small, ruined farm building – it must once have been a shepherd's hut or abandoned farm worker's cottage. I'd paint that on the left of my canvas and in the foreground, I wanted to focus on the shapes and colours of the purple thistles and bright red poppies. Then on the right I'd paint the three cypress trees that stood like sinister sentinels guarding the entrance to the estate along the white road in the far distance.

I completed my sketches quickly and soon I was absorbed in the process of applying paint to the canvas. I was progressing well, painting in broad, impressionistic brushstrokes, enjoying this rare period of uninterrupted peace.

I'd just put down my brush to take a sip of water, when it occurred to me. The noise from the digger had stopped. I listened carefully. It seemed too early to finish work for the day. They could be taking a tea break. Without the distant clanking and hum of machinery, it was eerily quiet. I picked up my paintbrush and tried to concentrate on the sound of my brushstrokes and the swirl of colours on my palette.

Some while later, I looked up to see a figure in dark overalls approaching over the brow of the hill, heading down through the olive groves. From a distance and with the sun in my eyes, I wasn't sure at first if it was Matt or Antonio. The men were of a similar build and hair colour and today, they were both wearing navy workmen's overalls and dark glasses.

My first thought was that Matt had seen my car turning off the main road and was on his way to get me. Perhaps I was needed back at the farmhouse to deal with some issue with the electricians who were completing the rewiring of our system. Sometimes Matt made me feel like a schoolgirl caught playing truant from class.

When I got a better view, I saw it was in fact Antonio. I shrank back into the shadows of the trees and sat stock-still, knowing that a hunter would be alert for any movement. Although we'd bonded over the shooting lesson, the thought of meeting him alone again made me uncomfortable. For starters, Matt wouldn't like it if he found out. It would look like a secret rendezvous. He'd got the idea into his head that Antonio had a thing for me, and it was making him jealous and possessive.

I froze mid-brushstroke and my hand shook. I couldn't deny it – Antonio made me nervous. I held my breath as he moved out of my view behind a scraggly row of old vines in what must have once been a productive vineyard, then strode on purposefully in the direction of the old cottage.

Now, I was curious. He was carrying a bulky holdall of the kind used by builders for their tools. The door must have been boarded over with timbers, because he put down the bag by the door, then took out a small axe to prise it open with a few decisive blows. He looked over his shoulder before going in. *What's he up to?* I wondered.

Once he was inside, I dragged my easel further back into the undergrowth so that I'd be hidden from his sight line when he re-emerged from the derelict cottage.

I tried to get on with my painting, but now my viewpoint had changed, messing up my composition. I dabbed at the canvas, adjusting the colour tone and the depth while keeping half an eye on the cottage and listening to the banging and scraping noises that were coming from inside. I was trying so hard to stay focused that it was only when he'd walked past me, less than 30 metres to my left, that I noticed Matt this time, still in his workmen's clothes, coming out of the woods and heading towards the cottage.

The normal thing would have been for me to call out, and for Matt to come over and ask me how my trip to Montepulciano had been. It should have been nice for him to see how I was getting on with my painting and for me to ask him how the work was going at the pool. But I held back. I was still angry about the way Matt had spoken to me that morning, telling me I was letting myself go. I had no wish to talk to him – especially when dressed in my baggy painting T-shirt and smeared with paint. More importantly, I was curious to know what Matt was doing down here with Antonio. It seemed they had a secret they were hiding from me. I was determined to find out what it was.

Matt entered the cottage and immediately the banging and scraping stopped and there was silence. It seemed like an eternity while I waited there, paintbrush poised over the canvas, wondering what was going on. Then I heard voices, first urgent and low, then fast and heated. I thought back to the confrontation I'd overheard between them on our driveway some weeks ago. This was the second time I'd witnessed an argument – conflict and tension over some forced but unwanted collaboration.

They were speaking in Italian, so though their voices carried easily through the broken windows, it was just a babble of noise to me. Things must have got more intense, because soon I could hear Antonio shouting, then the sound of clanging metal and something crashing to the floor. I began to fear for Matt's safety.

Paintbrush in hand, I ran as fast as I could across the poppy meadow to the front door of the cottage, which I found barred. Antonio was still shouting. I hammered on the door but got no reply. I raced round to the back of the cottage in search of another way in. I flattened myself against the wall and listened through a window opening above my head. Antonio had calmed down. He was still talking loudly, but Matt's responses were faint and muffled. I held on to the broken sill and pulled myself up. I got a quick glance into the dark room before my arms gave way and I dropped to the ground. Antonio was standing above a gaping hole in the floor of the cottage. Matt was nowhere to be seen.

With shock, I realised that he must be down there – in an underground cellar or cave. I remembered Matt telling me that during the Second World War, some of the farm workers had dug fortified shelters for protection from stray Allied bombs, and to hide their money and other valuables from requisition by the occupying Nazi forces. Some underground cellars had even been used to shelter Allied soldiers escaping from combat in the south of Italy, local peasants opposed to the fascists risking their own lives to help them evade capture.

'They have other uses, of course,' Matt had said. 'Mafia contraband, undeclared cash income, unlicensed firearms... Don't be fooled by the picture-postcard beauty of Tuscany; every peasant round here has something to hide from the taxman or the police.'

I picked up a broken brick and was on my way to batter down the front door, when it flew open and Antonio marched out. His jaw was set. I pressed up against the rough stone wall, hidden by a thick fall of ivy, hoping that he wouldn't look over his shoulder. He strode across the meadow and up through the olive groves towards the main buildings.

As soon as Antonio was out of sight, I burst through the door, still holding the brick like a weapon. Matt, who was scrambling out of the cellar with his back to me, almost fell back into the hole.

'What the hell's going on!' he cried out.

I stood there in the doorway, adrenaline pumping, close to tears.

'That's exactly what I want to ask you,' I said weakly, letting the brick fall to the floor. 'Thank God you're OK.'

I wasn't expecting what happened next.

Matt recovered himself, leapt to his feet, stared at me for a second or two and then burst out laughing.

'I thought you were going to bash me over the head with that brick,' he said.

He took my hands.

'Danielle, you're ridiculous. I love you. You're the one who should be writing fiction.'

I stood my ground. 'No, don't gaslight me, Matt. I was trying to protect you. You can't laugh this one off. What are you and Antonio playing at, sneaking round the estate like a pair of smugglers? What are you fighting over? What are you hiding from me?'

Matt took me by the hand and steered me to the door.

'It's just farm business – nothing you need to concern your pretty head with. Come on – let's get out of here. It stinks. Antonio and I are going to clear all this shit.'

He was right. I almost gagged at the rotting, putrid smell. With my eyes now accustomed to the dark, I looked around and saw the debris: ash and charred wood from a campfire, scraps of litter, food waste, cigarette stubs, a cracked plastic lighter, the carcass of a small animal, an empty bottle of spirits and beer cans, and small piles of human faeces and soiled toilet paper.

'Someone's been having a party here,' I exclaimed, disgusted and disturbed to think of strangers coming and going on our land, defiling our property.

I let Matt lead me out into the daylight and we walked over to my easel.

'So that's what you've been up to,' he said gently. 'I've been trying to get hold of you all afternoon. I was getting worried about you.'

I stared at my painting while he looked sideways at my profile, then licked his thumb and rubbed it gently over my cheek to remove a streak of paint.

Then he turned to look at my work in progress.

'It's good,' he said. 'I mean, I know it's not finished, but I'm impressed.'

I realised it was the first time he'd complimented one of my paintings.

'You should get on – make the most of the daylight. I'll explain all this over dinner.' Matt waved casually in the direction of the old cottage and sat down uninvited close to my easel. 'I'm waiting for Antonio to come back, so if you don't mind, I'll stay and watch you paint for a while. I promise not to distract you.'

He leaned back on his elbow and chewed a blade of meadow grass, observing my every movement as silently as a cat.

I wasn't in the mood for painting anymore. Yet, I forced myself to finish off the section I'd been working on before the light faded, then I packed up my brushes and tubes, slowly and methodically.

'I'll see you later, then,' I said as I set off back to the car.

I was pulling off the track onto the main road, when I saw one of the farm vehicles approaching the junction. The driver wore a baseball cap and a mask, but I knew at once it was Antonio. He stared straight ahead and didn't acknowledge me when I raised my hand. I caught a glimpse of a dirty old trunk partly exposed under a sackcloth tarpaulin. In the rear mirror, I watched Antonio turning onto the rutted mud track leading to the old abandoned cottage.

My stomach tightened. I shivered and closed my window. The spring sunshine had waned, giving way to a granite-grey dusk, and the wind was picking up. Marcella had told me it was coming, *la Bora* – the bitter north wind that blows from the north-east all the way across the peninsula to the Adriatic coasts of Italy, Slovenia and Croatia – a wind strong enough to reverse the seasons.

Let's see what Matt's got to say for himself when he gets home, I thought.

Already I could feel the chill in the air.

THIRTY-THREE
THE HITCHHIKER

BY MATTEO J. ROSSI

Luca keeps close to the wall of the ancient church, where his grey jeans and hoodie blend in with the stone. While the car pulls up, he ties a bandana around his face and puts on a pair of dark glasses. These are more for show than for disguise. He's past caring if other punters recognise him.

The car pulls up behind the church out of the sight line of the spot where the Fiat is parked. A man gets out slowly – a caricature of the 'dirty old man'. His baseball cap and over-sized green anorak scream 'pervert'. He pads over with his hands in his pockets and positions himself behind a cypress tree within a few paces of the Fiat. He takes out a pair of small field binoculars, the kind 'twitchers' use for birdwatching. Observing the skylarks and the stone curlews would be his cover story if he were caught by the police.

When they get Luca's text, Nikki switches on the interior lights in the Fiat to improve the quality of the peep show. Now, a warm glow comes from inside the car. From his position, Luca can see Nikki's and Ted's writhing bodies. He knows that their 'victim' will be glued to the performance being played out for him on the back seat. The pervert has a ringside view.

The man is shameless, fully exposed with his trousers hanging round his thighs. He stands in the shadows, one fist holding the binoculars up to his eyes and the other fist beating between his legs. His shoulders are hunched. His lips are drawn back in a panting snarl. He's both scary and pathetic. It's almost too easy. If he weren't so repellent, Luca would feel sorry for him.

Luca removes the lens cap and approaches slowly. The man's sexual urges and the antics inside the Fiat are so compelling that he's oblivious to the sound of Luca's footsteps. Luca shoots half a roll of film before the man becomes aware of the flashing bulb and whirring shutter and lunges round, howling like a wounded animal.

The man makes to run at Luca and swipe the camera hanging from his neck. But Luca is younger and fleet of foot. He dodges back and grabs the crowbar placed strategically against the wall of the church. He raises the crowbar above his head and orders the man to get down on his knees with his hands behind his head. Then he begins to negotiate with the man.

It's difficult to negotiate effectively when your trousers are halfway down your legs, so Luca does most of the talking. It doesn't help the man's situation that Luca knows him by sight – a recluse who lives in the next village. The brother of the postmaster and a minor official at the town council.

'I know you,' says Luca. 'Filthy swine.' (*Sporco suino* – it sounds so much better in Italian.) 'Hand over your money and we'll give you the film. Or you can keep your money and we'll print the photographs – send them to the town council and to your mother. I know where you live. It's your choice.'

Nikki and Ted, hastily dressed, come up behind the kneeling man. Ted grips the man's wrists in a vice above his head while Nikki searches his pockets and pulls out a battered old leather wallet stuffed with cards, crumpled receipts, and assorted banknotes and coins. She counts the money. It's not a bad haul: three hundred and seventy-four euros and seventy cents. Enough for 'one night of ecstasy' up at the pool. And the loose change for her 'running-away fund'. He's been to the cashpoint. Friday night is the night he goes in search of prostitutes in the back streets of Florence, after whetting his appetite cruising lovers' haunts in the Tuscan hills.

The man whimpers and hangs his head – a coward caught in the act. He's discovered that scopophilia doesn't pay – or does pay, depending on which way you look at it.

Nikki stuffs the cash into the back pocket of her shorts while Luca opens the back of the camera, spools out the film and tosses it into the man's lap. Then Nikki kneels down in front of the man to taunt him some more. Her shoulders are bare. His cashless wallet is tucked into her cleavage. He wants it back – it contains his ID and his driving licence. She yanks up his head by his hair, then nods, inviting the man to retrieve the wallet with his teeth. He does so and as he raises his head, the wallet clenched between his jaws, she spits full in his face before collapsing back on her heels in a fit of giggles.

Suddenly, something snaps in her.

'Let's teach this fat pig a lesson,' she screams.

She leaps to her feet, snatches the crowbar from Luca's hand and swings her arm back, taking aim at his head like a schoolgirl preparing to smash a rounders ball.

THIRTY-FOUR
DANIELLE

I drove back to the main entrance, feeling once again the flash of incredulity that hit me each time I turned into the gates – that this country estate was now my home. From a distance, the farmhouse looked like an advert for one of those perfect Tuscan villas on the cover of a luxury Italian holiday brochure. It was only when you got close that you saw the broken shutters and the peeling paintwork and the crumbling brickwork, arousing a quiver of the uncanny as you approached the front door.

I skidded to a halt on the driveway and, leaving my shopping bags and painting gear in the boot, headed straight over to the site of the swimming pool where, judging by the chaos, the groundworks were well under way. About half of the patio had been broken up and excavated, leaving a mound of rubble and earth heaped up on tarpaulins next to the old pool. A skip was arriving the next day and the men would have the back-breaking task of shifting it one wheelbarrow at a time through the wood to the driveway.

We should have got a specialist company in to do the

groundworks, I thought to myself. *This DIY job will take forever.*

Matt had been so adamant that he and Antonio could do it themselves and I hadn't had the energy to fight him. Where the patio had been, they'd begun to dig the hole – marked out with stakes and ticker tape – where the foundations of the new infinity pool would go.

This looks like a crime scene, I thought.

I stared into the gaping pit, as if it might unearth an explanation for Matt and Antonio's bizarre behaviour. And then it occurred to me – first a fleeting thought and then with a growing conviction: Matt's insistence on doing the ground-works himself was nothing to do with saving money. Usually, he was only too keen to pay someone to do all the practical jobs rather than having to get his hands dirty himself. No, the reason he'd insisted on doing it this way was that some secret from the past had lain buried beneath the concrete slabs and he didn't want anyone beyond the confines of the estate to discover it. I thought of the big, dirty trunk I'd seen under the tarpaulin in the back of Antonio's pick-up truck.

They're in this together. Hostile and reluctant co-conspirators. There's something inside that trunk that they don't want anyone else to find out about: drugs, stolen goods – I let my imagination run riot *– buried treasure, firearms, a dead body...* No. Not a dead body. That was absurd.

When I got back to the kitchen, I saw that Matt had left a copy of his unfinished manuscript on the table for me. In the moment, it distracted me from ruminating obsessively over what could be hidden inside the trunk. He'd stuck a yellow Post-it note on the title page with my name and the words:

As promised!

Be kind xxx

I poured myself a generous glass of chilled white Vernaccia di San Gimignano and savoured the fresh mineral tones and distinctive almond aftertaste. With Matt's tuition, I was beginning to appreciate the unique qualities of Tuscan fine wines. During the lockdowns, tasting local vintages had been one of our shared pleasures. I picked up Matt's manuscript: *The Hitchhiker*. After all the secrecy, I was curious to read his story. It would pass the time until his return from the derelict cottage. And then I'd demand an explanation.

I settled down and soon became fully engrossed in Matt's story. Before I knew it, I was sixty pages in and on my third glass of wine. As I read, I reflected on what Matt had let slip since our arrival in Italy about his hippy girlfriend. Though they'd only spent one summer together, he'd once referred to her as the 'love of my life', letting those cutting words fall so casually without thought for my feelings. Was his teenage love the inspiration for the 'Nikki' character in his novel? So much of his time was now spent inside the head of his 'Ted' character. *Matteo's* identification with his fictional protagonist was so self-consciously transparent. The name – Ted or Teo – said it all.

How much of Nikki was an invention of my partner's imagination and how much his memory? Was the hitchhiker still a part of his life? Were they in touch on social media? Was he still in love with her? I berated myself for the absurdity of feeling jealous of a literary creation, but a lingering doubt remained.

I was deep in thought, when a sharp rap on the kitchen

window made me jump. Matt's face was close to the glass, looking in.

'Can you open the door?' he called through the glass. 'I haven't got my keys.'

'God, you made me jump!' I said, opening the front door. 'I didn't hear you coming. Why don't you ever carry a key?'

'Why do you lock the door?' Matt retorted. 'We're miles from anywhere. And it would only take a nanosecond to break into this old house. Why pick a lock when you can smash a window? There's no point locking yourself up.' Matt nodded towards the typewritten pages. 'So, what do you think?'

'It's good,' I said briefly.

Matt raised his eyebrows expectantly, waiting for more.

'No... I mean it's intriguing. I want to keep turning the pages.'

'Ah, damning me with faint praise,' said Matt with a rueful smile.

'I'd love to talk about it,' I said. 'I've got lots of questions. But first I need to understand what's happening between you and Antonio. What's in that trunk?'

'Just let me get showered and dressed, then I'll tell all,' said Matt. 'It's a long story.'

* * *

I placed the salad bowl on the table and two plates. I piled Matt's high with spaghetti Bolognese, since he'd announced that he was ravenous and in need of red meat after the day's hard labour at the pool. I took only a small portion. The afternoon's tensions had cut my appetite. I played with my spaghetti, twirling it on the fork and forgetting to put it in my mouth.

'So, what's going on?' I prompted again once Matt had sated his appetite and downed his first glass of red wine.

'It's complicated and it goes back a long way,' said Matt. 'I guess it starts with my great-uncle, Benetto Rossi. Remember the graffiti you saw on his death notice down in the town square? Well, I wasn't entirely honest with you about that. I didn't want to say anything at the time because, quite frankly, I was ashamed and afraid of what you'd think of my family.'

I touched Matt's hand across the table. 'We shouldn't have secrets.'

Matt took a gulp of wine and plunged in. 'My great-uncle had a bad reputation for taking an unhealthy interest in young people and especially young boys. In the summer months, he loved to fill the place with seasonal workers – students, hippies, travellers – you know the type. The atmosphere was almost like a festival. That's how I came to spend the summers here.

'He worked us hard, but he gave us lots of freedom. People came and went, we drank and smoked pot, we took drugs and had sex, and we partied from dusk until dawn. We were young kids, some of us away from our parents for the first time. When I found out about my uncle's sexual preferences, I was mortified to be related to him.'

'Oh my God, you poor thing. That must have been awful.' I nodded.

'Everyone knew he was a creep – a dirty old man. They put up with it for the free lodging and food and the summers of love.'

Matt stood up and cleared the plates.

'Don't get me wrong – he never tried anything on with me. I suppose because I was family.'

Then he made us coffees and lit a cigarette. Normally, I'd

have objected to him smoking at the table, but I decided to let it pass.

'Anyway, the last summer I was here, just after I finished university, there were rumours circulating at the farm of more serious incidents involving children. I knew that Benetto used one or two of his most trusted workers as groomers to entrap local boys with promises of free alcohol and weed. Then he'd bring them back to the farm for his own pleasure.'

Matt narrowed his eyes and gave me a telling look as he exhaled the smoke from his cigarette. Was he implicating Antonio? I wondered.

'Most of the boys were Roma gypsies or Albanian immigrants who no one cared a fig about. But one day, a boy was brought to the farm who, unbeknown to Benetto, belonged to a "respected" Tuscan family.' Matt did the air quotes with his fingers, knocking cigarette ash onto the table as he did so. 'Anyway, to cut a long story short, it turned out the boy's father had connections to one of the Mafia clans that had infiltrated Tuscany's business community.

'When the boy returned home the next morning and squealed under his father's beating... Well, you can imagine! Things didn't turn out well for my great-uncle. From then on he was their creature.'

He stubbed out the cigarette, grinding it into the ashtray.

'Oh my God! That's so awful,' I said, genuinely shocked. 'I thought the Mafia were down in Sicily. I had no idea they were active round here.'

'That's because you know nothing about the Mafia except what you've seen in *The Godfather*,' said Matt. 'Believe me, the Mafia have their tentacles into everything all over Italy. The Mafia clan with the most influence here in Tuscany is actually from Calabria... You know, on the map – Calabria is the toe in the boot of Italy.'

'This is all fascinating,' I said, 'and disturbing, but what's it got to do with the trunk, which I'm guessing you dug up from under the patio and are now hiding in the derelict cottage?'

'Ah,' said Matt, leaning back in his chair. 'You guessed right.' His voice was chillingly calm. 'It has everything to do with the trunk.

'Benetto had been on the fringes of low-level Mafia activity – black market trading of farm produce and wines, corruption of minor tax officials and the like. But when he was caught with his pants down, the Mafia closed ranks on him for dishonouring one of their own.

'All hell was let loose. Two Mafia thugs came to the house the same night and dragged him from his bed to that outbuilding over there.' Matt gestured in the direction of the outbuilding, which housed the old wine press. 'They gave him a beating that left him within an inch of his life. Then they gave him a choice: your manhood or the fingers of your right hand. He chose, and then they crushed his hand in the wine press. Twenty-six breaks in his phalanges and metacarpal bones, I remember. An accident, he told the hospital.'

I winced at the image of the torture that had taken place just a few metres from where we now sat drinking coffee.

'I guess it was symbolic and fitting,' Matt went on. 'Never again could he fire a gun or pleasure himself.'

I shook my head. 'Except with his left hand,' I murmured stupidly.

'And that wasn't the end of it,' said Matt. 'My great-uncle's "affliction" lay him open to blackmail and extortion, which is perhaps why the Mafia had a change of heart. A few days later, when Benetto was recuperating in bed, he received a second visit, this time from someone high up in the chapter.

'The man was very civil and polite to Loretta. He wore a suit. Come to think of it, he was dressed like an undertaker. He told Benetto they'd decided he was more useful to them alive than dead. The old man's estate, so remote, with its many abandoned cottages and back routes and hidden wells and secluded woods, was a useful resource for Mafia operations.

'Again, he was given a choice, a second chance. He could cooperate with the Cosa Nostra – allow contraband and drugs to be hidden on his land, weapons training to take place in his woods, his seasonal workers to act as couriers, vats of his wine to be siphoned off for every wedding, baptism and funeral… He could do all that graciously, in which case he'd live a quiet life. But if he refused, or if at any time in the future he were to put a foot wrong or breathe a word to the police, then they'd kill him and feed his body to the pigs. Or better still, kill Loretta and feed her body to the pigs!' Matt finished with a dramatic flourish.

I sat there stunned, unsure whether to take all this at face value or whether Matt had become carried away with his own rhetoric. He spoke as if reciting the next chapter of his book.

'You wouldn't believe it,' I said uncertainly. 'If it was in a novel, it would seem too far-fetched.'

'Sometimes truth is stranger than fiction,' he said. 'Read the local papers. You'll find tales of Mafia atrocities – even today.'

He grabbed a bottle of grappa from the shelf and filled a crystal tumbler.

'So, if you ask me what's inside the trunk, I'm afraid I can't tell you.' His voice slurred slightly from alcohol and exhaustion. 'All I can say is that at the end of that fateful summer more than ten years ago, Benetto woke me and Antonio in the dead of night and ordered us to collect a trunk that had been dumped at the gates of the estate. To carry it in silence up the driveway and through the woods. To bury it as deep as possible in the foundations of the new patio that we were digging for him up by the pool. To cover it with concrete slabs, never to speak of it again and to forget everything we'd done... forever.'

He raised his glass, drained the grappa, then banged it down on the table.

'When the Mafia tell you to do something, it's best not to ask questions.'

THIRTY-FIVE
THE HITCHHIKER

BY MATTEO J. ROSSI

Luca blocks the blow. Nikki is fast and furious, but she can't compete with his bulk. He grabs her wrist and wrenches the crowbar off her. She fights him like a cat for a second or two and then springs away when she comes to her senses – murder isn't part of the plan.

Cowering on the ground, the man struggles to pull up his trousers. The boys are having none of that. Luca wields the crowbar above his head while Ted rips them off. He's had enough experience in the rugby scrum to know his strength and not be intimidated by some pathetic middle-aged creep grovelling at his feet.

Quick-thinking, Nikki whips out her phone and takes a picture as the man runs back to his car half-naked – his humiliation complete. Ted picks up the man's trainers that were dragged off in the de-trousering and takes aim. He flings them slowly, ferociously, one after the other. Again, his rugby skills come into play. Thump... thump... on the back of the man's head. Luca yells after him in Italian.

'If you go to the police, you'll find your dirty ass displayed on every social media channel in Italy with the hashtags "*fottuto pervertito*" and your name. So, keep your mouth shut!'

The three conspirators are sky-high and fall about screaming with laughter as the man drives off.

Luca chucks the ignominious man's trousers into the back of the Fiat – best not to leave any evidence at the scene in case the police are sniffing around – and drives back to the *fattoria* at breakneck speed. They might turn a blind eye, but then again, they might poke their noses in and make a pretence of prosecuting the case.

Back at the cottage, Ted and Nikki make love again, this time with real passion. One of the summer workers who Nikki befriended with free childcare in mind spent the afternoon with Harry. The girl is in love with Nikki (though the dumb thing doesn't know it yet) and will do anything for her. Turns out she's good with little children and has fed Harry and bathed him and put him to bed. So, Ted and Nikki have the downstairs all to themselves.

Meanwhile, Luca contacts his 'associate' – a self-styled would-be mobster drug dealer connected to a local chapter of the Calabrian Mafia whose day job is working as a foreman in a leather factory located near Parma. The drop takes place in an abandoned cottage on the far side of the estate.

That night, the poolside party is wild. Luca's *spacciatore* – drug dealer – delivered a varied tasting menu of questionable provenance and quality in exchange for their vigilante booty, but no one's complaining.

Nikki takes turns with the boys. Variety is the spice of life.

Ted is too stoned to care.

In the early hours of the morning, with Nikki curled up like a kitten in Ted's lap on the deckchair, Luca lights a fire. Ceremoniously, he drops the man's trousers into the flames.

The cloth is stained with engine oil and grime. The three of them watch as it catches and flares. The acrid smell of perversion fills the air. Like a pagan rite, the damning remains sparkle and swirl up and away into the night sky. When the smoke clears, the stars look brighter than ever and dance before their eyes.

THIRTY-SIX
DANIELLE

We stayed up late that night reading in bed. Me – *The Hitchhiker*, and Matt – *The Beast of Siena*. My nerves were on edge and I tensed up every time I heard the mournful call of a tawny owl hooting in the distance or the high-pitched scream of a red fox, so similar to the cry of a woman in distress. Someone had left a tap on outside in the yard and the sound of running water filled my head, making it impossible for me to concentrate on the words on the page.

'Any chance you could go down and turn off the tap?' I said, not wanting to go downstairs again on my own.

There was a locked doorway at the far end of the landing, which always made me feel uneasy when I passed it at night-time.

'The tanks will run dry and it's a criminal waste of water.'

Matt didn't hear me at first, absorbed in his reading. Eventually, he closed the book and went down. Having turned off the tap, I heard him pottering in the kitchen for a while, putting on the kettle and making himself a drink. In the mean-

244

time, I picked up his book, curious to see what he was reading that was so engrossing.

He was halfway through a chapter entitled '*Catholicism and Scopophilia*'.

'What does that even mean?' I said out loud and then skimmed a few paragraphs at random:

> *... because, traditionally, so many young people in Italy lived with their families until they left home (families often with strict Catholic values), the only way they could spend time alone together was by driving out into the wilderness... A high percentage of Italian babies were conceived on the back seats of cars in the 1970s and 80s... As this trend became local knowledge, the young lovers gained a following of voyeurs, who went out to the beauty spots to spy on them, and this in turn attracted vigilantes, who took photographs of the voyeurs and blackmailed them for the negatives... So there were circles of crime around this habit of young people meeting in beauty spots to make love. In this context, it may be said that Catholicism became a catalyst for scopophilia (sexual stimulation or satisfaction derived principally from looking; voyeurism)...*

What a simplistic deduction, I thought with distaste, rereading the last sentence. The author sounded like an apologist for these perverts. This must be where Matt had got the idea for his honeytrap vigilante scene that I had just been reading. I recalled the image of 'Nikki' about to whack a voyeur with a crowbar. The title of the next chapter was '*Topography of Terror in the Tuscan Hills*'.

'This man's got a thing for alliteration,' I muttered crossly.

He seemed to trivialise the horror of the true crimes he

described, cashing in on personal tragedies. There was nothing on the cover to indicate whether the author – J.P. Hitchkins – was a man or a woman, but I felt sure no woman would have written this account, which of itself seemed voyeuristic.

The 'Topography of Terror' chapter contained photographs of various sites and a map pinpointing the exact spot where the series of murders had taken place, highlighting their geographic features. The map was marked with crosses and arrows to show the movements of the attackers and their targets at the location, along with typed annotations giving the names of the victims, time and date, and the means of death: 'multiple gunshot wounds', 'strangulation', 'rape and genital evisceration'.

It was a brutal and macabre tally. Matt had added his own markings to the map – red biro ticks against certain sites, presumably those he'd visited, like a hiker ticking off Munros. With sinking heart, I realised that one of the ticks referred to the site we'd visited together, not long ago, when he'd taken photographs of me asleep on the picnic rug.

I heard Matt coming up the stairs and quickly replaced the book on his pillow. I didn't want to get into a conversation about it now. Something more pressing was playing on my mind.

'Why were you fighting with Antonio this afternoon,' I said, 'down at the ruined cottage?'

'Fighting is a strong way of putting it,' said Matt, unfazed. He got back into bed. 'Let's just say we had a lively debate about how we should deal with the object we unearthed at the swimming pool.' He hesitated for a few seconds. 'Antonio wants to inform the police. It's alright for him. He's a single man. I must think of you, and Loretta too. For reasons I explained to you over dinner, I believe we should keep the thing hidden while the workmen are on site installing the infinity pool, then bury it as soon as possible under the new patio and never speak of it again. To do anything else would not only put us, and especially my great-aunt, in danger, but would also be a huge betrayal of trust. Antonio made a solemn vow to my great-uncle to keep his secret safe – we both did.'

I listened gravely, unsure whether or not I could take Matt's words at face value.

This would explain Matt's conflicted emotions at the time he learnt of his inheritance, I reflected.

As if he could read my thoughts, Matt continued earnestly:

'Why do you think Antonio was given a life interest to remain living on the estate in Benetto's will? Why do you think I had no choice but to take up my inheritance? Because the secret that was buried underneath the patio had to remain hidden from the outside world... forever.'

I was bursting with questions, but for Matt the subject was closed. He pressed his finger to my lips.

'Do you know the word, "*omertà*"? It refers to the Mafia code of silence. Being a police informant is the worst possible violation of that code. Within Mafia circles breaking *omertà* is punishable by death.'

He turned off the lights and drew me into his arms.

'Forget you ever saw the bloody trunk,' he whispered into my ear.

Then he slid down between the covers and silenced me with kisses.

* * *

At breakfast the next morning, I showed Matt the story in *Your Tuscany* about the man sent to prison for stealing and deliberately crashing a car to escape living at home with his insufferable wife.

'You might find this entertaining,' I said. 'We got side-tracked yesterday, so I forgot to give it to you.'

'Side-tracked' was an understatement. Matt's revelations about his family's involvement with the Mafia had been a body blow. I was still reeling. This had implications for our life here in Italy now. It might explain why I'd felt cold-shouldered in town on more than one occasion. Matt chuckled over the article and then handed the magazine back to me.

'I'll know what to do if you keep nagging me, then,' he joked.

I thumbed idly through the pages while eating my breakfast. The magazine contained mostly trivia. There were no Mafia stories, but there was one other news item that caught my eye.

'Hey, look, Matt. There's a mention of *the Beast of Siena* murders here.' I pointed to the article. 'What a coincidence.' I read it out loud:

> Police are appealing for witnesses to an incident that took place near the village of San Pietro when a young woman was assaulted while out jogging in the early evening of 26 April. The victim ran out into the road and flagged down a passing car to escape her assailant. Luigi Santini, owner of nearby Bar San Pietro, noted that the attack took place within metres of the Chiesa della Madonna – the site of one of the most notorious 'Beast of Siena' murders, which terrified the local population in the late decades of the last century.

Police have warned the public to be extra vigilant. They say the number of reported incidents in the countryside has increased during lockdown because more people are taking exercise on their own and fewer people are in work. However, police chief Alberto Gianni dismissed any connection with historic serial killings, believing the attack to be an isolated 'lone-wolf-type incident'.

Matt glanced over briefly.

'San Pietro... that's close to where I got knocked off my bike. That brings it home. You should take care, Dani. We're so remote out here. That's why I don't like it when you go off walking or cycling alone, or setting up your easel in the middle of nowhere.'

*   *   *

It was market day when I went back to Montepulciano about three weeks later to collect the fabric for our bedroom blinds. The shutters were still broken and every morning, the sun streamed straight in. I loved waking up bathed in sunlight, but it drove Matt nuts. Once he got into a bad sleep pattern, it took him weeks to get over it.

There was an air of celebration in town because it was the first time the market had been held since the beginning of the last lockdown. The flags were out. The streets were crowded with shoppers. People had heard the news of the grand reopening and had travelled from neighbouring districts to stock up with provisions at the market stalls. Here, the produce was fresh and abundant. And it was so much more enjoyable shopping in the open air, rather than queuing in the scruffy, cramped supermarkets in the hill towns, where stocks were limited and tired.

I'd collected my package of fabric and decided to have a browse in the market for some Italian specialities. At last, my Italian bank card had arrived in the post, so I was able to withdraw cash independently without relying on handouts from Matt. It was a long time since I'd been in among so many people at such close proximity and I found myself more interested in people-watching than looking at the stalls. Heads oscillated in a moving canvas of masks and face coverings. It was a pickpocket's paradise.

I liked the feeling of being anonymous in the crowd. However, gradually I began to notice other features that differentiated individuals when facial recognition was compromised – like the way people walk, their particular gait. I'd read somewhere that everyone has their own distinct way of walking, as unique as a fingerprint. Your voice gives you away too, I reflected – though not being a native Italian speaker, I was less attuned to the subtle differences of the language. Masked Italians sounded all the same to me – loud and excitable.

As for me, the instant I opened my mouth, I became identifiable. My faltering Italian and strong English accent drew attention, as I was about to see. I was by a market stall piled high with hand-made soaps in a vast array of colours and fragrances, struggling to communicate with the stallholder over my purchases, when I heard my name.

'I recognise that voice! Hello, Danielle. *Ciao.*'

I looked up and there was Sofia, her spoken English clipped and perfect. Immediately, she stepped in and translated for me. The assistant who had served me at the Casa di Tessuti earlier that morning had told me it was Sofia's day off.

I was surprised to bump into her here – so elegantly dressed, she seemed out of place in the crowd.

Today, Sofia beamed at me from behind a red silk mask. It seemed she had a different mask to complement each of her outfits. She was wearing a shift dress that showed off her curves and tiny waist. She'd compensated for her lips being hidden behind the mask by applying dusky eyeliners and winged eye shadow and black mascara. Her hair was almost black, gleaming and sleek in the sunshine like a racehorse groomed for competition.

Marcella had told us that as well as working in the fabric shop, Sofia was a talented seamstress who was building her reputation as a clothes designer. When the shop closed at the start of the pandemic, she'd set up her own business designing and making silk masks, which she sold online and exported all over the world.

'Is that one of your own designs?' I asked, pointing to her dress.

She nodded.

'And the mask?'

She nodded again.

'Come, come with me,' she said. 'I'd like to buy you lunch. It's such a beautiful day and today we must celebrate. Bars and restaurants are allowed to start serving food again at their tables as from today. Did you know?'

She led me to a dimly lit trattoria tucked away on the ramparts of the town, where she greeted the owner.

'Everything is half price today, eh, Marco.' She laughed, taking off her mask. Her lips were bright red. 'Today, we are going to... What is it you say in England? *Eat, drink and be merry...*'

Marco guided us through the gloom of the dining room

out onto the terrace and the blinding glare of the midday sun. He led us to a table in the dappled shade of an olive tree with a far-reaching view over the hills and brought over a bottle of Prosecco with three glasses.

'*Sulla casa* – on the house.' He smiled.

We clinked glasses with Marco.

'*Saluti* – greetings.'

I felt out of practice, reconnecting with community and social life, and strangely exposed as I removed my surgical mask. I'd almost forgotten how to smile.

Sofia's radiant smile faltered when she saw my whole face unmasked for the first time and she glanced quickly at Marco. They exchanged looks and their complicit body language signalled an understanding of something concerning me. It lasted only a fraction of a second and then the three of us were raising our glasses in celebration of the new freedoms. Now she couldn't take her eyes off me.

It felt good to be doing this with new acquaintances... and, much as I loved him, all the more liberating for being here without Matt. I wasn't sure if I'd end up being friends with this glamourous businesswoman, but it was nice striking out independently and socialising with someone outside my narrow world at the estate.

Sofia treated me to the half-price menu, though I didn't get a free lunch. I was still sipping my Prosecco, when she opened her shoulder bag and took out a selection of masks.

'This is your colour,' she said, picking out a small cellophane package containing four silk masks in a palette of greens and blues.

She held the masks up to my face and showed me my reflection in a make-up mirror.

'See how your eyes *pop*.'

Ten minutes of sales patter and compliments later, I handed over one hundred euros and became the grateful owner of the masks.

Once her deal was done, Sofia turned the conversation to me and Matt, firing questions without paying much attention to my answers.

'How are you and Teo liking your new life in Tuscany?' she asked.

It took me an instant to realise Sofia was referring to Matt and that he had a past life associated with his Italian identity that belonged to her and not to me.

'And how are the renovations going at the farmhouse?'

I told her things were going fine. She seemed to know more about the progress of the building work than I did, so I guessed she'd been talking to Marcella. Matt was right – everyone knew everyone else's affairs in town. After what he'd told me about Great-Uncle Benetto, it didn't surprise me that he chose to stay away.

'I'm so pleased to get the fabric for our bedroom windows,' I said. 'At least we can then have one room that feels like home.'

We ate pasta with home-made fresh basil pesto sauce and drank chilled white wine from the Val d'Orcia. Sofia's easy chatter gave me a headache after the long silences I'd become accustomed to up at the farmhouse. While she continued to ply me with wine, I gave in to her charms, let down my guard and hinted at how difficult it had been adjusting to a new way of life and how isolated I'd felt at times.

Sofia opened up, too. She talked about the frustrations of living at home with her elderly mother and father. Because her parents were 'vulnerable individuals', the whole family had been strictly shielding for many months. It was only since the Casa di Tessuti had reopened that she'd regained her liberty.

'It's wonderful to have some female company,' I said. 'And someone who speaks English so perfectly! I miss my girl-friends. Just that thing of being able to meet up for a quick drink after work or down at the gym. I hadn't realised how important it was to me until I left London.'

Sofia patted my hand. 'You have Marcella.'

We laughed.

'Marcella is lovely,' I said. 'She's helped me so much. But the language barrier makes it hard to communicate.'

As the bottle went down, Sofia grew bored of talking about our building work and steered the conversation to the past. She was effusive.

'I've known Teo since we were this high,' she volunteered, tapping the table top. 'Marcella looked after me at the farm-house when I was a little girl. She took me with her when she went to clean because my mother worked in the leather factory and couldn't afford to pay for a childminder in the holidays.

'Later, when I was a teenager, I helped Marcella with her cleaning job during the school holidays and Loretta gave me pocket money for my work. Teo came here every summer with his parents as a young boy, back to the *madrepatria* as we say, the *motherland*. Sometimes he'd stay on with his great-uncle and aunt after his mamma and papà went home – I think because the marriage was close to breakdown. His parents were always tearing each other apart and having him around just added to the tension.'

I could feel the wine going to my head as Sofia prattled on smoothly about the family connections, dropping names of relatives I'd never heard of and losing me in the thread of her explanations. She was a cousin of Antonio (second or third cousin – I didn't quite catch it – everyone seemed to be related here), who had been born and always lived at the estate.

'Antonio's father was Benetto's gamekeeper like his father before him,' Sofia explained. 'When Antonio's father died, he took over the role.'

A gamekeeper born and bred, I reflected. No wonder Antonio walked around as if he owned the place.

Sofia refilled our wine glasses while she took a breath, then she was off again.

'Teo and I were like cousins, too.' She took a sip of wine and smiled as if remembering. 'I was what you'd call a tomboy then. *Maschiaccio* – that's how we say it in Italian.' Her red lips pouted as she enunciated the word theatrically. 'We played hide-and-seek around the farm and in the woods. It was me who taught him how to set traps and to shoot. Sometimes we would sneak off for the day with an old hunting rifle. Benetto never bothered to lock his weapons away. It's a wonder neither of us got killed.'

Looking at Sofia sitting there immaculately put together and manicured and made-up, it was hard to imagine.

'Teo is two years older than me. So, of course, aged twelve, I found him so cool with his British clothes and CD collection and his cool English accent.' She laughed. 'That summer I had a crush on him.'

It was beginning to grate, hearing this woman referring to my partner by another name and describing their childhood escapades and intimacies.

'Then the summer visits stopped,' Sofia told me. 'Teo's father walked, or I should say drove, out of his life – literally. He forced mother and son out of the car during a family squabble and left them stranded at the side of a motorway before driving off into the sunset, never to be seen again.'

'Oh my God! That's awful.'

Matt had never mentioned the manner of his parents' break-up to me and I wondered if Sofia was exaggerating for dramatic effect.

'After Matteo's father abandoned them, Benetto offered financial support, even though his English mother refused to let him see his Italian family. She wanted nothing more to do with any of them... any of us, I should say,' Sofia corrected herself. 'We were all lumped together as *the Italian Mafia* in the mother's mind.' Sofia smiled sadly. 'Teo's mother became depressed and began drinking. She took opioids and died two years later from an overdose.' Sofia stabbed her plate, twirling spaghetti with extravagant expertise. 'After that, things went badly for him: a miserable time at boarding school, some drugs and petty crime. It was understandable – being a victim of such trauma as a teenage boy was bound to leave its mark.'

My lunch partner seemed to have forgotten that she was talking about Matt, my life partner. Then she remembered, threw back her head and gave a little puff on her cigarette.

'But you know all this,' she said. 'I must be boring you.'

In fact, Matt had revealed very little about his sad and troubled youth. He'd given me only the sketchiest details. By the time I met him, he was a successful commissioning editor lauded by all in the publishing world, with a reputation for scathing wit and arrogance in the knowledge that he could make or break a writer's career.

'No, no, please continue,' I said. 'What happened to Matt's father? He never talks about him. Did he ever come back?'

'As far as I know,' said Sofia, 'Matt never saw him again.

He disappeared – out of choice, they say – to escape his debts and his crimes and his family. Some say he ended up in Latin America. He's probably dead now.'

What a dysfunctional family! If Matt sometimes seemed damaged and difficult, I could now understand why.

'When Teo's mother died,' she said, 'Benetto stepped in again. He paid for Teo's university studies and invited him to work in the vineyard in the vacations. They had no grandchildren or children of their own... because of the tragedy, you know,' Sofia whispered conspiratorially. 'So they treated him like a long-lost son. How do you say it? The *"prodigal son"* – *figliol prodigo.'*

It was sad to think that Matteo's inheritance was based on the unhappy combination of degenerate parents and family tragedy. No wonder he'd struggled to come to terms with it.

'Benetto must have spent a fortune on Matt's education,' I remarked out loud. 'Oxford, then Harvard...'

Sofia rubbed her fingers together and nodded meaningfully at me. *What was she hinting at? Mafia money?* She ordered another bottle and filled up our glasses. I'd lost track of time.

'I hooked up with Matteo the summer he came back to Tuscany,' said Sofia. 'He was no longer the carefree and fun-loving kid I remembered. He'd become hard and closed. He hid his trauma well. He never spoke of the disappearance of his father, or the death of his mother, and he overcompensated by being funny and cruel and unstoppable. Always the live wire of the group, pushing things to the limit. Always up for one last dance or one last drink or one last line of cocaine before calling it a night. He was devastatingly attractive.'

Sofia drawled over the words like a Fifties movie star.

'Every teenage girl in town wanted to be his girl, but he

played it cool. His only male friend was my cousin Tonio – yes, the very same. The other boys resented him, but the three of us hung out together.' She hesitated. 'Teo and I'–she glanced in my direction–'we had a summer *fling*, I guess you'd say, though I don't think you could call it a romance. There was intimacy, of course. But we were never close emotionally. Something inside him was dead – perhaps because of his father and mother.'

This was more sharing than I was comfortable with and no doubt Sofia would have been more discreet had she been sober. Was Sofia the girlfriend Matt had spoken of? Somehow, I couldn't imagine them together. *The 'love of his life'? Surely not? She's not his type,* I thought. Nor could I identify her with the character of Nikki in Matt's fictionalised teenage love affair.

'Enough of Matteo,' said Sofia gaily, realising at last that she'd overstepped the mark. 'And Antonio? How are you all getting along?'

I looked down at my plate.

'To be honest, I can't make my mind up about him.'

Antonio worked hard and was always very willing to help us out with practical jobs on top of his farm management and gamekeeping duties, but his constant presence at the farmhouse still made me uneasy, particularly given what Matt had told me about the family's brush with the Mafia. There was a peculiar tension, something electric crackling in the air whenever he was around.

'He comes with the property.' Sofia shrugged.

'The old man must have been very fond of him,' I said. 'Even if we wanted him to leave, we couldn't ask him to go. He has the right to remain living on the estate until the end of his days. We're stuck with him...'

I stopped short, knowing I was treading on thin ice. Of course, Sofia must already know that Antonio had been granted a life interest to remain living in the gamekeeper's cottage under the terms of Benetto's will – but did she know why?

'Unless you kill him!' Sofia said ironically. Then she pushed her plate away and lit a cigarette.

'He seems a decent guy,' I said without conviction. 'Actually, he's teaching *me* how to shoot.'

Sofia raised her eyebrows and I could see that she was impressed.

I decided to probe her further with my confidences.

'I think it's because Antonio's a hunting man that he puts me on edge – that watchful instinct. I feel his eyes on me all the time. He stalks round the property with his hunting rifle popping up when I least expect him. He and Matt are thick as thieves, but they're always getting into fights. I don't know what to make of it.'

'Antonio is a good man,' she said. 'He wants to protect you. He sees it as his duty guarding the estate. Crime may be more hidden away than in the big cities, but it's here, too. Only the other day, a woman was attacked not far from where you live when she was out running. You must take care.' She pushed her plate away and took a sip of wine. 'Think of Antonio as your bodyguard – not your stalker,' she said lightly.

Just then, Marco came over to clear our plates and tempt us with dessert.

'You have to try the tiramisu,' Sofia insisted. 'Marco's tiramisu is the best in the world. Nothing like the creamy mess they serve up in London!'

Marco brought us two spoons and we tucked in greedily.

'I think Antonio likes you,' Sofia teased. 'Perhaps that's

why he's always following you around. Whenever I bump into him, he can't stop talking about you. You remind him of someone...' She gazed deep into my eyes.

Is she flirting with me? I wondered.

'He's right. Something in the eyes – I noticed the first time I met you.'

She reached out and touched my lips with the tips of her fingers and now I was sure she was flirting with me.

'And when you took your mask off... well, your smile, it took my breath away.'

Just when I thought I couldn't eat or drink another thing, Marco brought over goblets of Vin Santo dessert wine and almond *cantucci* biscuits for dipping. Eventually, it was closing time and we rose from the table, giggly and flushed like a pair of drunk schoolgirls.

Sofia insisted we take a tour round the ramparts so she could show me the views. She linked arms with me as we walked unsteadily over the cobbled paths.

On our way, we passed through a dark alleyway where the town's death notices were posted. It reminded me of Benetto's death announcement with the graffiti insult '*pedofilo*' scrawled across it which I'd seen in nearby Sangiari.

'Was Benetto a bad man?' I asked Sofia.

'I never speak ill of the dead,' she said with exaggerated seriousness.

We walked on in silence for a little while, then Sofia said pensively, 'We know so little about our loved ones... We spend our lives being suspicious of their movements and their texts and their parallel lives. We imagine their deceits and yet we carry on living with them, giving them the benefit of the doubt. Loretta never stopped loving him.'

Glancing, at her left hand resting on my arm, I noticed for

the first time that Sofia was wearing a wedding band and yet she hadn't mentioned her husband once. Perhaps she was speaking from experience.

'You know the woman who stays with a man she suspects of committing a crime or having an affair... Why? Why does she stay? Is it because she accepts there's violence and betrayal in the world and there's nothing she can do to change it? Is it because she believes all the bad stuff is a fiction going on inside her head? Or is it because she chooses to give the man she still loves despite everything the benefit of the doubt – because everyone is innocent until proven guilty.'

'Yes... but Benetto...' I pressed, hoping to get something more out of her.

'Let's just say Benetto liked the company of young people. Maybe he had his weaknesses and maybe he kept bad company...'

We reached the viewpoint set on an escarpment at the highest point in town and stood by the stone wall to take in the spectacular view of the setting sun and the vertiginous drop below.

'There were always lots of young people up at the *fattoria*,' she said. 'Every summer, Benetto let them come to help with seasonal jobs. He liked having young kids around. It was like a hippy commune up there. They ran feral. He paid them a few euros a week – nothing like a real wage – but in exchange the kids got food and lodgings and freedom from their parents. And the drugs... And he got... well, certain benefits. She shrugged again in that peculiarly Italian way.

'We had parties every night – God they were craaazy. Then one day *she* turned up and suddenly *she* was all Teo had time for. He was smitten.

'She was wild – a firecracker – and she was beautiful. We were all a little in love with her – even the old man.

'Matteo dropped me like a stone, of course. I was cancelled, before that was even a thing.' She gave a rueful smile. 'He ignored all of my messages. If our paths crossed at the *fattoria*, he looked right through me. I lost him.'

'I have no idea who you're talking about,' I said impatiently. '*She?*'

'Teo never could drive by...' Sofia spoke softly, into the void. 'After what his father had done, he couldn't leave someone standing by the side of the road. He picked her up on the Siena highway... You must know who I mean, surely? *L'autostoppista*. The hitchhiker.'

Sofia turned. I felt her eyes on me, staring at my profile, lit by the setting sun.

Then, casually, as if it were an afterthought, she added, 'You look so much like her, you know.' And almost under her breath, she murmured, 'It's like seeing a ghost.'

'Stop! Why are you telling me this?' I interrupted, close to panic. 'It's all in the past.'

Sofia touched my hand. 'The past can come back to haunt you.'

THIRTY-SEVEN
THE HITCHHIKER
BY MATTEO J. ROSSI

Most nights Ted creeps out around midnight to share Nikki's lumpy single mattress in the corrugated shack where she's set up home. A few days have turned into a few weeks and Ted's grandma has grown fond of mother and child. There's no more talk of moving her on. But in an old Catholic family, *lo scandalo* – scandal – must be avoided at all costs and Ted is under strict instructions not to entertain Nikki in his bedroom. *La nonna* – the grandmother – is blissfully unaware of what goes down there at Nikki's after dark, or up at the pool, in the moonlight.

Nikki's *baraca* – shack – is far too close to Luca's for Ted's liking. It's distrust, as well as lust, that keeps him awake, staring up at the ceiling beams, and drives him from his comfortable oak bedstead in the main house night after night. When he wakes in Nikki's bed one weekday morning, she's nowhere to be seen. Once again, Ted is left holding the baby – literally.

'That stupid, irresponsible girl will make me late for work,' he mutters to himself.

Ted's taken on so many caring duties for Harry that he's beginning to feel like a surrogate dad. The little boy is unpredictable – one minute a mischievous bundle of joy, the next a headstrong monster screaming his head off. Sometimes Ted wonders if there's something wrong with him. He doesn't know much about kids. But Harry must be almost two years old and still not talking. Not one word. That can't be normal, surely?

Nikki gets angry whenever he makes any comment. She's not a good mother – which may explain the boy's difficulties. She spends part of each day off her head on alcohol or cocaine. She blames the boy's father.

'The poor kid was traumatised by his dad, violent and abusive. Can't have been much fun for Harry, watching that bastard beating me up. That's why I had to get away. It's not surprising he doesn't talk.'

It lifts Ted's spirits to hear Harry squealing with delight when he slings him up to his shoulders or tickles him on the ground. But this morning he hasn't got the patience for the little boy's whining demands.

'She's his bloody mother. This is her job.'

Ted can't bear to think where Nikki could be, but he can't go looking anyway, because Harry is yelling for his breakfast and has just peed on the floor. One spilt Ribena and two spattered *Weetabix* later, Nikki saunters into the cottage, skirting past the kitchen table and into the shower without a word of explanation or thanks.

'Negligent bitch,' says Ted, but without any real conviction.

His fondness for Harry is inseparable from his passion for Nikki – fiercely possessive of her and fiercely protective of her boy. Nikki – the love of his life – as careless with his feelings as she is careless with her child. Carelessness is her defining characteristic, part of her sex appeal. Sometimes (when she goes too far) it makes him want to kill her.

* * *

When Nikki comes out of the shower, Ted confronts her. It's something of a giveaway that she walked in wearing Luca's oversized flip-flops and slopping black coffee from one of his cracked old pottery mugs onto the tiles.

'I was with Luca,' she says defiantly. 'You don't own me. But it's not what you think.'

There are red marks in the hollow of her neck.

'We're planning something for Saturday. I'll tell you about it this evening. A new set-up... High-risk but brilliant.'

THIRTY-EIGHT
DANIELLE

'Where have you been? I was worried sick about you.'

Matt's first words when I got back from Montepulciano after my long and boozy lunch with Sofia came as no surprise. I'd already seen the ashtray full of cigarette butts left on the front step. He'd been sitting outside watching and waiting for my return.

I looked at my phone – five messages and seven missed calls. I hadn't thought to check it once.

'Sorry, my phone was on silent,' I said.

The fact I'd been out enjoying myself while he'd been stuck in his study working was frustrating enough, but the thing that really annoyed Matt was that I'd drunk so much that I'd had to leave the car in town and order a taxi to get home. He kept going on about the waste of money and announced that he had 'an important business meeting' in Florence the next day and needed the car urgently.

'Don't worry. I'll ask Marcella to drive me to Montepulciano first thing in the morning to collect the car,' I said, tossing the car key onto the kitchen table.

'If it's still there,' grumbled Matt. 'You'll probably find it's been stolen or towed.'

'Your old girlfriend got me drunk. Blame her,' I slurred, collapsing into a chair. 'That woman can really drink.'

Matt's jaw tightened. 'Who the hell are you talking about?' he said.

'Sofia. Remember her? Second cousin of Antonio or something.'

'I remember,' says Matt. '*Girlfriend?* No way! I hung out with her one summer and then I couldn't shake her loose. She was a nightmare.'

'That's not the way she tells it,' I said.

'Haven't you got anything better to do than gossip about me with that silly stuck-up bitch?' said Matt.

I brushed past him, holding the new fabric for our bedroom curtains.

'You never tell me anything, Matt. Perhaps if you were more open about your past, I wouldn't have to hear it second-hand from other people.'

* * *

Later that evening, I settled in the kitchen with a mug of tea, some biscuits and Matt's manuscript, which I was now more curious than ever to continue reading. Having listened to Sofia, I wondered whether Matteo's teenage lover was the model or at least the inspiration for the character of Nikki, the hitchhiker, in his novel. I'd been disappointed to find that the later chapters of the manuscript seemed to be missing.

'I'm still working on the ending,' he'd said.

'Why all the secrecy?' I'd asked only last night.

I knew the novel was unfinished. He was still trying to resolve various scenarios and plot twists in his head.

'Sometimes it helps to try out your ideas on other people.'

'And sometimes, it only makes you more confused,' he'd replied crossly.

I heard scuffling outside the window. Probably a rodent or a bird. I looked out into the dense black and then pulled across the threadbare curtains. I was spooked by the thought that Antonio might be out there with his rifle doing his rounds of the estate and watching me.

As it happened, I didn't need to trouble Marcella for a lift because it was in fact Antonio who had made the noise, appearing at our front door with Matt's bike. He'd ordered the spare parts and replaced the buckled wheel and the broken chain, cleaned off the mud and oiled it. It looked as good as new. This cheered Matt up no end. He clapped Antonio on the shoulders and fetched a padded brown envelope from his study, which I imagined contained a generous cash payment for the repair.

'Ah! excellent,' said Matt. 'I feel the need for some exercise. I'll cycle to pick up the car right away. It's a long way but it's all downhill.' He grabbed the key on the way out. 'I can throw the bike in the back for the drive home.'

I followed Matt onto the driveway.

'Take care. It's pitch-black out here. At least wear your helmet,' I shouted after him as he pedalled away.

Then, I remembered Matt didn't have a helmet he could use anymore. The hit-and-run driver who knocked Matt off his bike and into the ditch had crushed it under the wheels of his car.

Antonio was still hovering in the shadows as if there were something he wanted to say to me. After Sofia's disclosures, his presence made me feel more self-conscious than usual, especially as we were alone. I had a searing headache from excessive alcohol and coffee consumed over lunch and was desperate to be alone. I was about to close the door, when it occurred to me that now, while Matt was away from the house, would be a good opportunity to return the clothes Antonio had lent me. I motioned for him to come in and sit at the table.

'The police found the driver of the hit-and-run,' said Antonio quietly. 'They're investigating... One of the guys at the station is my friend. He tipped me off. They want to speak to Matteo.'

'That's a good thing, isn't it?' I said uncertainly. With a growing fear in the pit of my stomach, I got the story out of him. The police had found some orange-coloured plastic fragments with the badge *Specialized*. Not many Italian cyclists used that brand. Antonio looked deep into my eyes. His tone was grave.

'Please can you pass on the message?'

'Of course,' I said, confused by his serious tone.

'Wait here,' I said. 'I've got something for you. I'll only be a few minutes.'

I grabbed a screwdriver from the toolkit under the sink and ran up the stairs. I'd never got round to extracting from behind the bath panel the clothes I'd borrowed from Antonio that winter's day when he'd rescued me from the storm and taken me back to his cottage. The T-shirt and trackpants had been damp when I hid them. They were probably now rotting away. I'd intended to wash and return the clothes to Antonio some day when Matt was away from the farm. The task had been forgotten among all the other chores.

I prised the panel away with the screwdriver and pulled

out the fusty, mildewed pile. I stuffed Antonio's T-shirt straight into an old plastic bag – it was only good for the dump now. Then I spread the grey jogging pants out on the bathroom floor. I looked at the label inside the waistband: Top Shop UK, size 8, petite. That was a brand I knew well – my go-to store for shopping on Oxford Street when I was a teenager. A name had been scrawled in black marker pen on the white tape inside the waistband – faded but still visible: *N. Farrell.*

I sat back on my heels and breathed deeply.

N. Farrell... could that be Nikki Farrell? I wondered.

* * *

'Who did these belong to?' I said, holding out the jogging pants when I got back to the kitchen.

Antonio looked taken aback by my brusque tone.

He shook his head. 'I can't tell you... I mean, I don't know. One of the girls who worked here in the summer. They came and went. I had many girlfriends.' He made of light of it. 'English girls like Italian boys. And they have reputation for being... I think you say *"easy"* – unlike good Catholic Italian girls with their fierce Italian mammas.'

I wasn't going to be fobbed off that easily. I pointed to the black letters.

'Did these belong to a girl called Nikki?'

Antonio stood up to leave.

'I'm sorry, Danielle. It was a long time ago. What does it matter now?'

I gave up. I handed Antonio the plastic bag containing his rotting T-shirt. It was my turn to apologise.

'I'm sorry. I forgot.'

'Ah! my favourite,' he teased. He stuffed the jogging pants into the bag with his old Harley Davidson T-shirt. 'These are fit only for the bonfire!'

'You still have my clothes,' I blurted out.

'Ah, yes,' said Antonio, half smiling. 'And now I must go.'

I stood in the doorway watching him walk away.

Antonio turned. 'Shall we do another shooting practice Saturday?'

I nodded.

'Come to my place at ten. Then you can get your clothes.'

I closed the door.

I could feel my cheeks burning.

'He must think I'm such a fool!'

I was making myself a cup of tea, when there was a soft knock at the door. Antonio was back. Unexpectedly, he leaned forwards to kiss me. I angled my head, anticipating a peck on each cheek Italian style, but instead his lips brushed against mine, first very gently, then with more assurance, until we kissed deeply. Then he turned abruptly and walked away without looking back before I had the chance to say another word.

I stood with my back to the front door, my fingers pressed against my lips, blood pumping in my ears, trying to process what had just happened and unsure whether I felt outraged or elated – my emotions were in such turmoil.

I forced myself to be calm. What just happened was an aberration and not to be repeated. Undeniably, there was a chemistry. Until now, I'd misinterpreted the tension that fizzed between us. But relations between the three of us living in such proximity on the estate were already too complicated and fraught. Life would be unbearable unless I trampled this spark. I forced Antonio and the kiss out of mind.

* * *

The next morning, Matt told me his 'business' in Florence.

'I'm going to see Great-Aunt Loretta,' he said.

I'd almost forgotten that she was still alive, as Matt rarely mentioned her. Immediately I felt guilty. Here we were living in among the remains of her life and yet so unconnected with her, as if she'd already departed this Earth. Unceremoniously we'd rifled through her things, ripped out her decorations and her furnishings, dismantling her past.

I pleaded with Matt to take me along.

'I'd love to meet her,' I said. 'It seems only right I should get to know her since we're living here in her house. And I've never been to Florence. We could have lunch together in the city and look around in the afternoon.'

'She's away with the fairies,' he said. 'Advanced dementia. It'll only confuse her if you're with me. And she doesn't speak a word of English. No offence, but your Italian is so bad that you won't understand a word of the conversation.'

I was disappointed. Once again, he was freezing me out of his past.

'Stop sulking, Danielle,' he concluded. 'It's not a social call. I need the old lady to sign some papers to do with the farmhouse and my inheritance.'

With Matt out of the house for a few hours, I decided it would be a good day for Marcella to clean Matt's study, which hadn't been touched for weeks. Matt had left it locked, as was his norm when he went out, but as I expected, Marcella knew where all the spare keys to the rooms in the house were kept.

Over the weeks we'd begun to bond and though our conversation was very limited, there was an understanding between us. When I tried the door and it didn't shift, she tapped my arm and winked at me over her mask. In the brick-work behind the stove, she dislodged a loose brick and took out a dented tin box (no doubt a present from one of the English relatives, since it had *Betty's All-Butter Shortbread* printed on the side) from the cavity behind.

I wondered idly what else was squirreled away in the recesses of the house. A rambling old house like this held many hiding places.

Marcella rummaged around in the tin until she found the key ring she was looking for, holding a few rusty old keys. She carried in the cleaning bucket and mops and I followed behind. The wastepaper baskets were full of Matt's screwed-up sheets, the windows were streaked and there was dust everywhere. While Marcella mopped and polished, I stood over Matt's desk putting his papers together. I tried the draw-ers, looking for a hole punch. They all opened save for one that was locked. I took the key ring and tried the smallest key, which fitted the lock.

Unlike the other drawers filled with a random assortment of 'stuff', this drawer contained only an old shoebox, on which Matt had written the words: Writing Resources and Materi-als. The shoebox was full of newspaper cuttings – yellowed with age – dating from about seven years previously. It also contained the parts of the corkscrew, bloodied and broken, that Matt had snapped on our first evening in Italy.

I looked again at the markings carved into the olive wood – a heart shape with the initials N and T. Beyond repair, *Teo* must have kept it for sentimental reasons.

When I turned to the press articles and looked more closely, I began to suspect that these news stories weren't simply a starting point or inspiration for Matt's fiction but something of personal significance. They were cuttings from the regional press, mostly from one of the Tuscan dailies, the *Gazzetta di Firenze* – the local paper read by his great-uncle.

I wondered if these cuttings had belonged originally to Benetto. Matt could have come across them when clearing out the study. I'd seen stacks of old copies of the *Gazzetta* down in the cellar, some of them chewed up by rats who had used the shreddings to build a nest in the abandoned guitar. In fact, I was intending to take the newspapers to be recycled as soon as the facilities reopened.

All the cuttings in the old box related to the same incident. Whoever had collected them seemed to have an obsessive interest in this one murder crime. I struggled to understand the headlines, but the faded pictures told the story: a young attractive girl, little more than a teenager, tanned, hippy top, ripped denim shorts, beach waves in her hair, standing at the side of a white road, half turned to the camera, with a big smile and her arm stretched out to thumb a lift. That same picture was reproduced in many of the cuttings.

I recognised the word '*autostoppista*' that Sofia had used the day before to describe Matt's girlfriend. Was this the hitchhiker news story that had inspired Matt's novel? The article had the title '*La Scomparsa dell'Autostoppista*'. The words '*la scomparsa*' were repeated several times in the body of the text.

I pored over the article, trying to decipher its meaning, and while I did so, I became conscious that the rhythmic sound of Marcella's mop had stopped. She was looking over my shoulder, her mop poised over the bucket and her eyes fixed on the photograph in the news story. She glanced at me anxiously and then without a word, she went on quietly with her mopping. I went out to the kitchen to get my phone and typed the words into Google translate.

First:

La Scomparsa. English translation: *Disappearance*.

And then:

La Scomparsa dell'autostoppista. English translation: *Disappearance of the* hitchhiker.

* * *

I took the dusty shoebox upstairs to our bedroom, away from Marcella's watchful gaze. Painfully, I worked through the translation of the top article, typing the phrases into my phone and noting down the translation on a sheet of Matt's computer paper:

> *The discovery of a body has been reported in the Province of Brindisi. Following a tip-off, local police yesterday recovered the decomposed body of a young woman showing signs of violence, partially buried near to a railway on the outskirts of the city. The body was first discovered by railway workers, who raised the alert when it was exposed in the railway escarpment after a landslip. A source close to the investigation said that the cause of death remains to be determined, but the victim appears to have suffered multiple blows to the head and injuries to her torso. A sexual motive for the death hasn't been ruled out.*
>
> *Theories and speculation abound concerning the identity of the victim. One rumour is that the body may be that of missing Irish hitchhiker, Nicola Flanagan (inset photograph), who disappeared over three years ago.*
>
> *Flanagan went missing while hitchhiking through Italy*

from Tuscany to the port of Brindisi, Puglia, where it was thought she may have been intending to take a ferry to Greece – ferries leave regularly from Brindisi for Mainland Greece, as well as Corfu, Kefalonia and Croatia. The hitch-hiker was last seen caught on CCTV footage on 29 August 2011 at a motorway service station near Orvieto, where she took a lift with a truck driver. She was reported missing five weeks later by her estranged partner in London.

Though police haven't confirmed this, there's also been speculation that the case may be a 'copycat killing' motivated by the 'Beast of Siena' serial murders that took place at the end of the last century and have never been fully solved. Detectives have said that the details are too disturbing to make public but that certain barbaric methods and ritualistic 'markings' on the body used by the killer or killers of the Brindisi victim bear resemblance to those used in the Beast of Siena attacks.

It's hoped that this inquiry may resolve the case of the Irish hitchhiker's mysterious disappearance and may also shed new light on the many unanswered questions in the long-running 'Beast of Siena' investigations.

There was a long postscript:

Beast of Siena killings: Over a period of more than twenty years, ten couples were killed in the Tuscan countryside around Siena. The women were mutilated. Most of the victims had been attacked in their cars while making love parked up at local beauty spots. Under pressure, the police eventually charged Pietro Patriani, a Tuscan pig farmer with a record for murder and rape and with family connections to the Calabrian Mafia.

Other suspects were arrested and charged, only to be released when the evidence against them wasn't robust enough to sustain their convictions. Despite his denials, Patriani got multiple life sentences – only then to be freed on appeal. Patriani died suddenly four years ago, before the retrial that had been ordered, taking his secrets to the grave. Others are still serving lengthy jail sentences for their part in the serial murders.

The boss of Tuscany's murder squad, Inspector Giuliano Giacone, believes that behind Patriani was a mastermind: 'Maybe an individual, or a group linked to the Mafia or even a satanic cult.'

He's written a best-selling thriller, drawing on his investigations.

I slid my handwritten notes under the mattress and took the shoebox back to the study. It had taken me almost an hour to translate the article with the help of the Italian translation app on my phone – long enough for Marcella to polish the woodwork and the windows and scrub the stone floor. I noticed her eyeing me quizzically as I entered, but she said nothing.

I indicated that she should go upstairs to clean and once she was out of the room, I quickly photographed all the remaining articles. Then I locked the shoebox away where I'd found it before returning the key to the tin and the tin to the cavity in the wall.

Looking back, I don't know why I didn't ask Marcella more directly about the news story – she could so easily have confirmed whether or not the pretty, smiling face in the newspaper photograph was that of Matt's former girlfriend or that of a stranger. There was the language barrier, of course. And the fact that I wasn't sure if I was right in sensing an unspoken complicity between us. Her concerned looks could just as well have been because she thought I was behaving badly, intruding on the family's private papers.

On reflection, I think there was another reason why I didn't seek reassurance from Marcella. The mere act of revealing my anxieties to someone else would take them from the realm of fantasy into something that could conceivably be real and true. From fiction to fact, literally! Until now, my fears were as insubstantial as a bad dream. But if I were to voice them, they would take shape and solidify.

I put on my trainers and took myself off for a walk.

The *fattoria* had too many ghosts. I needed to get away and breathe the fresh air. Outside, the sky was cloudless blue, the fields a vibrant green, and the hot yellow sun beat down relentlessly. The cicadas were singing. It was impossible to feel melancholic. Out here, all of my imaginings seemed absurd.

Just think things through calmly and rationally, I told myself, getting into my legal mindset. *You're finding causes and drawing conclusions on the flimsiest of possible coincidences. The reference to the 'Beast of Siena' in the newspaper article isn't a sinister coincidence but most likely what drew Matt's interest to these cases in the first place,* I reasoned. *He probably came across the newspaper article and then ordered the book as part of his research for his novel.*

When translating the press cutting, I'd noticed that the chief investigator himself had written a best-selling thriller based on the Beast of Siena murders. I mused on the symbiotic relationship between crime in the real world and fictional representations of it. On the one hand, there was chief investigator Giacone using his lived experience of the murders to inspire creative fiction. Then there was Matt using a true crime book about the same murders to invest real-life authenticity into his novel. There was a certain irony in that.

Preoccupied with my thoughts, I followed the path to the swimming pool and surveyed the site – still a muddle of diggers, and holes and mounds of earth and debris. *Nicola Flanagan*, the name of the missing person referred to in the article, had caught my attention like a flashing neon sign. But on reflection, there were no grounds to imagine this was a sinister coincidence, either. On the contrary, it was probably because Matt had seen and registered the name Nicola that he'd come up with the name Nikki for his fictional character. It was all perfectly normal.

I decided it was time to get a grip. I'd allowed myself to become overwhelmed by paranoia. Like so many, my mental health had been affected by the lockdowns and the sense of dislocation exacerbated by our move to Italy. Generalised anxiety was clouding my judgement and affecting my whole being. I needed a reset. It was time to stamp out my morbid fantasies and to rebuild some trust and romance in our relationship... And to put a stop to this silly flirtation with Antonio.

THIRTY-NINE

THE HITCHHIKER

BY MATTEO J. ROSSI

Nikki is silent and morose. Ted wonders what he's done to offend her. As far as he knows, he's done nothing wrong – quite the reverse. He does everything he can to keep her happy. And maybe that's where he's going wrong. His devotion gets on her nerves. She despises the fact that she's the centre of his universe – makes her feel trapped, she says. She admitted to him once that she likes a man who treats her rough. 'And I'm not just talking about the sex,' she said. Well, it sounds as if she got what she deserved with Harry's dad. Careful what you wish for...

Goodbye, Mr Nice Guy!

Nikki's simmering resentment reaches boiling point later that week. Ted has been 'particularly clingy and needy' all evening, she says. He's in a sulk because she and Luca bunked off work at the *fattoria* that afternoon. He watched them driving off in Luca's car, top down, Nikki throwing back her hair and screeching like a hyena as they 'broke out' of the estate. They were 'doing a recce', as Nikki put it, for the planned weekend activities.

'I wish you could come, too,' she'd said. 'But I really need you to look after Harry. Promise I'll make it up to you.'

Once Harry's in bed, Ted hopes Nikki will 'make it up to him' as she promised and suggests they get an early night. Nikki has other ideas. She rejects the notion of 'sex on demand'. She grabs her bikini and a towel and flounces off up to the pool.

'It's such a beautiful night. I can't go to sleep.' She dismisses him curtly. 'Sweet dreams! See you in the morning.'

Ted lies on the narrow mattress listening to the sound of splashing and laughter coming from the pool. He's been labouring all day then dealing with Harry and he really would like an early night. But not without Nikki. He's not going to lie here – babysitting – listening to Nikki cheating and making a fool out of him.

He pulls on a pair of jeans and the baggy T-shirt Nikki sleeps in that lies dumped on the floor next to the bed. He goes into Harry's room. All is quiet. Then he makes his way up to the pool. As the pool comes into view, he sees Luca – Luca who is taller and stronger and more tanned than Ted – grab Nikki and swing her effortlessly up into his arms across his body. She clings to his neck and shrieks with delight as he races for the edge to take a running leap into the deep black water.

When they surface, laughing, and flicking hair and flighting in each other's arms, Ted stands above their heads looking down. Nikki's bikini top has come loose in the water and Luca swings it triumphantly above his head.

In his left hand, Ted holds a rock. First Luca, then Nikki, look up to meet his eyes. Instantly, the laughter stops. They tread water silently.

'Ted,' says Nikki very softly. 'Ted, are you OK?'

FORTY
DANIELLE

I was in for a surprise when I got back to the farmhouse one afternoon in late June. I'd been preoccupied with freelance work for my law firm the past few weeks and any free time had been spent with setting up my art and photography studio in one of the outhouses adjacent to the main courtyard. Marcella and Antonio had helped with the clearing and decoration of the outbuilding, and we'd passed many companionable hours, scrubbing and sanding and plastering and painting.

I now had a wonderful light-filled space for my artwork and a walk-in ventilated cupboard with black-painted walls for my darkroom. I could lose myself in there for days at a time. Antonio and I both acted as if 'the kiss' had never happened, treating each other with exaggerated politeness and respect. I put it down to him being Italian. Hot-blooded, macho, competitive and impulsive. He'd wanted to prove something to himself.

That sunny day in June, I'd been painting in the cool of the art studio since breakfast. It was only when I began to feel hungry and realised that I'd forgotten to break for lunch that I ventured out into the glaring sunshine and headed towards the farmhouse in search of a drink and some fresh fruit. The Land Rover was on the forecourt and there were women's voices coming from the kitchen, speaking in Italian. When I put my head round the door, I saw a little old lady sitting at the table. Marcella was fussing over her, pouring out black coffee and serving up *dolci* while Matt looked on, stony-faced, from the corner of the room.

Matt glanced over at me, nodded and gave me a long-suffering smile. The two women were deep in conversation and chattered on, unaware of my arrival. The old lady was tiny, hunched over her coffee like a little black bird – she was dressed all in black with wiry grey hair, pulled back in a tight bun. She had bright beady eyes and a kind face, which contrasted with the severity of her clothing and hairdo. I supposed this must be Great-Aunt '*Zietta*' Loretta. I stood still and let the women talk, not wanting to interrupt.

Soon, Marcella sensed my presence. She was about to introduce me, when Loretta jumped out of her chair, sprightly as a young girl, and came over to grasp my hands. She beamed at me with a gappy smile. There were tears in her eyes.

I shut my eyes and let her kiss me on both cheeks. It was the first time a stranger had embraced me since the start of the pandemic and I was touched by the old lady's warmth.

'*Nicoletta, cara mia...*' she said – my darling. '*Ciao, bella Nicoletta.*' – hi, beautiful.

* * *

I felt bad for not having invited Loretta to the farmhouse sooner. She should not have been a stranger to me at all. She was the only close family relative of Matt's that I might have the opportunity to get to know. For Matt, the social distancing rules had been a convenient excuse to avoid having her to stay. Because of her age and mental weakness, Loretta was a 'vulnerable' person. Legally, however, she was part of our household, with a life interest to reside at the property, so she'd have been able to come and shield with us. Matt had chosen to keep her at arm's length. In his eyes, she was a nuisance and an unwanted encumbrance.

Having met this sweet old lady, I knew the real reason why Matt didn't want me to have any contact with her. She was confused and her mind was trapped in a time warp. Although I pretended not to have noticed, it was obvious to me that her reference to Nicoletta was a case of mistaken identity – my presence (or perhaps, more specifically, my appearance) had conjured up a phantom still very much alive in her imagination. Not wanting to cause a scene while she was visiting, I didn't confront Matt directly about this.

Instead, I said vaguely, 'Your great-aunt seems to be mixing me up with someone from your past.'

'I'm sorry, darling,' Matt countered, also skirting round the unspoken question. 'She won't be here long.'

He guided me out to the terrace for a private talk while Loretta and Marcella chatted in the kitchen.

'Now you can see why I didn't want you to come with me to Florence the other day.'

Matt was chain-smoking again, so I knew he was tense.

'And why I didn't want her to come and live with us. She's just a crazy old woman.'

'Don't be silly,' I said. 'She's family and this is still her home. She's welcome to stay as often and for as long as she likes.'

Matt stubbed out his cigarette and took my hand.

'You're too nice. She's confused about everything,' he said. 'Thank God she's not living here.'

From our spot on the shady terrace, we watched Marcella showing Loretta the new flower beds and the vegetable garden. Loretta held Marcella's arm tightly as she leant to pick and smell the fragrances in among the herbs and flowers. Meanwhile, Matt updated me on his visit to Florence that morning. He told me his 'business' couldn't have gone better.

'At first, she was stubborn,' he said, 'but in the end she signed all the documents I put in front of her – though only when I bribed her with the promise that once the paperwork was done, I'd bring her back to the farmhouse.'

Under this emotional pressure, Matt had required Loretta to sign a power of attorney in his favour and other documents giving him the right to remortgage the farmhouse and deal with all estate assets at his sole discretion.

Matt was very pleased with himself.

'Poor woman thought I was bringing her home for good this very day. I didn't lie to her, mind you.' He laughed. 'I told her she was coming home today and, you see, I kept my word. She's here now – for tea.'

'You're so heartless,' I scolded. 'I can't believe you could be so cruel as to manipulate a poor old lady with dementia.' That wasn't true, of course – I knew that Matt could be very unkind when he chose to be. 'Don't keep her away on my account. I'd be perfectly happy for Loretta to come back and live here.'

It wasn't long before Loretta tired of the bright sunshine and came over to where we were sitting on the terrace. Her mood had changed. She was restless and distracted.

Marcella offered to take her up to the bathroom, but

Loretta protested and clung to my arm, dragging me to my feet with surprising strength and tenacity.

'I'll go,' I said, smiling at Loretta and taking her hand.

She had no need of my support climbing the stairs and she hurried ahead, every creak and twist in the treads familiar to her. I marvelled to see that though so confused about people, the old lady's sense of place remained strong, anchored by muscle memories ingrained in her subconscious.

At the top of the stairs, Loretta turned very deliberately, not right, to the bathroom, but left, to the locked door at the end of the landing. My heart sank. She yanked the handle up and down several times trying to get in. Finding it locked, she began to panic.

A week or so earlier, Matt had told me that the key was lost. When I suggested breaking down the door, he'd made a sick joke, saying his uncle's coffin was locked in the room. Then he'd told me it was just an old cupboard full of junk and to stop fretting about it. I'd stopped taking him at his word. It didn't look like a cupboard door. It looked like all the other bedroom doors in the farmhouse and from the outside of the building, you could see its window shutters, permanently closed. I always sensed an uncanny chill when passing by the door and unconsciously looked the other way when reaching the top of the stairs. But I had wanted to confront my fears. A potent lingering memory had drawn Loretta instinctively to the door and now I wanted to see for myself what was inside.

Loretta was becoming more and more agitated. I tried without success to divert her to the bathroom, but she wouldn't move.

'Just a minute, please,' I said. '*Solo un minuto per favore. Ma torno presto...* I'll be back soon.'

I had no idea if my crude phrasebook Italian was making

any sense. I left Loretta by the door and raced down the stairs. I wasn't sure if I believed what Matt had told me about the key being lost. Soon, I was back in the kitchen reaching for the loose brick and the tin key box hidden behind it in the cavity wall. I tipped the keys out onto the table and spread the pile. Most of them were blackened and old-fashioned in design. I collected a handful that I thought might fit the lock and went back upstairs.

I found the right key easily enough. It turned stiffly in the lock. You could feel that the room had lain empty for years – a thickness in the air that made it hard to breathe. It smelt musty with a hint of lavender. The setting sun coming through the slats patterned the space with bright lines and shadows.

It took a while for my eyes to make out the furniture. Every surface was coated with dust and there was a scattering of dead flies on the windowsill. A large, old-fashioned wooden crib took up most of the space in the small room. There was also a narrow table and a wicker rocking chair. The effect was like one of those sinister *Hand that Rocks the Cradle* movies. The crib was still made up and a traditional *Steiff*-design teddy bear with mohair fur lay at the foot of the mattress.

Loretta picked up the teddy bear and hugged it to her face. It was in almost pristine condition and must have been worth a fortune. I stroked my hand over the patterned woollen blanket, which I imagined had been lovingly crocheted by Loretta. A crucifix was nailed to the wall above. A pall of sadness hung over the cot. We stood side by side, our hands touching on the carved side rail. There was no need for words. Tears ran down Loretta's face as she sobbed silently.

Places where terrible things have happened often become defined by those events. They're seen as blighted somehow or unholy. I knew of the tragedy that had befallen Loretta's infant son, Lorenzo. It haunted my dreams. And I didn't want our new home to be defined by whatever sense of horror and pain might linger here. I wanted our renovations to breathe new life into the property and drive out the sadness. In our interior designs, I insisted on white walls and bright colours for the furnishings. Our home should be like a summer's day – filled with fresh breezes and billowing curtains and light. That afternoon, standing in the dead infant's room, I felt all of my efforts being overwhelmed by the ghosts of times past, escaping from behind closed doors and inside locked drawers, to cast their shades over the whole property.

* * *

Later that evening, Loretta left in great distress – supported by Marcella and almost frog-marched out of the door by Matt. She clutched the teddy bear that I'd pushed into her hands.

'Couldn't she stay the night?' I pleaded. 'It would be kinder for her to leave in the morning. She's tired and emotional now.'

But Matt was firm. Her carer would be waiting for her in Florence. All of her medications were there; she needed 24-hour support. We'd arrange another visit in a week or so and maybe invite her carer to come along too, to make things easier to manage. I couldn't argue with that.

But still, saying goodbye was upsetting as Loretta clearly didn't want to leave her old home and couldn't understand what was going on. For the second time that evening, I had to watch her cry.

* * *

As soon as I heard the Land Rover accelerating away up the hill, I collapsed onto a chair, emotionally exhausted by Loretta's visit. I held my head in my hands. If I'd learnt anything this afternoon, it was that I couldn't take Matt at his word. Matt had lied (there was no other word for it) about the hidden nursery behind the locked door. Perhaps he'd lied with my best interests at heart, not wanting to upset me, but it made me doubt whether or not I could trust him about anything else – in particular, his story about the trunk.

I was driven by a kind of madness to get to the bottom of the mystery that was poisoning my relationship with Matt. This was no time for self-indulgence. I stood up and made myself a strong coffee. I knew that the round trip to Loretta's apartment on the outskirts of Florence would give me about three uninterrupted hours. I intended to make use of them.

I went back to the loose brick in the wall and this time I took all the keys with me, stuffing the tin box into my leather art satchel in which I usually carried my paints and brushes, along with wire cutters, a screwdriver and hammer for good measure. Finally, I grabbed a torch as it was getting dark.

I ran up the path leading past the swimming pool and over to the far side of the estate. The area around the pool was now a full-scale building site, as the excavation of the old patio had been completed by Antonio and Matt and the swimming pool contractors were on site laying the foundations for the new infinity pool. The black outlines of machinery and mounds of rubble and earth lent an air of menace to the scene in the gathering dusk. I hurried on past. I was heading for the derelict cottage where I'd observed Antonio and Matt meeting in secret and acting suspiciously only a few weeks previously.

The path was in darkness under the trees and more than once I tripped on uneven stones and tree roots. I was reluctant to switch on my torch in case the beam of light caught Antonio's attention as I made my way across the estate. So I stumbled on, praying that Antonio wasn't looking out of his window or, worse still, out night hunting for wild boar, as I knew he often did. After our close encounter on my doorstep, I couldn't imagine anything more disconcerting than running into him in the woods and feared he might follow if he saw me heading for the ruined cottage.

Soon I was out of the woods and could see the cottage in the distance. I had to steel myself to keep going. In the evening light, it resembled a witches' coven. I'd gone over and over in my head what I'd observed that afternoon while painting *al fresco* in the fields, but could still make no sense of it. I'd witnessed Antonio transporting a trunk dug up from under the flagstones where it'd lain buried for many years, to a new hiding place inside the abandoned building. Matt had provided an explanation of why he and Antonio had had to dig up the old concrete patio themselves, rather than paying the contractors who were excavating the site of the new infinity pool to do it for us – The discovery of the trunk by our contractors had to be avoided at all costs. The secret had to stay hidden within the confines of the estate. It was a sordid tale of Mafia and mutilation and fear of retribution. But now I doubted its veracity...Matt had a vivid imagination. He could have made the whole thing up.

'And even if it is true,' I said to myself, 'Matt and Antonio might have made a solemn oath to Great-Uncle Benetto never to open the trunk or speak of it again, but I'm not bound by that promise.' I was burning to find out what was inside. 'Surely it's better to know what we're dealing with. *Better the devil you know...*'

The front door of the cottage was boarded up with thick

planks. Antonio must have sealed the entrance on his way out. I skirted round the building looking for a way in. There was a small window opening just above my head with only one shutter precariously attached. The other had rotted away or been broken off in the storms. I looked around for something to raise me up and noticed a heap of tumbledown stones. Laboriously, I carried them one by one until I'd created a new pile below the window, high enough for me to climb onto and lever myself up to the window ledge. Once again, I was glad of those online yoga and HITT sessions that I'd done during the lockdowns. I was fitter and stronger than I'd ever been.

I clambered through the window opening and let myself drop to the floor. Immediately, I regretted it. Had I gone completely mad, coming here after nightfall? It was pitch-black inside and with the front door sealed, I had no idea how I'd get out again. I swung my torchlight around and located the metal trap door that blocked the entrance to the underground chamber. I'd do what I had to do and then find a way out as soon as possible.

The metal door was locked with a big padlock. I searched frantically through the old shortbread tin and found the matching padlock key. Using the hammer as a lever and ripping my nails in the process, I managed to lift the metal panel to reveal the entrance to the small underground cellar where I'd seen Matt. The cellar was empty save for the large mud-caked trunk that I'd glimpsed in the back of Antonio's pick-up.

Carefully, I lowered myself in, fearful of being trapped within the claustrophobic hole. The trunk was triple padlocked, so I searched once again through the keys but none of them fitted. This lent some credence to Matt's explanation that Benetto had been ordered to bury and 'disappear' the trunk for a third party.

Assuming Matt told me the truth, then it's not surprising that the keys aren't here, I reflected. *If the contents of the trunk were so top secret, whoever gave them the orders to bury it would have kept the keys or thrown them away.*

There was nothing for it – I'd have to break open the trunk. I hesitated. Could my act of defiance lead to reprisals against Loretta or against us? This was all so foreign to me. Matt would be angry when he found out what I'd done, but I'd come this far – there was no turning back. I wasn't bound by any oath of secrecy.

It took all of my strength to hammer the screwdriver behind the fixings of the padlocks and lever them off. The clatter of metal reverberated horribly round the cellar and I prayed that no one would hear. My hands shook as I lifted the lid. I don't know what I thought I'd find – Drugs? Weapons? Black market liquor? Mafia contraband? Anything that would substantiate Matt's account about the Mafia's involvement in this bizarre affair. I desperately wanted what Matt had told me to be true because I needed to know I could trust him.

* * *

The reality at first sight was more banal – no drugs, no guns – and yet more sinister, lending substance to my worst nightmares.

It looked as if the trunk had been packed in haste, with someone's belongings thrown in at random. Not wanting to touch anything, I shone my torch around and poked at the contents with the screwdriver. I made out some old, ripped trainers, a worn beach towel, strappy heeled sandals with one pointy heel twisted at a grotesque right angle, some half-used cosmetics and a few well-thumbed and water-damaged paperbacks of the genre that have pictures of vampires or scantily clad women on the front cover, and a black bin liner containing a bundle of clothes. None of it looked of any value.

I found a pair of vinyl gloves in my jeans pocket (these days we all carried them all the time as many shops required customers to wear disposable gloves) and tentatively pulled out a screwed-up item of clothing from the black bag to see if it was marked with initials or labels suggesting a link to the girl Matt's great-aunt knew by the name of *Nicoletta*.

It was a pink stretchy bodycon dress in a shiny synthetic material. I didn't get as far as checking for a label or initials or a name. The instant I shone the torch on the fabric, I froze. The dress was spattered down the front with big stains, the deep red-brown colour of dried-up blood. I don't know how long I sat there staring, the beam of the torch illuminating the stains like an accusation, while a wave of fear swept through me. Then I slammed down the lid and climbed out of the cellar with shaking legs.

That night, it would be impossible to sleep. Sofia's words about the mysterious *autostoppista* the first time we went out for lunch would play round and round in my head like a broken record.

'There were so many rumours about that girl running wild. She was a bad influence and would do anything to get her next fix,' Sofia had said. 'When she wasn't drunk or stoned, Benetto used her to run *errands*, if you get my meaning. To put it plainly, she worked with the old man as a drugs courier for the local mobsters and as a groomer of young boys for his own pleasure. And Teo was besotted with her –

completely under her spell. Antonio, too. The boys adored her.

The police never took action against them, but her little gang caused havoc in our community that summer. And then suddenly, it was over... Rumour has it, they all fell out. Teo went back to England and the girl hit the road, hitchhiking south through Italy on her way to the Greek islands. At least that's what Marcella told me. Nobody asked too many questions.' Sofia's dark eyes had been fiercely piercing.

'All summer she is everywhere...and then suddenly, she is gone... *pouf*! Disappeared... *è sparita*...' Sofia had exclaimed loudly and raised her hands to the skies.

'Never to be seen again.'

FORTY-ONE
THE HITCHHIKER

BY MATTEO J. ROSSI

The sky is beginning to lighten in the east when they get back from the pool. The front door is wide open. Nikki goes into the cottage first while Luca and Ted linger for one last cigarette, gazing numbly at the early morning sky. They hear doors opening and closing, something falling to the floor, Nikki calling Harry's name. A few seconds later, she hurtles out, ashen-faced in the grey light, suddenly sober.

'I can't find Harry. He's not in the cot. I've looked everywhere... Don't just stand there like a pair of idiots! For fuck's sake, help me!'

Her voice rises to screaming pitch and the three rush in, circling inside the cottage stupidly, opening cupboards and looking under beds and chairs, behind the shower curtain and chest of drawers – anywhere that not even a child half his size could hide. He's nowhere.

Nikki starts to scream at Ted. 'You were with him... I left you looking after him. It's your fault. You left him alone. The door was open. You didn't even lock the fucking door.'

Ted doesn't answer back. He doesn't point out that she

never locks the door. That in fact she lost the key weeks ago. That she routinely leaves Harry alone after she's put him to bed. That Harry is her child and her responsibility...

Instead, Ted says very quietly, 'I shut the door. If the door was open, Harry must have woken up and come looking for you.'

'Or someone walked in and took him,' said Luca, ever the loudmouth.

Nikki is a quivering wreck. She can barely stand.

Ted issues the orders.

'Nikki, you stay by the cottage. Keep calling his name. Harry can't have gone far and may find his way back if he hears your voice. Luca, you go back to the pool. He could have heard all the commotion and gone to find his mum. Search the area and keep watch. It's the most dangerous place for him there with the deep water and all the machinery and trenches round the building works. I'll run back to the farmhouse and raise the alarm. Then I'll get the truck and start searching the woods.'

Unusually, the farmhouse door is bolted. Teds bangs the heavy iron knocker furiously against the solid oak door. The shutters open at the first-floor window and his grandmother's grey head appears, dishevelled and scared. He shouts up in Italian: '*Il bambino è andato*,' – the baby is gone.

For a moment she says nothing, just sways at the window as if about to fall.

He wonders if his grandmother's still dreaming or gripped by a waking nightmare of déjà vu, reliving the loss of her own infant son.

FORTY-TWO
ACKNOWLEDGEMENTS

Somehow, I managed to hold it together long enough to padlock the metal door of the cellar before seeking a way of escape from the derelict cottage. I zipped the padlock key into the inner pocket of my satchel. I was planning to keep it myself, not return it to the tin. The window opening I'd dropped down from was too high to climb up to from the inside and the front door was so heavily barricaded that I knew it would be impossible for me to smash through. More importantly, I didn't want Matt or Antonio to know that I'd broken into the cottage and forced open the trunk – at least, not until I was a safe distance away from the farmhouse when, with Sofia's help, I intended to call the police.

Having seen the contents of the trunk, I was at a loss to know who to trust. Had it contained valuables or drugs from some historic crime, Matt's story of hiding something for the Mafia might have been believable. Then I could perhaps have lived with the idea of honouring the oath of silence to protect the family from reprisals. But a girl's bloodstained clothing and her personal things – that filled me with fear. Why would anyone go to the trouble of hiding these worthless things, fit only for the trash, if not because they constituted incriminating evidence of some violent crime. Whoever was responsible for this, mobster or monster, the secret could not remain buried.

This screams murder, I said to myself. *What horrifying event could have led to this trunk being buried under our patio, and how did Matt and Antonio get mixed up in it?*

In the darkness, I felt my way round the walls, lighting up sections with the torch as I went. The beam must have disturbed a bat and I almost died of fright when it darted past my head to the opposite wall. I was close to panic, when I noticed moonlight filtering in past a small ventilation grate about halfway up one of the back walls above a primitive wood-burning stove. I got the screwdriver and the hammer and, using all of my strength, managed to bash the rusty old grating away from the crumbling brickwork then reach through to rip away at the ivy that had grown over it on the outside. Being petite, I figured the new hole in the wall would be just about big enough for me to wriggle out.

I was in bed with the lights out before I heard Matt's car pulling up outside the house. Matt would know immediately that there was something badly wrong if I tried to speak to him now. I was trembling so much that I'd struggle to get the words out. Of course, it was still likely, I told myself, that Matt and Antonio had no idea what was inside the trunk and had simply been following Benetto's orders to bury it. But I couldn't take the risk. I needed some excuse to get away from the farmhouse. Time to think. Opening the trunk had been like opening a Pandora's box of suspicion and uncertainty and evil. The bad thoughts unleashed inside my head wouldn't go back in the box.

Though I was wide awake, high on adrenaline, I pretended to be asleep. I heard Matt banging at the door a few times, then cursing. Once again, he hadn't bothered to take his house keys. Eventually, I heard him scrabbling around under the flowerpots. He'd remembered that I'd grown tired of him refusing to carry a key and now left a spare one for him there.

I heard Matt come quietly up the stairs. The bedroom door opened and I felt his presence in the room. He stood there listening to my breathing. I concentrated on taking long, slow breaths, mimicking sleep. Eventually, he moved away and back down the stairs. Then I heard him pacing round the farmhouse – doors opening and shutting and floorboards creaking as he moved from one room to another until I heard him enter the study.

The trusting part of my brain told me that Matt was probably working late on his manuscript to catch up for lost hours that had been spent with Loretta earlier in the day. I heard the faint hum of the shredder. He was just shredding old drafts. The paranoid part of my brain told me that Matt had picked up on my suspicions and was destroying the 'evidence' I'd found in the news cuttings.

Evidence of what? asked the trusting part of my brain.

It was when I heard the front door opening again that I almost lost it. I stood behind the shutters and peered through the slats, following a small plume of light from Matt's mobile phone torch dancing along the path that led through the trees towards the cottages. He was wearing a dark jacket and carried a small rucksack. As if he could feel my eyes upon him, I saw Matt stop and turn to look up in the direction of our bedroom window. There was something shifty in his demeanour. I drew back and shivered in the cold air. Where was he going at this time of night?

It was almost midnight, but I decided to call Sofia anyway. There was no one I could trust to speak to at the *fattoria*. Beyond the boundaries of the estate, she was the only person I knew well enough to call on for help. At coffee the other day, we'd spoken of going shopping together in Florence. Despite the late hour, Sofia sounded as resourceful and sparky as ever when she answered her phone with a confident '*Pronto*.'

I got straight to the point.

'Sofia, I need your help. I have to get away. And I need to speak to Loretta. Please can you take me to Florence for the weekend?'

The swimming pool contractors had completed the work installing the pool liner and the surround for the infinity pool. I knew that Matt had set aside this weekend to prepare the surface and lay the flagstones for the new patio. Time was running short if wanted to tip off the police. But before taking this step, I wanted to have another conversation with Loretta, this time with Sofia as my translator. And frankly, I was scared to be here on my own when Antonio and Matt discovered that I'd broken into the cottage and smashed the seals on the trunk.

'I'll call in sick,' said Sofia with no hesitation.

And the matter was settled.

When Matt came to bed about an hour later, he snuggled up to me. His skin was still cold and with that mossy damp smell of the woods.

'Where were you?' I asked sleepily.

'I had to work late,' Matt said vaguely. 'Then I went for a walk to clear my head. Let's sleep now, darling,' he whispered. 'It's going to be a hard slog tomorrow.'

Why would Matt need a rucksack for an evening walk? I wondered.

'Sofia's offered to take me away for the weekend to Florence,' I murmured, unsure what his reaction would be. 'All expenses paid – well, except for my shopping.'

'That's nice of her,' he said. 'Sure, why not. You haven't had much in the way of female company since we've been here and I'll be working flat out all weekend with Antonio. The pool guys are coming back on Monday to test the systems and fill the pool, so we need to get the patio done before then.'

'That's so exciting.' I rested my head in the hollow of Matt's shoulder. 'Thank you for all your hard work.' I ran my fingers over his torso. He was tanned and his abs were ripped from manual labour out in the Mediterranean sun. 'You're becoming more Italian every day,' I murmured. 'I can't wait to dive in for our first swim.'

'And you're becoming more beautiful every day,' said Matt, stroking his hands over my body.

I stayed awake for a long time after Matt had dropped off to sleep, staring up at the ceiling, surprised at my ability to dissimulate and trying to make sense of the situation.

'It's Benetto,' I said to myself, chilled by the thought that Matt's great-uncle, and my benefactor (in the sense that I was now living in his property), may have been mixed up in the death of a young girl and that my partner, knowingly or unknowingly, had been involved in hiding the evidence of that crime. This would explain the insults on Benetto's death notice. Also Matt's reluctance to have anything to do with the locals. And the veiled hostility I'd sensed directed towards the family and even towards myself. Benetto was dead. But now we had to atone for his sin and face the backlash.

* * *

After our first lunch out, Sofia and I had struck up a firm friendship, meeting for a walk or a coffee in town once or twice a week. She always introduced me full of smiles as her *'amica inglese'* and I'd detect an exchange of knowing looks from behind the masks. Sofia was always praising my figure and my hair and my complexion.

'You English girls have such beautiful skin,' she'd say. 'It's all that mist and rain.'

However, she clearly despaired at my lack of taste when it came to my dress sense.

'English women have no sense of style,' she said.

It was a constant refrain in the Italian media. She'd been nagging me for a while.

'All the designer clothes shops have reopened now,' she said the last time we met for coffee. 'It's the perfect time to go shopping before all the tourists come back. Things are quiet. The city is beautiful. There are sales everywhere. They're desperate to get people back into the shops again.'

It was the right time to allow Sofia to initiate me into the art of dressing in Italian chic. A perfect alibi.

In the midnight phone call, Sofia had arranged that we should meet at the café in our local town at 9 a.m., so that we could 'fortify' ourselves with espressos in preparation for a long afternoon of 'retail therapy' in the city. Although he'd responded well to our proposed trip, it was clear that Matt disliked Sofia. He'd already told me he didn't want Sofia setting foot on our property and the feeling was apparently mutual. We'd already had a few day trips together in Sofia's car, but she never offered to come and pick me up from home and always dropped me off at the bottom of the track. She seemed to have a superstitious phobia about coming anywhere close to the farmhouse. She refused to set foot on its soil, as if the whole place was contaminated.

The meeting point suited me well, as I didn't want Matt finding out about my plan to drop in on Loretta. Discretion wasn't Sofia's strong point. If Loretta said anything to Matt in the future, I could simply deny it all and make out that the visit was a figment of her confused imagination. With Sofia, it was different.

Over coffee, Sofia set out her plans for our weekend in Florence.

'Today is for shopping,' she said. 'I know all the best designer boutiques and they all know me.' She rubbed her manicured fingertips together delicately. 'I'll get you good discounts.' She sipped her espresso. 'And then, of course, we must visit the leather shops for handbags and shoes. *Firenze* is the leather-crafting capital of the world. It would be criminal to return without a new handbag!' She patted her own soft cream leather satchel appreciatively. 'Then Sunday is for cathedrals and galleries.

'First stop, of course, the Uffizi art gallery to see '*Nascita di Venere*' – you know, '*The Birth of Venus*' by Botticelli, with Venus rising from her shell above the oceans,' said Sofia. 'You can't miss the chance to see this masterpiece when the galleries are empty. In normal times, the view is blocked by fat American backsides.' She laughed wickedly.

I let Sofia chatter on. The shopping and sightseeing were just a pretext to get away from the *fattoria*. The only thing I really cared about was the planned detour on the way back. On Sunday afternoon, we'd pay a visit to Loretta. I would get Sofia to act as my translator. Matteo would be none the wiser.

If I really was a dead ringer for the girl Loretta knew by

the name of Nicoletta, this gave me a chance to find out everything I could about her and where she'd gone. Our resemblance might be enough to trigger the old lady's memories and give me a way into her troubled mind.

FORTY-THREE

THE HITCHHIKER

BY MATTEO J. ROSSI

His grandfather isn't at the cottage when Ted raises the alarm. He's spending the night at a neighbour's place, says Ted's grandmother – Thursday night is *Briscola* night – as addictive as poker and even more cruel. He makes up a six who get together every week for an evening of drinking and gambling over cards.

The old man is a seasoned player but, of course, there's an element of luck involved. Ted's grandma knows whether he's won or lost before she unbolts the door. After a good night, he serenades her loudly below the window when he stumbles back at dawn. When the cards have gone against him, he hurls his boots at her shutters until she comes down the stairs to let him inside.

The car keys are hanging in the hallway because Ted's grandfather is always too intoxicated to drive home. He knows these hills like the back of his hand. He'll track his way back on foot through the woods from the neighbouring *fattoria* as proficiently as a dog, even when dead drunk. Ted grabs the keys and a lantern and jumps in the car. For the next three hours, he drives up and down the tracks that criss-cross the estate, stopping every hundred metres or so to walk into the woods and shine the lantern, calling Harry's name.

Luca scours the area of the swimming pool, shining a torch into the deep water and searching the site where they're laying the patio. He directs the beam of light into the trenches and under mounds of earth, between the wheels of the digger and inside the cement mixer – anywhere a small body could be hidden or trapped.

Meanwhile, Nikki is beside herself, checking the house again and again, then circling the perimeter in ever wider circles, racing down one path and then another. Each time she hears a rustle or a crack or thinks she sees a flash of colour, in her mind it could be the movement of a tiny boy. Just two words bang inside her head to the beat of her throbbing migraine: *bad mother, bad mother, bad mother*. This time she fears her luck has run out.

Bad news travels fast. Within the hour, the woods are alive with people from the local community – friends and acquaintances and hangers-on – who have heard about the child's disappearance. Everybody wants to help – or to gape. There's much goodwill but no coordination. Nikki is tearing her hair out. All of these strangers wandering about, interfering in the search, wanting to talk, getting in her way, slowing her down... And her darling baby, vulnerable and lost... She wants to scream at them to go away.

Ted's grandma is on the point of calling the police, when Luca says he has an idea.

'Let me check the old cottage on the other side of the estate,' he says.

He remembers seeing Ted's grandfather taking Harry for a

walk round there the other day. He sets off at a run down the track while Nikki paces manically up and down near the pool, sucking on a cigarette as if her life depended on it. The area round the pool is a building site, with mounds of rubble and earth and equipment everywhere. Harry isn't much more than knee-height. He could so easily have fallen into a trench or been buried in a heap of debris from the groundworks. She imagines the worst.

Nikki is on her third cigarette and about to pass out, when she hears Ted's voice shouting from a distance.

'Nikki, I've got Harry... We've found him! He's safe.'

She charges towards them, dropping her cigarette and losing her flip-flops in her haste. Harry is like a flying angel, perched on Ted's shoulders. Nikki elbows Ted in the face as she grapples to get Harry into her arms. In her panic, she startles her little boy. She smothers him with kisses and crushes him close to her chest. He looks into her frightened eyes and begins to cry.

'Where did you find him?' asks Nikki. 'He's not hurt, is he?'

'He seems OK,' says Ted. 'No injuries as far as we can tell. I didn't find him. My grandfather found him. He was walking back from Patriani's place after one of his nights of drinking and cards. Says he found Harry walking down the track towards him on the other side of the hill. The man's still drunk. He was bloody vague. Thank God he had the sense to bring him back.'

Just as Harry's sobs begin to subside, the sound of sirens fills the air.

'Shit,' says Ted. 'Someone must have called the police.'

They both know the score. If the police search the estate – for sure, if they have a sniffer dog – then they'll find the stash of drugs the threesome have locked away in the cellar in the derelict cottage near to where Harry was found.

Nikki's had run-ins with the Italian police before.

'Do something quick,' she says. 'If we get arrested, who will look after Harry?'

Ted knows why she's so scared, because they've spoken of it before. If she gets into trouble with the police, Harry's dad will be notified. The man's a brute, a monster. She's been on the run from him for weeks. If her abusive partner finds out where she's staying, he'll be out on the next flight to take Harry home. There will be hell to pay.

'I'll run back to the farmhouse and tell everyone that all is well,' says Ted. 'Mother and child reunited and in need of privacy and rest.'

Ted arrives at the farmhouse just in time to witness an awkward stand-off between his grandfather and the police. His grandfather has been interviewed by the police in the past – allegations of 'inappropriate behaviour' made by certain young students who worked at the *fattoria* at harvest time. The police don't pay much attention to complaints brought by young foreigners – especially when they drink to excess and smoke pot and don't cut their hair. But the disappearance of an infant and his fortuitous 'discovery' by the old man sets alarm bells ringing. Rumours buzz in the close-knit Tuscan community like flies around a turd.

Ted's intervention relieves the tension. His grandmother hands out coffee all round. Within minutes, the police are on their way, with warnings about child welfare and offers of parenting classes for Nikki. No official report has been made.

'Do you think we should call a doctor?' says Ted once the police and the people have left and calm is restored, and

Harry is tucked up safely in bed. 'Get him examined properly?'

Nikki refuses. She doesn't trust doctors any more than she trusts the police. As far as she's concerned, they're all part of the same hostile group, intent on taking Harry away from her.

But Ted has a nagging concern. Something tells him Luca's suspicions were well founded when he went in search of Harry down at the old cottage and discovered Ted's grandfather walking towards it holding Harry in his arms. Harry may have had a lucky escape.

FORTY-FOUR
DANIELLE

When we arrived at the apartment where Loretta was staying in a residential suburb of Florence, we were met at the door by her carer.

'She's not having a good day,' said the carer to Sofia in Italian.

We followed the carer into a bedroom. The shutters were closed and it took a while for my eyes to adjust. Loretta was in the gloom sitting on an armchair in the corner of the room. She was hunched over, cradling the teddy bear from her dead son's crib. The carer stood to one side while we approached and gave our greetings. She didn't react for a minute or two but eventually she looked up. She glanced briefly at Sofia and then turned her eyes on me, reaching out her hand to touch my face. The skin on her fingers was almost translucent.

'She looks as if she's seen a ghost,' Sofia whispered in my ear.

The carer prepared drinks for us in the dining room while we persuaded Loretta to come through. We chatted for a while of inconsequential things, though Loretta took little part in the conversation, taking tiny sips of cordial and picking crumbs from the cakes. I had the same impression as on our first meeting – that Loretta identified me with a familiar figure who was as real to her now as in the past.

I'd prepared a list of questions. I wanted to ask Loretta about her relationship with Benetto, his work, his business associates and his dealings with the seasonal workers on his farm. I wanted to ask her what she remembered about the young woman she called Nicoletta who had been in a relationship with Matt – when she arrived and when she left, and the circumstances of her disappearance.

It was soon obvious that we'd get very little from questioning Loretta in her current mood. It didn't help having the carer and Loretta's cousin hovering in the background listening in.

In the brief moment when they left the room, Sofia said quietly, 'Basically, you want me to ask Loretta if her husband was a murderer and a member of the Mafia!' She raised her eyebrows dramatically. She nodded to the doorway. 'These things can't be spoken out loud. It'll be all round the town.'

I was beginning to understand why Mafia networks and crimes were so pervasive in Italy and so hard to prosecute. Fear of reprisals. Rumours abounded, but when it came to searching for the truth, there was a conspiracy of silence. Bury your secrets. Let the dead bury the dead. Don't dig up past wrongs. This seemed to be the Italian way.

As we drove away from Loretta's apartment, I turned to Sofia.

'Should I go to the police?'

Sofia almost snorted with laughter. 'On a Sunday evening?'

She pulled up the car at the side of the road.

'Perhaps you should speak to Matt first. And see what he has to say about that.' She pointed to the small brown package resting on my lap that Loretta had given me as a parting gift. 'Why don't you call him now, from my car. You're safe here.'

I took out my phone and with Sofia sitting beside me, I dialled Matt's number. Before he had the chance to say a word, and before I lost my nerve, I told him I'd broken into the trunk and what I'd seen inside it, adding I thought we should contact the police.

'You can't keep Benetto's secret any longer,' I said.

We'd agreed that if Matt responded suspiciously or aggressively to my phone call, I'd spend the night at Sofia's home and she'd accompany me to the police station in the morning. We'd get a better reception from the police on a Monday morning than late on a Sunday evening (when only duty officers were on site), if I wanted to make a report.

In fact, Matt was unexpectedly calm and reasonable in his response.

'It's OK, Dani. You can relax. I'm at the police station myself. Can't talk now. I'll update you when I get home.'

His words took the wind out of my sails.

* * *

Sofia dropped me at the bottom of the drive, reversed at speed and disappeared in a cloud of dust, leaving me to trudge up the hill, laden with my suitcase and the packages from our shopping trip, and to face Matt alone at the farmhouse on his return from the police station. It was just before sunset on a midsummer's Sunday evening and I was struck by the awesome beauty of the place, so peaceful and calm after the bustle of Florence. Exhausted from my first foray into city life after almost a year in the countryside, I looked forward to a long shower to wash away the grime and germs of unfamiliar crowds.

Before going inside, I went to see the new infinity pool. The cover was over it. The pool engineers would be back to fill it and get it functioning in the morning. The whole site was eerily quiet. I could see that Antonio and Matt had made great progress in my absence during the weekend, concreting and laying the flagstones for the new patio surround. There were still piles of rubble and mounds of earth to be cleared, but it would be stunning once the work was completed. It was such a burden off my shoulders to think that Matt had decided to inform the police about the buried trunk that had blighted this spot and our relationship. His change of heart restored my trust in him...up to a point.

I entered the house and as if on autopilot, knocked softly and let myself into Matt's study, which today was unlocked. The first thing that I noticed was that the light on the shredder was flashing. The container was full and needed emptying. I pulled it out and put my hand into the strips. I could feel from the texture of the paper and its greyish colour that Matt had been shredding newsprint. The shoebox came to mind and, sure enough, when I checked the desk drawer, it was unlocked and empty – the old shoebox and all the yellowed newspaper cuttings had gone.

The corkscrew was still there in its two broken parts. So much had happened since our first night when Matt had injured himself opening a bottle of wine. I held the pieces in my hand, its olive wood handle carved with the initials 'T' and 'N' linked by a heart.

'Of course! The initials stand for *Teo* and *Nicola*. So stupid of me. I should have thought of that sooner.'

Matt must have been distracted, because as well as leaving his study unlocked, he'd also left the document containing his draft manuscript open on his screen. Matt had given me the impression on the phone that he'd gone to the police station of his own free will, but I began to wonder if in fact the police had come to the house to take him away for questioning as the state of his study suggested a hasty departure.

I opened the document and scrolled quickly through the latest draft of his novel, not sure what I was looking for.

My eyes lighted on a passage:

*Nikki is as careless with his feelings as she is careless with the health and safety of her child. Carelessness is her defining characteristic – part of her sex appeal. Sometimes (when she oversteps the mark), **it makes him want to kill her**.*

Those last words jumped off the page as if highlighted in bold. Was this a rare moment of introspection on Matt's part?

I scrolled on to another passage:

As the pool comes into view, he sees Luca – Luca who is taller and stronger and more tanned than Ted – grab Nikki and swing her effortlessly up into his arms across his body. She clings to his neck and shrieks with delight as he races for the edge to take a running leap into the deep black water.

When they surface, laughing, and flicking hair and flighting in each other's arms, Ted stands above their heads looking down. Nikki's bikini top has come loose in the water and Luca swings it triumphantly above his head.

In his left hand, Ted holds a rock. First Luca, then Nikki,
look up to meet his eyes. Instantly, the laughter stops. They
tread water silently.

'*Ted,' says Nikki very softly. 'Ted, are you OK?'*

That passage made me feel suddenly cold. The words
'Ted holds a rock' jumped off the page... and the detail that
Ted was left-handed.

'Matt is left-handed, too,' I muttered out loud, drawing
another parallel between Matt and his protagonist.

Hadn't the victim recovered near Brindisi (who might
have been a hitchhiker called Nicola Flanagan) been battered
to death with a rock? I thought I remembered that from the
press article. I checked the translation that I'd typed into my
phone:

... the victim appears to have suffered multiple blows to
the head and injuries to her torso. A sexual motive for the
death hasn't been ruled out...

It was my imagination that had embellished this finding,
leading to my false 'recollection' that the article stated that the
victim's injuries had been caused by a rock.

'Don't jump to conclusions,' I told myself sternly. 'Innocent until proven guilty. This is Matt's story, not yours.'

* * *

In the distance, I heard the Land Rover approaching on the
white road that led to our property. I clicked off Matt's document and left the study, closing the door behind me.

I picked up the packages I'd abandoned in the hallway
and started to carry them up the stairs. I didn't want Matt to
trip over the evidence of my spending spree on designer outfits

the minute he stepped through the door. But those packages were nothing compared to the small brown package that I now placed carefully in my new leather shoulder bag for safe-keeping.

Loretta had disappeared into her bedroom to find the package and pressed it into my hands just before we left. She'd squeezed my hands with her papery old ones and Sofia had translated for Loretta, playing along with her delusions. Loretta had spoken each phrase slowly and clearly, pausing for Sofia to communicate it to me.

'Loretta says you left this behind... She found it under your mattress and has been keeping it for you all these years. She always knew you'd come back. She knew you'd never leave without saying goodbye.'

Sofia had smiled at me in complicity as we humoured the senile old lady. When I looked down, I understood the impor-tance of this gift. In the old lady's spidery handwriting, the envelope was addressed simply to 'Nicoletta'.

I'd resisted the impulse to rip open the sealed package immediately. This gift was something private and personal – certainly not to be opened in front of Sofia. Would the contents provide the clue to what was real and what was imag-ined? Or would they contain another narrative, as unreliable a source of truth as all the rest? Much as I longed to open it, I knew I had no right to. If this belonged to Matt's old girlfriend, then I was duty bound to share it with him – but I would do so, in my own time.

* * *

Matt breezed through the door full of confidence. He was wearing shorts, a T-shirt and aviators. He didn't look like a man who had just been interviewed by the police. I was on the point of handing over the sealed brown package Loretta had given me, but something held me back.

'How did you get on at the police station?' I said.

'Oh, fine,' said Matt. 'One of the policemen is a mate of Antonio's. I know him a bit from way back. We were drinking buddies that summer.'

'Are they coming for the trunk?' I asked tentatively.

'No,' said Matt. 'They had more important things on their mind. A recent incident – not some old historic crime. They wanted to talk to me about the hit-and-run. I've lodged a complaint against the driver, in fact.' He paused. 'Actually, it's a bit more complicated. A woman who was out jogging in the same area claims she was sexually assaulted by a cyclist.'

Instantly, my ears pricked.

'She managed to escape and flag down a car – turns out it's the car that knocked me off my bike. She was in the car at the time. She's...ahh...pointing the finger at me. It's a false accusation, of course... Lots of cyclists take that route. The driver of the car that picked her up and ran me down was her husband's boss. The woman's must be lying to get him off the hook for the hit-and-run.'

'Surely no one would lie about being sexually assaulted. The woman must have had injuries.'

Matt looked at me coldly.

'Are you taking their side? I didn't say she lied about the assault. I said she lied about it being me.'

* * *

While Matt prepared iced gin and tonics for us both and went out to drink his on the garden terrace and to lay the outdoor table, I prepared a simple dinner of pasta with basil and sundried tomatoes together with a green salad. We clinked glasses.

'*Cin cin!* I needed this,' said Matt, taking a long drink.

He seemed in a pretty good mood. As if a weight had been lifted. I took a deep breath.

'We stopped off at Loretta's flat on the way back,' I said. 'She sends you her regards.'

Matt almost choked on his G & T.

'I wish that interfering bitch would keep away from my family,' said Matt.

I knew, of course, that he was referring to Sofia.

'Don't blame Sofia,' I said. 'I asked her to take me there. I felt bad about the way your great-aunt's visit here ended last time – with her in tears. I wanted her to know that she can come and stay with us any time. She's always welcome.'

Matt stabbed at his pasta. 'The old woman's so out of it now. There's no point confusing her even more by bringing her over here.'

'I wouldn't write her off yet. Her mind is still quite sharp in some ways – just stuck in the past. She was obviously confused about who I was...' I hesitated. 'Kept calling me Nicoletta.'

Matt expertly twirled the pasta on his fork and said nothing.

'Who was Nicoletta?' I persisted, with a Freudian slip into the past tense.

'I haven't a clue,' he said. 'How should I know? I only spent the summers here. Probably a friend of hers, or one of the maids from long ago.'

I pushed away my plate. I'd lost my appetite.

'You're lying to me,' I said. 'She was young and pretty.

And she was English. That's why Loretta's confusing her with me.'

'Don't flatter yourself,' said Matt, deliberately misinterpreting me and trying to deflect me with his sarcasm.

This time I was determined to get everything out into the open.

'There's no point trying to keep up the pretence. I spent an hour chatting to Loretta with Sofia acting as translator. Your aunt may be confused, but she's not crazy. She remembers that summer and your girlfriend and the fact that suddenly, she went away... disappeared from one day to the next. Your great-aunt Loretta welcomed me like a long-lost friend, a revenant from the dead...'

Matt went to get himself a cigarette and sat at the table smoking.

'Sofia's poisoned the old woman's mind against me – And yours,' he muttered bitterly.

These days he was getting through almost a packet a day. He wouldn't look at me – just inhaled deeply again and again and tapped the ash into his pasta.

I tried to stay calm.

Eventually he stubbed out his cigarette.

Matt looked at me now, long and hard, and forced a laugh.

'You're the one who should be writing murder mystery novels,' he said contemptuously. 'You're as mad as Loretta.'

FORTY-FIVE
THE HITCHHIKER
BY MATTEO J. ROSSI

It's that hour after sunset, the 'blue half-hour', when the light is luminous, the wind drops, and all is silent and still. The mountains are sharp in the distance and every leaf on the olive branch above his head is clear and defined. Ted lies in the hammock, watching and waiting. Nature 'takes a breath' before the drama of night.

Inside the cottage, Nikki buzzes with excitement. Showered and spritzed with cheap cologne, she disentangles herself from Harry, draped round her neck like a sloth, and puts him down on the floor, where he clings to her legs and wails for attention.

'For God's sake, can you take him out for a walk or something?' says Nikki to one of the seasonal workers – a placid, overweight Polish girl who is babysitting for the night. 'I've got to get ready to go out.'

Getting ready involves shaving her legs (already as smooth as a peach), applying shades of dusky *Moonlight-Blue* eye make-up and *Shocking-Red* lipstick, and pulling a skintight bright pink sleeveless and backless bodycon over her head. The dress is more flesh than fabric, thinks Ted when she walks out into the yard. A silver clutch bag and a pair of heeled open sandals with long leather straps that tie in a criss-cross around her calves complete the look. Hardly the most appropriate outfit for hitchhiking.

Luca and Nikki staked out the spot the other day. Just beyond the junction where the road out of Sangiari joins the main highway to Siena, there's a lay-by with a few picnic tables and a clump of trees. Set back from the road, an embankment slopes down to the railway line. It's an established stopping place for the Italian equivalent of 'white-van man', since there's a primitive concrete toilet block next to the parking area and most weekdays, between nine and five, a mobile kiosk serving tepid fizzy drinks and slices of rubbery pizza.

Nikki is in high spirits on the drive over, flirting with Luca in the front seats. Tonight is the night she gets her running-away money for her onward trip to Greece. She's bored to death of Tuscany, with its endless vineyards and rolling hills as far as the eye can see. Nothing ever happens.

Ted sulks in the back, nauseated by the spectacle of Nikki virtually 'giving face' to Luca while they sing along to some idiotic love song.

Luca pulls into the lay-by, wheels squealing, having almost overshot the entrance thanks to Nikki's antics at his side. Nikki jumps out by the toilet block, says she's desperate for a pee. She's been alternating vodka shots and Bacardi and Coke all evening to get herself psyched up.

In the cracked mirror above the sink, her naturally radiant face looks distorted and grey. She opens her clutch bag and touches up the red lipstick. She musses up her hair. She replaces the lipstick in the clutch bag next to the open pack of cigarettes, the sachet of condoms (two missing), the twist of brown paper containing a handful of pills and the flick knife. All her essentials are there. Be prepared – that's the trusty old Scout motto, isn't it? Can't be too careful!

She walks over to the verge and positions herself strategically just before the turning. With her arm extended, her thigh gaping through the slit in her bodycon and an unlit cigarette hanging from her lips, she puts herself out there – an easy target for the punters.

Meanwhile, Luca and Ted drive 200 metres up the road, then turn off into a neighbouring field. Luca bumps the Fiat over the ruts in the field to park up between the vines. The plan is for them to walk back through the vines to the lay-by and lie in wait inside the men's cubicle.

A few cars drive by without stopping: families, couples, a man in an expensive Mercedes, who swerves almost to a stop and then drives by slowly, rubbernecks shamelessly but thinks better of it on seeing that Nikki is little more than a child. Nikki has her story prepared: she's thumbing a lift to the next town, where the sleazy Friday night disco will be in full swing. She's not in any hurry to get there. Her boyfriend just dumped her. Left her at the side of the road. Bloody prick. She needs a shoulder to cry on. Then maybe he (or she?) could join her at the disco.

The first car to pull up isn't what she had in mind – four kids on the way to the disco – matching leather jackets, white T-shirts, slicked-back greasy hair and acne. She was hoping for a mild-mannered rich middle-aged pervert – someone who would be satisfied with a fumble and a handjob in the front seat before she dispossessed him of his fat wallet and jumped out of the car. This lot must be younger than her and almost as skint.

The boy in the front passenger seat, sallow-skinned and with deep-set eyes and a long nose, leans out and leers at her while the ones in the back make lewd gestures. She holds out her cigarette for a light, planning to send them on their way.

But the meathead in the back has other ideas. He gets out, opens the car door and motions for her to get in. He's tall and big, too much pasta and ice cream as a young child. The original lardy kid who was bullied at school, now transformed into a muscle-bound hulk by heavy weightlifting and steroids.

In the blink of an eye, she senses he's the mean-spirited, vengeful sort who gets what he wants by throwing his weight around – literally. She backs away. She'd be asking for trouble getting in the car. She may be reckless, but she's no fool.

Nikki turns on her heel and heads towards the concrete toilet block. Luca and Ted should be hiding in the men's toilets by now – ready to intervene if things get too intense and pounce at the appropriate time if things go to plan. The other boys get out of the car, confer excitedly in Italian and then amble across the scrubby grass to join her, lighting cigarettes and cracking open cans of beer. Nikki plays along and humours them for a while, countering their attempts at sexual banter delivered in comically bad English with long-suffering but indulgent female scorn.

She'll take anything they're offering – pot, cocaine, cigarettes, alcohol – and then get rid of them... send them on their way as fast as possible. There are no rich pickings here. They're just time-wasters. And even she can't take on all four of them.

Nikki takes a can of beer and shares a spliff and then another. She's hoping that any minute Ted and Luca will come out and help her. What are they playing at? Surely it's obvious that this isn't going to plan.

'Let's start the party,' says the meathead.

They crank up the music on the car stereo, bring out more cans, and the bony skinhead who was sitting in the front passenger seat pulls a small plastic bag containing white powder from the inside pocket of his leather jacket. Four beers, two spliffs and a line of white cocaine later, Nikki has lost control of the situation completely.

The boys take turns dancing with her – necking and thrusting and grinding – putting on a show for the others, who look on, smoking and sniggering and shouting insults in Italian. She always loves to be the life and soul of the party, so she's into it – up to a point.

The skinhead is the first to cross the line, putting his hands up her dress and ripping off her thong. She pulls away, but he's having none of it. Two of the others start to slow clap. Soon he's got her back up to the wall, crushing her head against the concrete as he forces himself onto her.

The driver (the others call him Romeo, but she can't tell if that's his real name or if they're taking the piss) is the 'sensible' one of the four. He pulls the meathead off her. But not out of any concern for Nikki's welfare. They're in full view of the road, now with a steady stream of passing Saturday night traffic. He says something in Italian and nods towards the door of the men's toilet.

Nikki remains calm. Luca and Ted should be hiding in the cubicles, ready to pounce, grab the boys' cash, phones, bank and identity cards, together with their cigarettes, their drink and their drugs... before beating the shit out of them. They deserve it. Nikki silently curses Luca and Ted for waiting so long to intervene. She'll give them hell. She's had to entertain these teenage clowns on her own all evening with nothing to show for it. Thank God her ordeal is almost over.

But she is so wrong. It's only just begun...

FORTY-SIX
DANIELLE

I was tired of Matt gaslighting me. I'd seen what I'd seen. I got up from the table, scraped my leftover pasta into the bin and slammed the plate in the sink. I'd planned to be cool and strategic, to bide my time. But suddenly, my anger rose. Impulsively, I pushed past Matt. He watched me ominously but didn't react, and I had time to run out of the house and in among the trees, taking a shortcut in the direction of the old derelict cottage.

I'd expected Matt to stop me or give chase, but I heard nothing as I sprinted through the woods, dodging loose stones and low-hanging branches. It was almost ten o'clock, not long after sunset on that midsummer evening. The sky was light apricot and grey above the treetops. I arrived panting and struggling to catch my breath. I was surprised to see that the front door of the cottage was no longer boarded up. In fact, it hung loose on its hinges, a few inches open.

I went inside. The metal door to the underground cellar was padlocked. I'd brought the padlock key, which I'd kept hidden on my person throughout the weekend. I was determined to have another careful look at the contents of the trunk. Unless Matt had a very good explanation then this time, I'd take pictures and report it to the police.

I crouched to open the padlock and at that instant, the front door swung open, revealing Matt – a dark, looming silhouette, backlit by the rising full moon. I refused to be intimidated and carried on jiggling the key in the padlock, my task made more difficult by the fact that Matt was casting a shadow across the cellar door.

'You're wasting your time,' said Matt sardonically. 'It's a new padlock. Here, I've brought you the key.' He tossed a key ring across to me.

The new padlock opened easily and Matt assisted me by heaving open the heavy metal cellar door.

'Look inside,' said Matt. 'What do you see?'

For a second, I was scared. Matt looked so serious. Was he going to force me into another of his sick mind games – another method writing exercise? Locking me in the cellar so that he could embody the visceral experience of knowing I was terrified and completely under his control? I could imagine him standing there calmly above the metal door, while I panicked in the dark, and he asked me coldly to describe my fear.

Matt grabbed my elbow and dragged me forwards until I stood looking down into the black hole. He took out his phone and shone the phone torch around very slowly. The cellar was completely empty – an empty, concreted underground chamber. The trunk was gone.

I struggled to get free and shoved Matt to one side, with a force born of fear then ran out of the door.

'Don't come near me,' I screamed. I held up my phone. 'One step closer and I'll call the police.'

Matt grimaced. 'You'll struggle to explain your story to the local police in Italian,' said Matt. 'A hitchhiker spent a summer here and then she went on her way. And this all happened ten years ago. And you come up with a cock-and-bull story that she was murdered. I'd like to be a fly on the wall for that one. They won't believe you. They'll think you're some highly strung English bitch gone stir-crazy in the lockdowns.'

That stung. I stood my ground. Matt came no closer, seeing that this time, I wouldn't back down.

'What have you done with the trunk?' I screamed.

I looked up and saw Antonio jogging towards us down the grassy slope. He must have heard the commotion. Matt turned and saw him too, raising a hand to acknowledge his arrival.

Matt stood at a distance. Now that Antonio was within earshot, he talked quietly to calm my nerves, as if I were a desperate person about to throw myself off a bridge.

'Shush. Your imagination is running riot. It's OK, Danielle. We can sort this out. I know things have been difficult for you living out here in isolation what with the language barriers and being cut off here from all of your family and friends. You need therapy.'

Antonio stood beside me. His presence gave me the confidence to speak out.

'What happened to her, Matt? What happened to your girlfriend who disappeared without trace that summer? Did you kill her? In a fit of uncontrollable rage. Did you find her in the swimming pool making love to another man?' Antonio's hand brushed softly against mine. 'Did you batter her to death with a rock?'

Behind Matt, the moon hung heavy and low, casting his face into shadow. He came closer.

'Danielle, I don't know how I can help you. What are you doing? You've lost your grip on reality. Hacking into my computer? Reading my drafts? Just remember – it's fiction, Danielle. I'm not writing an autobiography or a confessional. *Nikki* was not my girlfriend. And I'm not *Ted*.'

He held up his hands in a gesture of exasperation.

'It's a story.'

It was all very well for Matt to get angry, but it was difficult to separate the protagonist's voice from the writer's in his story. There were so many parallels and resonances between the fictional world that Matt had created in *The Hitchhiker* and the things I'd learnt about this place in the past. The correlation between Loretta and the grandmother figure, or between Benetto and the fictional grandfather, was plain for all to see. There were even references to Patriani – a name with which I was familiar from a passage I'd read in *The Beast of Siena*. *Patriani* was the name of one of the people who had been convicted of murder in the serial killings. And, of course, there were parallels between Matt and Ted (the names made it obvious), and between Luca and Antonio. Most obviously, there was the fact that he had set his story in Sangiari, indeed on this very estate.

Matt had blurred and conflated fact and fiction in many places. So, it was natural to assume that the character of Nikki had also been based on a real person – a real person who had been Matt's girlfriend and lover – a real person who looked a lot like a younger version of me - a real person called Nicola. My interactions with both Sofia and Loretta suggested this was the case.

Was Matt trying to rewrite history? To convince himself

and others that his fictional story was what had really happened or what he wished had happened. Was he seeking to create a new reality so that he could start afresh in a place where certain people had long and dark memories of what he was truly like that summer? Was his chimerical goal to write a different ending to his own story 'in real life'?

FORTY-SEVEN

THE HITCHHIKER

BY MATTEO J. ROSSI

Romeo puts his arm behind Nikki's waist and steers her firmly towards the door of the men's toilet block with the others trailing behind. She doesn't resist. Her assailants are about to fall into the honeytrap, she thinks.

What Nikki doesn't know is that Luca and Ted aren't hiding in the cubicles, ready to pounce and dispossess the boys of their cash and their stash. In fact, Luca and Ted never made it to the men's toilet because two bored police officers driving along the Siena highway saw them turning into the vineyard and pulled up on the roadside to find out what was going on. Suspecting drugs, the officers had ordered the pair out of the car, made them take off their jackets and their shoes, empty their pockets and submit to a body search. Then they were ordered to sit on the track in among the vines with their legs crossed and their hands above their heads while one of the officers carried out a search of the car.

The officers weren't in any hurry. They took their time. They found nothing actionable in among the trash in the back of Luca's car apart from an empty bottle of Bacardi and a skip load of empty beer cans. That was sufficient cause to give Luca a breathalyser test, which miraculously Luca passed – just. They gave Luca a written warning for trespass on private land and Ted a stern talking-to, and then they drove off.

In the time it takes Luca and Ted to get themselves dressed, throw everything back into the car and reverse out of the vines, the police car arrives at the lay-by. Seconds later, they hear sirens wailing.

'Shit, I hope Nikki's not in trouble,' says Ted.

* * *

Meanwhile, Romeo opens the door to the men's toilet and follows Nikki inside. The other three teenagers crowd into the doorway, blocking the only way out as they prepare to watch the show. The stink of urinals and worse makes Nikki gag. The cubicles are empty.

Where the fuck are they?

This wasn't part of the plan.

Caught in her own trap.

Don't panic. Give them something. Play for time, get out of this unharmed.

Nikki has always been a drama queen – she switches into performance mode. Romeo goes first. Unexpectedly strong, he hitches her up onto the urinal effortlessly and pushes her legs apart. As they start to make out, the chanting begins, and clapping and foot-stamping. The spectators unleash a tirade of obscenities in English and Italian, inciting their mate to go all the way.

She recoils, struggles to get free, shoves him off with all of her strength. He hesitates, some last vestige of decency and self-respect holding him back. That's the cue for the skinhead to jump in and take his turn. The skinhead has no such restraint. He's ruthless and wiry with muscles of steel. He pins her hands to the mirror above her head and rams her skull against the glass. Bang... bang... bang... Behind him the chanting continues, and the cheering and the stamping of feet. Limp as a blow-up doll, she submits. Powerless. But inside her head she's as fierce as a tiger. The next one will die.

Her bag fell on the floor under the urinal and her flick knife is inside the bag – the flick knife that she uses for cutting up fruit for her little boy – but she grew up on the most deprived council estate in Hackney and at fifteen years old was gang leader of *ChicFlicks'* the most feared and revered girls' gang on the block – so she knows how to use it to protect herself. When at last the skinhead turns away, she leaps to her feet and sinks to her hands and knees on the floor. The ultimate degradation.

In seconds the meathead is behind her, down on his knees... can't believe his luck. And the chanting continues... and the laughter... and the obscenities... While he fumbles to pull down his jeans, she grabs for her bag, flicks open the knife and whips around, flexible as a viper, to strike the first blow. The blade of the knife enters his side, sinking deep into the newly exposed rolls of flesh next to his pelvic bone. The boy squeals like a pig being slaughtered. You could call it self-defence, but she doesn't stop there. A frenzied attack.

It's a few seconds before they hear the police sirens above the sound of his screams. By the time the other boys drag her off, the meathead is gasping his last breaths and collapses onto the filthy wet floor.

Romeo sticks his head round the door and shouts: 'Get the hell out of here! Run! It's the police!'

FORTY-EIGHT
DANIELLE

My alarm went off at six the next morning because I wanted to go for a run before the heat of the day set in. Perhaps Matt was right that I needed therapy. More importantly, I had to stay strong. We'd talked late into the night and reached a fragile truce whereby we both promised to be more open and honest with each other. Matt had asked me to be patient and pleaded with me to trust him for a little longer, when all would be resolved. I'd agreed to give him the benefit of the doubt.

Everything seemed normal and as it should be in the daylight. I put on my running gear and trainers and slipped out of the door, leaving Matt gently snoring in the bed. I was planning to do my usual circuit over the ridge past the swimming pool, then through the woods and out onto the white road that snaked down to Sangiari.

I slowed my pace as I ran past the new infinity pool. The pool engineers would be here shortly to continue with the job. There was still much that needed doing on the landscaping and I planned to work with a local landscape gardener to complete the designs. I stood for a minute trying to visualise where the new planting would go.

A splash of orange caught my eye poking out from a boarded rectangle of rubble and earth which was to be concreted over to form the base for a summerhouse. It was Matt's broken bicycle helmet, caked in mud. What was it doing here? I looked more closely. A wild boar or some other animal had been rooting around and dug it up. Why had Matt, usually so conscientious about recycling, dumped his helmet rather than disposing of it in a responsible way? And why would a wild animal have been attracted to it? *Of course. Matt's head injury. Because it smells of blood...His or his victim's?*

I remembered Matt's night walk before the weekend... with his rucksack which may have contained a bloodied helmet which he may have wanted to bury beneath a tonne of concrete...and my doubts returned. I shook my head. This paranoid madness had to end.

All was quiet when I came back into the farmhouse after my run. Matt was upstairs sleeping. After our talk, Matt had stayed up most of the previous night intending to finish the draft of his novel. He'd missed his deadline three times already and his editor was losing patience.

'Surely a few more days won't make any difference,' I'd said before going to bed.

I could see that Matt was emotionally drained and exhausted, but he was determined to get it done.

'I need closure.'

Softly, I pushed open the door to Matt's study.

His manuscript was open on the screen of his computer.

The text ended mid-sentence. So, he still hadn't made it to the end...

I placed the brown package addressed to 'Nicoletta' on Matt's desk. I hadn't opened it. I'd kept it safe in my bag. I scribbled a note:

Loretta gave me this – she insisted I should have it. It belonged to your girlfriend, Nicola. Loretta found it underneath her mattress in the old cottage when the place was cleared after she'd gone. Your great-aunt kept it for years, waiting for 'Nicoletta' to return. In her confusion, she still thinks I'm the girl who went missing so long ago. I thought I should give it to you as you're the person Nicola was closest to. Perhaps it will help you write the ending to your story? I hope it brings you peace.

Much as I burned with curiosity to rip open the sealed envelope and find out what was inside, I knew I had no right to keep the gift for myself.

FORTY-NINE
THE HITCHHIKER
BY MATTEO J. ROSSI

The three teenagers who had been stamping and cheering are gone, leaving the fourth, prostrate on the floor, with Nikki kneeling at his side. They sprint to their car and tear away down the highway. Suspecting a stolen car, the police officers U-turn their vehicle and pull out of the lay-by in hot pursuit, with sirens blazing and blue lights flashing.

Within seconds, Ted and Luca appear, having run across to the toilet block through the fields. The toilet is a scene of carnage.

'What the hell happened?' says Ted.

'What the hell happened to you?' says Nikki.

There's no time to lose. Someone could pull off to use the facilities at any time.

Ted is hysterical.

'Call an ambulance. Call the police!' he yells over and over again.

Nikki is having none of it.

'If we call the police, I go to jail,' says Nikki. 'And then what happens to Harry? His father will get him. He's a monster. I'll die before that happens.'

She's more cool-headed than the three of them put together.

'Those bastards gang-raped me. I acted in self-defence. This fat pig had it coming.' She kicks his side softly. 'His mates won't go to the police. Look at the way they fled the scene. They don't care about him. They won't risk getting banged up for aggravated rape.'

Leaving the kid there isn't an option. They need time to work out Nikki's plan of escape.

Luca gets an old blanket from the boot of his car (an improvised picnic rug from their pervert-entrapment stings) and they wrap him up as best they can. He's a big guy – twisting him onto the blanket is bad enough – dragging him over the grass to the top of the embankment is back-breaking. Nikki stands by the roadway keeping watch and signalling when the coast is clear while Luca and Ted do the heavy lifting.

Out of nowhere, it occurs to Ted that killing is the easy part. It's disposing of the body that takes real guts.

At the top of the embankment, they roll the boy out of the blanket and his body hurtles in a crazy roly-poly down the steep side to land with a sickening thud in deep undergrowth close to the railway line. Then they run.

Luca and Ted meet Nikki back at the car and Luca drives to the *fattoria* more sedately than he's ever driven in his life. With Nikki covered in blood and a blood-soaked old rug stuffed in a plastic bag in the boot, it wouldn't be the best time to get pulled over by the police.

Back in Nikki's cottage at the *fattoria*, the babysitter is sent packing and Nikki stands under the tap in the yard scrubbing herself clean. She throws a few things at random into her rucksack – Harry's clothes and toys, a couple of books, a handful of clothes for herself, her toothbrush and hairbrush, and the flick knife (scrubbed clean of the meathead's blood) – then grabs her guitar and she's ready to go. Ted wakes Harry gently and settles him on the back seat of Luca's car.

They all jump in and drive 150 miles down the motorway in the direction of Naples.

As dawn breaks, Luca pulls up on the verge of a slip road and Ted helps Nikki and Harry out of the car. Ted says his last goodbyes in a tender embrace that he wishes would go on forever. Then he gets back in the car and Luca starts the engine. He watches with blurry eyes through the rear window while the image of Nikki, hitching a lift to the port of Brindisi with Harry by her side, gradually recedes into nothing.

FIFTY
DANIELLE

Thank God it was Friday and finally the pool contractors had left for good having spent the week finishing off the installation, filling the pool and testing the systems. The infinity pool was ready for use. Tuscany was in the throes of a heatwave and I'd spent as much time as possible working in my air-conditioned art studio, where I could hide away from the men and their incessant noise. At last, I had the place to myself.

I wandered out onto the patio deck and lay down on the cool terracotta flagstones with my eyes closed and my hand dangling in the water. Matt and Luca had worked like dogs to get their part of the work done to fit in with the schedule of the pool contractors. Now, the place exuded peace and calm at the end of the sultry day.

On impulse, I pulled my sundress over my head and dived into the pool.

The water was both invigorating and soothing. Once again, my mind strayed to the trunk. I felt sure Matt had reburied it here under the new patio during my weekend absence in Florence. I was still trying my hardest to give Matt the benefit of the doubt and trust in his innocence. His Mafia explanation was so difficult to believe, but the alternative was too fearful to contemplate.

The trunk and its secrets were once again encased in concrete. The truth would never be exposed. I'd held back from notifying the police for fear of unknown Mafia retribution if Matt's warnings were really true. In particular, I'd feared my actions could put Loretta in jeopardy and more selfishly, I'd been scared of how Matt would react towards me. Now I had to let it go. Matt had promised to tell me everything soon.

I settled into a rhythm and relaxed into a state of mindfulness. Slowly, my head began to clear – and it was then that the image came into my head. An image so intense and compelling it filled my whole consciousness. A vision of a girl's body wrapped in sackcloth, buried deep in the earth below where I swam. Fleetingly, a memory came back to me of the ghostly presence I'd seen floating Ophelia-like in this very spot on our first night at the *fattoria*. Was it the blood-stained clothing, conjuring these images? In the liminal space, between water and sky, the infinity pool was giving up its secrets.

I dived down to the bottom and swam a full length underwater as if to get closer to the truth. I reached for the edge, gasping and breathless. The vision was gone. For now, the mystery remained as opaque and impenetrable as the sheet of white marble lining the bottom of the pool.

When I surfaced, I heard bicycle wheels spinning on the path, then footsteps approaching softly over the flagstones. Strangely purified and empowered by the water, I was no longer afraid. I swam to the side, and Matt came and sat beside me at the edge of the pool. I couldn't look at him. I rested my arms on the stone and turned my eyes to the palette of blues stretching to the horizon.

'There was a girl,' said Matt quietly. 'She was *the one*... you know what I mean? My love for her was more pure than anything I've known before or since. I could have died for her. I loved her to death.'

I said nothing. There was nothing I could say to that. I looked into the distance, my eyes fixed on the line where the water met the sky.

'We had a wild summer, it's true. She was a free spirit that nothing and no one could tame. She drank too much and she took drugs. She had a past. She came from a broken home and was running from her partner who was a brute. The bastard was more than ten years older than her and used her as a punchbag for all of his issues. She was hitchhiking from London to freedom - the beaches of the Mediterranean. I picked her up by the side of the road and we spent the summer together, but I was only ever a detour on her journey of escape.

'She got us into trouble, our gang of three – me, Antonio and her – stealing money to buy alcohol and drugs. She selected our targets, always from among the local thugs and perverts. She got off on thinking up the most fucked-up ways of entrapping and humiliating them. She was the gang leader. She didn't really care that much about the money, though she called her share of the takings her "running-away money". Turning the tables on some misogynist sexist creep was her idea of a good night out.'

Matt rocked forwards and held his head in his hands.

'But one night, things went horribly wrong. She got hurt... and she fought back. And, well, someone died.'

His words came out in between choking guttural gasps

like an animal in pain. I'd never seen him this way – so vulnerable and broken.

'She went away... I had to let her go. I dropped her at the side of the road. She was planning to hitchhike to the south of Italy, then a ferry from Brindisi to Athens to join a friend who worked in a bar on one of the Greek islands. I never saw or heard from her again.'

For a long time, I said nothing.

Was this the truth or his reimagined version of the past?

It looked like she'd left in a real hurry. Backpackers don't usually leave so many of their things behind. In my darkest moments, I'd imagined a narrative in which Matt was the bad guy, hiding something monstrous that had happened in the past. I truly longed to believe in Matt's version, but there were parts of his narrative that didn't fit.

'What about the trunk?' I said. 'The bloodstained clothes.'

Matt sat there for a while, saying nothing, struggling to compose himself.

Then he said, 'We were trying to protect her from being caught by the police. Some of her stuff was, well, you know... incriminating. Drugs... stolen goods. She needed to get away fast, to disappear without trace.

'The police were on the trail. She left in the darkness of night. After she'd gone, we cleared out her stuff from the outhouse where she slept and bundled it all into the trunk. I'd been labouring with Antonio, putting in the patio for the old swimming pool. So, we buried the trunk under the concrete foundations.

'We worked like a pair of maniacs, in the moonlight, all through the dead of night. When Benetto saw the patio the next day all finished ahead of time, he suspected something.

But he had his own secrets, which we were keeping for him, so he said nothing.'

We were both silent for a moment and all you could hear was the light splash of water against the side of the pool.

Eventually, Matt said, 'You were right. What you saw in the trunk were her clothes. I'm sorry I lied to you. But it wasn't her blood. I swear that on my life.'

'And?'

I pressed Matt for more information.

'I've already said too much. I promised her that I'd never speak of that night. She chose to disappear. She was in a controlling and violent relationship. She didn't want to be found. It wasn't so much the police she was afraid of as her partner in England. That's all I can tell you.

'Nobody missed her for a while. Eventually, the partner started asking questions and the police got wind of the fact she'd been staying at the *fattoria,* but her secrets were safe with Antonio and me... Until you came along.'

When the police investigations led to nothing, Matt's girl-friend became another 'missing person', one of many thousands of cases of missing persons recorded by the police each year in Italy – another shadowy absence diffusing anxiety and fear through the local community. Little wonder they spoke of her no more.

Matt couldn't even bring himself to utter her name.

What more was there to say?

Inside my head, I was thinking a teenage hippy back-packer might leave behind a soiled party dress and some tattered trainers and old few books, but she'd never leave behind her guitar. It was still in pieces on the woodpile. In the winter months, we'd burn it on our stove. Only yesterday, I'd taken away a piece to draw in my studio as part of a still life. It was the upper section of the fret board, where you place your fingers to make the chords. Some of the strings were still attached, snapped and curling. When I turned it over, I saw the initials 'NF', scratched into the wood on the back.

I had one last question for Matt.

'What happened to her little boy?'

'She never had a little boy, Danielle,' he said. 'She was single, young and free. The little boy you read about in my story was a figment of my imagination. The little boy was me.'

He clasps my hands to help me out of the water and I notice that he's wearing a *Breil* wristwatch that I haven't seen before.

FIFTY-ONE
THIS SUMMER

All summer long, Danielle has swum at the infinity pool. Each day she's in the water before dawn, in time to watch the bright orange disc of the sun rise behind the summit of Monte Amiata turning the sky from grey to purple to pink. It's the best possible start to the day. She loves feeling of the blood pulsing through her veins, and her limbs cutting through the water, the sweet fresh air filling her lungs as she swims lengths across the surface of the pool. She's more alive and in tune with the great outdoors than she's ever been before.

Sometimes Matt joins her for an early morning swim. Sometimes he sleeps in. Sometimes he goes for a bike ride instead and they meet afterwards for breakfast on the terrace – a feast of succulent watermelon, peaches and plums, accompanied by cream pastries and strong Italian black coffee. More often they come to the pool together in the early afternoon, when the sun beats down and even the lizards are hiding in the shade. Matt is always the first to dive in after a long, cramped morning in front of his computer. After they swim, they rub sun cream into each other's backs and push their sunbeds up close. Occasionally, when they hear Antonio working in the fields far away on the other side of the estate, they make love.

Antonio doesn't intrude on the couple at the pool. He is, after all, their employee – a worker on the estate – and this is their home. The pool is Danielle's domain. Every now and again, she asks him to join them for a late-afternoon cocktail or an evening barbecue at the poolside. Antonio is 'barbecue king', so that gives them both a night off from the cooking.

Danielle doesn't know it for sure, but she suspects that discreetly, with a hunter's guile, Antonio keeps an eye out for her safety when she's at the pool. (He doesn't want history repeating itself.) The woods behind and to one side of the clearing provide cover – the ideal terrain for close observation. Antonio knows exactly where and when to position himself behind a tree or in a hollow so that even if Danielle or Matt were to glance in his direction, they wouldn't see a thing. The sunlight would be blinding.

Encouraged by Danielle, Matt joins a local cycle club that meets on a Wednesday evening. It'll do him good, she thinks, to socialise with other men his age, apart from Antonio. After a long ride, the riders congregate at a local bar and drink and play pool into the early hours of the morning, undoing all the benefit of the evening's fresh air and exercise.

When Matt is out, Danielle takes herself off to the pool for an evening swim. The sunset is even more spectacular than the sunrise. It's nice to have someone to share it with. Most Wednesday nights Antonio joins her in the pool and sometimes, when the evening is sweet, they stay on to watch the shooting stars and swim naked in the moonlight and enjoy passionate midnight sex on the white marble steps. Then in their erotic fantasies, Dani and Nikki become one and the same.

One Wednesday night Matt has a migraine and comes home early from the bar after cycling club. He hears voices and laughter and sees two bodies intertwined and oblivious in the shallows of the pool. On his way back to the cottage, Antonio sees Matt's tracks circling the pool – broken branches, flattened grass, footsteps on the sandy soil. Tomorrow he must be extra vigilant.

Danielle gets up just before sunrise as usual for her morning swim. Although she's tired from her exertions of the night before she fears that changing her routine would arouse Matt's suspicions. She doesn't know it, but Antonio is already at his post. Feeling fragile, she lowers herself gently into the water and begins her lengths: one, two, three, all the way to thirty.

Meanwhile, Matt stands at the edge of the pool, holding a rock tightly in his left hand, his face in the shadows of the rising sun. He's very still and quiet. Danielle hasn't heard him. She doesn't look in his direction. Her eyes are either on the sunrise or face down in the water.

It's not until she's climbing out of the pool that she feels Matt's shadow looming over her and looks up to see his body leaning towards her. Her mobile phone is clenched in his right hand. He hurls it to the ground, and it smashes on the flagstones of the patio. In his left hand he holds a big, jagged rock directly above her head.

The next instant, a shot rings out across the valley and Matt is tumbling head first into the pool. She dives under the water to escape being showered in his blood.

When the shot no longer reverberates and the sound of splashing water stills, for a moment there's silence. Then

Antonio comes crashing out of the trees and is pulling her out of the water – and issuing one order after another like an SAS commander.

Danielle sinks to the ground and cradles her head in her arms. Antonio tells her that the police are on their way. He tells her that they identified the body of the hitchhiker found near Brindisi.

'Her name is Nicola Flanagan.'

Antonio looks pleased with himself. Fibres recovered from the victim's wrists matched the fibres of a braided friendship bracelet that he, Antonio, had found in Matt's wallet some months ago and given to the police. Matt had lent him his wallet to pay for the hire of the equipment used for the excavations at the infinity pool on the day he took Danielle to the hot springs.

'I knew it, as soon as I saw that friendship bracelet,' says Antonio, shaking his head.

It turns out Antonio's mate at the Pienza police station tipped him off yesterday that they were coming to arrest Matteo this morning...once again, they're too late. The police also wanted to question Matt in connection with a recent case of attempted rape, says Antonio with satisfaction.

He's saved them the trouble.

Antonio throws the rifle into the water – not his usual weapon but the rifle that Matt once used for target practice. Then he takes off his gloves. He'll burn them later.

'I shot him in the face so it'll look like suicide,' he says. 'Now, go and do exactly as I told you.' He kisses her quickly on the lips. 'And then we'll be OK.'

FIFTY-TWO
DANIELLE

Antonio told me to go to Matt's office. I sit shaking from head to toe, wondering if I can keep my nerve and follow Antonio's orders.

The notebook is on Matt's desk in front of his laptop.

Nicola Farrell, Summer 2000.

'Nicola Farrell', not 'Nicola Flanagan'. Are they one and the same person?

I remember the name I saw scrawled in the jogging pants Antonio gave me to wear when he rescued me from the storm. 'N. Farrell'. It seems Matt's girlfriend had been using a false surname to hide her identity while she was living at the farmhouse.

A single white bloom that Matt must have picked from our flower border this morning is placed across the cover of the notebook. The petals are still damp with early morning dew. The Breil wristwatch is beside the notebook, too. Matt must have retrieved it from the trunk before reburying it. The packaging and my scribbled note to Matt are screwed up in the wastepaper basket.

Matt liked to leave things tidy. Maybe he had a premonition of what the day would bring.

The notebook is worn and stained. It smells faintly of cigarettes and coconut suntan oil. She wrote her name on the front cover in big childish lettering. I can imagine her sitting in the hammock or by the pool with her notebook on her knees, writing up her thoughts day by day.

As I flip it open, a passport falls at my feet. It's an Irish passport. Matt's girlfriend was Irish, not English.

I pick up the passport and turn to the photo. Her face looks back at me, serious and unsmiling and familiar. I could be looking in the mirror. Nicola Flanagan. Her passport expired seven years ago. And that's when I know for sure. She never made it to Greece.

* * *

Sadly, I turn to Nicola's diary. The record of a summer: first entry in June, last entry 12 September – 12/09 – the numbers Matt used in his computer password. Was that the date he killed her, late that night, battering her to death with a rock up by the swimming pool, before driving 150 miles down the motorway in the direction of Naples and dumping her body down a railway escarpment? And what part did Antonio play in all of this? The rifle shot may have saved my life, but it also silenced Matt.

With shaking hands, I open the cover. Are these the usual ramblings of a teenage girl? Or will they fill the gaps in Matteo's manuscript? The parts that are too painful to write... the story's silent twin.

Later when I get the chance to read the notebook, perhaps I'll understand why a young Irish girl, whose real name was

Nicola Flanagan and who moved from London to Dublin when she was only twelve years old, chose some years later to conceal her true identity and travel to Italy. Here, she went by the name Nicola Farrell, embodying the persona of a beautiful, wild, rebellious English hitchhiker who had suffered and would suffer too much at the hands of men.

* * *

I hear the sirens from the brow of the hill. It's my *five-minute call*. The police are on their way. It's time to go.

'Get into the headspace,' I say sternly, recalling the shows I took part in as a young girl and reliving for real that stomach-churning excitement that grips your entire being in the seconds before the curtain goes up.

I stand, push back my hair, straighten my sarong, pick up my towel and the notebook, and set off towards the infinity pool, preparing myself for the most difficult performance of my life.

NEXT SUMMER

The final scene is set at the infinity pool next summer. The pandemic is over. Tourists have returned to Tuscany. The *Fattoria dell'Amore* features on three of the main holiday booking sites for luxury accommodation in the Val d'Orcia. It was sold on to a holiday rental management company for a knock-down price as a 'stigmatised property'*. (*Definition: property that buyers or tenants may shun for reasons that are unrelated to its physical condition or features. These can include the death of an occupant, murder, suicide, and belief that a house is haunted. *Wikipedia*) Such forced sales are highly sought-after by rental businesses, yielding a big return on their investment.

There are three young children playing in the pool – two sisters and their little brother – leaping on and off a giant white inflatable unicorn. Their shrieking and laughter jars in the stillness. A woman lies on the sunbed, sipping an iced gin and tonic and reading a book – most probably, a psychological suspense thriller from the best-seller list that she picked up at the airport – something with '*Girl*' in the title, no doubt, in bright yellow lettering on a dark background.

Every now and then the woman glances up at her offspring splashing in the water. Little does she know what dark secrets lie buried deep below its shimmering surface. She marvels at the view from her sunbed. There's nothing but sunshine and water and dazzling blue sky from the tips of her red painted toenails all the way to the horizon. She smiles and waves to the little ones then she goes back to her book.

ACKNOWLEDGEMENTS
WITH THANKS...

Thank you so much to everyone at Head of Zeus, with special thanks to my three brilliant editors, Hannah Smith, Thorne Ryan and Martina Arzu – for their commitment to *The Infinity Pool* and their patience while I wrote it (or failed to write it) through successive lockdowns when home life was chaotic and the opposite of isolated.

Thank you also to the artistic team at Aries, who have created a striking 'summery but sinister' cover for *The Infinity Pool* that absolutely captures the vibe of the story. And to assistant editor Bianca Gillam, and to all the marketing team who are always so helpful with everything relating to social media.

Thank you to the behind-the-scenes professionals who provided such useful (if occasionally brutal!) comments and brought their expertise to bear on the text. My thanks especially to Helena Newton, whose gentle copy-editing suggestions got me through the second draft and to Claire Dean for her meticulous proofreading.

Thank you as always to my wonderful agent, Hayley Steed at The Madeleine Milburn Literary Agency and to her assistant, Elinor Davies. I'm looking forward to being able to meet up 'IRL' again and talk about new projects.

Thank you in advance to all the lovely reviewers and bloggers who take the time to engage with this story. I love to read your comments and learn so much from them.

As always, I'm so very grateful to all of my family and friends – near and far – whose company and encouragement kept me going with this novel. My love and thanks above all to Louisa, Clara and Christine, for taking time out from their own commitments to read my drafts, and to chat through a multitude of scenarios and endings. Your ideas are always so inspiring! Love and thanks also to my father, Graham (ninety years young and always ready to offer support), and to my husband, Nigel, and, of course, to my son, Jack, whose full-volume Youtube videos fill my workspace (and headspace!) with sounds of rollercoasters and spin-cycles and jet engines while I write.

Thank you to all the friends who kept me sane through the lockdowns and the writing of *The Infinity Pool* – especially to Sara, Sarah, Rose, Heather and Janet – and to Denise, Carol, Joely, Helena, Kerry and Jill.

Special friends and generous readers.

For all the friendship and fun over the years, *The Infinity Pool* is dedicated to you.

ABOUT THE AUTHOR

CLAIRE S. LEWIS studied Philosophy, French Literature and International Relations at the universities of Oxford and Cambridge before starting her career in aviation law with a City law firm and later as an in-house lawyer at Virgin Atlantic Airways. More recently, she turned to writing psychological suspense, taking courses in creative writing at the Faber Academy and story writing for screen at the Professional Writing Academy. Born in Paris, she's bilingual and lives in Surrey with her family.